PENGUIN BOOKS
Senseless

Mary Burton is the critically acclaimed author of *I'm Watching You*, *Dead Ringer* and *Dying Scream*, all set in Virginia, USA, where Mary lives with her family.

For more information about Mary, please visit her website: www.maryburton.com

Senseless

MARY BURTON

PENGUIN BOOKS

PENGUIN BOOKS

Published by the Penguin Group
Penguin Books Ltd, 80 Strand, London WC2R ORL, England
Penguin Group (USA) Inc., 375 Hudson Street, New York, New York 10014, USA
Penguin Group (Canada), 90 Eglinton Avenue East, Suite 700, Toronto, Ontario,
Canada M4P 2Y3 (a division of Pearson Penguin Canada Inc.)
Penguin Ireland, 25 St Stephen's Green, Dublin 2, Ireland (a division of Penguin Books Ltd)
Penguin Group (Australia), 250 Camberwell Road, Camberwell, Victoria 3124, Australia
(a division of Pearson Australia Group Pty Ltd)
Penguin Books India Pvt Ltd, 11 Community Centre, Panchsheel Park,
New Delhi – 110 017, India
Penguin Group (NZ), 67 Apollo Drive, Rosedale, Auckland 0632, New Zealand
(a division of Pearson New Zealand Ltd)
Penguin Books (South Africa) (Pty) Ltd, 24 Sturdee Avenue, Rosebank, Johannesburg 2196,
South Africa

Penguin Books Ltd, Registered Offices: 80 Strand, London WC2R ORL, England

www.penguin.com

First published in the USA by Kensington Publishing Corp. 2011
First published in Great Britain in Penguin Books 2011
1

Copyright © Mary Burton, 2011
All rights reserved

The moral right of the author has been asserted

Set in 12.5/14.75 pt Garamond MT
Typeset by Jouve (UK), Milton Keynes
Printed in England by Clays Ltd, St Ives plc

ISBN: 978–0–141–04883–3

www.greenpenguin.co.uk

MIX
Paper from
responsible sources
FSC
www.fsc.org FSC™ C018179

Penguin Books is committed to a sustainable
future for our business, our readers and our
planet. This book is made from paper certified
by the Forest Stewardship Council.

Prologue

Saturday, April 1, Midnight

Duct tape muffled the woman's hoarse moans as a hooded figure stoked the glowing embers in the basement hearth. She had been screaming and struggling, hoping to get her captor's attention, since she'd started awake . . . was it an hour ago? Two hours? Down in this cellar prison, time leaked away like the drip, drip of water from an overhead pipe.

No amount of crying or rattling of chains against the stone floor diverted the shadowy figure's attention from the flames that hungrily danced and licked the logs in the ancient hearth. Twig by twig, her jailer tenderly fed the flames as a mother might nourish a child, never paying her a moment's attention. In this dank place, she was invisible, of no greater consequence than the three-legged chair leaning in the shadowy corner or the trash bags piled by the rickety staircase.

The hard, uneven stone floor dug into her back, cramping her muscles, numbing her skin and driving home the realization that there'd be no escape. She was going to die.

She closed her eyes, the thud of her heart mingling with the crackle of the fire and the clink of the andiron against the blackened grate cradling the logs. Since childhood, she'd been told she didn't deserve happiness or a full life. *Bad girl. You are a bad girl.* All her life, she railed against those messages, grabbing or stealing what she could to not only survive but also to prevail. Maybe the dark message funneled into her soul since the cradle was right. Bad girls always came to a bad end.

Despair rose up in her like a black storm cloud, wrapping around her throat and beckoning her to relent. It would be so easy to give in to her predestined fate. So easy just to close her eyes and let the darkness slide over her.

As she eased toward the mental abyss, ready to surrender to fate, a primal survival urge jerked her back from the edge.

No! You want to live! You deserve to live!

She opened her eyes and stared at her captor. He wasn't so large. He didn't look so strong. Or so evil. Perhaps she could wedge a bit of reason under his icy exterior and get him to take pity.

Drawing on what little energy remained in her limbs, she kicked and screamed, but he didn't shift his gaze from the fire.

God, what was he planning? What could he want with her? As her mind tumbled over increasing vicious scenarios, fear and panic reignited her struggles.

Please, God, get me out of this. A thousand promises, *I swears* and resolutions raced through her mind as she bartered with God.

And then a miracle came in the form of a loud thump from upstairs. The noise cut through the stream of *I swears.* She craned her neck toward the rickety staircase that led to the upper floor. Someone had arrived! Her heart pounded faster, harder and her stomach coiled like a tight spring.

She studied her captor's posture, searching for a sign. Was the upstairs arrival good or bad? Did this creep have some sick friend who'd come to enjoy this party? Or did she have a savior?

His narrow shoulders stiffened and an abrupt jerk of his head toward the door told her that the guest was uninvited.

Hope exploded. Maybe someone had come! Maybe someone had figured out that she'd been kidnapped.

Oh, God. Oh, God. Please send someone to save me!

She jerked against her bindings and screamed muffled pleas, projecting her voice beyond the tape.

Sunglasses and a hood hid a great deal, but she caught traces of a scraggly beard as he carefully laid down his iron and climbed the stairs to the first floor. He unlocked a shiny new padlock on the basement door, opened it and vanished.

Her heart thundered in her chest as she strained to listen. Above, the ceiling creaked as her jailer crossed the first floor in search of the intruder.

Someone, please, save me.

Floorboards creaked with the light tentative footsteps of the newcomer who moved about the upstairs freely. As the seconds passed, the footsteps grew more confident as if the new arrival wasn't expecting company.

Be careful! He's waiting for you!

She screamed until her throat burned, but the duct tape muffled her words, garbling all her warnings.

The intruder moved across the first floor. Her jailer remained still, lying in wait, like a snake ready to strike.

And then a loud scream, 'Shit!'

A scuffle followed. Bodies slammed against walls. Glass hit the floor and shattered. A subdued groan and something large slammed the floor, as if a body had crumpled under its own weight. And then silence.

The woman's heart jackhammered her ribs so hard she thought bones would crack as she frantically twisted her hands and stared at the door, hoping for a miracle. Who had won the battle? She struggled against her bindings, willing the hemp to snap even as it cut into her flesh.

Oh, God, save me!

Her mind tumbled as she imagined police storming into the basement and cutting her bindings as they explained in soothing tones that she was now safe. They'd ask her what had happened and she'd calmly explain.

'The last thing I remember was sitting at the bar in Moments, a little upscale place on the Potomac. It's a good place to hang out. Normal people, like doctors, lawyers and bankers, drink at Moments. It's not the kind of place crazy people visit. It's safe.'

She'd be sure to mention that she'd only sipped a single white wine and had spent most of that night chatting with the female bartender, killing time until her blind date showed. This had been her Saturday night routine for over a year.

Toward the end of the evening, a guy had settled beside her on a bar stool. He'd worn sunglasses, had a neatly trimmed beard and a nice oversized dark suit. He was a strange, still man who could hardly be classified as overly masculine. Her stepfather would have called him a

4

'Girlie-man.' He'd ordered vodka in a quiet raspy voice that had sent a chill whispering down her spine. But his drink had arrived and he'd sipped it without fanfare as if content to be alone. Ignoring him had been easy.

She remembered a woman walking into the restaurant and shouting someone needed to fix her flat tire. The shrill voice knifed through the hum of conversation and soft jazz.

Distracted, she had turned to see who was making so much noise. She'd classified the woman as unimportant . . . some nobody from the street. She'd returned to her drink, forgetting the woman even before she'd swallowed her next sip.

And then . . . then she'd woken up here – a dank, dark basement, tied to the floor.

Oh, God, how she desperately wanted to tell that story. To be saved.

Seconds passed – then minutes and then the steady sound of footsteps. Steady. Not rushed. Cautious like a rescuer or unhurried like a madman? Impossible to tell.

And still she hoped. What if her savior was just being cautious? He didn't know what was downstairs. He had to be careful so he didn't get hurt himself.

Please hurry.

The door at the top of the stairs opened and a silhouetted form appeared. Who was there? He descended the steps, carefully and deliberately moving into the light generated by the fire.

Her captor.

No savior.

No rescue.

Fresh tears welled and streamed down the side of her face, pooling in her knotted blond hair.

As if she were invisible, he passed her, his attention transfixed by the fire. He stoked the embers, whistling as he lovingly coaxed more life from the flames.

Tears ran down her face. *Look at me, damn you! See me as a frightened woman!* She was a good girl. She was from a respectable family. Sure she liked to party. What girl didn't? She'd told a terrible lie years ago, but it had haunted her almost every day of her life and she'd prayed for forgiveness. She'd donated to an animal shelter at Christmas. She went to church at Easter. She laid flowers on her stepfather's grave even though the bastard had never deserved respect. Christ, she'd just turned thirty.

Good people didn't die this way.

She didn't deserve this!

Her head slumped back as she tried to block out the panic and focus on what might get her out of this horror.

Oh, Holy Mother of God, this had to be a nightmare. It had to be! This did *not* happen to regular girls. It just *didn't*.

But the raw skin on her wrists and pain in her spine said otherwise. This wasn't a nightmare.

Fear fisted in the woman's gut as she stared at the man. Was he the one from the bar who'd sat down beside her? She couldn't tell, but sensed he had to be the one. Who else would do this to her? The one man she'd known who could be this cruel had died years ago.

'Finding you was easy, you know.' His voice sounded like sandpaper rubbing against wood. 'You didn't move more than five blocks from your parents' house.'

She stopped struggling, searching her brain for any clue to his identity. But as much as she tried to cut through haze and confusion, she found no answers. Fear rose up in her and she couldn't suppress a moan that sounded like an animal caught in a trap.

The guy straightened and turned. He wore a large bulky coat, making it hard to judge his size, maybe five-nine. As the figure moved toward her, his glasses reflected the firelight, which mingled with her terrified face. He pulled the tape from her mouth and the adhesive pulled off bits of the skin on her lips. She tasted blood.

'Surprised to see me again?'

The raspy voice sent a chill snaking down her spine. In the dim light she could see that he wore a wig and his beard appeared fake. Smoky glasses obscured his eyes.

She winced, moistening her cracked dry lips with her tongue. 'You were in the bar.'

'Yes.'

If she hadn't been trying so hard to ignore him in Moments she'd have seen he was a freak. 'You drugged me.'

'Yes.'

'Why?'

'Makes you more reasonable.' With a gloved hand he pushed up her shirt, exposing her flat belly.

'What are you doing?' Her white flesh quivered with fear.

Gently, he smoothed his hand over the pale skin. 'So pretty and clean. But we both know that you aren't clean, are you?'

'I'm a good girl.'

'No, you are not.'

Her mind reeled. *Make a connection. Let this freak see that I'm a person.* 'I have a family. Parents. A child.'

He circled an index finger around her belly button. 'You haven't seen any of them in a very long time. None of them want you.'

The words clawed at her insides. He was right. She'd lost contact with them all. She grasped for the right words that would cause delay. 'Someone was upstairs! Someone knows you are here. They know *I* am here.'

'He's trussed up like a pig for slaughter. I'll deal with him after you.'

Tears welled in her eyes. 'Please let me go.'

He arched an amused eyebrow. 'Can you imagine? A thief breaking into this house, tonight of all nights. Talk about timing.' A smile teased the edges of his beard. 'You can scream if you want.'

Her heart hammered so hard it rattled her ribs like a speeding freight train. Tears spilled down her cheeks. 'I'm not going to scream.'

The guy cocked his head. 'Why not? You've reason to scream.'

Oh, God. Please. 'I won't scream.'

The smile widened, revealing small yellowed teeth. 'We shall see.'

Words tangled with fear and caught in her throat. 'What do you want?'

'You.'

'Why? I'm nobody. You said so yourself. My family doesn't want me. I'm not worth the time.'

'No, you're special.'

Special. That's what her stepfather used to say. *My special little girl, it'll be our secret, won't it?* 'What do you want?'

'Not much really. All you have to do is lie still.' Gloved hands stroked her hair, the heavy-handed gesture pulling hard against her blond curls.

She winced. 'I want to leave.'

'No.'

Panic rose up in her throat. 'People will miss me.'

'No they won't.'

With quick, angry strokes, the guy jabbed a metal rod into the embers. Finally, he raised the tip out of the flames and inspected the glowing star-shaped tip. A four-pointed star.

Memories from long ago burned through her mind, forcing her to remember a time she'd worked hard to forget. 'What are you going to do with that?'

'You remember the star, don't you?'

'What are you talking about?'

'The star. And The Secret.'

Memories elbowed to the front of her mind. 'No, I don't remember,' she lied.

'Liar.'

'No, I swear.' She squirmed and tugged against her bindings but her struggling only tightened their hold.

He adjusted his sunglasses as he stared at the glowing red star. 'I promise you before I'm done, it'll be burned in your memory.'

Sobs fueled her hysteria. 'Please, I don't want to remember.'

He knelt beside her, the coarse fabric of his pants

brushing her hip. 'Your job is to send a message to the others.'

The others. 'You don't know about the others.'

'I surely do. I surely do. And soon everyone will know of their betrayal.' The scent of hot metal wafted around her, stirring up the old sin buried under a decade of wine and denial.

'Please.' Her gaze locked on the red tip of the brand and every muscle in her body tensed with terror.

'Starlight, star bright; the first star I see tonight. I wish I may; I wish I might; Have the wish I wish tonight.'

And then he touched the hot brand to her stomach. The metal seared into her flesh. Instantly, pain robbed her of breath and she couldn't squeak out a sound. Every nerve in her body convulsed. When he pulled the brand away, the pain lingered. Her heart slammed the walls of her chest, as if trying to flee the agony.

Glasses hid her tormentor's eyes, but a twitch of his lips betrayed a euphoric joy as if this moment had been a pleasure long denied. 'When I'm done, they'll see you and they'll know it's time to atone.'

Her lungs contracted, sucking in air.

She screamed like a wild animal caught in a trap.

Chapter 1

Monday, April 3, 9:15 P.M.

'What are you doing?' Eva whispered.

The fear in her voice fueled his excitement and anger as he dangled her star pendant over the dancing flames. 'You're so proud of your star necklace. So proud of being a Rising Star. Now you'll have it with you forever.'

As she pushed against the hearth to free herself, he shoved his full weight into her body. Her face scraped against the mortar, and when she whimpered, his erection hardened against her backside. As the metal star heated, she realized being raped again paled beside what he now planned. 'Josiah, don't do this. You've taken enough.'

'Not even close.' He removed the star from the flame, tossed it on the floor and then shoved her back, pressing her right shoulder into the hot metal. Instantly, it burned through her shirt and into her flesh.

She howled in anguish. His excitement grew. But as he reached for the hem of her skirt, agony turned her world black.

Eva Rayburn jerked awake, gripping the steering wheel of her truck, dragging in a lungful of air. Her muscles, as tense as a bow, braced for attack.

Seconds passed. No burning pain seared her flesh, and her muscles eased. Cocooned by the night, she heard only the distant sound of traffic and the chirp of a nearby grasshopper. The dream's smothering haze slowly eased its grip and the familiar came into focus. She was in the cab of her old truck parked on a suburban street corner. Safe. Okay. Years away from that terrible night she'd endured long ago.

'Damn it.' She rested her head against the steering wheel and drew in a deep, deep breath before slowly letting it leak away. 'Just the dream. Just the dream.'

She slumped back against the seat, grabbed the edge of her T-shirt and billowed the ends until the sweat dripping between her breasts dried. It had been years since she'd suffered through the nightmare, and its arrival didn't bode well.

Eva checked her watch, cursed herself for having dozed and then glanced toward the one-story house across the street. A '72 red Porsche was now parked in the driveway, signaling her guy had arrived home.

'Way to go, Eva,' she muttered. 'Sleep through the job.'

Eva tucked her long hair under a FLORIST ball cap, grabbed the bouquet of daisies and a clipboard and jogged toward the front door of the one-level rancher. She rang the bell, shoving aside a quiver of worry. An overhead bulb spit out a weak halo of light that ringed the cracked brick porch steps and a ragged welcome mat. Not a lot of light but enough to see her way quickly back down the stairs.

She'd been a part-time process server for about three months. The work fit well around her job as a waitress/bartender at King's Pub and her other gig as a night attendant at a homeless shelter. Normally, she didn't squeeze in a delivery between a shift at the pub and an overnight at the shelter, but her boss, Luke Fraser at LTF Processing, had promised her extra cash for this delivery tonight. The additional income had been too sweet to pass up.

Luke had described the job as a piece of cake. *Piece of cake*. Luke never paid extra for easy jobs, and tossing in that this was a divorce court summons for a guy nicknamed Bigfoot, she'd decided to play it safe and go with her florist delivery ruse. Eva adjusted her cap and rang the bell a second time. The faint scent of garbage rose from the daisies retrieved from the Dumpster behind a florist shop down the alley from King's. All she needed was a signature.

She rang the bell a third time.

Eva straightened her slim build to her full five foot one. Faded jeans hung on her slim hips and an oversized black hoodie swallowed her narrow shoulders and flat chest. As her mother used to say, she weighed one hundred pounds 'soaking wet.' The clothes, combined with her small stature, had most guessing she was a high school kid, not a woman in her late twenties. She hoped this guy pegged her for a kid because people generally underestimated kids.

Footsteps sounded behind the front door. Her heart kicked up a notch, but her chin stayed level and her stance relaxed. *Just a signature. Piece of cake.* Just serve him and then get the hell out of Dodge.

The door snapped open to one of the tallest men she'd ever met. The guy stood at least six foot six and had to have weighed three-hundred-plus pounds. A stained wife-beater T-shirt stretched across a wide chest and three days' growth of beard covered a lantern jaw. Bigfoot.

Behind him a table lamp lit a messy room furnished

with a worn couch and a flat-panel sixty-four-inch television airing a game show.

'I have a delivery for Bruce Radford.'

He snorted. 'I don't know what the hell you are selling, kid, but I don't want it.' His deep voice, raspy from cigarettes, telegraphed annoyance.

'I'm not selling. I'm delivering.' Extra attitude in the voice hid the nerves flexing in her belly. 'Are you Bruce Radford?'

Radford moved to close the door. 'Nobody here ordered any fucking flowers.'

She shrugged, still careful to keep her expression neutral. 'Like I said, I ain't selling anything, mister. Just delivering flowers. You Bruce Radford or not?'

Bloodshot eyes narrowed.

'If you're not, just say so. I'm too tried to play games. I'll tell the boss you refused the flowers.' She turned to leave.

'Who sent them?' He was more careful than she'd expected.

Eva paused and glanced at the clipboard, pretending to read. 'Some woman named Wanda.'

'I don't know a Wanda.'

'She's some hot chick that came into the shop at closing time. Red dress. Blond hair.'

The suspicion darkening his eyes faded a fraction. 'Blond?'

'Yeah. And big boobs.'

A hint of a smile tugged his full lips. He didn't know who the hell Wanda was but blond and big boobs suited him just fine. 'I'll take 'em.'

14

'So you are Bruce Radford?' The scent of stale pizza and beer mingled with his body odor.

'Yeah, I'm Radford.'

'Great.' Eva pulled a pen from behind her ear and held it out. For good measure, she tossed in a smile. 'Just need your John Hancock.'

Bruce studied the paper but in the fading light couldn't possibly read the small print. 'Must be the chick at Hanson Trucking. She's got a thing for me.'

She edged the clipboard closer, obscuring the page with most of her hand. 'Just sign here and I'll be out of your hair.'

Pursing his lips to hide a smile, Radford nodded. 'Cool.'

Radford grabbed her outstretched pen and scrawled his name in a sloppy mixture of print and cursive that reminded her of a third grader. 'Thanks.'

She shoved the flowers at him and tore off a copy of the delivery slip. 'You have a nice night.'

Absently, he took the slip. 'Sure.'

Eva moved toward her truck, praying the starter didn't act up and wishing she'd had enough gas in the tank to keep the engine running. *Just hustle across the yard and get behind the wheel before Radford figures out what he's really signed — an agreement to appear in court.* When he figured out he'd been tricked, he'd be one pissed hombre.

Eva fished her keys out of her pocket, got in the truck and fumbled in the dim light for the ignition. A glance over her shoulder told her Radford hadn't raised his gaze from the flowers, which he sniffed like a lovesick fool. He'd already forgotten about the delivery kid. Round one goes to Eva.

She cranked the engine.

Nothing. She tried the engine a second time. Still nothing. Crap. Another look at Radford had him studying the paper closely. The dumb schoolboy look morphed into confusion and then anger. 'Hey, what the hell is this?'

Tension fisted in Eva's gut. She cranked the engine. Nada.

What had her boss, King, said when he'd lent her the truck? Count to three and then try again. Shit. One. She glanced over at Radford who sprinted across the yard toward her truck. Two. He reached the street in seconds and had thundered halfway across the street when she lost her nerve and turned the key.

Click. Click. Click.

No engine roared to life.

Normally, she'd get out and tighten a few wires and the problem would be solved, but if she got out now, Radford would likely beat her to a pulp.

With the paper balled in his fist, Radford shouted, 'What the hell is this, bitch?'

She pulled in a deep breath. *Shit. Shit. Shit.* She locked the doors, wishing now she'd kept the engine running. Certainly, running out of gas a few miles from here would have been better than this mess.

Radford reached the door handle. Discovering it was locked he pounded his fist on the window. She jumped. Her hands sweated. Soon the battery would be dead.

He hit the window again, making it groan and flex under the assault. A couple more punches like that and it would shatter like a thin coating of ice.

'Bitch. Who the hell sent you?' he shouted. 'That damn

wife of mine sent you, didn't she? I ain't giving her a divorce. Greedy whore.'

Eva's focus remained on the ignition. Her hands steadied and her mind became oddly clear. She didn't bother with prayer, learning long ago that only she could solve her problems.

The fist smacked against the glass again and this time left a spiderweb of cracks. 'I'm gonna pummel your bony ass.'

Eva skipped counting to three and cranked the engine. This time the motor moaned and sputtered to life just as Radford hit the window a third time. Spiderweb cracks spiraled out from his fist, and if the glass had given way his fist would have landed on her jaw.

She shoved the gear into drive and punched the gas. Gravel sputtered under the back tires that struggled for traction.

Radford ran alongside, pounding metal with his fist. She gripped the wheel and held on tight. The truck picked up speed and Radford couldn't keep pace. A grin tugged the corners of her lips.

Bruce yelled obscenities, nearly tripped and released his grip. 'I'm going to kill you, bitch. I'm going to kill you.'

Eva held a white-knuckled grip on the steering wheel. She glanced in her rearview mirror and saw him running after the truck, his fist punching in the air. He finally stopped, bent over to suck in air, but took his gaze off her.

She plowed through a stop sign at the corner and drove several blocks before she slowed and rounded a corner. For several seconds, her heart pounded in her chest and sweat trickled down her spine. As her gas gauge hovered and sometimes dipped below empty, she drove for at least two miles before daring to really release the deep breath clogged in her lungs.

Adrenaline pumped through her veins, leaving her light-headed and, God help her, jazzed. She liked getting one over on bullies like Radford. Controlling bastards.

Luke owed her big time for this gig. A point she'd drive home when she reported.

She glanced at the clock on the dashboard. Nine forty-five. Good. She was ahead of schedule, but had chewed through the last of her gas. Digging in her pocket, she pulled out three rumpled one-dollar bills as she ducked into the first gas station. She pumped exactly three dollars' worth and started the engine. The gas gauge barely registered above E, but she knew she had enough to do her for forty miles. Just enough.

Eva got back on the beltway and headed toward Hanna's House. She spent Monday nights at the halfway house, working as a kind of nighttime attendant/go-to gal in the shelter. Most times her shift was quiet, although she had a night when two residents got into insane arguments over television remotes or who ate the last cookie.

She checked her watch. It was Sally's night off, and the shelter director would need her at the house on time. Eva hated to disappoint her. In her early fifties, Sally was a modern-day hippie who loved her tie-dye shirts, silver and bead bracelets and long hair. They'd met at King's six months ago, just days after Eva had moved back to Alexandria. Eva had been bartending, Sally had come in for a sandwich and the two had hit it off immediately. Sally had dedicated her life to helping people no one else gave a crap about, which in Eva's book equated to big points.

Eva glanced up and realized she'd strayed into a part of town she'd carefully avoided since her return to Alexandria. It was filled with stately brick homes, neat lawns and smooth sidewalks. Anyone would have described it as affluent, upper crust and a great place to raise kids.

Eva should have kept moving through the neighborhood but she continued to drive deeper into the web of streets until she reached the old stone house. She'd been to this house a few times for parties. She'd been the kid on scholarship who'd not quite fit in at the private college, but Kristen Hall, the school's reigning senior, had taken Eva under her wing and introduced her to the world of the elite. At Kristen's house, she was cocooned from the outside world and surrounded by sweet scents, pretty dresses and glittering lights. She'd ventured into a world away from her foster care home with its noisy arguments and greasy fried food smells. Each visit to the Halls' home fueled Eva's belief in fairy tales and happy endings.

Absently, Eva rubbed the scar on the back of her shoulder. God, she'd been so very wrong.

Shaking off anger and sadness, she pushed on the gas and slowly drove away. *No more memories. No more sadness. Eyes forward.* She'd chanted this mantra for over a decade.

Eva concentrated on the road ahead and the work she'd do at the halfway house tonight. The past was dead. Reaching for the radio, she turned it to a rock tune, full of words that pounded the memories from her head.

As she drove through Alexandria and cut her way toward the halfway house in the southeastern portion of the city, her stomach grumbled and she realized she'd not eaten since breakfast. King's had been slammed today. Her shift should have ended at seven but she'd stayed to help with the crush. She'd dashed out, forgetting the dinner her boss had bagged for her. Hopefully, the shelter had plenty of peanut butter and bread.

She looked forward to seeing who bunked down for the night. Maybe Tony, the ex-military boxer who'd just gotten out of jail, would have a new story to tell. He liked to relive the glory days in the ring and had sworn to control his temper. Or Pam. She just celebrated three weeks of sobriety. She talked of regaining custody of her kids and getting a job. There was Luna, a young teen runaway. Eva had been trying to convince the girl to get her GED.

Eva had driven halfway down the second block stuffed with one-story ranchers when she saw the distant flashing lights of fire trucks. As she drove closer, she realized yellow fire engines and cop cars crowded into the end of the shelter's cul-de-sac. She veered away from the dead-end scene and drove down a parallel residential road. Parking, she got out and cut between the yards that separated the streets.

Large floodlights, set up by the fire department, shone on the shelter. The unnatural light cast an eerie glow on the two-story frame house reduced by fire to smoking timbers. Even though the crews had contained the blaze Eva could still feel the residual heat burning her face.

Fire engines and dozens of cop cars surrounded the building, their bright red and blue lights flashing in the dark.

Eva's head spun as the old memories of another fire

rose up inside her and coiled around her chest. She could barely breathe and for a moment wanted nothing more than to bolt. Instead, she held her ground, shoving trembling hands through long black hair. She scanned the crowd for anyone that she recognized. Sally managed the shelter but she was nowhere to be found. And Neal, the evening manager, wasn't anywhere in sight either.

Oh, God. Oh, God.

Her mind tripped to the people who were to have spent the night in the shelter. Tony. Pam. Luna. She kept hoping she'd see them next to one of the EMS trucks, huddled safely under a blanket. But she didn't see anyone.

She hugged her arms around her chest, wanting to rush forward under the yellow crime tape and ask the cops about the building occupants, but she didn't. Since she'd gotten out of prison six months ago, she avoided the cops. Cops translated into trouble and she'd sworn never again to trust a cop or return to prison.

But her friends. God, she had to find out something.

Tucking her head low, she moved toward the edge of the growing crowd of onlookers mesmerized by the bright red flames. The heat would be so hot now that it could sear lungs and melt flesh.

Eva glanced toward an elderly man with wire-rimmed glasses and a Steelers sweatshirt that hugged a rounded belly. 'Hey, you know what happened?'

The man shook his head. 'Can't say. I was watching *The Price is Right* when I heard the sirens. I came out to look and saw the house in flames.' He nodded his head east. 'I live a block and a half away but could see the light of the flames as clear as day.'

She nearly choked on the lump of tension in her throat. 'You don't know how it started?'

'Nope.'

As the cop lights flashed, she resisted the urge to run. 'Anyone know anything?'

'Couldn't say.'

Emotion shortened her temper. 'They bring anyone out? I mean from the shelter.'

'Not that I've seen. The firemen just got the flames contained enough to get close to the building. There might be people around the back side.'

'Thanks.'

Eva hugged her arms around her chest and moved through the crowd, listening and collecting any bits of information that would tell her what had happened.

'Said it started just after seven.'

'Heard an explosion. Those old gas heaters are trouble.'

'Odd folks came and went from that place. Always knew that place was nothing but trouble. But looks like they brought in the big guns cop-wise. They're taking this seriously.'

Being near so many cops left her edgy and worried. Goons like Radford could be managed whereas cops equaled real trouble. She shoved out a breath and buried her emotions down deep inside. Prison had taught her that showing true fear not only showed weakness but also provided leverage for your enemies.

She focused on the fire. Who could have done this? Sally understood trouble often followed her residents and she was careful to keep the peace. They had code words. Security systems. Eva admired Sally's careful planning.

Her gaze skimmed the crowd of onlookers who looked shocked and terrified. Their sadness magnified her fears. As she turned to leave, her gaze settled on a lone figure standing just inside the yellow tape. His back was rigid, his arms folded over his chest. He wasn't weeping, whispering or afraid to look at the destruction. In fact, he glared at the dying embers with defiance.

Taller than most around him, this man had broad shoulders and a battlelike stance suited to an ancient warrior more than a modern-day man. When he turned slightly, the fire department's floodlights caught his profile. His chin was covered with dark stubble and jutted forward, as if anger chewed at his insides. Dark hair teased the edge of his collar and begged for a trim.

This one was a pit bull who gave off a big-time cop vibe. She'd bet money that nothing stood between him and a closed case.

A shiver crept up her back and coiled around her throat, choking the breath from her lungs. Cops determined to close a case a decade ago had stolen ten years of her life. *Just tell us you killed him, Eva. Just tell us . . .*

As she retreated, the cop turned as if guided by radar. His gaze locked on her like a hunter on a deer. She froze, refusing to show fear, all the while watching closely for any sign of trouble.

Eva swallowed. Her skin tingled and the muscles at the base of her spine bunched painfully. Not good. Not good at all. Smart ex-cons stayed off all cops' radars, especially at a crime scene.

It had been a mistake to linger. She didn't want to be noticed by anyone, especially a pit-bull cop. Carefully, Eva kept her expressions neutral as she slowly shifted her gaze away from his. She pretended to smile at something the man next to her said and made a nonsensical comment. Then, as if she were just another gal out for an evening stroll, she melted into the crowd.

Her muscles screamed: *Run, hide!*

But she didn't.

Experience had taught her that even the innocent looked guilty when they ran.

Chapter 2

Alexandria City homicide detective Deacon Garrison spotted the woman easing toward the back of the crowd. He could see she was short, slim like a boy, and had thick, long dark hair that skimmed the middle of her back and framed a pale face. She wore jeans and a hoodie that looked like it didn't keep her very warm. She could have easily passed for a teen if not for the intensity electrifying her stance.

For this woman, this fire was more than a night's diversion. It was personal, painful, and as much as she seemed to want to turn away he doubted she could. A tear trickled down her pale cheek and she swiped it away with an agitated hand. She didn't belong.

Whoever she was, she needed to be questioned before she slipped away. Instinct told him that she had information that would be valuable.

As he moved toward her, a man called his name. 'Deacon.'

Garrison turned to see his partner, Detective Malcolm Kier, duck under the yellow crime scene tape. Malcolm had a boxer's muscular frame, ink-black hair and a cynical nature rarely seen in men in their early thirties. He wore jeans, a gray sweatshirt and worn leather boots. His badge

25

dangled from a chain around his neck and his gun rested on his right hip. The last few days he'd hiked the Appalachian Trail and had returned to Garrison's message. Garrison and Malcolm were two members of a four-person homicide squad that served Alexandria, Virginia, a city bordered to the north by the Potomac River. The city was packed with a mixture of history, prosperity and poverty.

'I just heard about the fire.' Malcolm's accent held a hint of his central Virginia roots.

Garrison rested his hands on his hips and shifted his gaze back to the crowd. The woman had vanished. He searched the crowd, carefully going over each face in search of the woman. But she'd slipped away. Shit. He released a frustrated sigh, already wondering if surveillance cameras had picked her up. 'I saw a woman in the crowd. She was too wrapped in the fire.'

Malcolm frowned as he too searched the faces in the crowd. 'You want to sweep the crowd for her?'

'Yeah. We won't get near the house until the scene has cooled. Let's take five.'

'Who am I looking for?'

'Petite, long black hair, looks like a kid but she's older.'

The two swept the crowd for the next thirty minutes talking to people to see if anyone knew the woman. None did. A woman carrying a terrier had seen a hooded figure but hadn't noted in which direction she'd gone. Although the witness had commented the girl had electric blue eyes.

Garrison moved among the crowd, fending questions about the fire, wondering why the woman had captured his attention so quickly. Had seven years on the police

26

force honed in on an arsonist's vibe or had his tarnished knight-errant character chink simply responded to a woman's terror? Whatever stirred his fascination, he was wise to remember that waiflike appearances could hide dangerous, unsteady waters.

After forty-five minutes, they'd not found the woman. If she remained in the area, she'd hidden herself well.

'Any sign of her?' Garrison shoved calloused fingers through his hair.

'Nope,' Malcolm said. 'And no one seems to have seen her. She's vanished.'

Damn. Damn. 'Fine.'

'She set the fire?'

'I don't know. But something about that fire bothered her a lot.'

'Deacon Garrison.' The husky, unmistakable voice belonged to Lieutenant Macy LaPorta, arson investigator for the Alexandria Fire Department.

Garrison turned and spotted Macy standing between two firemen. She held up a hand. He'd seen the look before. Stay put.

Macy's five-foot-eight-inch frame was slight and willowy and she looked almost frail standing so close to two bulky city firefighters who each topped six foot. But only a fool categorized Macy as frail. She wasn't intimidated by anyone, regardless of physical size or rank.

Curly auburn hair stopped at Macy's jawline. Expertly applied make-up added color to her naturally pale skin and covered the band of freckles that trailed over the bridge of her nose. She hated the freckles.

As always, she was dressed neatly in dark pants, a white

tailored top and a dark blazer. Her brown eyes reflected a piercing concentration.

The fireman talking to her had his head bent forward slightly, as if careful not to miss a word. 'Yes, ma'am,' he said. 'I'll let you know as soon as it's safe to examine the structure.'

'Thanks.' Her gaze returned to Garrison and she moved away from the fire toward him. 'You two got here fast.'

'You never call unless there is a reason,' Garrison said.

Her glance moved between the two detectives. 'No, I do not.'

Garrison and Macy had dated a couple of years ago. They'd had a lot in common. The sex had been great. But in the end she'd wanted more. And *more* was the last thing he could offer. When her patience had worn thin, she'd told him now or never. He'd chosen never and broken up with her.

Macy had ranted and raved and called him a few names he'd probably deserved. But to her credit, when their paths did cross professionally she remained civil.

'So why have we been called to the scene of a house fire? I know it wasn't my winning smile.'

Macy nodded. 'We suspect arson.'

Garrison stared at the charred and smoking timbers that still hissed a protest as firefighters sprayed water onto the embers. 'Fatalities?'

'One.'

'How many people got out?' Malcolm said.

'Seven. And that was a miracle. Witnesses say flames engulfed the place in less than two minutes.' Macy rubbed the back of her neck and glanced toward the charred

28

timbers. 'Everyone was spared because they'd been in the front of the house watching television and when the smoke detectors went off everyone hustled out.'

'Where was the victim when the fire broke out?' Garrison said.

'That's the thing,' Macy said. 'She didn't die in the fire.'

'Where is she?' Malcolm said.

'In the backyard.' She crooked her finger. 'Follow me, gentlemen.'

Garrison and Malcolm followed Macy around the perimeter of the yellow crime scene tape to what had been the home's backyard. Fifty feet from the house lay an area roped off with red crime scene tape and in the center lay a body covered by a white sheet.

Macy moved up to the body, squatted and reached for the sheet. 'We covered her up to protect the evidence until we could get the blaze out. This close to the house it's a miracle she's not soaked in water.'

Garrison moved beside her, bracing as he pulled rubber gloves from his pocket and tugged them over his hands.

Macy folded back the sheet to reveal a woman's still, slack-jawed, sallow features. The fire had not touched her face and death had yet to rob her of what must have been striking looks when she'd been alive. Full lips, a high slash of cheekbones and blond hair that he imagined were just as much an asset to her as the large breasts hidden by the sheet.

'She doesn't look like the type who'd have been in the homeless shelter. She came out of that building?' Garrison said.

29

'I don't think so.' She rolled back part of the sheet to reveal stab wounds into the victim's heart.

Malcolm pulled on gloves as he moved to the other side of the body. Both detectives squatted next to the body and studied the deep and jagged wounds. 'She reminds me of the woman we found near the Metro stop a few months ago. Stab wounds are similar.' That victim had been identified as Eliza Martinez, age fifty-seven. She'd lived alone, worked as a domestic and her only daughter had died of cancer a year earlier. She didn't use drugs nor had she ever been arrested. Neighbors had said she was a nice woman. 'A good Catholic,' one neighbor commented. Loved it when her grandson visited. No one understood why anyone would have wanted to kill Eliza. So far the case remained unsolved and growing colder by the day.

'This victim's wounds look deeper, which suggests a lot of rage,' Garrison said. 'Martinez had a single knife wound to the chest and she wasn't naked. In fact, the killer had covered her face with a towel.'

'There is another big difference between the two victims.' Macy pulled the rest of the sheet down and a rush of worry shot through Garrison's limbs. The woman's belly had been branded four times with four-pointed stars, which encircled her navel.

'Shit,' Malcolm said.

Garrison studied the red, angry stars. Christ, the pain she must have endured. He could almost hear her screams in his head. 'Martinez certainly wasn't tortured like this victim.'

Garrison looked around the backyard, encircled by a

privacy fence. A back gate banged gently, as if someone had just passed through it. 'Any blood trail?'

'No. And there are no apparent signs of a struggle. Clearly, she wasn't tortured or murdered here,' Malcolm said.

'Why dump her here?' Macy said.

'That's what we need to find out,' Garrison said. 'You said you suspect arson?'

Macy nodded. 'I'd bet a paycheck on it.'

Garrison stood, the discomfort in his knees reminding him of his last days as an air force paratrooper. 'Why?'

'Hard to say. Intense, intense blaze that started out of nowhere near the back door. There appeared to be nothing near that door that could have accidentally just exploded like that.'

'How long before you know for sure?' Garrison said.

'Chances are I won't even be able to inspect the embers until tomorrow when the area is cooled and safe to investigate.'

'Let me know as soon as you have information.'

'If your killer set this blaze to cover his tracks, he didn't do such a good job,' Macy said. 'It was a long shot that the house fire would have destroyed the body.'

'I'm not so sure the killer wanted the body destroyed,' Garrison said.

'Why not get rid of the evidence?' she said.

Malcolm shook his head. 'If the body is obliterated, there is no one to admire his handiwork.'

Macy's gaze lingered on the body before she tore it away. 'Think he'll do it again?'

'I don't know,' Garrison said.

She shook her head. 'As unpredictable as fires can be, I understand they will kill me if I don't respect them.' She stared at the draped lifeless body. 'Whereas people, well, you never quite know where they are coming from. They are a mystery.'

Garrison couldn't tell if she referred to him or the killer. 'I don't want anyone near this body – including your men. The last thing I need is some nutcase trying to copy-cat this murder.'

Macy planted her hands on her hips. 'A few have already seen it, but I can trust them to keep quiet.'

Garrison met her gaze. 'I'm counting on that.'

Bristling at his tone, she raised her chin. 'You worry about your people and I'll worry over mine.'

The fire sparking in her gaze told him if he didn't back off, they'd land in a full-blown pissing match. Intensely loyal to the men and women who worked for her, Macy would go toe-to-toe with anyone who spoke badly about her 'crew.'

Garrison needed cooperation, not a turf war. And if Garrison was good at anything, it was convincing people to see things his way. He relaxed his stance, trying to cool off her temper. 'Have you spoken to the survivors of the fire or the shelter director?'

'That's your gig, not mine.' Still defensive, but breathing a bit less fire, she said, 'I'm just here to show you the body so I can get back to figuring out how that fire got started.'

Malcolm dusted imaginary dirt from his hands. 'Fair enough.'

Garrison grinned at Macy. 'And when you find out any-thing about the fire, you'll let me know.'

'You'll be the first.' She walked back toward the throng of fire trucks and let the controlled chaos swallow her.

'You have a knack for pissing her off,' Malcolm said.

'It's a gift.'

Malcolm muttered an oath. 'You dated her once, didn't you?'

'Yep.'

'Christ, man. Any woman in this city you haven't dated?'

'I never lie and I never make promises.'

'That why all the women love you?' Sarcasm dripped from the words.

Garrison ignored the comment. 'Forensics has been dispatched and should be here soon. The first priority is to run prints and find out the victim's identity. If by some remote chance the two murders are linked, we need to know.'

'The killings look as if they were done by different people.'

'That's my initial thought.' But he'd let the forensics play out.

'She looks classy,' Malcolm said. 'Doesn't look like she and the first victim ran in the same circles.'

'Doesn't mean they don't have something in common.' Garrison glanced at the dark roots peeking out from her blond hair. She appeared well nourished and didn't show any track marks on her arms. Her breasts appeared to have been enhanced by a plastic surgeon. He covered her body with a sheet.

'Want me to canvas the crowd again?' Malcolm asked.

'Yeah. And keep on the lookout for that woman in the crowd. She might have doubled back. I'll talk to the survivors.' Tonight promised to be long.

'Will do.' Malcolm peeled off toward the onlookers while Garrison cut back toward the front yard where the seven survivors were huddled under blankets and cradling cups of coffee. Each stared blankly – a sign of shock.

The group looked ragtag, worn and shell-shocked from the fire. Garrison's gaze scanned the group, beginning with a woman in her fifties. Wisps of gray hair escaped a thinning ponytail, and crow's feet highlighted brown sunken eyes and leathery skin.

At the opposite end sat a man – mid-thirties with a mocha complexion. He wore a thick hunting jacket two sizes too large, a tattered ball cap that read ACE, steel-toe boots, gray shirt and jeans covered with a half-dozen patches.

He'd have to talk to them all individually so one person's story didn't contaminate another's. Eye-witness testimony coupled with trauma often meant skewed memories.

'I saw what happened.' The man on the end with the ACE hat had spoken up.

Garrison slipped a hand in his pocket and pulled out a pack of gum as he strolled toward him. He offered the man a stick and waited patiently as the guy unfolded the wrapper and folded the gum in his mouth.

The guy nodded. 'Thanks.'

'Let's walk.'

'Sure.'

The two moved out of earshot of the other six survivors. Garrison learned long ago if he didn't rush the interview process he often learned more in the end. And a little kindness led to more information than hard-edged questions.

'Can I have the rest of that gum?' Ace said.

'Sure.' Garrison handed him the packet. 'My name's Detective Garrison.'

'I'm Ace.'

'Just like your hat.' Garrison pulled out a slim notebook and pen from the breast pocket of his blue sports coat.

'They call me Ace because of the hat.' Ace fumbled with the gum and then held it up to his nose. He inhaled deeply then shoved the pack into the pocket of his jacket.

'What's your real name?'

Dark brows knotted. 'I don't remember.'

Garrison smiled. 'Maybe it'll come to you.'

He knotted his brow as if it bothered him that he didn't know his name. 'Sometimes it does. Give it time.'

'Well, we'll just stick with Ace for now. Ace, what happened? How did the fire start?'

'I was watching the television. We were all watching *Entertainment Tonight.* I like Mary Hart. You watch *ET?*'

'No. Not much of a TV guy when it's not football season.'

'I love *ET.* Proves even the celebrities got their issues. Maybe if I'd had a handler like those stars I'd still be fine.'

'I suppose we could all use a little handler.' Hell, there'd been a time when his parents had stepped into his life and straightened him out. No telling where he'd have ended up if not for them. 'Did the fire start before or after the show ended?'

'Right at the end, thank goodness. I was just getting up to get water from the kitchen when I saw this flame in the front yard.'

'A flame?' Garrison jotted notes.

'Yeah. Some guy held a flame in his hand.'

'A Molotov cocktail?'

'Could be. I ain't never seen one before.'

'What happened next?'

'The flame carrier came right up to the house and tossed the fire bottle at the house. When it hit the house, it kind of exploded. If you don't believe me, then check the eyes.'

'Eyes?'

'Cameras. They are all around. They catch everything.'

Garrison's gaze swept around. 'Mostly homes around here.'

'There's a camera on the home on the corner. The guy is afraid of us. Doesn't like homeless people on his street. Uses the camera to watch us.'

'Which house?'

'White one on the corner.'

'Thanks. I'll check it out.' He rubbed the back of his neck with his hand. 'Know anyone that would want to burn the place down?'

'Some.'

'Like?'

'Always someone that's mad with someone here. Last week I got into a fight over the television remote. Darryl demanded the remote during *ET*. I got mad. We fought.'

'Darryl here tonight?' He wrote the name down, doubting if any of this would pan out.

'No. Ain't seen him in a week.'

'Do you know where he is?'

'No. He comes and goes. He ain't a regular like me.'

'Okay.'

Ace's nostrils flared. 'You don't believe me about the flame carrier.'

Garrison shook his head from side to side, letting his lips rise into a grin. 'I believe you, man. I believe you.'

Ace's eyes narrowed. 'You don't have to believe me. Just check the eyes. They're always watching.'

'I will. Thanks, Ace.'

Ace wiped his nose with the back of his hand. 'What's your name? I forgot.'

'Garrison. Deacon Garrison.'

'I'll remember.'

'Good.' Garrison patted Ace on the back. 'Where are you going to stay tonight?'

'Don't know.'

'Once I've finished talking to everyone I'll see what I can do about finding you a bed.'

'Thanks, Boss.'

'Ace, you ever seen a short, petite woman around? Dark hair. Looks like a kid.'

Ace hesitated, frowned as a child with a secret might. 'Could be a lot of people, I guess. Can't say for sure.'

He was lying. 'She moved through the crowd about a half hour ago.'

Ace flicked a foil gum wrapper. 'Sorry.'

Garrison leaned forward, close enough to invade Ace's space, but careful not to touch. 'You wouldn't be holding back on me, Ace?'

Ace dropped his gaze. 'No.'

'Good, because I don't want to get her into trouble. I just want to talk to her.'

'Sorry, Boss. Can't help.'

Ace was protecting the woman. But why? Was Ace a tarnished knight like himself or did he have a darker secret?

Garrison could kick himself now for letting her melt into the crowd. He hoped his hesitation didn't cost the investigation.

Chapter 3

Monday, April 3, 11:02 P.M.

Eva hovered in the shadows watching the scene. She'd seen enough to know her friends had survived the fire. The sense of relief that washed over her triggered a rush of tears. She brushed her tears away and noticed that tall cop who had surveyed the crowd several times since their gazes had locked had returned to the crime scene perimeter once again and was scanning the crowd. He frowned.

Eva pressed her body against a hundred-year-old oak. For several breathless moments she'd expected the detective to venture again into the crowd and close the gap between them. She had visions of handcuffs slapping on her wrists, of being lowered into the back seat of a patrol car and of a cell door locking her in an eight-by-eight concrete cell. Nausea churned her belly.

A few questions to the residents and he could find out her name and address. But she doubted any would talk. She got along well with everyone in the house and, like her, they distrusted the law.

Eva's heart hammered, warning her to leave and return to the pub. She'd been a fool to linger, but like the other onlookers, she'd been mesmerized by the scene's horror.

Shit.

Clenching her fists, she shook her head. 'I've done nothing wrong. I have *nothing* to fear.'

But as sweet as that mantra sounded, she knew the innocent got convicted all the time. They suffered. They went to jail.

She did not want to be on that cop's radar or any cop's radar for that matter. Cops were trouble. Period.

Forcing the stale breath from her lungs, she pulled in the cool night air and let the fresh oxygen fill her lungs. Dragging a trembling hand through her hair, she forced her stiff legs to move forward. Where had she parked her truck?

As she moved away from the scene her panic eased and she forced herself to concentrate. Relying on logic, she ticked through the questions colliding in her mind.

How had the fire started? The shelter's old building needed repairs, but for those very reasons the shelter director, Sally, had been so careful about maintaining the smoke detectors with fresh batteries. She'd had an electrician in just last week to fix a faulty breaker. Did an electrical issue cause the problem? And where was Sally? Had she been in the fire? She wasn't on the curb with the other survivors. Weren't Monday nights Sally's night off? She shouldn't have been in the building but that didn't mean she hadn't doubled back to check on something. That happened more often than not.

Oh, God.

With a sick heart, she glanced back over her shoulder as the fire crews pummeled the smoldering embers with water. That cop faced the fire, his hands on his hips and his head bent as he listened to the woman beside him. Eva turned, hurried away, grateful that he seemed to have forgotten her.

She moved down the small side street to her truck. Fishing keys out of her pocket she fumbled the key into the lock and released the latch. Climbing inside, she fired up the engine. Logic told her to get moving. Keep moving. It's what had kept her safe for ten years.

Don't stop for anyone. Don't care about anyone.

But images of the fire weighed her like an anchor. Despite tough talk of being the loner, she did care for the people at the shelter and the people at King's. She'd left friends and family behind too many times in her life, and now to possibly lose more friends was almost too much to bear.

Keep moving. Keep moving.

This time the engine had turned over on the first key turn. Slowly, she drove down the side street, carefully moving away from the scene. All the way home she maintained a light touch on the accelerator. A speeding ticket now could cause more unwanted problems.

Light traffic had her soon winding her way through the streets of Old Town Alexandria, the city's historic district. The area, chock-full of brick colonial buildings and uneven sidewalks, was now home to trendy shops, art galleries, restaurants and bars.

Eva turned on a small side street and then down a darkened alley. The alley led to the back entrance of King's Pub, where she'd worked for the last six months.

The owner, who'd found his business struggling these last couple of years, paid Eva a small salary but also gave her all the food she could eat and a room on the top floor.

In her mind it was the perfect arrangement. She had food, shelter, money to save for school and the time to find missing pieces of her past.

Eva parked in the spot next to the battered green Dumpster.

Two of the three lights by the back door were out again, leaving only a pale ring of light to mark the back entrance.

Eva didn't like the alley and always moved quickly from her truck to the back door. This quirk confused her boss, King, who pointed out she'd serve a subpoena on a bruiser like Bruce Radford but smelly alleys gave her the creeps. She'd never told King that something about the smell reminded her of prison.

Eva fumbled for the back door key and got out of the truck. She'd taken two steps when she heard a rustle behind her. She whirled around, keys clutched between her fingers like a weapon. Images of Radford and that cop bombarded her mind. Had someone followed her?

The scratching grew louder. The battered green Dumpster moved an inch or two.

'Who is it?' she demanded.

No answer.

'I've got a gun and I've called the cops.' Holding her breath, she slid her hands into her hoodie's front pocket, but captured only lint and a gas receipt.

A young boy peeked out from behind the Dumpster. Immediately, she recognized the dark hair, freckles over the bridge of his nose and the white Redskins T-shirt and torn jeans he wore almost daily. Bobby. The ten-year-old was King's foster son.

Social Services had provided scant information on the

boy's background. Mother died of natural causes. Father unknown. Extended family unwilling to take the boy. But Eva didn't need a full case file to see the kid had trauma in his past. The walking wounded recognized each other.

'You don't have a phone or a gun,' the kid said. 'You're too cheap to pay for a phone and too scared of guns.'

'Damn, kid. You scared the stuffing out of me,' Eva said. In the five weeks the kid had lived at the pub, neither had warmed to the other. The kid, like her, was another one of King's strays. 'What are you doing outside at this hour?'

He glanced behind him toward the Dumpster. 'I found a kitten.'

'Where?'

'Over there.'

'Have you seen it?'

'Just once. It's white and small. It has long hair. I heard it crying. I came to feed it.'

'Does King know you're out here?' She raised her hand to silence his reply. 'Of course he doesn't. He'd go nuts knowing you were running around at night alone. How did you get past the alarm?'

'I saw King press in the code. It's easy to remember.' The kid lowered his voice. '1984.'

'Great.' Her head pounded and this was the last thing she needed right now. 'Let's get you back inside.'

The kid frowned. 'But I've got to guard the kitten.'

'You fed him, right?'

'Milk and tuna.'

She now saw the two bowls by the Dumpster. Both looked untouched. 'He's not going to come out and eat if we keep standing here.'

'Why not?'

'Think about it. Would you take food from a stranger? And then eat it while he watches you?'

'No.'

'Neither would I. I'll bet that kitten is just as street-smart as us.'

'But . . .'

The kid hadn't shown much interest in anything these last few weeks. He went to school, did his chores and brushed his teeth, but he had been going through the day's activities in a stupor. She remembered being in the same funk after her mother died and she'd ended up in foster care. At least King cared about the kid.

She sensed if she didn't give him something now, he'd go to battle over this stray kitten, and hunger demanded she eat, not argue. 'We'll try to find him in the daylight.'

He frowned, staring at her through narrow eyes. 'Swear.'

Eva rarely made promises. 'Swear.'

'And you don't think anyone will get him?'

'He's pretty wedged back there because it's safe. He'll be fine.' She opened the back door. 'What is it about this place and strays?'

'Maybe it's King,' the kid said. 'Maybe he has some kind of magic.'

'Magic.' She wasn't sure what it was about King or why he collected strays like Bobby and her. The man had offered her a job while she'd still been living in the halfway house in Richmond just days after her release from prison. He promised honest work and an apart-ment in the attic. She'd not trusted him one bit and the last place she'd ever wanted to see again was her old home

Alexandria. So when he'd handed her a bus ticket to Alexandria, she'd refused him. He'd left her with the open-ended ticket and told her to contact him if she changed her mind. Bad job opportunities for ex-cons coupled with nagging questions about home had prompted her to take the bus to Alexandria and find King's. In the last six months, King had been good to his word. She had honest work and the apartment in the attic had started to feel strangely like home.

'Can we keep it?' Bobby said.

Eva shrugged. 'I don't know how to take care of a kitten.'

'It can't be too hard.'

She flipped on the kitchen light. 'I don't know, kid. This isn't my place.'

'Will you ask King if we can keep it? He listens to you.'

'I don't know about that.' She glanced up at the back staircase toward the second-floor apartment that Bobby shared with King. The dark staircase told her King was asleep. 'Hey, don't sneak out again, okay. King worries about you.' She tried to summon the stern voice of her mother, which she only barely remembered, but the effect seemed lost on the kid.

'Will you ask him about the kitten?' The boy's eyes held so much hope it squeezed her heart. 'Since you fixed the computer and saved him all that money he trusts you. Please, Eva.'

She shoved out a sigh. 'I'll talk to him in the morning. In the meantime I'm starving.'

Bobby fiddled with the frayed edge of his T-shirt. 'Do you think he can live in my room?'

Eva moved toward a wide stainless-steel refrigerator. 'Ask King.'

'Can we leave the back light on?' Bobby said. 'He's afraid of the dark.'

'Cats love the night. They've special eyes to see in the dark.'

'He's not like other cats. He likes the light.' Bobby slept with the light on in his room. His nightmares no longer came nightly but at least a couple times a week. He refused to tell King what terrorized him.

'Sure. Fine. We'll leave the light on and get those bulbs replaced. Hey, I'm hungry, are you?'

'Yes.'

No doubt King had fed the boy a grand meal. King was good at feeding people. But the kid was always hungry.

She pulled out six slices of bread, buttered each and popped them in the toaster. As she peeled the foil back from the meat, the back door squeaked open. Bobby was checking to make sure the floodlight was indeed on. She had no illusions about fixing the kid's life or even saving that damn kitten. Happy endings were for fools. 'Make sure you lock the door and set the alarm.'

Bobby flipped the dead bolt and punched the numbers on the security keypad like he'd done before. 'Done.'

Eva washed her hands, assembled a sandwich and placed it on a white plate. She slid the plate toward him, not saying anything as she turned to the refrigerator and pulled out a half-full gallon jug of milk. Filling two glasses, she set one in front of Bobby and kept the other for herself. Bobby reached for a sandwich.

'Wash your hands, kid. God knows what kind of germs that kitten carries.'

Bobby moved to the sink and stood on the small stepstool King had put down for him. He scrubbed his fingers using hot water and soap like King had showed him. His hands dried, he scooped the sandwich off the plate and held a half in each hand. He glanced at each, as if wondering if he could eat both at once. He opted for two large bites out of the one in his left hand.

Eva cut her sandwich and took a few big bites herself. Slowly, she sipped the milk and both ate in silence. When Bobby had finished the first half he took the milk and gulped half down, then turned his sights to the other half.

Eva placed another sandwich on his plate and continued to eat.

The boy ate everything placed in front of him and ended up drinking three glasses of milk. When he'd finished he tossed her his first glance. A milk mustache covered his top lip.

'Pie?' Eva said. 'Apple or cherry?'

He hesitated as if the choice was almost too overwhelming. 'Apple.'

Nodding, she cut him a large slice. He grabbed the fork she offered and jabbed into a juicy apple slice.

'I go for cherry,' she said, trying to keep her voice light as she cut herself a piece. 'But if I really had a choice I'd pick cake. Chocolate with extra icing.'

Bobby tossed another quick glance her way. He said nothing but kept eating as if fearing if he dallied the food would vanish.

'You like chocolate too?'

He nodded.

'Wise man.' She stabbed a cherry and a hunk of crust with her fork. 'But then I could tell from the minute I saw you that you were smart.'

He frowned. 'How could you tell?'

'You found that kitten.' Always paid to avoid trouble in prison. 'How'd you do it?'

'I heard it crying and I found its hiding spot. I'm good at finding hiding spots.'

'I can see that.' A part of her wanted to ask what he'd had to hide from. But she hated it when people dug into her past so she stayed out of theirs. If he wanted to tell her, she'd listen. But she'd not push. They ate their pie in silence and when they'd washed the dishes they checked in on the kitten one last time. 'He'll be fine. It's not too cold and you left him a milk and tuna feast.'

The kid frowned.

'Don't worry. That thing is a survivor.' *Like us.*

'Okay.' He hesitated, his hand on the knob. 'You're nice, Eva.'

'How can you be sure?'

He met her gaze. 'I know mean people.'

'Me too.'

She swallowed, remembering a moment of cruelty that had changed her life. Most days she could elbow the memories aside and forget about The Night that she'd died and become a different person. But for some reason, not tonight. It must have been the flames of the fire that had scored through her barriers.

Both were silent for a moment, until she said, 'Get to bed, kid. You've got school tomorrow.'

'I hate school.'

'Learn to love it. It's your ticket to a good life.'

'You don't go to school.'

'I will again one day. As soon as I can get the money together.'

He studied her with eyes that held wisdom far beyond his years. 'Okay.'

She walked him upstairs to the second floor and lingered as he slipped inside the apartment. She waited until she heard nothing but silence and then waited a few extra minutes to make sure he didn't double back.

She climbed the last staircase to her room. Entering, she locked the door behind her, checking it twice to make sure it was secure. For years she'd dreamed of sleeping with an open unlocked door and now she couldn't sleep unless the door was closed and locked.

Her room was small, but neatly organized as if she remained confined to an eight-by-eight cell. Furnished with twin beds, one covered with a blue comforter and the other pink, both chosen from the Goodwill store for warmth not style. She didn't need two quilts or two dressed beds, but maybe, just maybe, she'd have her sister over sometime. She should have called her sister months ago, but Eva had wanted to be someone with a real future and not an ex-con with a past dangling around her like a weight.

Between the beds was a desk and chair that she'd salvaged from a street corner. On the desk were used books she'd bought in the community college bookstore. *Intro to Literature. Trigonometry. The Internet.* Most women who'd reached their late twenties had long finished school or were on to graduate classes or careers. She was just beginning.

Nearly a decade lost.

An old bitterness rose in her but just as quickly she chased it aside. *Eyes forward.* That was her motto.

Eva flipped on the light in the small adjoining bathroom. She pulled down the hand-washed bras and panties hanging on the rod and tossed them on the second bed.

She turned down her comforter.

Eva headed back into the bathroom and turned on the tap. Gratefully, she stripped off her grimy clothes, which smelled faintly of smoke. She slipped under the shower's hot spray and savored the rush of water over her face and through her hair.

The emotion of the fire rushed through her, loosening the tight hold she normally kept on her emotions. Memories of another fire burned through from her subconscious. Despite ten years, she could still remember the moment, the coiling stench of hot metal burning her flesh before she'd blacked out. To this day she still shied from any kind of flame.

For the first time in a very long time, she let her guard drop. The tears came almost immediately, rushing down her cheeks and dissolving into the shower's spray.

As much as she wanted to believe that the fire was an accident, she just couldn't in light of the dream and The Anniversary, which was less than a week away.

Eva's survival instinct, like a clenched fist in her chest, whispered warning.

Leave Alexandria!

Something is not right!

Foolish to return!

No matter how much the fear goaded her to run, she refused. She now believed King or fate had brought her back to Alexandria for a reason bigger than a waitress job.

Crime reporter Connor Donovan reached for the beer bottle on the edge of his desk as he reread the letter from the managing editor. *Due to declining ad sales . . .*

The letter went on to say that crime reporting no longer sold papers like it once had. With twenty-four-hour cable shows and the Internet available, people didn't turn to their local paper for news.

'Christ, I am not a snot-nosed reporter writing for some hayseed paper.' He glanced at the awards on his wall and took another pull from the beer, which had grown hot and bitter. He crossed his loft apartment that overlooked the Potomac and opened the refrigerator, stocked with three six-packs of beer, a couple of cartons from the neighborhood Chinese restaurant and a few cartons of eggs.

Connor twisted open the top on another beer. He should slow the pace. He had another meeting with his editor in the morning and needed to be alert.

The phone rang. Connor ran long fingers through shoulder-length hair as he crossed the room to a thirties-style rotary phone. 'Donovan.'

'It's Marks.'

Elaine Marks on the assignment desk at the paper. 'We have a story for you to cover. Homeless shelter burned.'

'My stuff isn't selling papers anymore.' His petulant tone sounded childlike.

'You're gonna want to cover this story.' Her calm, clear voice reminded him of his mother.

'Why? Even if it was arson, who really cares about a shelter burning?'

She laughed, refusing to offer him an ounce of sympathy. 'My, my, you are in a snappish mood this evening.'

'See your paycheck cut by forty percent and then let's see how much you smile, sweetie.' The sourness of his demotion churned him like spoiled milk.

Elaine lowered her voice a notch. 'Stop your bitching and moaning. This story could have legs under it.'

'Then tell me.'

'Got a tip from someone from the scene just a few minutes ago. Cops found a murdered woman behind the shelter.'

He dug into the beer label with his thumbnail. 'And why should I care? Chicks get murdered all the time.'

She muttered an obscenity under her breath. 'Oh, man, you are gonna owe me the best bottle of champagne money can buy.'

'Spit it out, Elaine.'

'The victim had a funky brand on her stomach.'

'A brand?' He lowered the bottle from his lips. His stomach clenched a little excitement. 'What kind of brand?'

'Four-pointed star, baby.'

Connor didn't speak for a long moment as his mind tumbled through the past. The Sorority House Murder had been the series he'd done ten years ago that had landed him on the map. He'd gone from covering petty crimes to his own bylined column. The story's details had been a dream: a modern-day Delilah on scholarship who had killed her rich lover and then burned the sorority house to hide evidence. She'd cried rape, but friends testified she and the boy had been lovers. His little Delilah had simply gotten angry when lover boy had broken off their relationship. In the end, the jury had sentenced the girl to ten years in prison.

'You remember the star, don't you?' Elaine said.

'What are the chances that this story connects with the old story?'

'I don't know. Probably none, but who cares? You're clever. You can at least stir a little trouble with an alleged connection. Either way couldn't hurt. From what I've heard, your column is begging for a little sex and drama.'

Connor shuffled through the papers on his desk until he found a pen. 'I'll make it work.'

'That's my boy.'

'Give me the address.'

It was past midnight when Lenny Danvers stared at the brick colonial with dark windows, tall boxwood shrubs and two uncollected newspapers in the neat gravel driveway. The house's size and location said: *money*. The dark windows and newspapers said: *on vacation*. The boxwoods said: *cover and protection*. He'd been driving around for hours looking for this very combination.

The other houses on the street appeared dark and quiet, but to play it safe he parked his rented Saab at the end of the block and then jogged back to the house he'd just scoped. Quickly, he slipped behind the tall bushes and inspected the windows for signs of an alarm system.

Many rich folks had alarms but it amazed him how

often they left town with the systems disarmed. Maybe they figured their nice rich neighborhoods were safe from men like him, but last he checked, an invisible fence didn't protect the good parts of town from people like him.

He pulled a wedge from his dark jacket and worked it under the sill. He'd know in seconds if an alarm would sound. If it did, he had parked close enough to get back down the street and out of the neighborhood before the cops showed.

Jerking hard on the wedge, he forced the window to pop open. Adrenaline rushed as he scanned the yard behind him and waited for the *beep, beep* of an alarm system. He heard nothing but still waited, poised to flee just in case someone was home. But one minute turned into two and then five.

When he was certain no one was home, he pushed the window up higher, wincing as his bruised shoulder pinched. He rubbed pain from the shoulder, and then sucking in a deep fortifying breath, wriggled his slim body into the house. He'd been breaking into homes since Joey Welch had dared him in eighth grade to break into Mr Mullins's house and steal milk. Even to this day he could remember how sweet that milk had tasted. Now, at thirty-five, he was a seasoned veteran who'd broken into hundreds of houses.

He moved through the living room past Chippendale sofas and tables decorated with crystal lamps and porcelain bowls. The real payoff in houses was usually found in the master bedroom or study where owners stashed jewels and money. Folks who didn't set alarms often didn't hide their jewels.

This was all so easy and so predictable. Gravy, baby, gravy.

And yet, the stillness of the house, once catnip to him, unsettled his nerves. He couldn't move a step forward. His feet froze as if encased in cement.

Lenny dragged a shaking hand through his hair. The other night when he'd broken into that home in the southwest, it had been routine and easy. And then he'd heard the muffled cries of a woman coming from inside the house. The sounds, he realized, had drifted up through the air vents from the basement.

He'd been ready to get the hell out of the house when that crazy motherfucker had come out of nowhere and hit him with a club. The blow had dropped him to his knees. The second blow to the back of his head had knocked him out cold.

Why the son of a bitch hadn't killed him, he didn't know. It would have been easy to finish him off. But for whatever reason the guy had simply bound his arms and legs and left him.

When Lenny had woken up, he'd heard a woman screaming. The scent of burning flesh had permeated the house and he'd nearly vomited. Scared shitless, he'd pissed in his pants. Double joints and a lifetime of scrapes had gotten his hands and feet loose and he'd scrammed out of that house so fucking fast his head had spun.

Shit. Close calls were part of this business.

Even knowing that, he still couldn't shake off the sound of the woman's screams. Jesus only knew what that motherfucker had done to her.

He'd considered calling the cops, but in the end hadn't.

He'd been arrested twice and another conviction would send him to jail for a long time.

But what rattled him more now was the fact that he'd dropped his wallet when he'd hustled out the window. He'd been a dumb ass to even take the wallet. He should have gone back to get it but the idea of running into that sick son of a bitch again kept him away. Since Saturday, he'd stayed on the move, only catnapping in his car.

'Shake if off.' He moved toward the carpeted stairs, but before he could climb the first step, the woman's screams started echoing in his head. He jerked around expecting that crazy motherfucker. But the room was empty. 'Fuck.'

Lenny raised his hand from the banister and realized he'd forgotten his gloves. Shit. He'd left fingerprints everywhere. What the hell was he thinking? He reached in his pocket and pulled out his black gloves and then slid them over trembling hands. He wiped the banister with his shirttail and then retraced his steps back to the window. He wiped all around the sill and the jamb.

As he furiously wiped every flat surface, he kept getting the feeling that he was being watched. He saw that crazy son of a bitch in every shadowy corner. A crack of a branch outside nearly made him piss in his pants. But no one was there. It was just him and the fears that had gripped him since Saturday night.

He'd thought getting back to work would put his life back on track, but now he wondered if he'd ever shake the fear that this guy would find him and do to him what he'd done to that woman.

Please. Her screams echoed in his head.

Time slipped away from him and he wasn't sure how long he had been standing there when he shook off the funk. 'Shit. Man, get a grip.'

As he turned back toward the stairs, police lights appeared in front of the house. Flashing blue and red, lights from three cars illuminated his silhouette in the window frame. He glanced back over his shoulder. He could have run and vaulted over the back fence. His limberness and quickness had been his trademark. Instead, he raised his hands, savoring an odd sense of relief.

Maybe in jail he wouldn't hear the woman's screams.

Just after one A.M. Donovan parked at the crime scene. He checked the recorder in his pocket, grabbed a notepad from the passenger seat and pulled a ball cap over his head. Since he'd earned a byline at the paper a decade ago, he'd never run his picture or appeared on television. In fact, he'd been a little paranoid about keeping his identity secret. He rationalized that anonymity allowed him more access to a crime scene. Except for a few cops, no one knew what he looked like.

For a moment he just stood and surveyed the scene. The firemen flooded burned-out embers with more water, making the charred beams hiss and spit tendrils of smoke. At least a dozen fire and police vehicles crowded the end of the cul-de-sac, but most of the curiosity seekers had drifted away, likely deciding that the real excitement had passed. Many would wander back in the morning.

He suspected the medical examiner had long since removed the body, so he decided to visit the ME's office and see what he could dig up.

He recognized Detective Deacon Garrison and swallowed an oath. Garrison knew his face and resented Donovan's negative portrayal of a victim earlier this year. Garrison had sought him out, cornering him in a coffee shop. They'd gone head to head over the story.

Garrison's quick smile was a weapon he used to get information. Many said the city's top cop could squeeze blood from a turnip. So if he had been given this case, it meant something.

Donovan moved up to the yellow crime scene tape. 'Detective, got a minute?'

Garrison's gaze swung around. He smiled but his stance remained rigid and closed. 'Donovan.'

'The one and only.' He surveyed the charred rubble. 'Looks like you got one hell of a mess on your hands.'

'They pay me to clean up the messes.'

Donovan shoved a lock of hair off his face. 'So what did happen?'

'Can't say for sure right now. We're still sifting through it all.'

'Anything you can tell me?'

'No.'

Detective Malcolm Kier moved toward him, his muscles poised to fight. The city's newest detective looked tired and impatient. He'd only crossed paths with Kier once or twice but the man could be a raging bull when provoked. 'Who called you, Donovan?'

Donovan enjoyed pissing these two off. He shrugged, sliding long fingers into his pocket as he approached the yellow crime scene tape. 'Word gets around.'

'And when I find out who is passing around the words,

I'm gonna can them.' Garrison's smile belied the ice in his gaze.

Donovan had little regard for the source's fate because they most generally sold their information for less than one hundred bucks. As his old man used to say, if you're going to get off the porch, you best be ready to play with the big dogs.

'Go away,' Garrison said.

Donovan saw the detective's irritation as a good sign. Cops got irritated when they had secrets to hide. 'Can't you just answer a few questions for me? Come on, guys. Maybe sometime I could do you a favor in return.'

'No.'

'How many people died?'

'My office will be issuing a press release later today.'

'No sneak peek?'

'Nope.'

Donovan pushed his hands in his pockets. 'So I hear this place was some kind of halfway house. You talk to the director yet?'

'Let us do our jobs, Donovan.' Garrison and Kier turned and moved away.

'A little birdie told me the victim was mutilated. Did it happen postmortem?' He could have mentioned the old case he'd written about but the idea of helping Garrison irritated him.

That stopped both detectives. Garrison turned, unable to maintain even a pretense of good humor.

Bingo.

As Garrison moved toward him, Donovan pictured a prizefighter stripping off his gloves. 'That birdie got a name?'

Reflex almost drove him back a step. 'Can't say. You know I have to protect my sources.'

Garrison leveled a gaze designed to intimidate. His size added to the fear factor and Donovan struggled for calm.

'I'm right about the mutilation, aren't I?' Donovan pushed.

'Someone is jerking your chain, Donovan. Go find a real story.'

His instincts kicked into overdrive. A story simmered below the surface. A huge story. 'I've found one hell of a story.'

Garrison's and Kier's stances radiated pure fury.

Donovan possessed enough smarts to know when to cut his losses. Garrison, unlike his partner, kept a tight rein on his temper, but Kier's temper had gained a reputation as explosive. 'You'll call me if you find out anything?'

Garrison winked. 'Sure thing, sport. Consider yourself on my speed dial.'

'Sarcasm is the lowest form of humor, Detective.'

'I never claimed to be smart.' Menace threaded around the words.

Donovan swallowed a smile, not anxious to go head to head with Garrison just yet. He moved toward his car, his mind ticking with the things he needed to do as he slid behind the wheel. He pushed in the car lighter.

Why dump a body here? And why the fire? Some might say coincidence linked the two stories. Fat chance. One way or another, they fit.

The lighter popped and he pressed the hot tip to the end of a cigarette. Tobacco embers glowed and smoke rose before he replaced the lighter.

Donovan puffed his cigarette and then flipped open his cell phone. He dialed and had to wait only two rings.

'What the fuck do you want, Donovan?' The gruff voice was thick with anger.

Caller ID was not his friend. 'I need for you to find someone for me.'

'Who?'

'Eva Rayburn.'

'You going to pay on time?'

'I swear.'

Silence followed and then the guy shoved out a breath. 'Give me what you have.'

Donovan grinned and gave the private investigator the particulars.

'Might take time.'

'I don't care what rock you have to dig under, but find her.'

'You have a last known address?'

'Virginia Penitentiary.'

'How long has she been out?'

'A year, maybe less.'

'I'll see what I can do.'

Chapter 4

Angie Carlson's stomach tumbled with nausea the instant her eyes opened. She lay on her back and stared at the white ceiling of her bedroom as she counted to ten and drew in slow deep breaths. Cautiously, she raised her head as if handling antique crystal. Immediately, her temples pounded and her stomach lurched violently. Collapsing back against the pillow, she muttered a curse. Too many glasses of wine with her TV dinner last night had knocked her out cold. Now fully awake, she really regretted the number of drinks she'd downed. 'It's just an upset stomach. A headache. I can deal with this.'

Steeling herself, she rose slowly and swung her legs over the side of the bed. The wood floor pricked her feet but she welcomed the distraction. Chilled toes trumped queasiness any day.

Moistening her lips, she moved out of her bedroom and down the center hall of her house. Located off Seminary Road near the Capital Beltway, the house had been built after World War II and came complete with plaster walls and crown molding in each room. Large fireplaces with marble mantels dominated the living room and original hardwood floors ran throughout the house.

The place was neat, clean and organized, but to say

she'd attempted any kind of decorating would be an exaggeration. The kitchen hadn't been updated in thirty years but she didn't have an eye for colors and fabrics and couldn't summon the patience to live among scaffolding and ladders. And considering her repertoire of meals included just toast and cereal, a fancy kitchen didn't matter.

Angie dug into her refrigerator past bottles of wine and half-eaten discs of cheese to retrieve a bottle of ginger ale. She untwisted the top, savored the fizzing sound and filled a clean glass from the cabinet. She sipped the ale, enjoying the burn even as she prayed the liquid would stay down.

She leaned forward over the sink and stared out her kitchen window into the small yard that she paid a boy from the neighborhood to maintain. A large century-old oak provided protection from the summer sun but hogged so much water and light it choked the grass. A small round wrought-iron table and three matching chairs rested under the tree. She'd paid a small fortune for the table and chairs because she'd imagined leisurely Sunday breakfasts at the table. In the last two years she'd had a grand total of two meals in the shade.

In the last few months, her days had been consumed with her work as a defense attorney in the small but growing law firm of Wellington and James. In a regular year junior partners rarely had much free time, but this last year had demanded a punishing schedule. Her life had been consumed with her defense of Dr James Dixon, a successful plastic surgeon who'd been accused of attempted murder.

Dixon, who frequented prostitutes often, had been suspected of killing several missing women whom he'd hired for sex. But no solid evidence linked the doctor to the missing women. Then a prostitute, Lulu Sweet, had fled his hotel room, screaming that he'd tried to kill her. Police had their first concrete evidence against the doctor. They'd arrested him for attempted murder. Angie had been able to demonstrate that the prostitute had lied about her drug use on the stand. In the end, she'd torn the young woman apart. The witness's testimony had been struck and Angie had planted enough seeds of reasonable doubt in the jury's mind to get an acquittal. Dr James Dixon was now a free man. She'd become a minor superstar in the law community and had received offers to practice at larger firms. She'd opted to stay with Wellington and James.

Angie had asked Dixon if he were guilty and he'd sworn he was innocent. Despite nagging doubts she'd taken the case. She'd become a lawyer because she believed in the justice system, which demanded every defendant receive a good defense. And she'd delivered her best to Dixon.

That ideal had been as shiny as a new penny when she'd been in law school. She'd had visions of saving the world's downtrodden from an unjust system. But five years of practicing defense law for too many clients like Dixon had tarnished that ideal. Now dreams of justice had been replaced by nightmares featuring the victims of her clients.

Angie sipped her ginger ale and turned from the window. Charlotte Wellington had promised that once the Dixon case had been resolved, Angie could do more pro bono work. Perhaps now she could get back to the law that had once excited her.

She took her ginger ale into the shower, setting it on a small tiled shelf before she turned on the hot spray. Closing her eyes, she dunked her head under the hot water, letting it wash over her pale skin. She lingered under the hot spray as long as she could before shutting off the tap and grabbing a towel. She dried her slim body and rubbed the terry cloth over her shoulder-length blond hair. Mascara added definition around her pale blue eyes and a little blush provided color to her cheeks. She chose a silk blouse and a dark pants suit and sensible flat shoes. A slim, gold crucifix dangled around her neck.

She grabbed her purse and briefcase and headed out the front door and hurried to her car. She slid behind the driver's seat. As she backed out of the parking space, her cell rang. Caller ID told her it was the office.

She flipped open the phone. 'Angie Carlson.'

'Doll, it's Iris.' Iris Stanford ran the offices of Wellington and James. A paralegal/administrator/mom, she kept the firm's three attorneys organized. Right now the two firm's named partners, Charlotte Wellington and Siena James, were out of town. Just Angie was holding down the fort so she'd stayed tethered to her phone. 'You got a call from your on-again, off-again client, Lenny Danvers. He's been arrested again. He's made bail but wants to see you.'

She checked her watch. Lenny knew all the bail bondsmen that worked all night. 'He always wants to see me.' Another tarnished penny. Thief, drug addict, manipulator.

'He says it's important.'

'It's always important.' She checked her watch. 'Does he want me to defend him?'

'He didn't say anything about defense. He says he's got information on an active murder investigation.'

'That's a new twist.' Two months ago he'd faked a heart attack to delay his testimony. Another time he'd had a breathing spasm. 'Since he's not requesting my counsel, let him stew. I've got other things to do.'

'Whatever you say, doll.'

Garrison and Malcolm had been at the crime scene for the better part of the night. They had interviewed all of the shelter survivors and released them from the scene so that a city bus could transport them to another facility.

Malcolm rubbed the back of his neck as the bus drove away with the shelter residents. 'No one else other than Ace saw the man with the bottle of flames.'

Garrison had hoped for corroboration of Ace's account. 'It's disappointing.'

As the night had waned, Ace's memory had drifted and he had a harder and harder time with the details. And a search of all the surrounding homes had not produced a camera. No 'eyes' watched the shelter.

Garrison slid his hands into his pockets, staring at cold embers of the halfway house. 'According to Macy, the fire's point of origin was the front door. She found traces of accelerant, which was likely gasoline. That's consistent with Ace's story.'

Malcolm shrugged. 'Low tech but effective.'

Forensics had sealed as much of the backyard as they could and swept it for any evidence. They'd photographed the area, sketched it and bagged several things – plastic food wrappers, a half-eaten apple and dozens of cigarette butts. But as Garrison replayed the scene of the body and how it had been so carefully laid in the yard, he doubted this killer had been careless enough to leave behind DNA evidence. It took time and planning to kidnap a woman and hold her for several days. 'The medical examiner called about our Jane Doe?'

'About a half hour ago. A branding iron likely burned the star shapes into the victim's skin. She's running a toxicology screen for drugs, but results will take days or weeks. Jane Doe had no track marks. Teeth were good, suggesting access to dental care. Recent breast implants and a nose job.'

'Prints shown up yet?'

'Not yet. But if we don't have a match she said she could check the implants for serial numbers.'

'Okay.'

'I've been able to track down the director of the shelter, Sally Walton.'

'What do you know about her?'

'Just what I could get from her night manager. She told him she is fifty-two years old and has a Masters in Social Work. She also told him she has run several other shelters over her career. She came here less than a year ago. He says she's dedicated to her work and is a caring woman. The neighbors love her.'

'And where is she?' Garrison said.

'Monday nights are her night off. I just reached her on her cell phone and told her what happened. She sounded pretty torn up. She'll be here by seven.' Malcolm checked his watch.

'Good. I want to ask her about that woman.'

'You're still stuck on her?'

'She's connected to all of this. I'm certain.'

Eva finally gave up on a good night's sleep around seven A.M. She rose up and swung her legs over the side of the bed. The springs in her bed squeaked as she shifted her weight. She grabbed her clothes from the end of the bed and unrolled her yoga mat. She spent the next thirty minutes moving through dozens of fast-paced sun salutations until her body glistened with sweat. The physical release eased the tension not only in her body but her mind. She'd discovered yoga in a book in the prison library. She'd started to practice just looking to kill time. What she'd found was a practice that gave her a mental peace that enabled her to endure her time behind bars.

She tiptoed into the bathroom. A shower, clean clothes, hair brushed into a neat ponytail warded off the last hints of fatigue and gave her a sense of control.

Eva headed down the back staircase to the pub's kitchen and filled a teakettle with water and set it on the front burner. She turned on the gas flame and in the refrigerator found the tea bag she'd used yesterday, now carefully wrapped in a piece of foil. Each bag, she'd discovered, was good for two cups, three if she were really pushing it.

When the kettle whistled, she dipped the retrieved bag into a cup and poured hot water over it.

Helping Bobby last night stirred memories of her sister. She'd not seen Angie in over ten years. The last words they'd spoken to each other had been at Eva's sentencing hearing. Angie had cried when the judge had passed sentence and his gavel had smacked against his desk. Eva was seventeen. Angie had been twenty-one. Angie's eyes had been red from crying but Eva had possessed an odd calmness as if her soul had risen above her body.

The kitchen's back door opened and closed with a bang, startling her back to the present. A blurry-eyed King strode in the back door with a bushel of potatoes. He set the bushel down on a stainless-steel prep table. The morning chill had left a rosy hue on his lean face and gray hair stuck out from under a Redskins football stocking cap. At his full height he stood five foot four inches and had narrow shoulders and a lean belly. He reminded Eva of a leprechaun more than a King.

The cold of the morning market still clung to his leather jacket. 'I thought I heard you come in last night. Figured your shift didn't work out.'

'The place burned before I arrived.'

'What!'

The story even sounded odd to her. 'The place was charred rubble when I arrived. There wasn't much for me to do but leave.'

He tugged at his belt, as if readying for a fight. 'Damn, Eva. I'm glad you're okay.'

'I missed the whole drama.'

He cocked an eyebrow. 'You look like you slept five minutes last night.'

'Just about.'

'No wonder, seeing as the shelter burned.'

The nightmare had come again last night, waking her at two in the morning. Her sweat had soaked through her gown to her sheets so she'd had to lay bath towels over them so she could go back to sleep. Only, she'd not slept well at all. 'I guess.'

King kept a modest two-bedroom apartment over the restaurant. When he'd first offered her the room on the top floor her radar had gone on full alert. No one gave anything away for free. Everything in life came with a catch. She'd agreed, but the first week she had pushed a dresser in front of her door. But once he retired for the night and she heard no sounds coming from his apartment she had stopped moving the dresser.

'Me, I'm in a coma when my head hits the pillow, unless you're rearranging the furniture. Or Bobby is thundering about the house scrounging for food.' He shrugged off his jacket and tossed it aside. 'So what was he doing in the alleyway?'

'You heard that?'

'Hard to miss. I was on my way down when I heard you arrive. Sounded like you had things under control.'

'For the most part.' She shoved her hands in her pockets. Eva motioned to the potatoes. 'That all you bought?'

'Naw, I got a few more bushels. But I'm having them delivered. New farmer at the market and he's trying to beat out the competition. So he's offering to deliver.'

'Great. When will he be here?' She cradled her cup in her hands and took a sip.

'By ten.'

'Hey, I've got a bit of news.'

King shoved out a breath. 'What?'

'Don't look at me like I've blown something up.'

He arched a brow. 'Did you?'

'No. Bobby found a kitten.'

'A what?'

'A kitten. He was outside feeding it.'

King rubbed the back of his neck with his hand. 'And I take it you let him keep it.'

'First, he's going to need help catching it. The thing is living in the alley.'

Again he rubbed the back of his neck with the back of his hand. 'What the hell am I going to do with a wild cat?'

'Look at it this way. Bobby is just acting like you.'

'What's that mean?'

'He's taking care of strays. He's turning into a chip off the old block.'

Color rose in King's face. 'You are buttering me up now.'

She grinned. 'As fast as I can.'

'Damn it, Eva.'

'I'll do all the invoices for the next three months if you let him keep the cat.'

King grinned. 'You're starting to like the kid.'

'I didn't say that,' she grumbled. 'I'm offering a hand.'

He sighed. 'Fine. The cat can stay. Provided we can catch it.'

She kissed him on the cheek. 'You know you are the best.'

A faint hint of pink colored his cheeks. 'I got to get Bobby up and ready for school. He's got a spelling test today.'

She studied him and not for the first time wondered what made him tick. 'Why did you do it? Why help me and the kid?'

'Why not? We all get into jams now and then.'

'Very few people go out of their way like you, King.'

'I'm just a hell of a nice guy,' he grumbled. 'Now leave it at that.' The hard lines of King's face eased. 'What do you have planned today?'

She understood a 'back off' when she heard one. 'I want to go back to the shelter.'

'Why?'

'I want to know what happened.' The cops would still be crawling all over the place, but after a restless night of dreams that reminded her of a time when she'd been so helpless, she felt compelled to return.

'Do they know who set the fire?' King had been more like a father to her in the last six months than her own father had been.

'I don't think so, but I want to find out.'

'You be careful. You got a record and it ain't smart for ex-cons to be so close to a crime scene.'

She could have told him how she'd hidden out in the woods last night, almost too afraid to think. She opted to keep that to herself. 'I'll keep that in mind.'

Chapter 5

Tuesday, April 4, 8:00 A.M.

A patrol car followed a beat-up Gran Torino station wagon into the shelter's cul-de-sac and parked next to Garrison's car. A tall, broad-shouldered woman got out of the station wagon and surveyed the damage. In her early fifties, the woman wore faded jeans, a HANNA HOUSE sweatshirt and tennis shoes. Black tendrils of curly hair escaped a topknot and framed high cheekbones and sharp gray eyes edged by deep lines.

She wrapped her arms around her chest. 'Oh my God. Oh my God.' Tears rolled down her freckled cheeks.

Garrison moved toward her. 'Ms Sally Walton?'

'Yes.' Her voice trembled as she shook her head and stared at the charred remains.

Garrison shook her hand, noting tension had flattened her lips. 'I'm Detective Deacon Garrison, Alexandria City Police Department, and this is my partner, Detective Malcolm Kier.'

Malcolm stuck out his hand. 'I sent the car for you so you wouldn't have to drive.'

Silver bracelets jangled as Sally shook his hand. 'I wanted to drive my own car, so the officer followed me.' She closed her eyes and pinched the bridge of her nose. 'I'm always getting calls on my night off. Most of them were nuisance calls so, lately, I've turned off my cell phone.'

'Understandable,' Garrison said. 'Where were you last night?'

'My boyfriend's. His name is Charlie Jones. He works in a garage in Arlington. You want his number?'

'Yes, ma'am. I'm going to need to verify where you were.'

She dug a pad and pencil from her purse and scribbled names and numbers on it. 'Well, the sooner you can figure out I didn't do it, the faster you can find who did.'

'Yes, ma'am.' He studied her elegant handwriting. 'Can you tell us who stayed in the house?'

'I think so.' Sally had a rough, jagged tone to her voice that suggested a life of heavy cigarette smoking.

'Would you also write down the names of your residents and staff?'

'The officer told me none of my people were hurt.'

'We just like to be sure everyone's been accounted for.' Sally wrote the names down, her hand steady and sure. 'I've listed seven names. Six residents and one staff member. I starred resident names who supplied full names that I thought might be fictitious.'

'Fictitious?' Garrison said.

'I hadn't had time to verify their identities. Some may have lied about their last names.'

'That happens a lot?'

'All the time. But I always check on people. I don't want trouble. Yesterday was my night off and I was in a rush to get out. I didn't take the time to run background checks. It was cold, and turning folks away seemed harsh.' She

74

raised fingers to her lips. 'Did one of my residents do this?'

'I don't know yet.' Garrison glanced at his notepad. 'You only had one staff worker on call last night?'

'I was supposed to have two but my second night worker called to say she'd be late.'

'Did her call surprise you?'

'No, no. Eva is very reliable. She just called to say she'd have to work late – at her other job. She works three jobs. She's hustling to save money. I understood she'd be here as soon as she could.'

'You said her name was Eva?'

'That's right. Eva Rayburn.'

'And the other volunteer?'

'Beamer.'

'We spoke to him last night. He was in the front of the house watching TV with the residents when the fire broke out.'

'Sounds like Neal. He likes his television. I'm glad Eva wasn't on site.'

'Why?'

'She'd have been in the back of the house in the kitchen working. The kid barely sits down.'

Garrison thought about his victim. 'What does Eva look like?'

'She's short. Maybe five foot. Dark hair. Blue, blue eyes. Pretty girl. Could pass for a fifteen-year-old. Why do you ask?'

Eva matched the description of his mystery woman. 'We found the body of a woman behind the shelter. I'm trying to identify her.'

The furrow in Sally's brow deepened. 'Oh, God. Was the girl Eva?'

'Judging by your description, no.'

Sally pressed the heel of her palm to her forehead. 'Was this woman killed by the fire?'

'We're still trying to determine the cause of death.' He pulled a Polaroid of the victim's face shot before the medical examiner's office bagged her body. 'Would you mind looking at a picture of the woman?'

Sally straightened her shoulders. 'Of course.'

The lines on Sally's face deepened as she stared at the picture of the victim. Tears welled in her eyes. 'Poor woman. God bless her.'

'Do you know her?'

'No. I'm sorry.'

'You're sure?'

She drew in a breath and refocused on the picture. Seconds passed. 'Sorry, I don't know her.'

Garrison took the picture back and tucked it in his breast pocket. 'No problem.'

'What can you tell us about the people who were staying in the house?'

'What do you want to know?'

'Whatever you have at this point.'

'Two of the women had jobs as cleaning ladies at a local school. The men didn't work, but collected Social Security.'

'Did you have any trouble here recently?'

'No. In fact, it's been as smooth as glass. No fights. No contraband found. I knew trouble was bound to return. Looks like it did in spades.'

'What's your idea of contraband?'

'We do surprise searches every day. If I find something that breaks our house rules, I confiscate it. Knives or guns. Drugs. Alcohol. The usual troublemakers. If a weapon or drugs are found, the resident has to leave immediately, but if it's alcohol we sometimes cut them a second chance. The resident is issued a warning and if it happens a second time they're evicted.'

'You evict anyone lately?'

'It's been a couple of months since I had to kick someone out.'

'Who was it?'

'Oh, I'll have to go back and check my records.' She glanced up at the shelter. The charred ruins glared back at her. 'The files were in my office. They were destroyed.'

'And you don't remember this person's name?'

'Only that it was a woman. She brought drugs into the shelter. I tossed her out. She called me a few names.'

'Any threats?'

'Oh, yeah. In fact, Eva stepped between us. She's small, but the girl is strong and isn't afraid of a fight.'

'What did Eva say to her?'

Sally raised a brow. 'She spoke so quietly I couldn't hear, but whatever she said it had a real impact.'

'Ever hear from that resident again?'

'No.' Sally paused then snapped her fingers. 'Her name was Brenda.' She frowned as if burrowing into her memory and then shook her head. 'But the last name escapes me.'

'Anything else you can tell me about Brenda?'

'She worked the streets. Said she wanted to get her life together but she was just one of those people who seemed more interested in a bed and a hot meal than putting her life back on track.'

'Does that happen a lot?'

'Enough. But for every one hard-core addict that shows up here, two others really need us. Most of our residents just have trouble managing the day-to-day details of life, caused by mental illness.'

'Would you be willing to look at a few mug shots to see if we can identify this Brenda woman?'

'Sure. Sure, I'll do whatever I can to help. Where are my residents? I want to talk to them.'

'We bused them to the YMCA so they could shower and get a meal.'

'I'll need to check on them.'

'Sure. An officer can drive you.'

'He can follow if he wants, but I drive my own car. First the Y, then the station.'

'Sure.' Garrison pulled a card from his pocket. 'Call me if anything else comes to mind.'

Sally took the card. 'Sure.'

Chapter 6

Tuesday, April 4, 8:15 A.M.

When Eva approached the shelter, she parked on a side street like she had last night and again cut through the yards. When she rounded the corner her breath caught in her throat as she got her first daylight look at the burned-out structure. The old Victorian had collapsed into a pile of charred, smoking timbers. The scent of smoke still hung in the air. It truly was a miracle that anyone had gotten out alive.

'Eva.' The unknown man's deep voice caught her off guard and she turned, startled. The cop from last night stood only a few feet from her. She'd not heard him approach.

She faced him. 'I'm sorry?'

He raised an eyebrow. 'You are Eva Rayburn.'

Not a question but a statement. 'Who are you?'

'Detective Deacon Garrison.' He pointed to the badge hanging around his neck. 'You are Eva.' He glanced through the yards at her truck. 'And that is your vehicle?'

She could lie. But checking her license would be easy enough. 'The truck belongs to my boss. Toby King, owner of King's Pub.'

He nodded. 'You work at the shelter?'

'How do you know my name?'

He moved a few steps closer, but was careful not to get

79

too close. 'I spoke to Sally Walton a few minutes ago. She described you.'

'You've seen Sally?'

'Yes. She's fine.'

Some of the tightness eased in her throat. 'Good.'

'How many were staying at the shelter last night?'

Garrison stood well over six foot and she had to crane her neck to look him in the eye. 'They expected five or six. But often more show up by lights out. I was running late so I couldn't say.'

'Where were you?'

'I deliver subpoenas. You can ask my boss, Luke Fraser, at LTF Processing.'

'I'll do that.'

Eva resisted the urge to drape her arms around her chest. No need to feel defensive. In fact, sounding defensive fueled the flames of suspicion. 'Great.'

He hovered, clearly not finished. 'Do you know who was staying here?'

'I can jot down a list of who was here. We have regulars but I have no way of knowing. Didn't Sally know?'

'She did. Just double-checking.' He handed her a pad from his pocket. 'Write them down.'

Tense fingers gripped the pen and she wrote names in neat, precise handwriting. 'I don't know if these names are real or assumed. Sometimes our residents lie.'

'Do the best you can.' He smelled of soap. No after-shave. No frills. Neatly trimmed nails and a starched shirt projected a button-down, by-the-book image that would have been totally believable if not for an intense energy that seemed barely restrained.

She handed back the notebook, mindful not to touch him. 'Did anyone die?'

'We had one fatality.'

'Oh my God. Who?'

'I don't know yet.'

'Do you know how the fire started?'

'I hoped you could tell me.'

'Me? I wasn't here.' This moment mirrored another night ten years ago. Cops threw leading questions at her and interrupted when her answers didn't fit what they wanted.

'Come on, Eva, the other girls told us you and Cross were having an affair.'

She'd been up over thirty-six hours and could barely string two thoughts together. Her body ached. All she wanted to do was go home. 'We were not.'

'The girls said so.'

'The girls lied.' She was so tired that her words slurred.

The sheriff leaned so close she could smell the way his sweat mingled with his soap. 'You are the liar.'

Her mouth was dry. Her eyes burned. 'Josiah raped me. I'm the victim.'

'You had sex with him and in a jealous rage killed him.'

'No!'

'Yes.'

To her shame, she'd wept. God, but she was so tired. 'Why don't you understand? Josiah raped me and burned my own pendant into my flesh.'

'The fireman says the house fire heated the pendant and when you fell back it burned your skin.'

'No. Josiah burned me.'

'Tell me the truth,' he said so softly. 'And I will let you see your sister.'

'My sister is here?'

'She's outside waiting.'

She glanced up at him. She'd held strong while he'd yelled at her, but now that he came at her with kindness her mind tripped with confusion. 'I want to see Angie.'

'I know. She's waiting for you.'

The haze of sleep deprivation coupled with thirst and fear left her so weak. She just wanted the nightmare to end. 'Okay.'

'Okay what, Eva? Are you saying you killed Josiah?'

Shame burned in her belly. 'Yes.'

She wanted to leave and get away from Garrison who was drawing her into a web she feared would be impossible to escape.

'I saw you in the crowd last night.' Before she could deny it he said again, 'I saw you.'

Eva had learned to walk the tightrope between lies and the truth when she'd been in prison. Too many lies were hard to remember and too much truth endangered her safety. 'I was scheduled to work last night. I saw the flames and just kind of froze.'

'How long have you worked at the shelter?'

'About six months.'

'Why here?'

'Easy work. Good pay.'

She picked at a stray thread. Now the truth would serve her better than a lie because she suspected Detective Garrison ate liars for breakfast. 'I work at a pub called King's.

Sally is one of my patrons. A few months ago, she offered me the work and I never say no to work.'

'Mind my asking how old you are?'

'Twenty-seven.'

'You look ten years younger.'

'I get that a lot.'

'And where did you say you worked?'

'King's. It's in Old Town Alexandria. I tend bar and waitress. I also rent a room on the top floor.'

He nodded. 'Sally said you called last night and that you were running late.'

'You already asked me about that.'

'Humor me.'

'I also serve subpoenas for extra cash. Last night's delivery took longer than expected and I ran late.'

'How many nights a week do you work here?'

'Depends on my work schedule. One or two.'

'What was your schedule last night?'

If she'd been on time, she realized now that she'd be dead. 'Nine to nine. I was supposed to spend the night.'

'Being late looks like a lucky break.'

She glanced past him at the charred remains of the shelter. 'Yeah.'

'Sally said you had words with a resident six or seven weeks ago.'

'That's right. Her name was Brenda. She tried to stir up trouble and I stopped her.'

'How'd you stop her?'

'I told her to be nice.'

'That's it?'

'That's it.'

He suspected she'd phrased it much differently. 'Where can I reach you?' Garrison said.

'Why would you need to reach me?' He reminded her of a dog who'd just picked up the fox's scent.

'Just for good measure. Questions do pop up.'

She shoved her hands into her pockets. 'King's is in the phone book.'

'You have a cell?'

'Can't afford it.' Which was true. Landlines weren't totally extinct, plus she didn't like being tethered to anything, even if it was just a phone.

He appeared in no rush. In fact, she sensed he got a kick out of dragging this out. Cops. All control freaks.

'Any unusual phone calls? Any cars hanging around the shelter lately?'

'Like I said, nothing out of the ordinary.' A little digging into her past and he'd find out she'd done time. So be it. Her manslaughter conviction would haunt her forever.

He planted his hand on his hip. 'You sure about that?'

'Yes. I don't have a reason to lie.'

He lifted a brow. 'Let's hope not.'

Eva folded her arms over her chest, refusing to allow old fears to rise. 'If you have something to say then say it.' He could shove his silence and piercing gaze.

'Don't worry, Ms Rayburn. If I have something to say, I will.' Instead of rising to defensiveness, he kept his stance relaxed. 'You said you moved here six months ago. Where from?'

The shift in conversation robbed her of some bravado. 'Down by the Richmond area.'

'You know a little place downtown called Sid's?'

'Can't say I've been there.' After she'd been released from prison, she'd spent a few weeks in a halfway house in the Fan district. With only a hundred bucks from the prison system for a fresh start, there'd been no money for restaurants.

'It was mighty popular.'

'Maybe. I wouldn't know. I didn't stay in Richmond long.'

'It was off Hanover Street.'

'All I know is Eddie's on Franklin.' She walked past it daily on her early-morning walks. She'd walked just after sunrise because crowded streets triggered minor panic attacks. Funny, she'd longed for freedom for ten years, but after so much time in partial isolation, regular everyday things like grocery shopping and talking to people on the street overwhelmed her. Hell, her first month out, she kept asking for permission to go to the bathroom.

'I remember. Bar was constructed of lumber from an old mine.'

She ran her fingers through her long hair, not surprised he'd know a detail like that. Homicide detectives were good at the details. 'Care to quiz me about anything else?'

His quick grin didn't reach his eyes. 'No. No more questions for now.' He pulled a card from his breast pocket. 'But you'll be sure to let me know if you decide to up and move.'

She flicked the edge of the card. 'Why do I have to let you know?'

Steel glinted in his eyes. 'For now let's just call it a curiosity.'

No missing the thinly veiled order. This guy would

track her down if she left the area. And she'd bet a paycheck he'd find her inside a week. 'Sure.'

'Thanks.'

She turned to leave, anxious just to stuff distance between them.

'Ms Rayburn, why'd you move to Alexandria?'

Careful to keep the tension from her face and voice, Eva ignored the way her muscles clenched as she met his direct gaze. 'Curious. And more jobs.'

'Just that simple.'

'Sure, why not? You've never just gone with your curiosity for a new locale?'

'Maybe on vacation but not to live.' He grinned. 'Must be nice to be such a free spirit.'

Actually, it kind of sucked. She longed for roots and a real home. 'It's the best.'

'Mind if I ask you a favor?'

Crap. Favors never boded well. Still, her lips curved into a smile as she turned. 'Sure.'

He reached in his breast pocket. 'I'd like you to look at a picture.'

'Of?'

'A woman. We found her behind the shelter. She's dead.'

A sick wave washed through her limbs. 'I really would rather not.'

'The shot is just of her face.'

'Still, I'd just rather not.' A deep fear rooted in her bones.

'Please,' he said. 'Just one look.'

Why was she so afraid? She nodded, unable to speak.

He held out the picture, holding her gaze until she had the courage to lower it to the picture. The image nearly took her breath away. It was of a young woman, not any older than her. She had pale blond hair and a fair complexion. For just a moment, Eva couldn't breathe or clear her thoughts. She'd been labeled a murderer and yet never had looked into the face of death.

The woman's image teased memories on the edge of her mind, but she couldn't translate the shadowy images into words. Who was this woman? Had she seen her at the pub or maybe along King Street?

Eva cleared her throat. 'I don't know her.'

'You sure about that? You been staring at her a good while.'

'I guess it's just a shock to look at death.' She handed the picture back to him, trying to keep her hands steady. 'How did she die?'

'Can't really say right now.' He studied her a long moment. 'If something comes to mind, you'll tell me?'

'Sure.'

She moved toward her truck, praying her legs did not collapse. How had her life turned upside down so fast?

Angie nursed a cold can of ginger ale and a packet of crackers as she unlocked the front door of the law offices of Wellington and James. The firm was housed in a brick townhouse built in the 1890s. A black lacquer front door sported a large door knocker fashioned of brass. Flanking the entrance were twin sets of hand-blown windows underscored with iron window boxes filled with topiaries. The building was located on a tree-lined section of Cameron Street near the banks of the Potomac.

Charlotte Wellington had promised a partnership to

Angie if she could bring in the business. So far she'd delivered. For the last year, her days had been spent finding clients or racking up seventy-plus billable hours a week. They were scheduled to have a partnership discussion next week when Charlotte returned from her vacation.

Angie dropped her keys in her purse and with her foot nudged the self-locking front door closed. Oriental carpets, landscapes and subtle grass wallpaper gave the reception area a traditional feel that suggested old Virginia and money.

Charlotte always said lawyers needed to convey a certain level of class to get the right client. The one contradiction to the antique furnishings was the state-of-the-art security system Charlotte had installed just weeks before Angie had joined the firm. In the top corner of the room red lights blinked from three motion sensors. Charlotte insisted that everyone keep the front door locked. If a visitor arrived, they were buzzed inside. Charlotte Wellington developed an obsession with security after an armed man had forced his way into the firm a year ago and shot her. She'd barely escaped with her life.

Angie moved down the carpeted hallway to her office and set her large black purse on her desk. Three rows of neatly stacked folders rested in the center of her desk. She prioritized the next day's work before she left in the evening.

On the credenza behind her desk were only two pictures: one of her mother taken thirty years ago, and the other of two young girls dressed in matching blue dresses. It had been snapped fifteen years ago by their mom. Angie had been sixteen, and her sister was twelve. Angie had been living with her dad by then and visited her mother and sister only occasionally. They'd had a rare special day with their mom who treated them to the movies and lunch with dessert. Three years later their mom had died of cancer. Angie's father had refused to take the child his ex-wife had conceived during an affair. He'd also threatened to cut Angie off if she left school to care for Eva. So Angie's sister had been sent to foster care. To this day, Angie regretted that she'd not stood up for Eva.

Angie shrugged off her coat and hung it on the hanger dangling from the hook on her office door. She shoved her purse into the bottom desk drawer and sat down. The day promised to be jam-packed. Briefings to write. Motions to file. She thought about Charlotte, now on a long overdue vacation in the Florida Keys. Toes in the sand. Hot sun.

Sighing, she sipped her ginger ale and nibbled on crackers as she reviewed the wording on a brief that needed to be filed by tomorrow.

A knock on her door had her looking up at Iris, who stood in the doorway. In her late fifties, Iris kept her silver hair pulled in a French twist and she dressed in immaculate Chanel suits. She'd joined the firm a year ago after she'd discovered her late husband had lost all their money in the stock market. The double loss of a fortune and husband could embitter most women, but not Iris. She'd been born poor, she'd explained, and she knew how to work. She now ran Wellington and James with brutal efficiency. 'You look like death.'

'Thanks. I feel it.' Too much wine and too little food last night, but she'd never admit it.

Iris eyed her carefully. 'Flu's going around.'

'So I've discovered.'

Iris held a pink message slip between her delicate fingers. 'Mr Lenny Danvers is still very anxious to talk to you.'

Angie closed her eyes and pinched the bridge of her nose. 'Did he say what he wanted?'

'And I quote, "Ms Carlson will be pissed if she doesn't hear what I have to say to her."'

Angie drummed her fingers on the polished desktop. 'That's it? I'd be pissed.'

'That's what he said.'

'So I'm supposed to drop my morning routine and work him into my schedule?' Irritation, spurred by the nausea, crept into her voice.

Iris flicked the pink slip with a manicured finger. 'Don't shoot the messenger.'

'Sorry. Can you get specifics? I'm not jumping to Mr Danvers's request just because he needs some hand-holding.'

'Let me see what I can do.'

Her stomach tumbled. 'Bless you.'

'Want me to bring you a coffee?'

'God, no. But thanks.'

Iris hesitated in the doorway, studying Angie like a mother. 'Wow, you must be sick.'

Angie smiled, determined to keep up appearances. 'I'll live.'

'I'm not so sure.' Iris's gray eyes narrowed. 'Are you sure you're okay?'

'Just got a bit of a bug. As you said, the flu is going around. I'll be fine.'

'Right. The flu. I'll report back.'

Alone, Angie cradled her head in her hands and tried to concentrate on the documents in front of her. But as much as she wanted to read, her wobbly stomach wouldn't allow it.

When Iris reappeared, she felt almost relieved. 'Yes.'

'Danvers on line three.'

'Okay.' Angie sucked in a breath and picked up the receiver. 'Mr Danvers.'

'About time I got you. Christ, you're my attorney.'

'I represented you once, Mr Danvers. And as I remember, you made me look like a fool when you faked a heart attack. And you still have invoices outstanding.'

'Yeah, well, I'm not crying wolf this time. And I'll get you the money.'

'What do you want?'

He dropped his voice a notch. 'I got information on a murder.'

'Really?'

'Yeah, really. I can help the police.'

She'd give him points for the sincerity in his voice. 'Tell me.'

'Not over the phone.'

'Why not?'

'Look, someone just posted bail for me.'

'And why were you in jail?'

'The usual. Breaking and entering.'

'This is at least your third strike. How did you get out? Bail would have been high.'

'Exactly, but someone posted it.'

'You have a girlfriend, from what I remember.'

'It wasn't her. She don't love anybody that much.'

'You've a guardian angel?' Angie rubbed her temples with her fingertips.

'Or the killer wants me back on the streets.'

'Don't you think you're being a bit paranoid?'

'No. Look, if you want information on this murder, meet me at the Fort Ward Park in one hour.' Fort Ward was a park that commemorated the Union camp that defended Washington, D.C., from the Confederates. It could be reached easily and provided open spaces as well as wooded areas.

She glanced at the stack of briefs on her desk and then at the digital clock on her desk. 'You're kidding.'

'I ain't kidding. Ms Carlson, this killer is a nut and I can tell the cops who it is.'

'What do you want?'

'Immunity. Lots of it.'

She picked up her pencil and doodled boxes on a legal pad. 'Lenny, that is not enough. I've got to give the cops more.'

'Tell them the killer burned his victim.'

Her stomach turned. Years ago, her sister had been burned by her attacker. 'What do you mean, "burned".'

'I'm not sure. But I could smell it. I could hear her scream.'

The urgency in his voice cut through her malaise. 'Where did this happen?'

'That I ain't saying until I have a deal with the cops.'

'Which jurisdiction should I call?' The Northern Virginia area was comprised of two cities and several counties.

He paused, then said, 'Alexandria.'

That meant Garrison. Shit. 'I swear I will bury you if you are lying.'

'I ain't lying. Get the cops there and I'll supply an address.'

'Who knows if they will deal?'

'They'll deal with you. You're kinda like Wonder Woman.'

'Wonder Woman.' Bitterness dripped from the words. Once upon a time she'd been a wet-behind-the-ears, fresh-faced lawyer who was full of fire and determination to protect the innocent. Then she'd realized most of the people in the system weren't so innocent or were working an angle. She didn't feel like Wonder Woman anymore.

His voice raised a notch. 'So you'll deal for me?'

'You haven't offered me much.'

'I will.'

For the first time in a long time, Angie considered the victim before her client. 'I'll make some calls.'

'Make it quick. Fort Ward. One hour.' He hung up.

Angie tossed her pen on her desk. 'Damn it.'

'What did he want now?' Iris said.

'A meeting at Fort Ward. With the cops.'

'Tell me you are not going to bite. The guy is a con art-ist. He's just jerking your chain.'

'I'm not so sure this time.'

'Look, anyone who can read knows you're a sucker for a defendant. All that work you did on Project Innocence and those boys you got out of jail. He's playing you.'

'He won't be the first.' She glanced again at the paper-work. If she went to the park she'd lose at least two hours.

She'd be here until midnight. But better to work here than drink alone at home.

Iris's voice sliced through the silence. 'Which cops are you calling?'

'Garrison.'

'Oh, he'll be so thrilled to talk to you again.' Sarcasm dripped from the words. 'Few have seen that man mad but you managed to accomplish that feat when you got his suspect acquitted.'

Iris referred to the Dixon case. After the verdict, Garrison had been angry, but his partner, Kier, had been the one that had cornered her later on the courthouse steps and called her scum. She'd shrugged it off for Kier's benefit but the detective's words had left a bitter taste in her mouth.

'We're all big boys and girls, Iris. I'm just offering them information.'

She retrieved Garrison's number from her cell and hit Call. He picked up on the second ring.

'Detective Garrison.'

'Detective. Angie Carlson with Wellington and James.'

'Yes, Ms Carlson.'

Ice crackled through the phone. Clearly, deep emotions simmered in the detective. 'What can I do for you?'

She brushed a strand of hair from her face. 'One of my clients has information that might be of use to you.'

'Really? I can't wait to hear this one.' Normally, he didn't let his frustration or anger show.

'I wouldn't be calling if it wasn't credible.'

'Shoot.'

'One of my clients appears to have stumbled upon a

murder in progress, or at least that's what the guy said. Anyway, he believes the killer burned his victim.'

'Say that again,' Garrison said.

'He says your victim might have been burned.'

A heavy silence hung in the air for a moment. 'Did he say anything else?'

'Nope. The rest he'll tell you in person.' She expected him to laugh it off.

'I'll meet with him.'

Angie buried her shock. 'He said Fort Ward in one hour.'

'I'll meet you at the entrance in one hour.'

'Great.'

'Carlson, don't speak to the media about any of this. If it leaks, your client doesn't get a deal.'

The menace in his voice had her hackles rising a little. 'You've got my silence until the meeting.'

Chapter 7

The image of the pale woman with full slack-jawed lips and high cheekbones niggled Eva's mind. Who was she? Why did she seem so familiar? It bothered her that she shared a sense of connection with this woman – this murdered woman. Her only alibi was Bruce Radford and he'd never help her. If the cops really dug into her past they'd learn about her record.

Damn.

She had nothing to be ashamed of or anything to feel guilty about. The law should be on her side in this matter. But too many years in prison had taught hard lessons. Right did not always win.

Her hands trembling, she jerked open the back door to the kitchen and found that King had peeled most of the potatoes and had set them in a pot on the stove to boil. Whistling the theme to *Gilligan's Island,* he appeared happy, as he always did. She never could figure out how the guy remained so positive.

She was surprised to see Bobby sitting on a stool at the end of the butcher-block countertop. He ate a bagel with cream cheese and had a half-full glass of milk in front of him. 'Bobby, I figured you'd be at school now.'

'I'm sick. King said I could stay home with him and Merlin.'

'Merlin?'

'The cat,' King said. 'Bobby and I went out and got cat supplies.'

'You've caught it?'

'Not yet,' King said.

'But we will.' Excitement sparked in Bobby's eyes.

When she'd been a kid, she'd never missed school. Her mother had seen skipping as akin to waste. And one of her mother's old admonishments rose in her before she caught herself. Let the kid have a day with the kitten.

Bobby glanced up from his bagel. In the morning light she could see a sprinkle of freckles on the bridge of his nose. 'King says Merlin eats like a horse.'

King glanced toward Eva as she shrugged off her jacket. 'Merlin eats more than you do.'

Eva smiled. 'That's saying a lot.'

'Remember when you first tripped through my front door?' King spoke easily, as if they'd broken bread a thousand times before. 'You ate all the leftover meat loaf I had.' He looked at Bobby, his lips twisted into a wry smile. 'Drank five glasses of milk – nearly a half gallon.'

When she'd showed up at King's she'd not eaten much for a couple of days. The bus ride from Richmond had stretched from the expected two hours to four thanks to traffic snarls. The thick air on the bus coupled with constant stopping and fears of returning home had twisted her stomach into knots. But when she'd arrived at King's and smelled his meat loaf her stomach had growled with hunger.

Eva sat on the stool next to Bobby and spread cream cheese on her bagel. 'These are great, King. I love fresh bagels.'

'I never met anyone that didn't like bagels. Glad I got extra.' King kept his tone even and light as he continued to chop. Both pretended this was just another day and this kid who had just dropped out of nowhere belonged at the edge of the table eating a bagel.

'Good call.' She took a couple more bites. 'So what's on the menu for tonight?'

King laughed. 'Potatoes. Wings and the usual burgers and chili dogs. Good bar fare.' The pub had a limited selection but 'the eats were good and cheap,' as King enjoyed saying.

'Let me know what you need done today. I don't have any subpoena deliveries.'

'That reminds me, that Luke fellow called. He wanted to know how the delivery went. He also said the cops called asking if you had a job last night.'

Garrison had wasted no time. 'I'll give him a call back.'

King tossed her an annoyed glance over the top of his half glasses. 'I don't like that fellow.'

Refusing to engage in an old argument, she popped some bagel in her mouth. 'He's okay.'

'He puts you at risk. Tosses you the worst jobs he has on his books. Almost as if he wants you to find trouble.'

'They are the best-paying jobs.'

'Because nobody wants them, Eva. And,' he said, lowering his voice, 'he's a little too well acquainted with you.'

'What's that mean?' Bobby asked.

'He wants to date Eva,' King said.

'He won't,' Eva said. Life was complicated enough right now without a man mucking it up.

Aware that Bobby was studying their volley of conversation as if it were a tennis match, she shrugged and tossed the kid a smile. 'I'll buzz him this morning.'

King swallowed his retort when he caught Bobby's gaze. He grunted and lapsed into silence for several minutes before saying, 'So how did your errands go this morning?' He didn't mention the fire, mindful of Bobby.

'Fine,' she said, glancing to the boy who still stared at them both, trying to figure them out. 'Didn't pick up anything new.'

'Really?'

She inclined her head toward the kid. 'I might try back later.'

King grunted, clearly not happy. 'Maybe tomorrow.'

Eva tore another piece of bagel but didn't eat it. 'I can go today.'

He shrugged his shoulders. 'No rush. That reminds me,' King said. 'You got a letter. Came in the mail yesterday. Just got it from the P.O. box this morning.'

He dug under his big white apron into the pocket of his jeans and pulled out a rumpled brown letter. He handed it to her.

A frown creased her brow as she glanced at the simple bold handwriting. Her name, King's post office box and no return address. Who would ever know she lived at King's?

Refusing to borrow trouble she tore open the back flap with her thumbnail and pulled out the neatly creased newspaper article. The paper was brittle and yellowed on the edges.

Dated a decade ago, the article's headline read FIRE DESTROYS SORORITY HOUSE.

Eva's blood pressure dropped, making her light-headed. She glanced at the envelope and searched for a return address or a postmark. Alexandria postmark with no return address.

She reread the headline. FIRE DESTROYS SORORITY HOUSE. She flipped the article over, and written on the back in red ink was the word *Atone*.

Atone. Atone for what? She'd spent ten years in jail atoning for sins she wasn't so sure now that she'd committed. Now she was rebuilding her life. What did she have to *atone* for? Instead of being scared she grew angry. Someone in town had recognized her, remembered her history and thought it would be a laugh to jerk her chain. Outrage burned inside her.

'Bad news?' King said.

Eva carefully folded the paper. 'Just a bill.'

'How could you have a bill? You never spend money.'

'Don't worry about it.' She crammed the article into the back pocket of her jeans.

King grunted. 'Something wrong?'

'Nope. All good.'

Someone knew about her past.

Eva coaxed a faltering smile for King and Bobby. 'No worries, boys. No worries.'

King arched a bushy brow.

Even Bobby had stopped eating and stared at her as if he were trying to read her mind.

Eva bit into her bagel, doing her best to look casual. 'You two look so serious. Really, it's nothing.' To change the subject she said, 'That computer professor at St Margaret's said I could come by the lab anytime after I audited his class.'

'You should go,' King said.

Eva shook her head. 'I'll skip today. I can help find Merlin.'

King shook his head. 'No, you go. I see the way your eyes light up when you get back from one of those classes. The kid and I will trap Merlin.'

The boy's brow knotted. 'I don't like school but I like reading.'

She smiled. 'What do you like to read about?'

'Cowboys. And boats.'

'I'll bet you are good,' Eva said.

'I am.' Tension suddenly radiated from his little body like a clenched fist. He'd remembered something from his past.

'It's okay,' Eva said. She had similar moments. She'd be discussing something that didn't have to do with anything and then the past would blindside her.

Bobby sighed. 'Aren't you too old for school?'

'You're never too old.' Eva shrugged. 'I didn't get a chance to go much when I was younger. I'm doing a little catch-up.'

'Why didn't you go to school?'

'Good question,' King said.

The brains that had earned her a full college admission and scholarship at sixteen hadn't saved her from a manslaughter conviction. 'Lots of reasons.'

'Like what?' Bobby said.

'Like it doesn't matter now.' She dug her fingers through

her long hair and checked her watch. 'I better get going or I'll be late for class.'

'Go,' King said. 'The boy and I have a kitten to trap.'

Bobby studied Eva. 'You're coming back?'

'Of course. I'll be gone just a few hours.' Going to the computer lab would mean on-line time and the chance to check on kids matching Bobby's description.

The boy picked a fresh bagel from the tray. 'Not everyone comes back.'

'Yeah, well, I will.'

He thrust his lip out. 'Even if you don't, I'm not a baby. I can take care of myself.'

Garrison and Malcolm pulled into Fort Ward's stone entrance exactly an hour later. This time of year, the trees had begun to bud and the land looked a little less barren. Still, the air remained chilly and likely few tourists meandered about. Garrison parked at the main entrance lot, which was empty. He checked his watch.

'So what is Carlson selling?' Malcolm said. 'She's always working an angle.'

'I don't know. But her guy might have a lead on our Jane Doe's murder. I've got to hear what the two have to say.'

'That woman irritates the shit out of me,' Malcolm grumbled. 'I doubt she has a conscience.'

'Who knows? She might.'

'How can you say that? She was a barracuda in the courtroom.'

'Just doing her job. And she won the Dixon case fair and square. I don't like it but it's done and over.'

Malcolm shifted in his seat toward his partner. 'How do you do it?'

'Do what?' Garrison kept his gaze ahead as he tapped his fingers on the steering wheel.

'You never seem to get pissed.'

Garrison was gratified his smile could mask so much. 'My motto is simple. Don't get mad. Just get even.'

Malcolm shook his head. 'I want both.'

Garrison laughed. 'Doesn't always work that way.'

A sleek black BMW pulled up next to the driver's side of Garrison's car. Angie Carlson, her eyes shielded with dark glasses, got out of the car. She moved around to the back of her car as Garrison shut off the engine and slid out. Malcolm followed.

Carlson's arms were crossed and she tapped her foot. Garrison noted tension around her mouth and the fact that she'd dropped a little too much weight. She usually never showed emotion but he guessed, like him, she paid a price somewhere along the line for the stoicism.

'Thank you for the meeting, Detectives,' Carlson said.

Garrison nodded. 'Where's your client?'

She checked her watch. 'He said he'd be here.'

'Let's hope he shows and is not wasting my time,' Garrison warned.

A crease furrowed her brow. 'I've already outlined the consequences. I don't have time for wild-goose chases either.'

'All right.'

The trio waited several more minutes, an awkward strained silence hovering around them. Finally, Carlson's phone rang. She glanced at the number, frowned and flipped it open. 'Lenny, where are you?' She listened, her scowl deepening. 'You said you'd be here!' As she listened she flexed and unflexed her fingers. 'Sure, he's standing right here.' She handed the phone to Garrison.

He accepted it. 'Detective Garrison.'

'Is this really Garrison?' The mousy voice on the other end of the line sounded nervous and agitated.

'It is.' He'd met Danvers once when he worked Burglary and could almost picture the man dragging his long, bone-thin fingers through his wispy black hair. No doubt he had a lit cigarette in his other hand, the ash dangling and ready to crumble. 'What do you have for me, Mr Danvers?'

'I want a deal.'

The muscle in the side of Garrison's face tightened. 'You said you were going to be here.'

'And have you haul my bony ass to jail? Couldn't take that chance. Give me a signed deal and then we'll meet.'

'Tell me what you have first.'

Danvers chuckled. 'I want a deal in writing before I talk.'

Garrison glanced at Carlson, who stared at him stone-faced. He cupped his hand over the receiver. 'You said he was going to be here.'

She shook her head. 'That's what he told me.'

Garrison swallowed an oath and then said to Danvers, 'Call me when you're ready to talk. I'm giving you back to your attorney.'

Malcolm pushed away from the car. 'I knew this wasn't going to pan out.'

Carlson lifted her chin and said loud enough for

Danvers to hear, 'He's not my client. He never paid his last bill and I've never once said I'd continue to represent him.'

'Looks like you're screwed. No deal and no attorney. Have a nice life, Danvers.' Garrison hung up.

Malcolm raised a brow but said nothing.

Carlson leaned a little closer in anticipation, but she was too smart an attorney to say what was on her mind.

They waited in silence just a few more seconds before the phone rang. Garrison handed it to Carlson. 'I believe that's your client.'

She flipped open the phone. 'Angie Carlson.' She stared at them. 'You're in luck. He was just about to drive away but I think I can flag him down.' She waited a beat and then handed the phone to Garrison.

'Make it fast, Danvers. You're pissing away my time.'

'Okay. Okay. I was at this house on Saturday night. Nice house. Well-manicured lawn. Looked like the people were on vacation. You know, my kind of place.'

'Keep talking.'

'I get inside and the place is just empty. Nothing. Not a stick of furniture. I was getting ready to leave when I heard a moaning sound coming from the air vents. I thought I'd heard wrong and then I heard it again. It was an awful sound. Like a wounded animal. I moved toward the kitchen to look for basement stairs. And then some-one hit me from behind. When I woke up I was tied up like a pig and a woman was screaming. I could smell some-thing burning. Like flesh. I wiggled loose and ran like hell.'

Garrison stared at the barren horizon. 'You left this screaming woman?'

'I was scared.'

'You never called the cops to report this?'

'Like I said, I was scared.'

Scared that his bony ass would end up back in jail for ten to fifteen years for breaking and entering. 'Did you see who hit you?'

'Just a flash in the corner of my eye.' He sounded breathless.

Garrison had no concern for whatever fear Danvers felt now. He'd left a woman in the hands of a monster. 'That doesn't tell me a whole lot, Mr Danvers.'

'I want my deal in writing and then I'll talk more. I can tell you where the house is located – where I'll bet he killed that woman.'

Garrison smiled. 'Mr Danvers, you are out on bail. If you don't tell me what you know I'll have every cop in Northern Virginia looking for you.'

'No one is going to find me. Not you. Not that crazy motherfucker.' He inhaled and exhaled deeply. 'I dropped my fucking wallet at the house. He knows where I live.'

'Then you better come in so that I can protect you.'

'I give you an address and then you still put out an APB on my ass and I go back to jail. You've got to know this breaking and entering is my third strike. I can't risk being put away for the next ten years.'

'Just give me the address.'

'I don't want to go back to jail again.'

'I can do that.'

Danvers shoved out a sigh. 'I want my guarantee in writing. I'll call Ms Carlson at six this evening, and if you've got my deal, I'll text you the address. Once you've found the killer, then I'll reappear.'

Connor Donovan balanced a cup of double espresso and a box crammed full of notepads, scrap pieces of paper and articles on his hip as he shoved the key into his mailbox lock, wiggled it a couple of times, yanked up and then turned the persnickety lock to the right. He'd gone by the medical examiner's office last night hoping to find someone who might tell him something about the woman's body found at the shelter. But no one had talked, no matter what he offered. So he'd headed to his storage shed and dug through old file boxes, trying to find his notes on the Sorority Murder story. He'd dug out five boxes from deep in the shed when he'd hit pay dirt and discovered the box of missing notes.

His eyes itched as he pulled the mail – mostly junk and bills – from the full box. He shoved the lot under his arm next to the box, closed the box door and headed up the stairs to his third-floor apartment. He never took the elevator and he always walked when he could. His hours for getting to the gym proved next to impossible but he liked the fact that his waist was as trim as it had been when he'd been doing more fieldwork.

He unlocked his front door, entered and kicked it closed behind him. Polished hardwood floors and white walls were the first thing most visitors commented about. He liked the sleek barren look – fewer distractions when he wrote.

The large living room had a long, low black couch,

which sat across from a coffee table and a wide-screen television. The only pictures on his wall were photos he'd snapped during his travels. U.S. soldiers raising an American flag in Baghdad in front of a schoolhouse. Snow falling on a young blond teenage girl with braids in Munich. A girl in Madrid on a scooter, arms wrapped around her boyfriend's waist as she grins over her shoulder. A Russian soldier crossing the cobblestone street at the Kremlin in Moscow while a handful of schoolchildren watch. Each photo represented a story assignment and each offered a perfect conversation opener.

He set the box and mail on a sleek black slate table that sat under a white dome chandelier, but kept his espresso. The galley-style kitchen glistened with chrome and polished black granite countertops. It looked sleek as hell, but he rarely used it.

Donovan sorted through the mail, tossing the ads and bills in separate piles. The last piece was an oversized manila envelope that was hand addressed.

His sister occasionally sent him articles of interest. But Nadia lived in Europe now and the postmark on the envelope was local. He tore open the envelope, anxious to start digging through his old files. He pulled out a single piece of paper and glanced at the handwritten note. REPENT OR ATONE.

'What the hell?' If the mail hadn't been delivered to his apartment building he'd have balled it up and tossed it away. He'd had his share of crackpots contacting him over the years. But this one had come to his home. And he'd always been so careful about hiding his identity from everyone.

Donovan stared at the note. He could call the cops but what could they do? 'Keep your eyes open,' they'd say.

He didn't need to waste a half a day at a police station to know he had to be careful. He carefully folded the letter and replaced it in the envelope. He'd tuck it in the file with all the other hate mail.

Repent or atone.

If the letter had been a mindless rant like all the others, he'd have shoved it out of his mind. But the simply written words rattled through his mind as he opened the box and mined for gold.

Red Horseman had been on-line for just under an hour when *Drama-Girl* came into the chat room. *Drama-Girl* and *Red Horseman* had hooked up a few weeks ago in the chat room for single professionals living in the Washington, D.C., metro area. Immediately, they'd struck up a rapport and *Drama-Girl* quickly found she anticipated their chats.

Drama-Girl was lonely, bummed that her parents' thirty-year marriage had ended in divorce and her own affair with a married man had dissolved. Toss in the fact that *Drama-Girl* also felt the weight of her ad sales job, which had grown more and more competitive in the last year.

The chat rooms helped her unwind. My boss is an ass.

Red Horseman responded, He just doesn't appreciate the work you do. You've told me how hard you work.

Drama-Girl liked the fact that *Red Horseman* was her age and an ambitious professional. He, too, worked long hours and was feeling the pressures of the economy. I should have his job. He thinks he knows how the work gets done but he has no clue.

You will have his job one day. I have confidence in you. You are going places.

Drama-Girl glanced up from her laptop through the glass walls of her office. The mail boy had paused at her door and slowly sorted envelopes. I'll own this company one day.

I'd bet on it. I keep telling you how smart you are.

Thanks. You always make me feel so good. No one else understood her like *Red Horseman*.

She'd sent him pictures. The first few were sweet, safe. When *Red Horseman* had sent her a picture and she'd been pleased to see a darker, smokier version of Brad Pitt, she'd been so thrilled. Maybe she had found the one. Luv your eyes! Too cute!

God, she'd just passed her thirtieth birthday and was falling for a guy she'd never met. She'd read all the warnings, even watched those reality To-Catch-a-Bad-Guy-type shows but *Red Horseman* wasn't like them. He never asked anything of her and gave her so much support. He was real, genuine. She could feel it in her bones.

So she'd sent him more explicit pictures. When she'd said she'd wanted to hook up, *Red Horseman* had suggested they go a little slower. He wanted her to be sure. It touched her that he was looking out for her well-being.

But *Drama-Girl* was anxious and so certain of her feelings. Waiting was overkill. Hey, let's meet. I'm leaving town on business in a few days and I want to see you before I go. I am so sure of you.

The cursor blinked for several moments as if the machine was deep in thought. Are you?

His smiling picture stared at her, fueling feelings of a deep spiritual connection. I am very sure. When?

I'm leaving in three days on my trip. Tonight? Her fingers trembled with anticipation as she drummed them nervously on her desk.

Great. Where?
There's a bar on Prince Street.
Renegades?
Yes.
I know it. Nine work?
It sure does, babe.
I can't wait.
Neither can I.

Chapter 8

When Garrison returned to his office, Lieutenant LaPorta sat in one of the two metal chairs in front of his desk, her long legs outstretched, ankles crossed. Her head tipped forward as she studied the screen of her BlackBerry. LaPorta had always liked her gadgets, whereas he simply tolerated cell phones and pagers as necessary evils.

He passed by her and dropped his keys on the desk. Shrugging off his jacket, he hung it on the back of his chair. 'What do you have?'

She typed a message into the BlackBerry. 'Where's your partner in crime?'

'Kier? Tracking down backgrounds on a couple of our witnesses to the fire.'

She hit Send. She tucked the BlackBerry in the pocket of her dark blazer as if she had all the time in the world. 'The fire was definitely arson. We tested the area for chemicals and the kitchen area lights up like a Christmas tree. I suspect gasoline, judging by the scent, but tests will confirm. A Molotov cocktail tossed at the front door as your witness suggested would have set the place ablaze.'

He leaned back in his chair wondering why the murderer would set fire to the shelter. Had someone in the shelter seen him dump the body? Or was the killer sending a message? 'Any of the residents test positive for accelerant?'

'No. They were all clean. And none so far have any arson priors or reasons to burn the place.' Her BlackBerry beeped. She glanced at it but ignored the caller. 'Any word on your Jane Doe?'

'I'm headed to the medical examiner's office in a few minutes. She'll be doing the autopsy in an hour. No match on prints yet. And so far no missing-persons reports match her description.'

'You've got yourself a puzzle, Garrison. And as I remember, you like puzzles.'

He grinned, hoping to dodge the personal stuff. 'Sure, why not?'

She studied him a minute. 'That's why we didn't work. I'm just too straightforward. An open book. No mystery to be untangled.'

'That's a good thing.'

'Not in our case.'

He tensed, unsure why she'd chosen now to revisit the past. Not sure what to say, he said nothing.

'Have you ever wondered why we didn't work? That's a puzzle I've never been able to crack.'

It hadn't worked with Macy or anyone else – not since his wife had died. Life with Susan had been a roller coaster – ups and downs. And in the beginning it had been great. Then the mood swings became more pronounced. She either couldn't sleep for weeks on end or would crash and not be able to get out of bed for days. Taking care of Susan had become a job unto itself. And still he'd loved her and tried to make it better. They'd been married fourteen months when he came home and found her dead. She'd committed suicide. That had been a decade ago, but since then he'd not been in any relationship for the long haul.

'I never lied to you, LaPorta.' And he hadn't. He'd also never promised what he couldn't deliver. A normal life. A family.

'You have a way of drawing people in and making them believe they're special.'

An awkward silence settled between them. 'I'm not sure what to say.'

Macy usually didn't struggle with emotions and it surprised him she did now. 'Nothing to say, I guess.'

'What's this about?'

Suddenly she straightened, as if realizing her terrible slip. 'Sorry. Don't know where that came from.' Color flushed her cheeks as she rose. 'I'll keep you posted if I find out anything more about the fire.'

He stood. 'Great. Thanks.'

As Macy left his office, Garrison listed all the attributes that made Macy perfect for him. Smart, logical, independent. He respected and admired her, but had never loved her. Maybe Susan's death had damaged him and left him no good for anyone.

His mind took an unexpected turn back to Eva Rayburn's sharp eyes and smoky voice, which had remained with him all day. She was like a cool, smooth pond, but he suspected the waters below the surface were deep, murky and even turbulent. But was she a firebug or a killer? That he didn't know.

A puzzle.

Macy was right on one score.

He liked puzzles.

Butterflies chewed Eva's stomach when she knocked on the door of Mark Givens, director of financial aid at St Margaret's College. She'd sat in on a few classes and had discovered just how much she'd missed college and learning. She'd done some studying on-line in prison, but it had not been the same as sitting in a room full of students or talking directly to a professor. So on a whim six weeks ago, just days before the spring deadlines, she'd applied to the college and to the scholarship program, knowing without help she'd not be able to afford full-time college.

She'd been accepted two weeks ago to St Margaret's, but had yet to hear from Financial Aid. She'd been dreading this visit for days.

Eva pushed open the door. 'Dr Givens.'

Dr Givens raised his dark gaze up from a stack of papers on his desk, peering over horn-rimmed glasses that magnified his eyes to owlish proportions. He'd shorn his dark thinning hair close to his head and his white button-down shirt and black slacks exactly fit his trim body. As always, he studied her as if trying to peer into her brain.

'Eva Rayburn,' she supplied. 'You said you might have news on my grant application today.'

'Rayburn. Yes, I have your file.' He pretended to not quite remember her name, but she sensed he'd not forgotten the ex-con. Few did. He turned to the bird's nest of papers on his desk and rooted through them. Several seconds passed before he found her paperwork. 'Have a seat.'

Eva held the strap of her backpack so tight her knuckles ached. For so many years she'd told herself that wanting too much was dangerous. Much like venturing off the porch and racing to the car before the neighbor's pit bull attacked.

But in the last six months, she'd found it harder and harder not to want more. She wanted to go to school, wanted a real college education, wanted a normal life. Still the memory of her year at Price haunted her. She'd reached and been punished for it. For ten years she'd licked her wounds, fought off anger and resentment and in the darkest hours of night dreamed again of what might be. Those dreams had grown hungrier and hungrier with each year and now it seemed they were demanding to be fed.

And now she was reaching again. And she'd never been more terrified.

'Has the committee decided on my scholarship?'

He nodded. 'You have excellent college board scores. Perfect, in fact. I first assumed the results were wrong but you took them twice. Scored perfectly both times. That doesn't happen often.'

'I'm good with tests.'

'And we received your transcripts. You earned all A's throughout your first and only year of college. Excellent essays on your application.'

'Yes.'

'The only thing working against you of course is your criminal record.' He peered over the edge of his glasses. 'We don't get many students who have served time for manslaughter.'

Eva lifted her chin, refusing to cower. She'd served her time. 'No, I suppose not.'

'Your manslaughter conviction gave the committee pause.'

Eva sensed the 'But' coming and had to fight a crushing wave of disappointment. She'd heard all the reasons she couldn't be hired in Richmond or why she couldn't rent a room. But instead of cowering or showing any sign of sadness, she trained her gaze on his, wanting a direct connection when he rejected her. 'What are you saying?'

'Your paperwork said that you killed a young man from your college, Price University.'

She'd been up-front about all the details. 'Yes.'

'I spoke to the warden and to your parole officer.'

No doubt he'd asked about all the gruesome details that most were afraid to ask her directly. *Why did you kill that boy? He raped me. How did you kill him? I don't remember. They say I hit him in the head with a fireplace poker. Why did you burn the house down? I don't remember.*

She had the vague sense of an old scab being scraped open. 'And?'

'Both had very good things to say about you. They believe you deserve a second chance.'

The breath she'd been holding seeped from her lungs. The warden had been kind to her, recognizing her need to learn. Her parole officer had given her used books to read.

Eva nodded, again fearing her voice would crack with emotion. Maybe she'd read him wrong.

'We are progressive here at St Margaret's. We're not a big university but we believe what we do here has value. And we believe in second chances.' He smiled and he held out his hand. 'You're one of the strongest applicants we've had in years.'

Hope flickered. For an instant, her future flashed bright and shiny. 'Does that also mean I get the scholarship?'

He sighed. 'You did not get the award.'

Her lips flattened as she choked back hurt and anger. 'You just said I was your strongest applicant.'

'You are, and if it were up to me you'd have gotten the money. But we have a very conservative board of admissions. Some were uncomfortable about your past.'

'They accepted me to the school.'

'Yes. You are smart. No doubt. But the committee decided other students deserved the scholarship more.'

Bitterness twisted in her belly. 'More deserving.'

He grinned, oddly reminding her of a clown she'd once seen at the circus. Clowns were supposed to be happy, funny creatures, yet the one she'd seen had given her nightmares for a week. 'You've been accepted. There must be another way to find financing.'

'Without the money, they might as well have denied me.'

'We can defer your admission up to three years.'

'At the rate I'm saving, it'll take twenty years before I have enough.' Suddenly the walls in the room closed on her. Her chest tightened and for a moment the crushing confinement of prison returned.

Eva extended her hand, wondering how long her past would haunt her. When did people forget about the past and just let you live? 'Right. Thanks.'

His smooth palm wrapped around her hand. 'If it means anything, you had my vote.'

'You're not on the committee.'

'No.'

'Right. Thanks.'

Eva pulled her hand free and left his office. As she climbed down the building's stairs she could feel her anger growing. For so long she'd refused to dream or want. And now that she had opened the door to the future, her past had again slammed the door in her face.

She paused at the bottom of the stairwell, her hand on the door. She'd been branded a murderer and done her time for the crime. But in those lost moments, doubt taunted her. *Are you sure you killed him? Are you sure?*

For so long, she'd simply accepted. But acceptance had not only cost her ten years, it had also gnawed into her future. The time had come to reach into the shadows and embrace doubt. Good or bad, she needed to know what happened in the moments leading up to Josiah's death.

Eva yanked open the door, wincing as bright sunshine slammed her. She had to pause, as her eyes adjusted to the harsh glare. When her vision cleared, she headed for her truck, her long strides determined.

Twenty minutes later, grim determination had replaced the butterflies as she climbed the staircase to the second-floor computer lab at the college. She clutched a bag of fresh doughnuts as she walked to the teaching assistant's office. She knocked.

'Yep. Come in.' The deep baritone voice had her spine straightening.

She summoned a grin. 'Jeremy, I brought glazed doughnuts.'

Jeremy's chair squeaked as he turned from a desk piled high with bits and pieces of computers. Long black hair skimmed narrow stooped shoulders and framed a narrow face. His large green eyes, accentuated by the blackness of his T-shirt, bulged a little when he laughed. He reminded Eva of a hobbit. 'Back again?'

'We bad pennies keep turning up.'

He laughed. 'You must want a favor. Another computer lesson?'

Smile widening, she handed him the doughnuts. 'No lesson this time. I just need a little computer time.'

He dug a doughnut out of the bag and sniffed it. 'You know the way to my heart.'

Eva kept her stance casual. 'Is that a yes?'

Jeremy bit into the doughnut and closed his eyes in sheer pleasure. 'Sure. What are you looking for?'

'Just doing a little poking around.'

'No chat room this time?'

'Don't really have the time for it now.' The chat room had been a fascinating world to her where it seemed no one judged her, just accepted her at face value. She felt free when she surfaced. 'Just searching.'

'Swear.'

'I do.'

'Have at it,' he mumbled as he extended his hand toward a laptop in the corner.

Eva had met Jeremy a few months ago when she'd been sitting in one of his classes. She'd not had much access to computers while she'd been in prison and she'd soaked up all he'd offered about computers. She'd figured out quickly he had a weakness for glazed doughnuts and came armed with a dozen when she wanted to pick his brain. Soon she was doing advanced searches on her own and even helping him.

She sat down in front of the computer and typed:

'Sorority House Murder.' Seconds later her search gave her a list of choices to choose from.

'Have you considered college?' Jeremy said.

'Sure. But the money is holding me up.'

'You're smart. I bet you'd get grant money.'

'Maybe.' She'd not told him about the scholarship and now was glad. Explaining why she'd been rejected meant explaining the past.

She selected an article and waited while it loaded. The article had been written over a decade ago and featured a picture of the sorority sisters who had testified against her. Sara. Lisa. Kristen.

They were the key to those missing minutes because they'd been there. They had testified that Eva had swung the fireplace poker and hit Josiah hard enough to kill him. They'd been so certain, so unified in their stories. They couldn't, wouldn't have lied. Would they? They'd been her closest friends.

'So who are those chicks?' Jeremy said.

She clicked out of the article, hit the print button and glanced back at him. His lips glistened with doughnut glaze. 'Ancient history.'

'The look on your face said otherwise.'

'What's that mean?' She grabbed the printout from the printer and tucked it in her pocket.

'Babe, you look like you could kill.'

Garrison and Kier arrived at Wellington and James just minutes before six. They showed their badges to the security camera and the receptionist buzzed the front door open.

'Pretty bad when you need security to protect you from your own clients,' Malcolm said.

Garrison scanned the reception area's lush interior. 'Everything has its price.'

The receptionist escorted them back to the conference room where Angie Carlson stood at the head of a long mahogany table. Dark circles hung under her eyes and she stood stiff and straight like a nun ready to dish out penance. 'I haven't heard from Mr Danvers yet.'

'I have the deal. And it took some doing, considering your client's record.'

'I represented him a couple of months ago. He's not my client now,' she said. 'I called you because I thought he could help.'

Malcolm snorted. 'Mighty generous.'

Carlson's gaze flickered to Malcolm and for a moment Garrison imagined he saw sadness in the icy depths of her eyes. 'Would you gentlemen like to have a seat? Mr Danvers isn't the most punctual.'

The detectives sat, as did Carlson. She drummed neatly trimmed fingers on the polished table. On the wall, a clock ticked. No one spoke, but the tension between the three could be cut with a knife.

At a quarter after, Garrison checked his watch. 'How late does he usually run?'

'It's hard to say. Let's give it a half hour.'

'Sure.'

Malcolm settled back in his seat. 'What's your angle on all this, Carlson?'

'No angle, Detective. Like I said, I thought I could help.'

Malcolm leaned back in his chair and knitted his fingers together. 'I find that hard to believe after you put that scum Dixon back on the street.'

A muscle tensed slightly in her jaw. 'I've no angle on this case.'

Garrison understood his partner's anger, which mirrored his own. But the goal here today was to get information from Danvers, not get a pound of flesh. 'We appreciate your help, Ms Carlson.'

'Thank you.'

Malcolm raised a brow but kept his comments to himself.

At six-thirty Garrison and Malcolm rose. Normally, they'd not have waited for anyone this long. But this wasn't about them but the victim. 'Do you have Danvers's last known address?'

She nodded and from her jacket pocket pulled out a slip of paper. 'His girlfriend and he have an on-again, off-again relationship. Give her a try. If I hear from him, I'll call you.'

He flicked the edge of the paper with his thumb. 'Thanks.'

In the car Malcolm said, 'She's jerking our chain.'

'I don't think so.'

Fifteen minutes later, they arrived at the brick apartment complex located on the west side of Alexandria, not far from Interstate 95. They parked in front of the building and crossed the sidewalk to the building's front door, which surprisingly was unlocked. They pushed through the entryway, found the apartment number 3-B and climbed to the third floor. Hard rock music blared from the apartment's interior. Garrison knocked and when no one answered, he pounded his fist on the door.

'Okay. Okay.' The woman's voice mingled with a guitar solo. Her voice sounded rough and heavy. Seconds later the music shut off and footsteps moved toward the door. It opened partway thanks to a chain on the inside. 'What do you want?'

The woman had a wild tangle of black hair and wore an oversized T-shirt and pajama pants. 'We're with the Alexandria Police. I'm Detective Garrison and this is my partner, Detective Kier. Your name is?'

'Tracy Henderson.'

He held up his badge so that she could see it. 'Ms. Henderson, we're here to see Lenny Danvers.'

She cocked a plucked brow. 'He ain't here.'

'Where is he?'

'I don't know. I'm not his mother.'

Garrison didn't trust anything Danvers had told him and wanted to test some of the statements. 'You bailed him out this morning.'

'I did not. That bastard knows I'm not putting another nickel into him.' The heavy scent of tobacco drifted around the woman. 'I haven't seen him in days.'

'Where do you think he went?'

She shrugged. 'How do I know? He never tells me anything.'

'Who do you think bailed him out?'

'Likely he's got another girlfriend.'

'Mind if we search the place?'

She lifted a brow, her expression teetering between amusement and annoyance. 'Have at it.'

Garrison and Kier walked into the one-bedroom apartment. The room was furnished with a beat-up green couch, a couple of salvage yard end tables and a coffee table constructed of boards and cinder blocks. Scattered pizza boxes on the furniture and floor and several full ashtrays left a lingering stale odor in the room. Down a short hallway, the bedroom had only a mattress and box spring on the floor and a single beat-up nightstand. Discarded clothes covered the floor. The closet had clothes for a man and a woman.

'Any of his clothes missing?'

'Not that I can tell. And that's his duffle on the closet floor. I've been here all day, so if he came by to grab stuff, I'd have seen him.'

'Does he have another place where he crashes?' Criminals were creatures of habit and had favorite hiding spots.

'Like I said, I'm not his mother.' She reached to the nightstand by the mattress and picked up a cigarette and lighter. She lit the tip. 'Seems he's crawled under a rock, but he'll turn up. People like him always do.' She puffed the cigarette. 'What's he done this time? More breaking and entering?'

'He's connected to a murder case we're investigating.'

That had her lowering her cigarette. 'Lenny is a lot of things but he isn't a killer.'

'He may have witnessed something while he visited a home.'

She shook her head. 'Just like that dumb-ass to stumble into trouble. He's got the crappiest luck in the world.'

'Are you sure you don't know where we can find him?' Malcolm's annoyance punched through the words. 'We have reason to believe he could be in trouble.'

This time she considered the question. 'Sometimes he goes out to Leesburg.'

The picturesque small town was located about forty miles west of Alexandria. 'Where?'

'A house that belongs to a friend of a friend who travels a lot.' Her eyes narrowed. 'Do you think he could be in trouble?'

'Maybe.'

She shoved out a breath. 'He's not supposed to be in this house, if that's where he is.'

'I don't care about that. I just want to talk to him.'

'It's on the Fifteen Bypass.'

'You have an address?'

'I've only been there once. I don't have the address but I do know it's on the left side of Fifteen Bypass as you're heading north and there are huge white boulders marking the driveway.'

'Thanks.'

'If you find him, is he gonna be in trouble?'

Garrison and Malcolm moved toward the front door. 'He'll be in bigger trouble if we don't find him.'

Chapter 9

Tuesday, April 4, 8:00 P.M.

Garrison and Malcolm rolled into the station just after eight. Garrison had called Leesburg police and given them a description of the house on Route Fifteen. They asked them to check it out and Leesburg PD had agreed.

But Garrison had a growing sense of urgency that Lenny was in trouble. Too much rode on this deal and Danvers knew Garrison would hunt him down if he ran. Perhaps the thief's dropped wallet had led the killer to him.

The detectives grabbed sodas and crackers from a vending machine, knowing there'd be no time for a real meal. When they pushed through the doors of the conference room they were met by a tall, willowy brunette, Detective Jennifer Sinclair, who stood next to a white presentation board. She'd pinned pictures of the victim on the board as well as Danvers's DMV photo.

Beside Sinclair stood Detective Douglas Rokov. His height, broad shoulders, bulky frame and dark hair testified to his Russian heritage. His folks had moved to the States from St Petersburg weeks before his birth. Douglas could speak both Russian and English like a native.

Garrison set his soda on the table and shrugged off his jacket. 'What do we have so far?'

'An ID of your victim,' Jennifer said. 'Turns out she

did have prints in the AFIS system.' The computer system stored hundreds of thousands of prints of those who'd been arrested.

'Her name was Lisa Black and she was arrested for prostitution in a swanky hotel in D.C. three years ago,' Rokov said. 'Remember that scandal with Congressman Webber?'

Garrison rested his hands on his hips, nodding. 'He sat on the Defense Committee and he was caught using tax dollar money to pay for hookers.'

'The one and only. Well, our victim, Lisa Black, was the prostitute that he was with when he got busted. That's how she earned her one and only arrest.'

'Only one arrest?' Malcolm said. 'Don't tell me her arrest set her on the straight and narrow?'

Rokov grinned. 'Doubtful. She's from a well-to-do family. Private high school and college. Lots of attorneys.'

Malcolm shook his head, grumbling, 'I hate attorneys.'

'But what's her story? Why was she hooking?' In Garrison's seven years on the force, he'd seen all kinds of crazy motivations.

'We asked around. Until four years ago, she worked as a marketing director at a very successful engineering firm in Fairfax. Office rumor had it she had a sex addiction. When her stepfather died three years ago, she inherited millions. She quit her job and booked an eight-week vacation to Argentina. When she came back, no one recognized her. She'd had surgery done on her nose, eyes, lips and boobs.'

'After the surgery, the few friends she had said her obsessions got worse,' Sinclair interjected.

Rokov checked his notes. 'She has an apartment in a

high-rise in Crystal City, but we've not had a chance to visit it.'

Garrison checked his watch. 'Any word from the medical examiner?'

'The medical examiner had to push back Black's autopsy. Said if you came by about nine tonight, she'd have a report.'

'Okay.' He took a long gulp of his soda, amazed at how thirsty he'd become. He filled them in about Danvers and the Leesburg police. 'Call me if you get word from Leesburg PD.'

'Consider it done.'

Garrison glanced at Black's DMV photo. 'Rokov, go over to Eliza Martinez's house and have another walk around. Forensics still has the house sealed. I've been over the house dozens of times but maybe your fresh eyes, plus the details on Lisa Black, will spark something.'

'What connects the rich-girl nymph to the fifty-something Catholic domestic?'

'Right now, just a gut feeling.'

Garrison quickly obtained a search warrant for Lisa Black's apartment; by eight-thirty, Garrison and Kier stood in front of Lisa Black's door waiting as the building manager unlocked it.

The manager, Ralph Pemberton, a short man, with thinning red hair and thick glasses, reminded Garrison of the goofy troll dolls his sister had as a kid. 'I haven't seen Ms Black in a few days. Is she all right?'

Garrison smiled. 'We just need to have a look at the apartment.'

'She is always so nice to me,' Mr Pemberton said. 'I mean she's such a lovely woman. She didn't have to be nice to me. Not everyone is nice.'

Garrison nodded. 'I've heard good things about Ms. Black.'

'That stuff that happened a few years ago in the city wasn't her fault.'

'What stuff?' Garrison wanted the manager's perspective.

'That mess with the senator and his buddies.'

'Ah.'

'The lawyers got her off.'

'Then she must have been innocent,' Malcolm said.

The manager nodded, missing the sarcasm. 'That's what I said.'

'Did she have a lot of visitors in the building?' Garrison said.

'No. No. She never had any visitors. But she went out almost every evening. She liked people. A pretty girl should be around people.'

'You keep tabs on her?' Malcolm said.

Mr Pemberton shrugged. 'She always looked so pretty. Seeing her always brightened my day. So yeah, I looked from time to time. No crime.'

'No crime at all,' Garrison said lightly as he stared down at the little man. 'Thank you. We'll take it from here.'

'You want me to come into the unit? I know every nook and cranny of all the units.'

'No. That won't be necessary.'

A frown advertised his disappointment. 'Right. Sure.'

'When did you see Ms Black last?'

'Four or five days ago.'

'Which was it?'

The manager scrunched his face as if flipping through the days. 'Four days. Saturday morning. She said she had an appointment. Sometimes she's gone for days at a time on business, so I didn't worry.'

'What about her mail?'

'Post office boxes are in the lobby. They're around a corner. You can't see them from the main entrance.'

'Do you have access to her mail?'

The little man leveled his shoulders. 'I have a spare key.'

'Would you mind getting the key for me?'

His brows furrowed. 'Seems kinda wrong going through her stuff.'

'It needs to be done.'

'What's going on?' Nerves heightened the pitch of his voice. 'What's wrong with Ms Black?'

'She was murdered.'

The older man's face paled three shades and his lips quivered. 'How?'

'Can't say right now. Can you get that mail key?'

'Yeah, yeah, sure.' He fished a trembling hand into his pocket, pulled out a ring of keys and handed two keys to Garrison.

'You might need the other key. Each unit has a storage shed off the patio.'

'Thanks.'

The detectives moved into the apartment. Each pulled on rubber gloves and unfastened the clips to their gun holsters. Garrison, right hand on his weapon, flipped on the lights.

A large picture window dominated the main room, decorated in a sleek and modern style. Twin bleached couches and sparkling glass end tables rested on a soft white carpet that iced the pale wood floor. All the furniture faced an enormous fireplace hand crafted with white marble and scrubbed so clean Garrison doubted it ever held a fire. Mirrors hung on the walls, but no plants, flowers or personal touches warmed the room.

'She's got a thing for clean,' Malcolm said. 'Maybe she felt just a tad dirty.'

Garrison nodded. 'Could be.' He let his gaze roam the room, trying to understand Lisa Black. But the sterile room offered him little. 'Let's have a look at the kitchen and bedroom.'

'I vote kitchen first. Can tell a lot about a person by looking at their kitchen. Heart of the house.'

'What does your kitchen tell us about you?'

Malcolm kept his gaze locked ahead and alert to the unexpected as they moved into the kitchen. 'Me? I love to cook. Cabinets are stocked with all the basics for a killer marinara and the freezers have steaks. One thing I can't stand is a bad meal.'

Garrison reached the end of the hallway first. Malcolm hung back, ready to react to any nasty surprises as Garrison flipped on the overhead lights. Florescent lights flickered on, reflecting off top-of-the-line stainless-steel appliances, white marble countertops and shiny silver gourmet pots hanging from a pot rack. As sterile as the rest of the condo, the kitchen appeared just as unused.

Malcolm opened the refrigerator to find five bottles of

champagne and three cartons of cottage cheese. 'The breakfast of champions.'

Garrison shook his head. 'Even I do a better job than that.'

'What? Beer and cold cuts?'

'And eggs and cheese. When I want a real meal, I head to my folks' house.'

'Amen to that.'

Malcolm checked the drawers, stocked with a set of glistening Shun knives. 'Damn, it's a crime this stuff hasn't been used.'

The pantry was barren and the counters and floors perfectly clean. 'It's like she never lived here.'

'Or was one hell of a neat freak.'

Garrison opened and closed the drawers. 'She might have used the place as a base of operation.' In the last drawer he found a packet of matches. Embossed in gold on the black cover was Moments, Washington, D.C. 'One of her haunts?'

'Could be.'

They moved into the bedroom, which like the rest of the condo lacked any personal touch. A round bed with a white satin coverlet covered the room's center, while mirrors reflected from white walls above the headboard. When the sun was up, the mirrors caught the morning light from large sliding glass doors, which faced east. On the west wall, a smooth dresser displayed neatly lined up antique crystal perfume bottles.

Garrison opened the closet door and switched on the light. The closet was filled with all types of clothes from sleek business suits, to leather skirts to costumes that ranged from Snow White to a pirate. 'Interesting collection.'

'My, my,' Malcolm said, standing in the doorway. 'Whatever her man wants.'

'Clearly she hooked up with a lunatic.'

'But where?'

'That's the question. But I'd like to check this place out.' He tossed the matches to Malcolm.

Malcolm snatched the packet out of the air. He unfurled his fingers. 'Moments.'

'It's swanky, from what I remember.'

'Sure.' Malcolm glanced in the closet. 'The costumes appear to be the only variable. The rest of the place has no personality.'

'Even the costumes represent make-believe personalities.' Garrison glanced out onto the patio. 'Manager said the unit had a storage closet.' He pushed open the sliding glass door and found the key that fit the lock. He opened the door and pulled on the light string. 'Shit.'

'What?'

Both stared into the five-by-five closet. The walls had been painted a pale blue and were covered in bright posters featuring foreign cities. Rome. Paris. Madrid. And on the ceiling, Zurich. A plush mattress warmed the concrete floor. Blue sheets, several down pillows and a handmade pink and white quilt made the space almost cozy. Nestled between the mattress and the wall was an eight-by-ten-inch hand-painted wooden box. On top of the box, rhinestones spelled out the word LISA.

Garrison ran his hand over the back of his neck. 'She lived in the storage closet.'

'The one place that was all her own.'

Images of the frail, badly mutilated body found behind the shelter flashed in his mind. She'd suffered a horrible death but clearly demons had haunted her for some time. 'Hell of a life when you feel at home in a storage closet.' He reached into the room and grabbed the box. The box was filled with dozens of personal mementos. A child's diary, complete with a little lock. A handful of pictures featuring a younger Lisa with unidentified friends. A silver cross on a delicate chain. And buried on the bottom was a diary.

He opened the book and discovered the entries appeared to be gibberish. The letters made no sense. 'She keeps her journal in code.'

'Interesting. What's so scary you have to hide it so thoroughly?'

'I don't know.' Garrison thumbed through the pages of precise handwriting. Just as he reached the end, a pendant shaped like a four-pointed star fell to the ground. He picked it up. 'What do you think?'

Malcolm studied the pendant. 'Looks a lot like the brand.'

The star's rhinestones caught the shed's light, which dangled and swayed as if an imaginary hand had just nudged it. Specks of light danced on the wall. 'It does.'

'It's nothing all that special. Looks like a department store buy. I've a couple of sisters who had jewelry boxes full of that stuff.'

Garrison's sister had loved her baubles too. His parents had buried her with a red sparkly heart that he'd bought her a couple of weeks before she died. 'It meant something to her, otherwise she'd have tossed it like she did with everything else personal in her apartment.'

Time had chipped away some of the star's glass stones. 'Whoever gave this to her did so a long time ago.'

'Must have been very personal, otherwise it wouldn't be hidden away. I thought her killer might have been one of her boyfriends, but now I'm not so sure.'

Garrison shook his head. 'At this point, hell if I know. But we need to get this journal code broken and figure out what Lisa Black didn't want the world to know.'

A knock on the condo unit's front door had Garrison crossing the condo to answer it. Mr Pemberton stood on the threshold, holding a stack of mail in his hand.

Garrison frowned. 'I said I'd get the mail.'

'Found another key. Thought I could help. I want to help.'

Garrison took the mail, a muscle in the side of his jaw tensing. He had no way of knowing if Pemberton had removed anything from the box.

Garrison sailed through the traffic where I-95 intersected with the Beltway. Locals called it the Melting Pot, and despite billions of dollars of road improvements, it was always clogged with commuter traffic even on a good day. Toss in a fender-bender, or bad weather, and the line of cars slowed even more. But at nearly nine in the evening, the traffic was light.

The thick scent of bleach greeted them when they pushed through the metal doors of the medical examiner's autopsy room. The tiled gray floors had a dull polish and florescent bulbs cast an overbright light on the room.

Dr Amanda Henson, a tall, slim redhead, stood next to a stainless-steel table, which held Lisa Black's nude body. Under the harsh lights the star brands looked redder and angrier. Dr Henson had just cut the Y incision into the body's chest and with pliers snapped through the first rib.

Only in her mid-thirties, Henson wore her auburn curls in a tight bun generally favored by much older women. Dark horn-rimmed glasses framed vivid blue eyes and off-set a splay of freckles over her cosmetic-free face. She always wore white Dansko clogs and no jewelry. A high slash of cheekbones, full lips and a trim silhouette under her shapeless scrubs kept her from looking plain and men wondering what she looked like dolled up.

'Just in time, gentlemen.' A rib snapped.

Malcolm slid his hand into his pocket, doing his best to look relaxed, but Garrison had come to recognize the move as a mental bracing. 'Would hate to miss the show.'

'So what do you have?' Garrison said.

'I took her liver temperature and can tell you she died late Saturday or early Sunday. She has four distinct star-shaped burns on her body. Three knife wounds into the chest and abdomen. The burns didn't kill her, and I doubt most of the stab wounds killed her.' The doctor pointed to a section of slashed skin by the victim's neck. 'This one killed her. It serrated her jugular.'

'What kind of knife would make wounds like that?'

'Long. Serrated edge.'

'And the burns?'

'Done at least a day to a few hours before the stabbing. Whoever burned her wasn't in a rush.'

'How was she burned?'

The doctor set down her pliers, pulled off the glove on her right hand and punched a few buttons on a computer keypad. The screen monitor switched from a sandy beach to a photo of the brand. 'I'd say the killer used a metal branding iron heated in a fireplace.'

'Why do you say that?' Garrison asked. 'Some branding irons are electric.'

She outlined sections of the picture with her fingertip. 'Faint traces of ashes in the wounds. If its heat source is electricity, then there'd be no need for fire.'

Garrison moved closer to the screen and held up the bagged necklace star with the rhinestones. 'An identical match.'

Dr Henson arched an eyebrow. 'Where'd you find that?'

'Lisa Black's apartment.'

Dr Henson returned to the table, pulled on fresh gloves and reached for a section of rib cage.

Malcolm shoved out a breath and took a step back. 'Can you tell me anything about Ms Black?'

'She appears to be well nourished, though a bit on the thin side. Nails appear healthy, no track marks, no evidence of old fractures, no birth defects.'

'Tox screen?' Garrison said.

'Prelims are clean but that could change.' Dr Henson set the rib cage on a side cart draped in surgical batting. 'I did do a vaginal swab and pelvic examination. No signs of sexual assault or recent intercourse. Judging by the shape of her uterus she's never had children.'

'Anything else?'

Her brow knotted as she studied the brands on the victim's belly. 'When I first examined the burns I noticed they were uneven. Meaning a couple were light and a couple progressively deeper.'

'Which suggests?'

'I'm redoing my kitchen and to save money I'm doing a little stenciling on the walls.'

'Dr Henson, do you digress?' Malcolm said.

'When, Detective, have you ever known me to make small talk with you?'

Malcolm shrugged. 'Never.'

'Exactly.' She peered through her safety glasses into the body cavity, looking at the heart. 'The first burns were tentative, as if the killer was experimenting with the branding iron.'

'The killer was practicing and getting a feel for the process.' Garrison ground his back teeth.

'Makes me think this is the first time the killer has done something like this. But judging by the burns on Ms Black, the killer gained confidence quickly.' She glanced up at him. 'Which leads me to believe, he's just getting started.'

'Why do you say that?'

'The number four seems to be a recurring theme. Four stars. A four-pointed star. Four stab wounds.'

'And so far only one victim.' Garrison shook his head. 'He's not finished.'

Garrison studied the clear brands placed in a neat circle on the victim's belly. 'Forensics scraped under the nail beds. Let's hope they come up with foreign DNA. I can only hope the killer left something behind.'

Dr Henson shook her head. 'So far, I've found nothing on the body. No hair. No semen. Nothing. I'd say you have one organized killer.'

'No one's perfect, Doc. All killers forget something. We just need to find it.'

Eva shut the water off in the ladies' room and reached for the paper towel dispenser. It was empty. She checked under the sink and found the towels she'd just stocked this morning gone as well. What was it with paper products? There were days it felt like they evaporated into thin air.

Her hands still damp from the washing, she pushed through the door, her gaze skittering to a blond waitress behind the crowded bar. Betty, a fifty-something waitress, could keep the bar moving for short periods of time, but more than fifteen minutes and she fell behind and orders got jammed. Alcohol was King's best moneymaker, and Eva understood that each order dropped meant lost revenue.

Still distracted by the lost scholarship and the articles she'd read about her sorority sisters, she wasn't paying attention and nearly tripped over Bobby who stood right by the door. She yelped in surprise. 'Good Lord! You nearly scared me to death.'

Bobby frowned and tears filled his eyes. 'I'm sorry.'

Immediately contrite, Eva shoved out a breath. 'Bobby, you've got to stop walking around the pub like it's covered with eggshells.'

'I'm sorry.'

She knelt in front of him. 'Don't be sorry. I didn't mean to scream like a little girl. I just didn't expect you.'

'I'm sorry.'

She smiled and patted his shoulder with drippy hands.

'It's not even worth being sorry about. Hey, what are you still doing up? It's past nine.'

'King said I could put food out for the kitten.'

'Any luck catching Merlin yet?'

His eyes brightened. 'No, but I am getting close. I almost caught him today.'

'Keep feeding him, and he'll warm up to you.'

'I will.'

'So you're headed to bed?'

'Yes. King says lights out now. Will you take me upstairs? King is busy and doesn't have time to check under the bed for monsters.'

King had mentioned their ritual. Every night King searched the boy's room for monsters. 'Wait just a minute while I go to the basement and get towels. And then I'll run you upstairs.' She dashed down the rickety stairs and clicked on the light at the bottom. A bulb swung from a rope. The place smelled of must and old brick. Most of the other gals waiting tables at the pub didn't like the basement. But it didn't bother her. Spiders, cobwebs and ordinary frights had lost their fear factor since her journey to hell and back.

Eva found the towels on a shelf by a locked root cellar and dashed back up the stairs because Bobby hovered at the top peering into the basement, his eyes wide with worry. 'See, no worries.'

A deep furrow creased his brow. 'It's dark down there.'

'Dark never hurt anybody.'

'You're not scared?'

'Nope.' She smiled. 'Help me put these towels away and then I've got to get the bar prepped.'

'Okay.'

'Are you afraid of basements?' Learning any information about Bobby might help figure out his story.

'Yes.'

'Is there a basement where you lived?'

'My grandmother had a basement.'

'She did?' Another clue to his family. 'Where did she live?'

'Far from here.' A note of suspicion seeped into his tone.

Back off or push? He might open up if she nudged him a little more. It might also send him deeper into silence. She'd never been one for the safe route. 'Isn't your grandmother worried about you?'

'No.'

'She has to be.'

'She died.'

'I'm so sorry. You must miss her.'

'I do. She baked cookies when I visited.'

Eva glanced down at the child, into dark brown eyes that reflected maturity far beyond his years. She laid her hand on his shoulder. 'How did she die?'

He glanced up at her but hesitated before he spoke. 'It was her time. She was old.'

'Her time? That sounds like something an older person would say. Who told you it was her time?'

'Nobody. I heard that line on TV once.'

'Your grandmother and mother are dead. What about your father?'

'I never knew him. Mom said he died before I was born.' He pulled his gaze from her and scanned the shelves lined with boxes. 'I can put the extra towels away.'

'Okay.' She loaded the towel dispenser. 'Shove the extra towels under the sink. That would be a big help to me. Then we head upstairs.'

His eyes brightened, his need to please reflected in his eyes. Her heart twisted. She'd been that way once – so eager to please that she'd have done anything. She'd been a fool.

'Sure, Eva. I'll do a good job. Can I help with anything else?'

'Yeah, you can get upstairs and brush your teeth. It's well past nine and you need to be in bed.'

His lip curled out into a pout. 'I don't like sleeping. I have dreams.'

'Read a couple of the books King got you for school.'

'I don't like reading.'

'Reading or bedtime.'

'I'll read.'

They passed through the kitchen; Bobby said good night to King, and Eva followed the kid up the back stair-case. Fifteen minutes later she'd checked under the bed and the race car quilt on top, in the closets and even behind the blue curtains. She picked a baseball book from a stack by his bed. 'I'll leave the light on, okay?'

He nodded stiffly. 'Okay. Did you check the windows to make sure they were locked?'

'Twice. Locked tight. No bad guys are getting in this room.'

He eased his grip on the sheets a fraction. 'Okay.'

He conned her into reading a few pages of his book. When she handed him the book, she hesitated.

A kiss good night didn't seem right. He wasn't her child.

But just to get up and leave felt rude. She settled for a pat on the head. 'I'm right downstairs if you need me or King.'

'Thanks, Eva.'

Eva moved down the steps, wondering who had messed Bobby up so badly. No child should be so terrified of his own shadow.

Customers inundated the bar and several patrons held up glasses, trying to catch Betty's attention. Eva slipped behind the bar and made quick work of serving several of the more impatient customers.

She set a cold beer down in front of a guy who just about lived at King's. 'Here you go, Stan.'

Stan, an older man with thinning hair and a double chin, pouted just as Bobby had. 'No one takes better care of me than you, Eva.'

'We aim to please, Stan. Need anything else?'

'Not now.'

Betty greeted Eva with a grateful grin. 'Thank God. I can't keep up with all the drinks.' She tucked a stray blond curl behind her ear and checked the notebook in her hand.

A man at the end of the bar waved his glass impatiently and called for another Vodka Collins. Betty moved to go but Eva smiled. 'I got it.'

Eva mixed the drink, remembering this was the man's third round and he liked four cherries on a toothpick in his drink.

'How did you remember he likes extra cherries?'

She never told anyone she could recall details very easily, but most noticed quickly. 'Don't know.'

'God, I wish I could remember things like you. It's all I can do to remember whether a sandwich order is toasted or not.'

'It just takes practice.'

'I've been at this three years. You haven't been here six months.'

'I've always had a good memory.' Photographic was more accurate. Facts, figures, details stayed with her. Of course, the irony was that she could not remember the most critical minutes before Josiah died. She had reason to kill Josiah and a part of her believed she had struck the fatal blow. But as the years had passed, the not remembering haunted her. Those minutes likely were the real reason she'd accepted King's offer. Those minutes drove her to the computer lab to search out what she could about Lisa, Sara and Kristen. And now it seemed those minutes controlled her future.

Betty tucked her pencil in her starched hair. 'I never would have figured King would do the foster parent thing.'

'He seems like a natural.'

'I heard after his wife and kid died it changed him. I guess no one figured he'd want parental responsibilities again.'

King had lost a wife and child. She'd never known. Her heart twisted and ached for him. His unending patience with Bobby now made so much sense.

'You know what happened?' Betty said.

'I never ask about anyone's past.'

'Why not?'

'None of my business.'

145

'Aren't you a little curious?'

'Nope.' The only past she cared about now was her own and those missing minutes.

Sara Miller, a.k.a. *Drama-Girl*, sat in the bar nervously tracing the glass rim of her second gin and tonic. In the background a guy played a jazzy/bluesy song that reminded her of Bourbon Street in New Orleans. Young professionals, clad in dark suits and silk dresses, packed the bar, making her feel safe. She was glad she had chosen this place to meet her on-line guy, *Red Horseman*.

She'd been looking forward to this all day. The stress at the office chewed on her constantly these days and she needed a break. For years she'd worked backbreaking hours to stay ahead of the pack, but recently, work, which had been such a refuge at times, had felt like prison.

So much rode on this new client's ad campaign. 'It'll make or break the agency, Sara,' her boss had said. 'Show me you are still number one and get us the Impact Sports account.' And she had. At dinner tonight, she'd won the biggest contract the Fairchild Advertising Agency had ever earned.

But for the first time, she worried if she could actually deliver on the job. The payout would be huge, but it would require hundreds of hours of her time in the next month. As the firm's top account executive, she'd already been averaging one hundred hours a week and she didn't know from where the time would be carved.

Sara sipped her drink. She should have been at the office now, incorporating the notes from the client dinner into a memo for tomorrow's staff meeting. However, her thoughts were only for *Red Horseman*. She could break from work for a while.

Sara checked her watch. He was three minutes late. Which wasn't exactly late late but it felt like forever. She couldn't afford to stay too long. Like it or not, she needed to get back to her office to write that memo.

Her phone buzzed beside her on the bar and she glanced down, praying it wasn't her office. The display read *Red Horseman*. 'Please don't cancel.'

Hey, I think I've got the wrong bar, his message said. I'm down the street at King's. She hadn't been there in years – not her kind of crowd. Too working-class.

Smiling with relief that he wasn't canceling, she typed: I'm at Renegades just down the road.

Directions? I have no sense of direction.

His helplessness was sort of endearing. It was nice to be in charge once in a while. I'll come to you.

You're the best.

Sara paid her tab and headed out of the bar, whistling and feeling more excited about life than she had in a long time. Get a grip, her brain warned. You've only just met this guy on-line. He could be such a loser.

But they'd connected so well.

She moved outside, away from the noise and the smoke and into the darkness. For a moment she savored the quiet and clean air. Getting her car would be easy, but the night air coaxed her to walk. King's was only a few blocks away or less than five minutes if she hustled.

Shoving long fingers through her hair, she headed down the street, her high heels clicking on the cobble-stone street.

Halfway down the street, someone called out her name. The voice sounded husky, hoarse even.

'Hey, Sara! Where you headed so fast?'

Friendly, and at ease, whoever called out clearly knew her. No doubt she'd met this person at a business event where she elevated fake smiles and light conversation to an art form. But tonight she wasn't in the mood to play nice or guess Who Am I? She wanted to see *Red Horseman*.

'I'm in a rush,' she said, tossing a careless smile as she kept walking.

'Hey, I understand.' The person skimmed along the stone wall bordering the sidewalk, just in the shadows. 'Just wanted to say hello.'

She tossed a quick glance, ready to tell whomever to scram when a zap of pain shot through her body and her knees buckled. Another zap to her side and she landed facedown in the street.

Rough hands grabbed her and pulled her to her feet. Before her thoughts could clear, a van door opened and she was dumped inside. A needle jabbed her arm and the world immediately spun out of control. The last thing she remembered was the door closing.

Detective Sinclair's phone call caught Garrison and Malcolm as they were leaving the medical examiner's office. She had gotten Lisa Black's credit card receipts.

'Anything jump out at you?' Garrison said.

'Lisa Black preferred the upper-class hotels and bars in D.C. She likes expensive lingerie and good wine.' Her crisp voice cut through the lines. 'There is a D.C. bar she visited more than any other. It's called Moments.'

'We found matches in her condo from Moments.'

'I guess she figured she could hook up with a better kind of guy in a nice place.' Sinclair snorted. 'We all know bad guys don't have money.'

Garrison checked his watch. 'We'll swing by and see what we can find out.'

Malcolm rubbed the back of his neck. 'Going to be a long night?'

'Oh, yeah.'

'Where we headed?'

'D.C. bar called Moments. It's located in the Walter Hotel.'

'Can't wait.'

When they arrived at the hotel bar, a glittering marble floor, crystal chandelier and soft piano music drifting through the room, greeted them. The Tuesday-night crowd amounted to a few couples sitting at secluded side tables and a few people at the bar. 'I guess the regulars come later.'

'I suppose.'

Garrison spotted the bartender and moved toward her. Long blond hair swept into a twist accentuated her high cheekbones just as her crisp white shirt and tight black slacks showed off her figure.

She offered a cautious smile as if she'd already sensed they were cops. Likely, spotting cops was part of the job.

'What can I do for you, gentlemen?'

Garrison pulled out his badge from his pocket. 'I'm Detective Deacon Garrison and this is my partner, Detective Malcolm Kier. We're with the Alexandria police.'

'You're a little out of your jurisdiction, aren't you?'

'We'd like to ask you a couple of questions,' Garrison said.

She glanced up, her gaze full of challenge. 'About?'

'One of your regulars.'

'Man or woman?'

'Woman.' Garrison pulled out Lisa Black's Division of Motor Vehicles picture. 'You seen her lately?'

The bartender arched a neatly plucked eyebrow. She glanced at the customers at the end of the bar and noted their nervous glances. 'You're bad for business.'

'Answer my questions and we'll leave.'

'I'm not paid to answer questions.' She picked up a glass and started to polish it.

Garrison leaned forward and smiled. 'I can start questioning each of your customers.'

Blue eyes turned to ice. 'That won't be necessary. Let me see the picture again.'

Garrison pushed it across the bar toward her. 'Take your time.'

'Her name is Lisa, I think. She comes here a couple of nights a week.'

'Did she meet anyone here in particular?' Malcolm said.

'She met a lot of men. She liked variety.'

'Any one of these guys appeared questionable? Anyone that seemed like trouble?'

The bartender arched a brow. 'A two-thousand-dollar suit hides a lot of sins. And I don't ask for character references when people order drinks and tip well.'

'So no trouble,' Garrison said.

'No trouble.'

'When did you see Lisa last?'

'It's been a couple of weeks but I took last week off. This is my first night back. Is she in some kind of trouble?'

'She's dead.'

If this woman did know something, she carefully masked her thoughts. 'When?'

'That's something we're trying to figure out.' He pulled out his notebook. 'Now when was the last time you saw her?'

'One week ago to the day. She ordered her Chardonnay like she always did.'

'Business as usual.'

'Yes, and no. She looked great like she always did, but she was just a little off.'

'How so?'

She picked up a clean towel and started to polish an already-clean glass as if she needed something to do with her hands. 'Something was bothering her.'

'Such as?'

'I asked, and she mentioned past mistakes. I asked a second time for more details and she said something about the past coming back to haunt her. I pressed but she clammed up. She's a big girl and if she wanted to tell me something she would. I serve drinks. I'm not a priest.'

'What can you tell me about her?'

The bartender shrugged. 'She was popular. Never had trouble finding a date. That blond hair and blue eyes are like money in the bank. Plus she was clever.'

'How so?'

'She came from the world of the rich. You could tell by

the way she talked. She knew books and sometimes she spoke French. She knew etiquette.'

'What else can you tell me about her?'

'Hey, it's not like she and I really bonded. We just chatted.'

'About?'

'She talked a lot about traveling. She wanted to get out of town. She'd had a rich older boyfriend for a while but he had left her and she was talking about a change of scenery.'

'Did she ever mention the boyfriend's name?'

'No. But he was rich. Always had his bodyguard/driver with him.'

'When did they break up?'

'About eight months ago.'

'She go out with anyone more than once?'

'Not that I saw. I think long-term connections didn't suit her so well.'

'You remember any of the guys she hooked up with?'

'No. And if I remembered a name it was a first name only. I'm not a den mother.'

Garrison handed the bartender his card. 'The person that killed Lisa did some very nasty things to her. She did not die easy. I want to catch this guy.'

She set down the glass. 'Have you gone by the security offices? They tape all the entrances. They keep the tapes for at least ten days.'

'Do they tape the bar area?'

'They do.'

'Where can I find your security office?'

'Basement.'

Garrison and Kier left the bartender and the gawking patrons to ride the elevator down to the basement. It took just minutes before their badges earned them passage into the director of security's office. The brass plate on the door read: HANK MCMINN.

The director wore a navy blue jacket and khakis, which covered a lean frame. A crew cut accentuated the lines etched around his eyes. The guy had to be pushing fifty but Garrison sensed his reflexes remained quick and strong.

Garrison showed his badge and Lisa's picture, and explained the purpose of their visit.

McMinn studied her picture. 'Sure, we tape every public corner in this hotel. We've got a lot of higher-ups that frequent the place and we like to keep tabs. The cameras are well hidden, though. People here don't like to be recorded. But we've got to protect ourselves.'

'Understood. We're simply after Lisa and whoever she may have left with during the last couple of weeks.'

He swiveled his chair toward a computer screen on a credenza behind his desk. 'What dates?'

'Let's have a look at last weekend.'

McMinn pulled the digital tapes from Friday night. The three watched as McMinn scanned quickly through the hours. No sign of Lisa on Friday night. Saturday night she appeared at eight-seventeen and sat at the bar. She ordered and waited alone for several minutes before a man took a seat at the bar. He wore a nice suit but he'd chosen his seat so that his back was to the camera. At eight thirty-four a woman arrived at the club and screamed that she had a flat tire. Everyone, including Lisa, turned in her direction. The mystery man leaned forward and put something in her drink. Two minutes later, she stumbled out of the bar.

'He was in the bar,' Garrison said. 'I'm going to need all your tapes for the last few months.'

McMinn shifted, his stance now rigid and defensive. 'If the general manager gives the okay and the lawyers bless the exchange, I can give you tapes by tomorrow.'

Garrison handed him his card. 'If not, I'll get a warrant.'

Outside the hotel a light drizzle had come and gone and left the street wet and glistening. 'How much do you want to bet Mr Security has the hotel's GM and their attorney on speed dial?'

'That's why we're requesting a search warrant first thing in the morning. I trust them as far as I can throw them.'

The last thing Lenny remembered was sitting in the house on Route Fifteen watching a sitcom on TV. He'd had a couple of beers but his nerves still jumped with each creak of a branch outside.

And then his world had gone black. Just like someone had flicked a television off. Now the TV was back on – he was awake. But he wasn't in his secret place. He was in an apartment. Tied to a chair with a wad of cotton jammed in his mouth and held in place by duct tape. He jerked his hands, his panic growing with each yank, and he rocked the chair from side to side.

'Did your mother ever teach you that you shouldn't steal?' The voice came from behind Lenny. 'If she didn't, she should have.'

Lenny shook his head, recognizing the voice from the

other night. He screamed but the cotton muffled the sound.

'If you'd lived a good life, Lenny, you wouldn't be here now.' A gloved hand stroked the top of his head as his captor stood behind him. The gloved fingers had an oddly gentle touch. 'But you were a bad boy and well, bad boys have to be punished.'

Before he could scream again, a knife rose up from behind Lenny and plunged directly into his heart. For several beats, he felt the blood pulse through his body, spilling onto his shirt and pooling on the floor.

And then he felt nothing.

Chapter 10

The morning sun peeked over the horizon, bathing the graveyard in a soft pink. Dew glistened on the grass and the gray headstones didn't seem so harsh to Eva.

She'd avoided cemeteries since her mother's funeral and she'd been avoiding this cemetery since her return to Alexandria. She eased on the accelerator and drove past the neatly manicured stone pillars that marked the entrance. She wound down the smartly edged street and found the section she needed. Parking, she got out of the truck and walked the fifteen feet to the plot of graves portioned off from the others by its own stone fence. The etched sign on the gate read: CROSS.

This was the Cross family plot where Josiah Cross and his parents had been buried. Her car keys in hand, she got out and shivered as the morning cold passed through her jean jacket as if it weren't there.

Butterflies gnawed at her stomach as she pushed open the gate and walked up to the grave that belonged to Darius. The old man had lived sixty-one years. His health, from what she'd read, had been bad for years, but meanness kept him alive.

She didn't kneel by the grave, nor did she brush off the sticks that had drifted onto the site.

*

'I'm going to fight the confession,' Eva shouted to the bulky, powerful man before her. 'It wasn't right. The cops pushed me.'

Darius Cross rose from the metal seat in the prison's visiting room and leaned toward her. He smelled of expensive aftershave and hate. 'Do that and I will bury your sister. I will have someone take her to a faraway place and do to her what you claim Josiah did to you. And I promise you, no one will find her body.'

Color drained from Eva's face as she stared into eyes as dark as Satan's. She knew he would do as he'd said. Darius Cross did not make idle threats. If she didn't go to prison, Angie would suffer.

'You hateful son of a bitch,' Eva whispered. 'I hope you rot.'

She drew in deep even breaths and did her best to expel the anger. But it wouldn't let go of her and it festered and burned in her chest. Unable to stand here a moment longer, she moved to Cross's wife's grave: Louise Cross. Dead nineteen years. BELOVED WIFE AND MOTHER. What kind of woman married Darius Cross? Or birthed a monster like Josiah?

Eva moved to Josiah's headstone. IN GOD'S LOVING ARMS. The words made her sick. 'Let's hope it's the Devil's embrace.'

She noted the dates on his stone and realized that this Friday would have marked his thirty-second birthday. 'Happy Birthday, you son of a bitch.'

The report from Leesburg police came in just after the morning shift change: Lenny Danvers, aged thirty-five, had been found dead at 211 Riverstone Drive. The address belonged to a first-floor unit in an apartment complex.

Garrison and Kier headed out as soon as they got the call. The forty-mile drive out to Leesburg took over an hour and a half, thanks to early-morning traffic snarls along Route Seven and a fender-bender.

By the time they reached the Fifteen Bypass on the out-skirts of Leesburg, it was nearly ten-thirty. Minutes later they pulled into the Rock Creek apartment complex.

The apartments had been built in the late eighties, a time when the area's development had boomed. The com-plex would have looked modern and been considered luxurious twenty years ago but now time, combined with cheap construction, had taken a toll. Despite spring flowers by the entrance, the place looked worn.

Garrison spotted the two sheriff's cars flashing blue lights, bypassed the complex office and parked directly behind the patrols. Two deputies waited by their cars to ensure no one crossed the yellow crime scene tape that blocked off the first-floor unit.

The deputies were both short. The one on the left was younger and carried more muscle while the other guy looked as if he could drop twenty.

The slender cop held out his hand to Garrison. 'I'm Deputy Rollins and this is Deputy Finnegan. You get caught in that traffic?'

'Sure did. I hear you found the guy I'm looking for.'

Deputy Rollins nodded stiffly. 'We went by the other residence you mentioned yesterday and there were signs that someone had been there and a back door lock broken. This morning we got a call from a resident in this building about blood dripping from the ceiling. That's when we found your guy.'

Deputy Finnegan nodded. 'Management took one look inside the unit and called us. It is a damn mess. Never seen that before.'

'Would you show us?'

Rollins hesitated. 'Sure.'

The two deputies held back as if waiting for the other to go first. Finally, Rollins took the lead and led the detectives through the building's front entrance and up a flight of stairs to the unit marked 2-A, now roped off with red crime scene tape. Even from outside the apartment, the distinct sick-sweet smell associated with death soured the air.

Garrison pulled on gloves. 'Danvers made bail late Monday.'

'Then he died soon after,' Deputy Finnegan said. 'The killer cranked the heat in the apartment to over ninety. He also placed a space heater in the room with Danvers. The place feels like a sauna and smells . . . well, one breath and you'll get the point.'

Garrison studied the front door and the worn WEL-COME mat in front of it. 'No signs of forced entry.'

'Not at the front door,' Rollins said. 'But have a look at the sliding glass door by the patio. Someone wrenched open the lock with a crowbar. Killer must have broken the lock because it won't stay closed. It's barely cracked open now.'

'Has your forensics team had a look?'

'Not yet. We're stretched thin right now. But the apartment is secure.'

'Okay. Let's have a look around back.'

When Garrison opened the door, a putrid smell hit him

square in the face. Malcolm raised his hand to his nose while Garrison inhaled through his mouth. Both deputies turned away, looking as if they'd be sick.

Garrison moved across the beige carpeted floor, careful not to step on anything that might be of use later. Clothes littered the floor and a quick glance in the kitchen revealed dishes piled high in the sink and pizza boxes on the counter.

'This is the kind of stink that doesn't come off,' Malcolm said.

'Yeah.' He always kept a spare change of clothes in his locker at the station.

The smell grew worse as they moved to the back bedroom. Garrison peered through the open door to find the bloated, decomposing body of Lenny Danvers. His hands were tied to a chair and his feet bound together. Four stab wounds sliced into his chest.

Garrison leaned closer. 'Killed quickly and doesn't look like he was branded. Just stabbed.'

'The killer was taking care of a necessity, not getting revenge,' Malcolm offered.

'Reminds me again of that stabbing victim, Eliza Martinez. But I'll be damned if I see a connection between the two victims.'

Garrison studied the blood spatter patterns. It appeared Danvers had been stabbed from behind. 'Like Danvers, she saw the killer?'

'That's what it's looking like to me.' In the front of the apartment there was some commotion, suggesting Forensics had arrived. Garrison straightened. 'We need to zero in on Danvers's favorite hunting grounds. Maybe we can figure where Lisa was murdered and find something that connects all this to the killer.'

'Police have identified the woman found dead behind the Hanna's House shelter late Monday.' Eva was half listening to the television above the bar until she heard 'Hanna's House.'

'The victim's name was Lisa Black, age thirty-one, of Alexandria, Virginia.' Eva froze, the tap still spewing beer into the glass and overflowing on her hand. She shut the tap off and shook the liquid from her hand as she glanced at the screen, hoping to see a picture of the victim. But the news station was simply showing shots of the burned-out structure.

She wiped her hands before setting the beer in front of her customer. She grabbed the remote and backed up the picture on the screen. The face of a young blond woman flashed on the screen. Garrison had showed her a picture of the same woman but in his photo her eyes had been shut and her mouth slack-jawed. This DMV picture wasn't very flattering but she smiled and brightness illuminated her eyes.

Eva studied the face. Lisa Black had been one of the three that had testified against her. But this Lisa Black didn't resemble the woman she'd known at Price. Her Lisa had dark hair, was thirty pounds heavier and had a wide thick nose. Could it be the same person? This Lisa was bone thin and her high slash of cheekbones and a pointed chin suggested an air of sophistication the other Lisa had never known.

*

'God, Eva, you are so smart.' Lisa tucked a dark curl behind her ear. She grinned, her smile making her wide face look even broader.

'You are smarter than you think,' Eva said. 'Don't sell yourself short.'

'I just wish I could be more like you. And Kristen. You have brains, and well, she has the looks.'

Eva wasn't sure what to say to that. A part of her was flattered and a part sad for Lisa. 'Let's get back to the books.'

'Great. Kristen wants our house to win the Battle of the Brains next week. And I don't want to disappoint her.'

Could this be the Lisa that had sat on the witness stand and told the world that Eva killed Josiah?

Lisa, Eva, Kristen and Sara had been close friends in college. Lisa and Eva had met in a math study lab. Later, Lisa had brought Eva to the sorority house and encouraged her to pledge. Eva had been so thrilled to finally start making friends at Price. She'd been the seventeen-year-old genius who'd graduated high school early and won a full academic scholarship. A foster kid, she didn't have the extra money to do the fun things the other kids did. Plus, she'd looked so young, no fake ID got her into any bar or party.

She'd been so naïve then. So willing to please that she'd have done just about anything. Only later did she realize that Lisa had approached Eva because of Eva's reputation as a math wiz. She'd been no more valuable to the girls than a calculator.

'Well, you look like you've seen a ghost.'

Eva turned toward the familiar voice and smiled when she saw Sally sitting at her favorite bar stool. 'Why are you so pale and ghostly looking? You sick, honey?'

Eva shook her head as she wiped the bar. 'The news identified the woman at the fire. Just kind of creeped me out.'

Sally nodded, the laughter dimming in her eyes. 'According to the news her name was Lisa Black.'

Eva frowned. 'Why was she behind the shelter?'

Sally sat down and scooped a handful of nuts from a bowl. 'I don't know. Seems odd such a high-end girl would find her way to us. But you never know why people end up where they do.'

Her Lisa had come from money. There'd be no reason to seek a shelter. 'She doesn't look like the homeless type.'

'Maybe her issues weren't money. You'd be surprised what haunts people.'

Eva wasn't surprised at all. 'You're not going to believe this, but I think I went to college with her.'

'Think?'

'She looks so different. She's even changed the color of her eyes. But the more I stare at the picture the more this gal and the other seem the same.'

Sally raised a brow. 'No kidding? You went to school around here?'

Just cracking the door to her past sent a bolt of shivers through her body. 'It was just for my freshman year and it was a long time ago. She looked so different then.'

The older woman's eyes sparkled with amusement. 'Couldn't have been that long. You can't be more than mid-twenties.'

'Let me place your order. The usual?'

'You take such good care of me, doll.'

Sally's fishing for information had Eva's defenses

rising. Thankfully, the bar needed her to fill empty beer mugs, deliver a hot dog platter and refresh the peanuts. By the time she'd rung up a few tabs, Sally's sandwich was ready. Eva set the plate in front of her.

'I'm dying to know more,' Sally said. 'I mean, what are the chances that you'd know a dead woman.'

'Yeah. What are the chances?'

'So dish. Tell me about her. What was she like in college?'

The old barriers rose into place. Silly to be so guarded with Sally, but to talk too much about Lisa cracked the door even wider to her own past. And she wasn't in the mood for scaring off friends or losing a job. Not that Sally would run or King would fire her. But fear didn't always make sense.

'She was a good student. I liked her. But I haven't seen her since college. We lost track.'

Sally studied her tight features and, as if sensing Eva's tension, changed the subject. 'I'm already on the hunt for a new place to house another shelter.'

'Really?'

'Yeah. Met with the board today and they want to find a new home. Lucky for us it's an election year. A few local senators want to look like the good guys.'

Relieved to be talking about current stuff, Eva smiled. 'Hey, we take what we can get.'

'Yeah. But I'm no good at sweet-talking those hoity-toity folks. I never am all that comfortable around rich people.'

'Join the club.'

Sally bit into her sandwich, nodding her approval. 'Good eats as always.'

'I'll tell King.'

'How is the old man doing?'

'Great.'

'You know I heard something odd about him the other day.'

'Really.' Eva avoided gossip, even with Sally.

'Did you know that he lost his wife and son in a car accident?'

'I knew of a loss but no details.'

'A drunk driver killed them.'

'I'm sorry to hear that.'

'Seems King found the driver of the car and beat him to a pulp. He nearly killed him. King faced attempted murder charges but ended up with parole. Judge said he'd suffered enough. The drunk driver didn't see a day of jail time or parole.'

Eva shifted, feeling uneasy with the turn of conversation. 'I don't feel comfortable talking about King. This is his business. He doesn't poke in my life and I plan to stay out of his.'

Sally picked at the edge of her sandwich. 'That's what I like about you, Eva. You judge people as they come. You don't hold the past against them.'

Garrison and Malcolm waited at the Leesburg crime scene with the county forensics team and hung around until they had processed the apartment and removed the body. It was ten P.M. by the time Garrison dropped Malcolm off at the station. Malcolm bid him good night and slid wearily into his own car.

Tomorrow would prove to be another long day. With luck they'd be plowing through video surveillance and trying to identify the man that had sat next to Lisa before she'd vanished.

As Garrison pulled out of the police parking lot, he considered stopping by King's and talking to Eva. Something about her kept tickling the back of his brain. He'd learned to not ignore the sensation, but right now with less than five hours' sleep since Monday night, he understood he needed a few hours of sleep under his belt before he questioned her.

Garrison would have given his left arm just to go home and hit the sack, but he'd promised his mother he'd stop by. Today was the anniversary of his sister's death and in the last twenty years since Debbie had died, Garrison and his parents always got together, if only for a few minutes.

Debbie had died during her junior year of high school. She'd suffered from cystic fibrosis since birth and keeping her healthy and alive had always been a struggle. Many nights he'd sit up talking to her when her breathing labored. She mostly rambled during those long nights but he believed if he remained at her side death couldn't snatch her away. He always promised her that everything would be fine. The night of his senior prom, Debbie lay down to rest and her heart stopped. Their mother found her and called 911 but doctors declared her dead upon arrival at the hospital.

Many had assumed that the family would cope easily

166

with Debbie's death since it had been a part of their lives since her birth. But Debbie's death had been as unexpected and tragic as any accident. Garrison's parents wanted him to get on with his life and he'd done the best he could. He'd still played on the football team his senior year, escorted four girls to the prom and had told jokes to anyone who would listen. His mother stepped up her volunteer work and his dad split his time between whatever cases crossed his desk and tinkering with a Ford remodel. For at least a year they'd lived in the same house but had barely spoken to each other.

The anniversary of Debbie's death had been what had forced them together for a memorial service the school had sponsored. As Garrison watched the slide show featuring Debbie, he'd cried his first tears. His parents had held him as he'd let the sadness flow out like poison.

From that day forward, when he was in town, they gathered on this day.

He pulled up in front of the brick rancher, got out of his car and slammed the door. He reached the front door in three quick strides. He knocked and then opened the door. 'Mom, Dad, Carrie?'

His mother poked her head out of the kitchen door. 'There you are. I was getting worried.'

He crossed and kissed his mother on the cheek. 'Sorry. But you know how the job goes.'

'Please. I'm married to a thirty-year veteran of the force.' She squeezed his arm. 'Only too well. Are you hungry?'

'Starving.'

'Go on out to the garage and check in with your dad.

He's been working on that car for hours, grumbling about where you are. I'll bring you out a plate.'

'Thanks. Where's Carrie?'

'Sleepover at Julia's. She knows I'm a mess on this day so she decided to avoid all my sloppy tears this year.'

Mark and Eileen had adopted Carrie just after her fifth birthday. The lost little girl's parents had died in a car accident. The Garrisons still missed their daughter, but Carrie had fit perfectly into their lives. The little girl had helped heal the wound left after Debbie's death.

Garrison liked the kid. In fact she reminded him of Debbie – the way she played her music too loud, her talk of clothes and boys and the way she hugged their dad when she wanted something.

'Carrie hasn't forgotten that you promised to take her to the outlet mall.'

Deacon groaned. 'I'd hoped she had.'

'Kid never forgets a promise.'

The idea of schlepping around Potomac Mills Mall with a teenage girl made him want to hide, but he'd keep his word. 'Now I remember why I never promise anything.'

Eileen smiled. 'Sunday still work?'

'I'm in the middle of a case. It may have to wait.'

'She understands cases. But she'll know when you're done with it and are free.'

'That kid is destined to be a cop.'

He grabbed a cookie from a plate beside the stove and headed across the kitchen through the door that led to the garage. He found his father standing beside a workbench organized with military precision. Screwdrivers lined up in descending order like soldiers. Spare parts were boxed in neat little boxes that his father had labeled with a black marker in precise block lettering, and the car that Mark Garrison was restoring glistened as if it had just been washed.

'About time you got here,' his dad said. He set down the carburetor. 'Working?'

'Yeah.'

Mark reached below his workbench to a small refrigerator that he kept stocked with beer. The beer was supposed to be a secret from Eileen who monitored her husband's blood pressure like a hawk. But Eileen had discovered her husband's secret long ago. Maintaining the pretense had become a game.

His dad pulled out a brown bottle filled with a microbrewery beer. He twisted off the top and handed the bottle to his son before grabbing one for himself. 'Don't tell your mother.'

A smile played on Garrison's lips. 'Never.'

Mark held up his bottle. 'To Debbie.'

Garrison raised his bottle and clinked it against his father's. He took a long pull, needing the moment to wrestle the surge of emotion from his chest. Shit. He'd lost a sister. 'Their deaths never get easy.'

'Sucks.'

'How's Mom?'

'You know Mom. She keeps a smile on her face, but I caught her watching home movies last night. We bawled like babies.'

'Which ones did you watch?'

'Remember the beach vacation from hell? The one

where it rained and you and Debbie fought the whole time? You must have been in sixth grade.'

Debbie had felt good that summer so their parents had opted for the family's first vacation. 'Christ, she annoyed the hell out of me that week. She kept stealing my stuff so I'd have to track her down and demand it back.'

'That last night on vacation you two sang "Happy Birthday" to your mother. I taped it.'

'I'd forgotten about that.' For the first time in a long time his smile was genuine. 'Debbie had painted a mustache on me while I slept.'

His father chuckled. 'They weren't kidding when they said permanent marker. Of course the hearts you traced on her cheeks to get back at her didn't help the situation.'

'She had it coming.'

'So there are my two kids, looking like rejects from the circus, singing "Happy Birthday" off-key and as loud as they could to their mother.'

'Pretty bad.'

He heisted his beer and took a swig. 'Nope. Pretty great.' Mark sniffed back a tear and set his bottle down on the workbench with a thud. 'So tell me about your case before I bawl again.'

Garrison welcomed the distraction. He cleared his throat. 'Remember that fire at the homeless shelter on Monday night?'

'Yeah. There was a fatality.'

'The victim wasn't killed by the fire. She was stabbed to death.'

'Really?' His father's eyes sparked with a hunter's gleam Garrison had seen so often as a kid.

'The killer did something odd to his victim. He burned stars into her skin before killing her.'

His father frowned, his cop's mind working full speed now. 'Really. What kind of star?'

'Interesting you should ask. A four-pointed star. The killer used a branding iron.'

'Really?' Mark Garrison sipped his beer. 'Any forensics?'

'The killer is very careful. Organized. We thought we might have a witness, but the guy was found dead in a Leesburg apartment. Also stabbed.'

Mark took a pull on his beer. 'Were all the points of the star even or shaped like a cross?'

Deacon's attention sharpened. His dad's mind still worked like a cop's. 'Even. What do you know?'

Mark shook his head. 'There was a case in a small town thirty miles south of here about ten years ago. I didn't work the case but heard about it. The victim was branded with a four-pointed star.'

'Was she stabbed?'

Mark rested his hand on his hip as if sinking into the past. 'No. She lived.'

'Do you remember the particulars?'

He rubbed the back of his neck. 'The guy brutally raped her and then took her necklace, heated it on the stove and burned her skin. The prosecution turned things around and made it look like the victim and rapist were lovers. I remember being pissed for the victim.'

Eileen pushed through the door that connected the garage to the kitchen. She had a plate with a roast beef sandwich, pickles and chips. In her other hand she held an iced Coke. 'You two look deep in thought.'

'I was just telling The Boy about an old case. You remember the Price University case?'

Eileen set the plate on the workbench. 'I do. That was about the time we adopted Carrie.' She shrugged. 'Of course the two have nothing to do with each other. We mothers mark the time with our children.'

'What was the girl's name?' Mark said.

'I don't remember her name, but I do remember the case. I saw her in the news and she looked so lost. My heart went out to her.'

'Dad said she was burned with a star-shaped pendant,' Deacon said.

'Yes.' She dropped her gaze and frowned. 'As I remember, the girl attended Price University on scholarship. What did she and her friends call each other?'

Mark hesitated then snapped his fingers. 'The Shining Stars.'

'No, that wasn't it.' She frowned and then snapped her fingers. 'The Rising Stars. One of the girls had pendants fashioned up for each girl. They were in a sorority together.'

Mark nodded. 'That's right.'

'I don't remember how the rapist knew the girls. Maybe he dated one of them.'

Mark nodded. 'That's right. He came to the house the last day of the semester. Broke into the house, found her alone and brutalized her. When the other girls returned, the house was on fire. They barely saved the victim. The story got a lot of media attention because it involved a pretty girl and a rich boy.'

Anger burned hot in Deacon's gut. 'And the attacker? What happened to him?'

172

'The victim killed him,' Eileen said.

Grim satisfaction rose in Garrison. 'Really?'

'Not so good,' Eileen said. 'The boy was Josiah Cross and his father was Darius Cross.'

'The wealthy businessman?'

'That's right. He refused to believe his son could be a rapist. And he went out of his way to prove that the sex was consensual and the girl killed him in a jealous rage.' Eileen shook her head. 'Your dad told me he'd seen the case files. Said no way a reasonable man could look at her bruising and medical reports and believe they had consensual sex. But the girls from the sorority house all testified that they saw the girl kill the boy. Hit him with a poker.'

Garrison took a pull on his beer. 'What happened?'

Mark's lips flattened into a grim line. 'She was convicted of manslaughter and sent to jail.'

'Shit.'

Mark shrugged. 'Darius Cross would not be denied. He wanted his son's memory cleared and this girl punished. I'm not so sure if it has anything to do with your case.' Mark shrugged. 'Silly to recall an old case. I doubt the two are connected. The star brand jogged my memory.'

'When did you say this happened?'

'Ten or so years ago. While you were still in the air force.'

Deacon picked up a chip and ate it. 'Couldn't hurt to look and see if either of my victims were connected to the case.'

Moonlight glistened on the street as Eva draped one arm around a customer as she held up her other hand to hail a cab. The man walking beside her wobbled with each step and he smelled of the gin he'd spilled on his pants. He'd shown up at King's drunk about an hour ago. At first she'd not realized he'd had too much so she'd served him. But when he ordered his second gin and tonic in less than ten minutes she'd cut him off and called a cab.

'I'm fine, little lady,' he slurred.

At least he was a happy drunk. 'I know.' The cab stopped and she leaned him against the side as she opened the back door. 'Remember, come to King's tomorrow for your car key. We'll have it for you behind the bar.'

He gifted her with a sloppy boyish grin. 'I will never remember that.'

'I've tucked a note in your pocket just in case.' She guided him into the seat and fastened his seat belt. She gave the driver the man's address, which she'd gotten from his driver's license. 'Be careful, Harvey.'

His head dropped back against the seat. 'Will do, doll.'

She closed the door and the cab drove off. Her back ached and her feet had grown to the size of watermelons. Shaking off the fatigue, she went back inside. Over the next half hour, she cleaned the bar and put the chairs on the tables for tomorrow's cleaning. King remained in his office counting the day's receipts and preparing the night drop at the bank.

A dull headache throbbed behind her eyes as she eased open the door to her room. The light in the bathroom remained on and cast a soft glow on the twin beds. The clock on her nightstand ticked. It had been a long time since she'd not felt so alone.

Before her mother had died, she and her sister had been close. When Angie could visit they fought over the usual teen stuff: clothes, books, food or boys. But they'd also stayed up late at night whispering to each other in the dark about hopes and dreams. They'd been a team. Together forever. And then Mom had died, Eva had gone to foster care because her biological father had split and Angie's biological father wanted no part of Eva, the child conceived during the affair that had destroyed his marriage.

In the first days of foster care, Eva had barely been able to function and had thrown herself into her schoolwork. They didn't see each other for almost two years and that last meeting had been after her arrest.

Without warning, hot tears burned her eyes and spilled down her cheeks. 'Grow a backbone, Eva,' she whispered. 'Call your sister.'

She closed her eyes and thought back to the last time she'd seen Angie.

'We'll fight this,' Angie said. Phone to her ear, she sat on one side of the glass and stared directly at Eva. Her straight blond hair fell forward as she spoke, partially cloaking her face. 'I should have taken you myself after Mom died.'

'No. Let it go.' Darius had sworn to destroy Eva's family if she did not atone for his son's death. It was better to just let Angie go. She could do her time if she knew Angie was happy. 'I don't want to fight this.'

'Why not?'

'Leave it, Angie. Ten years isn't that long.'

'My God, you're only seventeen.'

'And I'll just be twenty-seven when I get out. Plenty of time to live.'

'Don't give up, Eva. What Josiah did to you was wrong. You should not be punished for defending yourself.'

'Let it go, Angie.'

Eva set down the phone and left the waiting room. She didn't turn back but could hear Angie pounding on the glass, begging her to look back. Eva didn't and she'd told the guards she wanted no more visitors.

A week ago, she'd been on the verge of calling Angie. Darius was dead and she'd been on the verge of claiming a new life. But the shelter fire, Lisa's murder and the article . . .

Even if she had more to offer than her talent for escorting drunks and collecting strays, she feared the past had risen from the dead to haunt her and endanger Angie.

The scent of cinders and smoke filled the basement room and mingled with the woman's whining. She'd been crying since she'd awoken, and her weak-willed noises had a way of grating. 'Shut up!'

'Please!'

'Please what?'

'Let me go.'

'Our business won't take long.' Lou ignored her cries and jabbed the poker into the anemic fire, cursing the fact that the hearth didn't draw as well at it should. 'Damn hearth needs cleaning.'

'Let me go.'

176

Her voice buzzed around Lou, no more important than a housefly and easy to swat away. 'No doubt the flue needs a good cleaning. But a cleaning doesn't make sense now. I'll be finished in less than a week.'

'Someone will find me.'

Lou laughed. 'That's what the last one thought. That she'd been saved. Turned out it was a no-account thief that stumbled into my house. He thought he got away from me but finding him, posting bail and tracking him to Leesburg was child's play. What thief carries a wallet?'

'Let me go.'

'You sound like a broken record. Playing the same tune over and over again. It's annoying.'

Lou turned to the woman, looking at her for the first time in hours. She lay on her back, her arms strapped above her head and tied to a support beam that ran floor to ceiling. Her feet were bound and tied to a twin beam.

Lou stoked the flames with the handle of the metal brand created especially for this moment.

'Please. Why are you doing this?'

Sara's blond hair no longer looked full and lush. Now it lay flat against her head. Her mascara smudged in a dark smear down her cheeks and her red harlot lipstick had faded to a pale, uneven blur. Her white blouse was gone, cut off and discarded, and her lacy white bra cupped full breasts.

'Because you've been so bad, Sara. You've broken so many rules.'

Sara pulled at her bindings and screamed. 'Help!'

'Scream all you want, sweet Sara. No one can hear.' Extra precautions had been taken this time. Lou had nailed the windows shut, dead-bolted the front door and spread broken glass over the front hallway. 'I've had my fill of unexpected messes to clean up.'

'Let me go.'

'No. Not just yet.'

Sara dropped her head back against the brick floor, rolling it from side to side. 'Why me? What have I done to you?'

Lou glanced into the hearth, letting the erotic dance of the flames draw its spell. 'You tore out my heart.'

'I don't even know you!'

Anger flickered to life and Lou jabbed the brand deeper into the hot coals. 'That makes it all the worse. That you could destroy a life and not even be aware.'

Tears filled Sara's eyes and trickled down her cheeks. 'Please. If I hurt you, I am sorry. I'm sorry.'

Lou removed the brand and studied the glowing red tip. A burning red star that was so beautiful. 'You are not sorry.'

'I am. I swear that I am.' Desperation made Sara's voice hoarse.

'You aren't. But you will be.' Lou turned and moved toward the quivering woman. Nothing had felt more right than this moment. Nothing. This was Lou's destiny. To rise up out of the ashes and to prevail.

Without guilt or hesitation Lou pressed the tip of the brand against Sara's belly. She screamed and the sound was filled with desperation and bitter fear.

The smell of burning flesh rose up, filling Lou with power. Sara passed out from the pain.

Lou removed the brand and stared at the red angry star

that would be forever embossed in this harlot's white perfect flesh.

Replacing the brand back in the fire, Lou reached for the bucket of cool water. Time to soothe the red angry burn. Time to revive Sara.

And then it would be time to begin again.

Chapter 11

Thursday, April 6, 9:20 A.M.

'Now tell me why we are at the Taylorsville Municipal Building?' Malcolm's question projected mild annoyance.

Garrison glanced at his partner. 'What's wrong, princess? Didn't get enough beauty sleep?'

Malcolm rubbed his eyes. 'Long night.'

'Another date?'

'Yeah.'

Garrison shook his head. 'Damn, boy. You know how to burn the candle at both ends.'

'You only live once.' He stretched a kink from his neck. 'So why are we here?'

'There's a case file I want to read.'

'What does a ten-year-old rape and manslaughter case have to do with our murder investigations?'

'I don't know, really. Something my dad remembered.'

'Your dad?'

'He was a cop for thirty years. The man has a memory like a steel trap and he remembered that the rapist burned a four-pointed star shape into his victim.'

Malcolm raised a brow, his interest growing. 'Really?'

'Might be nothing.'

'The Devil is in the details, man. And four-pointed stars aren't the kind of details that crop up often.'

They strode through the main glass doors of the municipal building and showed their badges to the guard on duty.

The guard picked up the phone at his desk. 'Sheriff Canada is expecting you.'

Five minutes later they sat in the sheriff's plain gray office waiting for him to find the file he'd had one of his deputies pull that morning.

'Sorry, it took me a few minutes,' the sheriff said. A tall man with a rounded belly, the sheriff had shaved his head and sported a thick, dark mustache. 'We store our older files in another building. We talk about computerizing but there's never enough in the budget to cover it.'

Garrison rose and shook his hand. 'No problem.'

Malcolm stood and introduced himself.

The sheriff sat behind his desk, pulled out a set of half glasses and opened the file.

Garrison and Malcolm sat down and waited as he read through the file.

Deep lines formed on the sheriff's face as he read. 'Oh, yeah, I remember this one. Nasty case.' He turned the file so Garrison could read.

'Happened at a university sorority house.'

The first image Garrison saw in the file was the charred structure, reduced to rubble and scorched timbers. It was a miracle anyone had survived. 'This the sorority house?'

The sheriff leaned over. 'It was.'

'My father is retired Alexandria PD. He said the girl killed her rapist.'

The sheriff nodded. 'That rape was never proven.'

Garrison turned the picture over and studied another

image of the burned-out Victorian house. 'What about the killing?'

'From what we could piece together, she hit him with an iron poker by the fireplace. Caved his skull right in and then she passed out from her injuries. Firefighters arrived in time to drag her and the boy out. Of course, the crew quickly figured out the boy was dead.'

Garrison flipped through the fire scene photos. 'And he did attack her?'

'That's what she said.'

'What did the medical examination reveal?'

'That Josiah Cross's semen was present in her and bruising suggested the sex was rough.'

'Rough and not forced?'

'His family claimed that the two had had a sexual relationship and that she enjoyed vigorous sex.' The sheriff shook his head.

'What was your assessment of the case?'

'I was just a brand-new deputy then. But I can't imagine any girl wanting what she got. He roughed her up pretty well. She had bruising on her face and arms and, of course, the burn.'

Garrison glanced up. 'My father said he branded her.'

The sheriff leaned forward and flipped through several photos until he arrived at a close-up of the burn on the girl's shoulder. A red angry star glared back from pale ivory skin.

That was the work of a sick bastard. 'Josiah Cross did this?'

'That's what the girl claimed. Defense said the house fire must have heated up the star and when she fell it burned her skin.'

'This the first trouble you had with Cross?' It had been his experience that warning signs preceded this kind of violence.

'No, this wasn't the first. Young Mr Cross had drunk driving charges filed against him and a waitress in the historic district complained he assaulted her.'

'What came of it?'

'His daddy got involved. All charges were dropped.'

'Really?'

'You'd have to have lived under a rock not to know that Darius Cross was rich and always would swoop in with attorneys and clean up the mess, but that didn't mean any of us forgot the messes that boy created.' The sheriff leaned back in his chair and folded his fingers over his belly. 'When Cross was twelve, he shot seven head of cattle at point-blank range. Just walked up to them and killed them for no other reason than to kill. The farmer caught the boy and called us. But Josiah's father ended up paying off the farmer twice what the cattle were worth.'

'Great kid,' Malcolm said.

'It didn't end there. As he got older he picked fights with other kids. Cross was a big kid for his age so he overpowered most anyone in his age group. He beat one boy bad enough to land him in the hospital. Again, Daddy paid. Darius Cross paid for that victim's college education. And then the waitress, like I said. She ended up with a brand-new car and quit her job. Some said she moved to New York. After that, Cross stayed clear of town.'

'What about the girl that killed him?'

'From a poor family and going to Price University

on a full scholarship. Apparently, she was as smart as a whip.'

'What else can you tell me about her?'

The sheriff lifted a brow. 'I've done a good bit of telling. Now you mind telling me why you are so interested in this old case?'

'I've a murder victim. Female. Branded with a four-pointed star.'

The sheriff frowned. 'I see.'

'I'd like to talk to this girl. There might be no connection, but the more I stare at this picture of her brand, the more I'm not so sure. They look too much alike.'

'I have no way of knowing what happened to the girl. As your daddy might have told you, she confessed to killing Cross and was sent to jail for ten years. She's got to be about twenty-seven by now.'

'Can you tell me her name?'

'Don't see how this connects.'

'It's a lead I don't want to ignore.' He smiled, wanting the sheriff to work with him, not against him. 'I've got to try.'

The sheriff shrugged and glanced at the file. He dug through the records, selected a photo and then handed it to Garrison. 'Here's her mug shot. Looks like she's not more than twelve but she was almost eighteen when this happened.'

Garrison took the picture and froze.

There was no mistaking the woman's identity. The eyes were different, harder, more guarded, but ten years had not changed her that much. 'Eva Rayburn.'

*

184

Kelly hated her early-morning jog. Yeah, she'd heard all the tripe about it setting the tone for your day and how it revved your metabolism, but that didn't change the fact that she hated it. Given half a chance, she'd have been at home, sitting in bed, doughnut and coffee in hand and watching the morning news like a civilized person.

But, no, she was out here on the WD&O jogging trail, dragging her fat ass along the river. Why? Because of that guy Leonard in accounting and the little black dress she wanted to wear on their date next week. All she needed to do was shed a couple of pounds and she'd be able to pull up the damn zipper.

Her lungs burned and her knees ached. 'Shit.' The word came out in a whoosh as she slowed her pace from a weak jog to a walk. 'There has just got to be a better way.'

She rested her hand on her hip, trying to ease the stitch in her side. She glanced ahead to the park bench a quarter of a mile away. 'Jog to the bench and you can stop.'

After a couple of false starts she sped from her walk to a jog. Her knees ached and groaned but stopping now only made restarting all the more painful. If she stumbled to the bench alive, she'd swear off the sweets for at least a month. Well, maybe a week.

Dropping her head, she pumped her arms, kept moving and chanted, 'Little black dress. Little black dress.'

When she reached the bench, she shoved out a sigh of relief and promptly sat down. She dropped her head between her knees and sucked in a breath.

She regretted the breath instantly. The air she pulled in wasn't sweet or restorative. It was foul and pungent and reminded her of the time a squirrel had gotten into her home's air ducts and died. Her whole house had reeked of death.

Death.

Kelly shot to her feet and glanced around her. Something had died around the bench. *Damn.*

She started to inch away. The last thing she wanted was to find a dead dog or raccoon or worse, a dead skunk. She heard dead skunks could still stink you up. Just her luck that she'd finally fit into that little black dress and smell of dead skunk.

Kelly had continued down the path just two steps when she spotted the flicker of pink fabric in the brush by the river. Halting, she took a cautious step toward the fabric. The closer she got, the stronger the smell. She shouldn't look but curiosity goaded her. Covering her mouth, she peered down and nearly retched.

The river reeds and grass tangled around a woman's body, which lay curled in a C-shape, face buried in the water.

Kelly backed up, unsure if she should scream or get sick.

She threw up.

Garrison's mind pondered the puzzle of Eva Rayburn as he and Malcolm drove to the office. He wound down I-495 and took the Telegraph Road exit and headed toward police headquarters on Mill Street. He was anxious to visit King's.

'It can't be a coincidence,' Malcolm said. 'The star in that old case and then the girl turns up branded at the scene of a fire along with Ms Rayburn.'

'Yeah, I stopped believing in coincidence a very long time ago.'

'What the hell kind of connection does our victim share with a dead rich-kid-rapist and the girl who killed him?'

'A little digging will turn up something.'

Garrison and Malcolm had been five minutes from their office when they got a call from the medical examiner's office. Dr Henson had toxicology results on the first victim.

Garrison detoured to the medical examiner's office and the detectives found Dr Henson in her office. She was on the phone but waved them in and pointed to chairs in front of her desk.

'Yes, sir,' Dr Henson said into the phone. 'His death would have been very quick.' The softness in her voice conveyed genuine concern.

Garrison presumed she was talking to a family member. Known for taking her time with grieving family members, Dr Henson patiently answered each question.

Finally, she hung up the phone.

She pulled off her glasses and squeezed the bridge of her nose.

'Bad case?'

She nodded. 'Brain aneurysm. The guy just turned thirty-nine. He'd been on a ladder and fell. Family and responding EMTs thought the fall killed him. Autopsy revealed the vessel burst first and then he'd fallen. He was dead before he hit the ground.'

'That's rough,' Malcolm said.

'Leaves behind a wife and two young kids.' She picked up some papers and tapped them into a neat stack. 'Some days I hate this job.'

Malcolm shook his head. 'I don't know how you do it.'

She arched a brow. 'You deal with death too, Detective.' 'You're knee-deep in it each day. I'll bet you got the smell on you every night when you go home.'

She shrugged. 'I don't notice it anymore.'

Garrison rested his ankle on his knee. 'Have you had a chance to look at Danvers?'

'He's next on the list. We've been slammed the last few days. Something about spring, I guess.'

'Spring?' Malcolm said.

'Warm weather. People seem to get out more. Doesn't matter if you exercise and eat right. If you fall off a ladder or get hit by a car, it's over.' She dug through her papers. 'And the suicides go up this time of year.' She rubbed the back of her neck. 'I don't have anything on Danvers yet but I do have preliminary toxicology results from victim Lisa Black.' Often it took months to get drug analysis results. Clearly, she'd pushed hard to get the answers back quickly.

'What did you find?' Garrison said.

'Cocaine. She was a user. Recreational, not toxic levels in her system.'

'How can you tell that?'

'She had an enlarged heart.' She glanced down at her notes. 'She also had Rohypnol in her system.'

'Rohypnol? A date rape drug.'

'It's cheap, fairly easy to get and can render a victim immobile.'

'Makes her easy to handle.' Garrison's cell rang. He flipped it open. 'Garrison.'

The uniform officer identified himself, and then said he was on the WD&O trail. Forensics had arrived. They had another branded murder victim. 'I'll be right there.'

Malcolm raised a brow. 'What?'

'Another body from our killer.'

'Shit,' Malcolm said. 'Two bodies in one week. What the hell is driving this guy?'

Dr Henson rose. 'I'll get on that Danvers autopsy right now.'

'The sooner the better. Whoever the hell this is, he's moving fast.'

Eva parked in the lot at LTF Processing just after ten. Luke had given her a call asking her to deliver three subpoenas. After her encounter with Radford the other night, she was cautious about another job. Luke had promised a bonus. So she'd agreed.

She moved into the industrial building. Pulling off her sunglasses, she let her eyes adjust to the dimmer light. She spotted Luke in the far corner sitting at his metal desk, leaning back in his chair and talking on the phone.

Luke was a tall, slim man who had to have been in his late forties but looked a good decade younger. He was fit and neatly dressed but his tanned skin came from a salon, and for some reason he always looked a bit plastic.

He hung up and grinned at her. 'Eva! Doll, how's it going?'

His grin turned her insides to ice. 'You have a few deliveries for me?'

'I do. And they should be a piece of cake.' He dug the papers out of his desk drawer.

She took the subpoenas. 'That's what you said about the last one. And I nearly got the crap beat out of me.'

He had the good sense to look embarrassed. 'I didn't know the guy would go postal. His ex's attorney said he wanted the divorce. That he'd be glad to be served.'

'I've got a couple of dents in my truck that say otherwise.'

'Sorry about that.' He handed her an envelope with cash.

She counted it and tucked it in her backpack. 'Sorry enough to do a little PI work for me?' She kept her tone even, knowing if Luke got a whiff of how much she wanted this he'd find a way to use it.

'What's that mean?'

'I want you to find a few people for me.' She handed him the printout showing the photos of Lisa, Sara and Kristen.

Blue eyes narrowed. 'Why these chicks?'

She shrugged. 'Time we had a chat.'

'Sure, why not? But PI time is expensive.'

'How expensive?'

'Like you owe me a couple of deliveries gratis. And maybe a dinner.'

'No dinner. And what kind of deliveries?'

'The legal kind. And yes to dinner.'

She ignored the dinner reference. 'Where do the deliveries go?'

'A small firm in Old Town. Wellington and James.'

Angie's firm. 'Really. Which attorney?'

'Carlson. And please get those done as fast as you can. She'll ride my ass if you don't. Hell of a stickler for details.'

Some things never changed. 'Sure. No sweat.' Sooner or later it made sense she'd deliver for Wellington and James. Alexandria was a small community. And if you were to ask a shrink he'd probably say she'd accepted the job knowing it would shove her in her sister's path eventually.

Luke flicked the edge of the photo with his finger, grinning. 'These chicks got names?'

'Just worry about the two on the right. Kristen Hall is the redhead and the blonde is Sara Miller.'

'Why not the first gal?'

'She's dead.'

As Donovan studied the old pictures of the ten-year-old crime, he remembered the thrill of covering his first real murder case. Rich boy and poor girl. Rape. Drugs. It had all the makings of a great story and it had panned out just as he'd hoped. By the end of the trial he'd had a byline.

Where the hell was Eva Rayburn hiding? And when the hell was his private detective calling in with a report?

'Units on the scene of the WD&O trail.' The voice squawked from the police scanner on his desk, which always remained on. *'Garrison is en route.'*

Garrison.

Donovan straightened. Garrison had to be knee-deep in the shelter fire and murder. Why call Garrison and not another like Sinclair or Rokov? Unless this murder was connected to the shelter murder.

His nerves popped like firecrackers as he jumped out of his chair, jammed bare feet into worn loafers and grabbed his keys and coat. This had to be worth seeing.

Within twenty minutes Donovan had headed through Old Town and south on Route 1. Within a mile, he spotted the police cruisers parked along the side of the river bike path.

With too many cops on the scene for him to park close, he found a spot a half mile down the road and hiked back toward the scene, arriving just as Garrison and Kier arrived.

Garrison got out of his car, his face an angry mask. Sunglasses shielded his eyes but when he looked in Donovan's direction, instinct demanded Donovan step back. Garrison wasn't a man to have as an enemy.

Donovan tossed him a small salute and edged toward the edge of the crime scene. He moved toward a crowd of onlookers and started to nose his way into a conversation.

'So what happened?'

An old man sporting a straw hat and holding a Yorkie's leash turned. Excitement glittered in his gray eyes even as he tried to look solemn. 'They've found a murdered woman.'

People by and large loved to pass on bad news. They took an unholy glee in sharing the bits of information they'd collected. It took so little prompting to get information out of this man. 'Murdered?'

The man leaned closer. 'I hear she was stabbed.'

'Damn.' Donovan slid his hands into his pocket. 'Who found the body?'

'That woman over by the EMT's truck. She's a jogger.'

Donovan's gaze followed the line of the old man's

outstretched hand and saw the heavyset woman huddled under the blanket. She sat in the open bay, chubby hands cradling a cup close to her lips. Her skin looked as pale as flour. 'Poor lady.' Already he wondered how he could get over to talk to her.

'I heard her scream,' the old man said. 'She'd just jogged past me.'

'Did you see the body?'

'No. Didn't have any need to look upon the dead. But I called 911.'

Like most, he was too afraid to stare at death, but still willing to talk about it.

'Damn. That must have been upsetting.'

The man shook his head as he scratched his Yorkie between the ears 'I didn't see the body but I could smell it. God-awful.'

'I'll bet.' If the old man hadn't seen the body, then talking to him was pointless. He needed to talk to the jogger.

'My Harry smelled it too and started barking like a madman. Harry's a smart dog. The best.'

Reminded Donovan of a drowned rat. 'I can see he's a smart dog.' Without making an excuse, he moved toward the yellow tape and the EMT truck. A couple of minutes – hell, even a minute – with the witness and he could confirm a connection to the last victim.

But a couple of uniforms stood by the ambulance, no doubt assigned to keep people like him away. He shifted his gaze over toward the yellow tape and spotted Garrison. He kept a tight hold on this case, just like the other.

'What did you know that you're not sharing, you son of a bitch?' he muttered. Donovan couldn't see the detective's features, but he could tell by his rigid posture that whatever he saw was rough.

Donovan needed to talk to that witness. If he could confirm a connection to the last killing he had one hell of a story, and if he could connect it to the story ten years ago then he could name his price.

Hovering close to the crowd, Donovan wanted to blend into the group of onlookers even as he watched the jogger speak to the EMT. She looked anxious and ready to leave.

'I just need to pee and have a cigarette,' she said.

'Can't help you with the smoke, but the Porta-Johns are over there. I'll walk with you.'

She held up her hand. 'I've been peeing by myself since I was two and a half. I can handle this.'

The uniform hooked his thumbs in his gun belt, frowning his worry. 'You shouldn't be alone.'

Rising, her jaw tensed. 'You want me to keep the door open so you can watch?'

The uniform shifted his stance, glancing down so that she didn't see him blush. 'That won't be necessary. The detectives are gonna want to talk to you, so hurry back.'

She brushed a strand of dark hair from her forehead. 'I've told my story a dozen times.'

'Might have to do it a dozen more.'

'Damn it.' She headed toward the Porta-Johns sandwiched between the river and the path.

Donovan waited an extra beat and then hurried toward her, positioning himself near the john. He pulled the pack of smokes he always kept close and lit one up. His window to talk to her would be very brief.

She vanished into the john, locking the door behind. She reemerged less than a minute later, rubbing her hands on her pant legs.

He took a deep puff on his cigarette and blew it out toward her.

The scent of his smoke reached her and had her turning. 'I don't suppose you have an extra?'

He grinned, reaching in his breast pocket for the pack. 'Sure.'

The woman closed the distance between them, her expression a mixture of joy and relief. 'God bless you.'

He jiggled the pack so that a couple of cigarettes peeked out of the opening enough for her to grab one. She took the filtered tip in her fingers and accepted the lighter he offered. She lit the tip, inhaling slowly as she savored the kick of nicotine. 'I keep swearing I'm going to quit.'

'Me too.' He grinned as he took another pull. He exhaled. 'But the butts always beckon. Especially when I'm stressed.'

She exhaled a lungful of smoke. 'I've had a day for the record books.'

'What happened?'

'Found a body.'

'Damn.' He inhaled and handed her the pack. 'You deserve the whole pack.'

She tossed him a half grin as she accepted the package. 'I don't suppose you have a bottle of Scotch in your pocket?'

'Sorry, the canteen is empty.' He glanced toward the crime scene tape. 'I'm Connor.'

'I'm Kelly.'

'Kelly. Nice to meet you.'

'Likewise.'

'So who died?'

'I don't know. I never saw her before. A woman. Stabbed. And burned.'

A soft breeze blew from the Potomac, and he did his best not to look rushed or impatient. If he rushed this, she just might shut down. 'Shit. How you holding up?'

'Ready to get the hell out of here. I've had it with the questions. Cops just won't let me go, like I committed a crime or something.'

'They can be a pain in the ass.'

'I just want to go home.'

'I bet it will be soon.' He pointed toward the scene. 'You know they found that other woman who'd been stabbed.'

Kelly nodded, staring at the glowing tip of her cigarette. 'I heard about it on the radio but I don't watch much television so I missed whatever else they said. Did she have crosses burned on her stomach too?'

His heart kicked but he kept his voice even. 'Cops didn't say. I'll bet it's been a bear of a case for the cops.'

The woman nodded. 'I shouldn't have looked at her body, but it was kinda like a car wreck. You look.' She took a long pull on the cigarette. 'And she was covered in these funky star-shaped marks. They looked so red and awful.'

Excitement burned to the tips of his fingers, which ached to type out this story. 'Damn. I'm sorry you had to see that, Kelly.'

'I don't know who would do that to a woman.'

'Some sick bastard.' Donovan glanced up and his gaze caught Garrison's. Busted. The cop's dark angry glare even caught Donovan short. No doubt the cop had murder in his heart now.

Donovan tossed his cigarette on the ground and crushed it with his shoe. 'See you around, Kelly.'

She glanced up, a bit of disappointment in her eyes. 'Hey, you don't have to go. In fact, if you're free . . .'

'Sorry, doll, I got to go.'

Garrison startled the two uniforms by the EMT truck with a blast of angry words. They both glanced in his direction and he knew if he didn't get moving he'd find himself arrested for interfering with a crime scene.

He turned to leave when he spotted Detective Kier headed his way. The guy moved toward him like a slow-moving freight train. Malcolm didn't look rushed, but when the impact came it would knock him off his feet.

Malcolm grinned. 'Going somewhere, Donovan?'

Donovan grinned back. 'Just leaving, as a matter of fact.'

'Oh, no, stay and chat a while. I know Garrison will want to have a word.'

Kelly looked between the two of them, her mouth slightly open like a dumb twit. 'Hey, what's the matter, Officer? The guy just gave me a smoke.'

Malcolm didn't remove his gaze from Donovan. 'He's a reporter, ma'am.'

'A what?'

'Meet Connor Donovan. A man who will say or do anything for a story.'

Donovan shrugged. 'I just gave the lady a smoke.'

Kelly tossed him back his pack of cigarettes. 'Asshole.'

She passed Garrison as she stomped back to the EMT's truck.

Garrison pulled off his glasses. 'So what did you find out?'

Donovan winked. 'I'll show you mine if you show me yours.'

Garrison didn't even attempt to flash his trademark grin. 'Back away from this, Donovan. I don't want you turning this into a circus.'

'Serial killers are hot stories, Detective. Readers need to know they aren't safe.'

Garrison tightened his jaw. 'You've no proof of a serial killer.'

'Witnesses at both scenes reported the victims had been branded with a star.'

He pulled in a long slow breath and let it out slowly. 'Don't print that.'

'You can't stop me.'

'No, I can't. But if you print that detail, I'll end up with another nutcase who will try and recreate what you've written.'

Donovan shrugged. 'You're being dramatic.'

'Do not print that detail.'

'Maybe you should do a better job of overseeing your crime scene and controlling your witnesses, pal. I've got a story to write.'

Garrison's blood boiled as he stared down at the murder victim. Shoving that bastard Donovan from his mind proved to be a challenge. Visions of punching the guy danced in his head.

Malcolm moved beside him. 'He's gone.'

'Great. Much like closing the barn door after the horse is gone.'

'Yeah.' Kier didn't bother to offer any platitudes. 'He'll print whatever sells papers.'

'I've called the department's public relations officer. She's going to try to get hold of the story.'

A gust of wind blew off the river, sending a chill through him. 'How long can she hold off the papers?'

'Depends on what kind of mood the editor is in, I suppose. But he knows how the game is played. He helps me now, I might be able to help him later.'

Malcolm shoved his hand in his pocket. 'You certainly sound reasonable.'

Garrison grinned, not feeling the least bit jovial. 'Good.' He shoved aside his anger and focused on the body. The four gruesome stars had been etched into her flesh in a circular pattern just like on the last victim. 'Whoever is doing this is no longer tentative. The stars are pronounced and clear.'

'Practice makes perfect.'

'She's young like the last victim. Maybe thirty and attractive when she was alive.'

'Yeah.'

Garrison nodded. 'The medical examiner hit the nail on the head. The killer's confidence is growing.'

'And now he's a cocky son of a bitch who doesn't need to set a fire to get our attention.' Malcolm rubbed the back of his neck. 'Why her?'

'I don't know, but I'd bet a year's salary none of this is random.'

'Why do you say that?'

'He's just too damn careful. Forensics hasn't found much at this scene either. This guy is smart. And he's picking his victims for a reason.'

'Hard to catch.' Malcolm drove strong fingers through his thick black hair.

'That's what I'm afraid of.'

'I did some checking on branding irons. They can be electric or can be heated up the old-fashioned way in a fire, just like Dr Henson said. You can order the damn things off the Internet. I've got Sinclair searching the top twenty Web sites and sending enquiries.'

'Good. I'm headed to King's. I want to talk to Eva Rayburn and ask her about the night Cross raped and burned that star into her skin. This all fits together but I just can't see it yet.'

'She hates cops.' Disdain seasoned the words.

Garrison didn't care about her likes and dislikes. 'She's just going to have to get over it.'

Garrison's mood had soured from bad to foul by the time he pulled up in front of King's Pub. It had been a long day at the crime scene. The forensics team had collected a lot of samples. He and Malcolm had spoken to everyone in the crowd and the medical examiner had promised to get right on the autopsy. But so far they weren't any closer to catching a very careful and methodical killer. And unless he had a missing person's report that matched the victim or her prints were in AFIS, the automated fingerprinting system, it could be much longer for identification.

He pushed through the front door of the pub. Laughter,

music and the clink of dishes grated his raw nerves as he studied the packed crowd. This wasn't the average tourist destination. There were a couple of folks with maps and cameras, but most of the patrons looked as if they'd just gotten off work. Some looked like the legal eagles and the non-profiteers. But most looked like ordinary folks . . . construction workers, tour guides and shop owners. This was a working-class crowd.

He spotted Eva Rayburn behind the bar. A thick rubber band bound her long hair in a loose ponytail. She wore no make-up but it didn't seem to matter. Her fresh, pale skin and bright eyes trimmed with thick lashes could easily look garish if painted too heavily. Her form-fitting red T-shirt drew his attention to a slim neck, small firm breasts and a trim waist. She seemed to do her best to downplay her sexuality, but somehow in the simplicity she'd managed to accentuate a feminine earthiness that he found far more attractive.

He watched as she talked to a short redheaded waitress as she filled five beer steins. With efficiency, she served the beers, took a dinner order and refilled two wines. Her movements were fluid and she seemed to handle the noise and chaos as if she'd been born to it. When he'd first seen her, she'd looked more like a kid than a woman. But watching her now, he could see she possessed a bearing and confidence that would make it impossible for him ever to think of her as a kid again.

He moved to the edge of the bar and took a seat on the corner stool. He grabbed a handful of nuts and waited for her to catch his eye. When she did, her smile faltered and the confidence that had just burned so bright dimmed.

Shoulders straightening, she moved toward him, her hips moving more like a swagger than a sway. 'Detective Garrison, isn't it?'

He liked the way her husky voice roughed up his name. 'Very good memory for names, Ms Rayburn.' He glanced at her name tag, which read DORIS. 'What's with the name tag?'

'I never bothered to order one. It belonged to the last girl who tended bar.'

She didn't bother with a menu, cocktail napkin or greeting. 'You came all this way to ask me about my name tag?'

'I've got a couple of other questions for you.'

'As you can see, I'm slammed right now. Can we do it another time?' A subtle tightening of her fingers around the bar rag signaled a tension that didn't show in her eyes.

'No.' Interviews always worked better if he could get the other guy off balance.

A frown flickered on her brow and vanished. Whatever emotions rose up in her had been expertly tamed. A trick, he'd bet, she'd learned in prison. 'I really can't talk right now, Detective. I'm working.'

'Great. I'm starving. I'll have a soda. And a menu.'

Her brow furrowed. 'You said you had questions.'

He grinned. 'I can talk and eat. You can work and talk. It's a compromise.'

She leaned forward and he caught the barest hint of fresh soap and lemons. 'Why can't we just do this later?'

He leaned in, noting the silver flecks in her eyes. 'I'd like to see a menu. And I drink real cola. No diets for me. Can't stand anything that's fake.'

Stiffening, she shrugged. 'You're playing me.'

He knitted his fingers together and relaxed his shoulders. 'I'm thirsty. And hungry.'

As she studied him, he could almost imagine her weighing her options. Fight or flight? Tell this guy to go fuck himself or play along? Smart inmates knew when to do both.

'You said cola?' The softness in her tone didn't hide the Fuck Off burning in her gaze.

'That's right.' His grin widened naturally. He enjoyed being close to her.

'Sure.'

Garrison worked on a handful of nuts as he watched her fill an iced mug with cola and then set it back in front of him. He might have a fight on his hands with her soon, but for now she didn't run.

She pulled a menu from under the bar and handed it to him. 'I'll give you a minute to look over the menu.'

'Hang on just a second, I have a question about the soup of the day.'

She hesitated. 'You're kidding?'

'I never kid about food.'

'Okay. The question?'

He pretended to think, knowing each passing second ticked her off. 'Tomato or cream based?'

Her eyes narrowed. 'Tomato.'

'Great. I'll have a bowl. With crackers.'

'Will do.' She returned in minutes with a bowl of steaming chowder with soda crackers on the side.

He had to admit the soup did smell good. 'Thanks. I'm surprised I've never been in this place before.'

'We don't advertise. Most of our business is regulars.'

He tasted the soup, which was delicious. 'I know I'll be back.'

'Great.' The word fell flat like a pancake.

'Make my sandwich roast beef on rye. Toasted. Spicy mustard. Two pickles. Tomato on the side.'

'Will do.'

'Aren't you going to write that down?'

'Don't need to.' She filled a glass with soda and lime and set it front of another customer.

Garrison glanced around the bar, guessing it would slow or clear out in the next half hour. Places like this bustled well into the night when they catered to tourists, but people who worked had to leave sooner rather than later. He'd kill time eating until the pace eased and then he'd ask his question. For the first time in a couple of days, he'd felt like he had landed in the calm waters that swirled in the hurricane's eye.

Garrison quickly realized that Eva really didn't have to write anything down. She remembered everything she heard and from what he could see she never made mistakes. When she served his order it was correct down to each detail.

But as he continued to stare at her, he could see she didn't move with the same fluid ease she'd had before she'd first spotted him. His presence put her nerves on edge. He liked the fact that she was so aware of him. When he'd been with Macy, she'd liked his attention and she'd wanted more of it. Eva didn't want more of him. He could have vanished into thin air right now and she'd have been happy.

When he'd finished his meal and sipped a coffee, he

waited patiently until she moved toward him to collect the plate.

'Can I get you anything else?' Eva said.

'Just the check and one question.' He reached in his coat pocket and pulled out the photo of Lisa Black taken by the DMV. 'Do you know her?'

She glanced at the photo on the bar. Tension crept into her face, adding surprising age to her teenlike features. 'You already showed me her picture. Besides, the news-caster reported her name.' She glanced around, seeming to hope that some patron needed her, but none did.

Her nerves had gone from tense to high alert. 'So what aren't you telling me?'

She pushed the photo toward him. For a moment she hesitated, as if weighing her options. 'I went to college with her.'

He hadn't expected truth. 'At Price?'

'That's right.' Her brow furrowed. 'How did you know I went to Price?'

'I've been to Taylorsville's sheriff's office. I read the case file on you.'

The color drained from her face as she glanced from side to side. She clearly didn't want anyone to overhear this. 'I've been careful to keep that part of my life hidden since I moved back.'

'I can appreciate that.' Knowledge of her past could prove to be an effective leverage that he wasn't afraid to use. 'How'd you know to look at Price?'

The confidence in her voice thinned, revealing the fear lurking behind. He elbowed aside the pity nudging him. 'Why'd you lie about knowing the shelter victim?'

'I didn't lie. I truly didn't recognize her. She's changed a lot since college. I only connected the dots when I heard her name on the news.'

He glanced around and noticed several folks at the bar were staring at them. 'Do you have somewhere more private where we could talk?'

She studied him as if weighing her options. Finally, she nodded over her shoulder. 'In the back. Let me just get someone to cover me for a minute.'

It took several minutes for her to find the redheaded waitress to cover the bar. When she did, she ducked under the bar and came around to his stool. He rose, leaving enough to cover the meal with a generous tip.

'We've a small banquet room off to the side. No one's using it right now.'

'Sure.'

Digging the key out of her apron pocket, she unlocked a set of French doors. She opened the door and waited for him to pass through before she closed it behind them. The doors muted the bar sounds but he could still feel the bass beat in his chest.

She smoothed long fingers down over her apron. 'What do you want to know?'

'First, I want to show you another picture.'

Eva tucked a stray strand behind her ear and tensed. Pale skin accentuated the red in her lips and the darkness of her hair and eyelashes. For a long tense moment she didn't breathe. 'Okay.'

He held out the Polaroid. 'Do you know this woman?'

She braced as she glanced at the picture. Her brows knotted as she moistened her lips. 'Her eyes are closed.'

'That's right. Do you know her?'

'What's she done?'

'You're good at asking questions, Ms Rayburn, but that's what the city pays me to do. How do you know her?'

Her gaze lingered on the photo. 'She went to Price too.'

A bolt of adrenaline shot through his limbs. A connection. 'What's her name?'

'Is she dead?'

'Yes. What's her name?'

She closed her eyes for a moment. Was it sorrow or relief that washed over her features? 'Her name was Sara Miller in college. I don't know if she got married and changed her name.'

'Do you know anything about her?'

She folded her arms over her chest. The gesture wasn't aggressive but defensive. 'Nothing since college. I've not seen her since my . . . trial.'

The word sounded wrenched from her throat. 'No one here knows about your conviction for manslaughter.'

Her eyes narrowed a fraction. 'King knows. He offered me the job while I was still at the halfway house. How did you piece my past together?'

'My old man served as a cop in Alexandria for thirty years. He remembered your case, specifically the star.'

She nodded. 'I've only been out six months but I learned quickly that people don't like ex-cons. Please keep my past private. I like it here.'

'Then why come back here? Someone is bound to recognize you.'

'Darius Cross died.' Her eyes narrowed. 'Maybe I wanted to dance on his grave.'

'You confessed to killing his son.'

Her jaw tightened. 'That's right.'

There was more but she'd locked that part of her past behind an iron door. 'It doesn't take six months to dance on a grave. Why stick around?'

She swallowed and he sensed a door slamming closed. 'Am I a suspect?'

'Should you be?'

She planted her hands on her hips. The fear had ebbed from her gaze and fire replaced it. 'I just know how it works. The cops get an idea in their head and then they look for facts to prove it. Doesn't matter if they're right or wrong. It only matters that the case gets headlines.'

'I'm here to catch a murderer. The rest doesn't mean anything to me.'

A bitter smile tipped the edge of her mouth. 'Everybody wants to get ahead and headlines and closed cases mean promotions. Do you know the sheriff in Taylorsville won his reelection based on my conviction?'

'He's been voted out since.'

'Great.'

He studied her face closely. From what he'd read of her file, she had a right to be angry. Any half-decent defense attorney would have seen to it she'd not gone to jail.

But showing her pity over a past injustice wasn't going to catch this killer. 'Did you know Ms Black, Ms Miller and you share an interesting trait?'

She folded her arms over her chest. 'Yeah, we went to school together?'

'It's more than that.' He studied her face closely. 'Both women were burned with four-pointed stars.'

Eva flinched as if he'd slapped her hard. 'I don't understand.'

'Whoever killed those women burned each woman four times with a star-shaped brand.'

She closed her eyes. A tear spilled down her cheek.

He studied her closely, wondering if she was an expert liar. 'Your attacker also burned you, didn't he?'

'You read the file.' She sniffed and swiped the tear away. 'And as you know, my attacker is dead.'

'Did you kill him, Eva?'

'What?'

He wanted to lay his hand on her shoulder as a gesture of comfort but he guessed she'd jump a mile in the air if he did. 'Did you kill the man that raped you?'

A painful sigh shuddered through her. 'The file says three girls saw me do it. Sara. Lisa. And Kristen. And I did eventually confess.'

'I went head-to-head with Darius Cross a few years ago. His mansion had been robbed and I was assigned to investigate. Darius Cross proved to be a real domineering pain in the ass throughout the investigation. Took all I had to handle him. A seventeen-year-old girl who'd been brutalized could easily have caved to a guy like him.'

'But the bottom line is that I confessed.'

'Did you kill him?'

Silence wedged between them. 'You're the first person that ever asked me if I killed Josiah Cross and wasn't expecting a "yes." Everyone else, including me, just assumed I did.' Shaking her head, she took a half step back. 'But the God's honest truth is that I don't know if I killed him or not. I blacked out. When I woke, the house was on fire, the fireman was dragging me out. Through the smoke I saw Josiah covered in blood lying on the floor.'

'And now two of the three women who testified against you are dead.'

'Are you accusing me?'

Tension goaded by fatigue seasoned the tone of his voice. 'I'm looking for a killer.'

She stiffened. 'You're looking in the wrong place.'

'One way or another you're connected.'

'What's that supposed to mean?'

'At this point I don't know.'

Eyes narrowing, Eva shook her head. 'I'm not going to be railroaded again.'

'I want to help you.'

'*Help* me. Like the cops helped me after my attack? That's rich.' Bitterness dripped from the words.

'If you wanted to avoid the past, there are better places to live than here. Why'd you return? And don't tell me you came back to dance on Darius's grave.'

She moved toward him until she stood toe to toe with him. He stood a foot taller but that didn't seem to intimidate her. 'I don't remember hitting Josiah with the poker. After he branded me, I passed out for several minutes. And those missing minutes have haunted me for nearly a decade. And right now they are dictating my present.'

'What's going on now?'

'You mean other than the fact that I've got a cop questioning me about two murders? St Margaret's turned down my scholarship application because of my record. I'm not the kind of person they want representing their school.'

He'd read her academic stats. It made sense she'd want to return to academia, a place she'd excelled. 'That's got to piss you off.'

'Sure. It stings. But I'll get over it.' Her face paled.

'I hear resentment in your voice.' He injected challenge into the statement, wanting to goad her.

'I'm sure you do. I've got almost ten years of it bottled up.'

'Would killing those women who testified against you ease some of that resentment?'

She lifted her chin as if she'd been cuffed. 'What?'

'Did you kill Lisa and Sara?'

'No!' The word sounded wrenched from her chest. 'No, I did not kill those women.'

He leaned toward her, letting his height rattle her shaky nerves more. He wanted her off balance and primed to blurt out whatever truth she harbored. 'Are you sure about that, Eva?'

She stumbled back a step. Tears glistened in her eyes and reminded him of a cornered animal. 'I didn't kill anyone!'

He closed the gap between them, continuing to hover over her like a wraith. 'Torturing and killing those women would be the perfect revenge. Make them suffer as you did.'

'No!' She stumbled back again and this time bumped into a table. She righted herself and scrambled around it until it rested between them. 'If you want to lay the murder of two women on me you'll have to do it all by yourself. I'm not going to make this easy for you. I'll get a real lawyer this time and fight you.'

He moved to within inches of her. He didn't touch her but made it impossible for her to move away. 'You sound afraid.'

'Damn right, I'm afraid. I'm afraid of you. And every other damn cop in this world.' Her breath rose and fell. Her pulse thrummed in the hollow of her neck.

She wedged her body along the wall, freeing herself from him. He let her go, watching as she hurried back to the bar.

Garrison stood in the room alone. He'd scared the shit out of her just as he intended. He needed to know if she was involved with the murders. The raw fear in her eyes said she wasn't, but he'd need evidence to back that up. Though he'd gotten the answer he needed, he realized shaking her up might have shut her down to him permanently. It wasn't like him to push unless absolutely necessary. He'd learned long ago that he got more information out of a suspect with a bit of kindness than with heavy-handed techniques.

So why had he pushed Eva so hard? Why had he wanted to shatter the wall of ice around her and force her to deal with him? Why did he feel a sense of relief when he'd gotten the vibe that she was innocent?

What had Macy said the other day? 'You like a puzzle.' Shit. He didn't need any more puzzles in his life. And yet his attraction to Eva was undeniable.

Back in the main room, he found Eva behind the bar serving drinks. Color flushed her cheeks and her hands trembled. He could tell her he thought she was innocent but she'd not believe him. He doubted she'd believe anything he had to say again.

But he needed her to believe in him. She was the key to this case, and if his instincts were on target she might very well be on the killer's hit list. He regretted now that he'd come on so strong. He thought back to her police file and the young girl who'd looked so lost. 'We'll talk again soon.'

She shook her head. 'You don't want to talk. You want a suspect. And I'm not going to be it.'

'We'll talk again. Like it or not, we're joined at the hip until this case is solved.'

As he turned to go, he saw a kid run out from the kitchen and back behind the bar. The kid ran right up to Eva and showed her a piece of paper. Her stony features softened and she took a moment to examine what the boy had given her. The kid seemed to beam around her. Who was he? A brother? A son?

There was a hell of a lot he needed to find out about Eva Rayburn.

Eva could barely concentrate or breathe as she stared down at the row of numbers Bobby had written down. She wasn't so good with stories or coloring but she could add numbers and that's what they had done for fun earlier today. They both liked puzzles.

But with Garrison so close, staring at her, she could barely breathe, barely concentrate on what Bobby was saying. When she heard the pub door open and close, she dared a glance back over her shoulder and discovered he'd gone.

Her shoulders slumped forward. 'You've done a great job, Bobby. I like the way you wrote the number five. It's not backward this time.'

'I traced your numbers a couple of times.'

The child reminded her of a dried sponge, starving for anything she could pour into his brain. She took the pen from him and wrote five more simple math problems. 'Add these up and then I'll check them. Once you're done we'll get you ready for bed.'

A normal kid would have balked at bedtime and math problems. But he nodded, so happy to please. 'Okay.'

'Monster check in five minutes?'

'Will do.'

His acquiescence broke her heart. The kid had been starved not just physically but mentally as well.

When he dashed back into the kitchen, she turned her attention to the rows of liquor bottles, pretending to search for something. She'd inventoried and alphabetized the bottles her first night and knew not only where each was located, but also how much remained in each. But she needed the pretense to gather her thoughts.

Just because Garrison had come here didn't mean this case would repeat the last. She'd done nothing wrong. Her arrival at the fire had been coincidence. And if he wanted to ram some cop theory down her throat, she wasn't having it. She wasn't a frightened kid anymore. She was an adult who'd read most of the legal textbooks.

She could handle whatever he threw at her.

Still, the star. Lisa had been burned with a star just like her. And so had Sara. The odds of a killer choosing a four-pointed star like the one that marred her shoulder were beyond calculation.

Eva grabbed a rag and started to polish glasses. She'd done her best to block out what had happened years ago.

And for the most part she'd done okay. She almost never stood in front of the mirror anymore and stared at the scar on her shoulder or cried at night when she felt alone. When Josiah had raped her, he'd killed the innocent girl. Prison had transformed that wounded girl into a harder, stronger woman.

But the past now screamed to be noticed. Who would have done this to Lisa and Sara? To kill them so savagely. She wouldn't have wished that on anyone.

She'd thought that once Darius Cross had died, she could return home and recapture some of the old life she'd had to forfeit. But maybe coming back had been a mistake.

Panic continued to churn in her belly when she took Bobby upstairs and got him ready for bed. He climbed under the covers.

'I can read you a story,' she said.

'I've read all my books.'

'All? That's great. Tomorrow, we will find more books for you. Maybe a chapter book or something we can read together at night.'

'Okay.' He exuded caution, not enthusiasm.

'I know it's hard to believe in promises, Bobby. But I'm not making a big one tonight. I'm just promising a new book and some reading time. Something simple.'

'Okay.'

Not a ringing endorsement but a touch less defiance. A kiss on the cheek still felt too over the top. The kid wasn't hers. They both knew foster care could be so temporary, and the fewer ties the better. She settled for a pat on his hand.

Eva left the light on as she had the other night and

went back behind the bar and finished out her shift. By the time she climbed the stairs to her apartment just after midnight, she'd convinced herself that sticking around was a bad idea.

The time had come to cut her losses.

She moved into the bathroom, closed the door before she turned on the lights to wash her face and hands.

Eva studied her expression as she'd done a million times since her attack.

A knock on the door had her looking down to find Bobby standing there. He rubbed his eyes. He wore one of King's oversized black T-shirts that read BAD TO THE BONE.

'Eva.'

'Hey. What are you doing up?'

'You're not going anywhere, are you?'

'Why do you say that?'

'You just looked mad tonight.'

'I'm not mad. Just tired.'

'Did I do something wrong?'

She knelt in front of him. 'No, honey, you haven't done anything wrong.'

'So you won't leave me.'

What could she say to him? She wasn't his family. She wasn't even family to King. She was a boarder with no roots. No plans. No alibis.

But he wouldn't hear any of that. All he'd hear is that she didn't want him. And she just couldn't do that. Not now.

'I'm not going anywhere tonight. Not tonight.'

'Mean it?'

'Yeah. I mean it.'

He took her hand in his and squeezed gently before he turned and left the bathroom. The warmth of his fingers against hers remained long after he'd gone to bed.

These last six months she'd been drifting. The time had come to stop drifting and to dig into the past and to really fight for what she wanted.

Chapter 12

Friday, April 7, 8:02 A.M.

Garrison and Malcolm arrived at Sara's office located at Fairchild Advertising minutes after it opened. Chrome polished elevator doors opened to a sleek front desk and sign that read FAIRCHILD ADVERTISING AGENCY. A young woman sat behind the front desk. Slim and smartly dressed, she looked as if she'd been plucked from the pages of a fashion magazine. She glanced up from her computer screen. 'Can I help you?'

Garrison pulled out his badge. 'We'd like to speak to Sara Miller's boss.'

'Sara didn't come in today.'

Garrison nodded. 'I know. Who is her boss?'

'Ross Fairchild. He's in a meeting.'

As Garrison tucked his badge back in his breast pocket, he smiled. 'I'd like you to interrupt that meeting.'

She raised a plucked eyebrow and injected authority into her voice. 'It's an important meeting.'

'This is more important.' He leaned forward a fraction. 'You need to get him.'

'Is Sara all right?'

'We need to see her boss.' Garrison had discovered that Sara's parents were both out of the country and unreachable for a week and none of her neighbors were home.

218

The boss was the next likely step until the others could be tracked.

She frowned. 'Sure.' She vanished around a corner.

A few minutes later, a tall, gray-haired man in a slim black suit appeared. He approached Garrison and extended his hand. Gold cuff links winked in the light. 'My name is Ross Fairchild. I understand you have questions about one of my employees.'

'We do. Is there somewhere private we can talk?'

'My office.' Fairchild led them down a carpeted hallway decorated with colorful advertising posters that clearly illustrated some of their more successful campaigns. Cereal. Watches. Cars. Fairchild Advertising seemed to do it all.

Fairchild opened the mahogany doors to his office. The wall behind his polished desk was all windows and looked out over the city and in the distance the river. Given different circumstances, Garrison would have admired the view. He glanced around the office, taking in the art, polished brass, antique oriental rugs and the credenza behind the desk filled with awards and pictures. A picture on the far end featured Fairchild and Sara Miller. He held a crystal award and she grinned up at him, adoration glistening in her eyes.

Fairchild took a seat at the head of the conference table. He looked annoyed. 'Please have a seat. Can I get you coffee?'

The officers sat down, each choosing chairs on his left. 'No. Thank you.'

He rested his flat palms on the table. 'So what is this about Sara?'

'Ms Miller's secretary called in a missing-persons report early this morning.'

'Yes. I asked her to. I asked her to keep the call quiet. I don't want rumors spreading.' A smile twitched at the edge of his lips. 'Sara is my most dedicated salesperson, and when she didn't show up Wednesday and Thursday, I got worried. I tried her cell and her home numbers but no answers. Have you found Sara?'

'When was the last time you saw her?'

A small frown creased his forehead. 'We had a breakfast meeting three days ago.'

'Which was when?'

'Seven A.M., give or take.'

'Did she seem upset or distracted?'

'She's a tense woman. Always has been. But that's what I like about her. Advertising is a very competitive business and I like to surround myself with people who are on the edge. Maybe even a bit neurotic about working long hours.'

'Lot of burnout in this industry.'

'Sure. AEs, account executives like Sara, don't generally have a long shelf life. Clients like working with younger people. It makes them feel younger. So they have to make hay while the sun shines, so to speak.'

'They're disposable.'

'Sure.'

'So Sara worked killer hours?'

Fairchild raised a brow. 'Nothing out of the ordinary.'

'What's ordinary?'

'Eighty, ninety hours.' Fairchild tapped his manicured fingers on the conference table's polished wood. 'Have you found Sara?'

'We did.' Garrison studied Fairchild's face closely. 'A

jogger found her body yesterday on the WD&O trail. She'd been murdered.'

The color remaining in Fairchild's gaunt cheeks drained away. For the first time his rigid posture eased. 'My God, how?'

'We're not releasing that yet.' Garrison glanced at Fairchild's smooth and perfectly manicured hands. No scratches or torn nails, something a killer might have if his victim fought back.

'I can't believe this. Not three days ago, Sara stood in this conference room laughing and smiling.'

Malcolm eased back in his chair. 'Did she date anyone?'

Fairchild shrugged. 'No, not that I'm aware of, but she didn't tell me everything.'

'Close friends?'

'No time for that, she said. She lived her job.'

'Making hay while the sun shined.'

'Exactly.'

'Did she notice any odd people around here? Sending her texts or e-mails.'

'I don't know.'

'I'd like to have access to her computer.'

Fairchild stiffened. 'I can go through it and send along any personal data.'

'I'll go through it.'

'That computer contains a lot of confidential business information. I can't just let it leave these offices.'

Malcolm leaned forward. 'I'm good with computers and I'll protect the information.'

'I've got millions riding on several campaigns. I can't have Sara's information leaked out.'

Garrison leaned forward. 'I promise it won't be leaked.'

Fairchild's frame stiffened. He'd recovered and retrenched to protect his business. 'I've seen how other police departments leak information. Accident photos, mug shots and police reports. No one knows how the information got out but the fact is that it did.'

Garrison could feel the muscles in his neck tighten. 'Nothing's ever been leaked from my department.'

'I can't take that chance.'

'You've no choice.' Garrison removed a slim sheet of paper from his pocket. 'I'll obtain a warrant to seize all of Sara's belongings, her computer and her files in an hour if need be.'

Fairchild nodded. 'Get your warrant.'

Malcolm cocked an eyebrow. 'A young woman was brutally murdered. That's got to mean something.'

'What's that supposed to mean?'

'The picture on your credenza. It's of you and Sara.'

'So?'

'The way she's looking at you suggests there were shared feelings.'

He brushed imaginary lint from his coat sleeve. 'I won the Chamber's service award that night. She was proud of the honor.'

Garrison sensed he'd hit a nerve. 'She's smiling at you like she thought more of you than just an employee would. She wasn't thinking about the award.'

His chin raised a fraction. 'You've no proof of that.'

The old man's reaction shredded Garrison's patience. 'You were having an affair with her, weren't you?'

His spine stiffened so much, it looked as if it would

snap. 'Don't even say something like that. Even a rumor can be very damaging.'

Garrison's gaze dropped to the man's ring finger and the gold wedding band encircling it. 'Did your wife know about the affair?'

Fairchild rose. 'You need to leave.'

Garrison stayed seated, knowing he'd hit a few major nerves. 'So that's a no? If you can't tell me I'd be happy to ask her.'

Fairchild fisted his fingers. 'It's time you left.'

Malcolm leaned forward, his muscular build radiating raw power. 'If you don't make me work for the computer, I can go out of my way to keep any damaging e-mails secret. You make me work for it and I promise you I will recover every bit of data and make it as public as I have to.'

Color rose in Fairchild's face as if he were teetering between anger and raw fear. 'I'm calling my attorney.'

'Do that,' Garrison said. 'Where can I find your wife?'

Lips pursed, Fairchild rose and his fingers pulled away from the buttons on his phone. 'Fine. Have a look at the computer. But if one word leaks out about our ad campaigns or clients I will have your job.'

Garrison rose, straightening his full six-foot-three frame. 'I really don't think you'd want it.'

Malcolm rose. 'Not nearly as glamorous as television portrays it.'

'We start early here.' Fairchild's gaze skipped between the two until finally he nodded. 'This way.'

They followed Fairchild down the corridors past open offices. With each open door they passed, more stunned employees glanced up at them. Several moved to their office doors to watch their boss.

At the end of the hallway, they reached a corner office whose doorplate read SARA MILLER. Garrison blocked the doorway, halting Fairchild's advance into the office. 'We'll take it from here.'

Malcolm sat behind Sara's desk. He opened the laptop and turned it on. 'Let me check her Internet history. Might give me an idea of what she had planned.' After three clicks of the button, he said, 'She checked out The Warehouse restaurant and O'Malley's Bar. 'She had reservations at The Warehouse for dinner. She had a client meeting at eight.'

Garrison frowned. 'Which client?'

In the doorway, Fairchild hesitated then said, 'Cross Industries.'

'Cross Industries,' Garrison said. 'As in Darius Cross of Cross Industries.'

'Darius died eight months ago. We were pitching to his son Micah. They're switching ad firms and it could be a big coup for us to get them.'

'You went after them?'

'No. They came after us. Asked us for a proposal.'

'Who contacted you?'

'Micah. He recently took over the firm after his father's death. He's looking to shape up the company image.'

Garrison glanced at Kier. 'Check her e-mail.'

Fairchild cleared his throat.

'How long did your affair with Sara last?' Garrison asked.

Fairchild moved into the room and closed the door. 'Does it matter? My wife can't find out.'

'How long?'

'I broke it off about six weeks ago.'

'How did Sara handle it?'

'I thought well. From the beginning I made it clear that we would never be forever. When the breakup came, she was composed. But in the last couple of weeks I noticed she'd lost focus. I assumed the breakup had finally sunk in and she was just having some issues.'

'How did she change?'

'Late for work. More argumentative. Nothing most would notice, but I did.'

'Did she find someone new?'

Furrows creased his brow. 'No. I don't think so.'

Garrison detected a note of jealousy in Fairchild's tone. He didn't want her, but didn't like the idea of her moving on to someone else. 'Did she ever mention Lisa Black?'

'That newscaster profiled her the other day. She died in a fire?'

'She was murdered.'

'Oh.'

'They know each other?'

'Not that I'm aware of.'

Garrison scanned the walls of Sara's office. Behind her desk were diplomas. An MBA from the Wharton School of Business. And next to it a BA from Price University. Price. Sara had gone to Price and so had Eva. 'Did she keep up with any of her friends from college?'

'She did have a reunion last year, but I don't know the details.'

Malcolm glanced up from the screen. 'If she did have someone new, they didn't communicate via e-mail.'

'Let's check her phone records for texts. Do you have her phone numbers, Mr Fairchild?'

Fairchild pulled his phone from his breast pocket, punched a couple of numbers and then rattled off Sara's phone numbers. 'I doubt you'll find much. She and I never texted.'

'She might not have worried about a paper trail with the new guy.'

Fairchild pursed his lips, but said nothing.

Malcolm packed up the laptop and glanced over at the wall behind Sara's desk. He frowned but said nothing. After they'd left, he said, 'Everyone talks via text or social networking sites these days. I'd bet a paycheck that if she had a guy, she communicated to him via text.'

'I think you're right. My sister's phone is just about glued to her hand. Dig into her phone records. I'll bet money she had a new guy.'

'Where you going?'

'After I drop you off, I'm headed over to Cross Industries.'

'I thought you might be.'

'This is the second connection I've had to the Cross family.'

'And Price University.'

'Imagine that.'

'The killer knew them from school or through the family.'

'Or both.'

The four girls sat in a circle around the stone fireplace. A hearty fire crackled and popped in the hearth, warming the room and chasing away the chill of the spring night.

Now as the flames flickered and cast shadows against the stone hearth, the girls sat in a circle, each a little tipsy from wine.

'We're out of wine,' Kristen complained. 'And I for one am not ending this night until I'm good and drunk.'

Eva glanced at her half glass of wine. Her stomach had soured and she wondered where she could dump the wine so that no one would see. At seventeen, she was four years younger than the older girls. Freshman year had been a struggle socially and it seemed she always came off as a dork. Now, this last night on campus in the sorority house, she wanted to come off as cool. For once, she wanted to feel a part of the group and not some tagalong kid.

Sara raised her glass. 'I could definitely use more wine.'

Lisa's lips rose into a lazy, sloppy grin as she brushed a dark curly strand from her round face. 'Me three.'

Eva smiled. 'Sure.'

'Well, if you girls want more wine then ante up.' Kristen always bossed the group around. 'I'm not paying for this alone.'

Each girl nodded, eagerly digging into pockets. Eva hesitated. She was the only girl that worried about money. She had about seven bucks left in her purse that was supposed to last her until tomorrow when her sister came to pick her up. Her summer waitress job began tomorrow night, but she'd not see a paycheck for a week. Unlike the others, Eva attended Price on scholarship and every dime counted. But this was her last night and she didn't want to come across as a cheap ass in front of her best friends.

Kristen glanced down at Eva's glass. 'Aren't you going to finish that?'

'Soon,' Eva said. She raised the glass to her lips and pretended to drink.

Kristen's eyes narrowed. 'You're not drinking that much.'

'I am too.' And to prove it, Eva took another sip. Her stomach coiled and she forced a smile to prove she wasn't about to throw up.

'Let me finish it,' Kristen said. 'I'm not buzzed enough.'

Eva handed the glass over to Kristen. 'It's good wine.'

'It's crap,' Kristen said. 'I've had glasses of the good stuff and this is crap.' She sipped the wine as if it had a foul odor. 'But it's got alcohol in it and that's all that counts.'

Sara glanced at Kristen. For the first time a hint of worry flashed across her face. 'There's no rush.'

'There's always a rush to get drunk,' Kristen said.

'She's drinking because Josiah isn't here,' Lisa said. 'He doesn't like it when she drinks.'

Kristen rose up on wobbly feet. 'I don't need my boyfriend's permission to drink or not. I do what I want.'

Eva rose, fearing Kristen would topple. 'We don't have to get more wine right this second. Maybe in an hour or two.'

Kristen frowned. 'No, it does have to be tonight. If I can still stand then I've not had enough.'

'What's wrong with you?' Sara rose and smoothed the wrinkles from her skirt. 'You're not yourself.'

Sara had finally voiced what each of the other three girls had whispered about all week. Kristen wasn't herself. She'd been moody, tired and sick to her stomach occasionally.

Eva ran her fingers through her long, dark hair. 'Are you feeling okay, Kristen?'

Kristen leveled her gaze on Eva like a lioness scoping prey. 'I'm fine.'

Eva held her gaze. 'I'm not so sure.'

Sara took courage from Eva. 'You're not fine.'

Lisa stood. 'You can tell us.'

Kristen pointed at each one of them. 'What is this — some kind of lame intervention? Get off my back.'

Eva had seen a scene like this play out in a movie once. Friends saw that their buddy was in trouble and rallied to help. In the end, the buddy was saved. 'You've been off for a couple of weeks.'

Kristen's face paled. 'What did you say?'

Lisa stared into her glass as if it held the meaning of life. 'You get sick in the mornings a lot.'

'Eva is right. You aren't yourself. You sleep all the time.' Lisa's voice faltered, as if she tossed matches toward gasoline.

Kristen's gaze didn't waver from Eva whom she clearly blamed for this new line of conversation. 'I'm fine. And I sure don't need advice from a girl who hangs out with the housemaid and her daughter.'

'I like Rebecca.'

Kristen leaned forward. 'She's a loser, Eva. She's going to be a maid just like her mother. A loser.'

Eva's temper rose. 'You're sick. You're tired. And you said you and Josiah had sex.'

Bracing, Eva waited for Kristen's explosion of temper. Here comes the storm.

But in that instant, Kristen crumbled. She let the nearly full glass of wine fall to the carpeted floor. Tears flowed down her cheeks.

Immediately, Eva's anger melted to pity. Crap. What had she done? Her sister always said that she shot her mouth off. 'Kristen, I'm sorry.'

The other girls gathered around Kristen like natives circling the settlers' wagons.

Lisa shot Eva a nasty look. 'God, why would you say such a thing?'

Sara shook her head. 'Eva. You are such a bitch.'

Kristen cried so hard, her shoulders shook for several minutes as the three just watched helplessly. No one knew what to say, as if sensing they played out of their league.

Finally, Kristen straightened and looked at Eva with red-rimmed eyes. 'You can't tell anyone. Especially Josiah.'

Eva shook her head. 'I won't tell.'

'Josiah is crazy,' Kristen said. 'I broke up with him last week, and if he knew about the baby he'd never let me go.'

The girls knew Josiah had a temper. Kristen had made excuses for him, but the girls always worried.

'You can't tell Josiah about this baby,' Kristen said. 'Swear.'

Each girl nodded.

Each girl swore.

'I didn't tell!'

The hushed desperate whisper rushed over Eva's lips as she jogged up the back staircase of the condo building. Eva had never told anyone about Kristen's baby. Ever. Even during the darkest times during the trial when she'd felt betrayed and alone, she'd kept silent.

And when Garrison had been at King's last night, she could have told him about the baby and maybe drawn heat away from herself. Kristen Hall was just months away from a huge wedding that would join two wealthy families. Maybe this wasn't about Josiah, the Cross family or Price. Maybe it was about keeping an old, dangerous secret.

Clutching her backpack, Eva pushed through the heavy exit door and stepped from concrete to plush carpeting. She moved down the hallway, her shoulders back, aware she did not fit in this sleek place. She glanced at the message from Luke and the address at the bottom. Wentworth Towers. Condo 7-C. She rang the front bell.

Her stomach bunched in knots as she waited. Finally, high heels clicked on the other side of the door seconds before it snapped open.

In the doorway stood a sleek, tall woman with curly red

hair and sharp green eyes that narrowed instantly. 'Eva Rayburn. You're about the last person I ever expected to see again.'

Eva clenched the strap of her backpack. 'Hello, Kristen.'

Brittle green eyes turned frigid. 'What do you want?'

She'd not expected a gushing welcome but she'd also not expected the coldness. 'Do you have time to talk?'

Kristen didn't open the door wider. 'Do you want money?'

Eva's body grew rigid. 'No, no money. I just wanted to talk.'

Kristen glanced behind her and then stepped out onto the hallway. She closed the front door behind her. 'What do you want, Eva?'

'Did you hear about Lisa?'

The flicker of emotion darkened her eyes. 'It was on the news. Sad. What do you want?'

Eva had always looked up to Kristen as had Lisa and Sara. Kristen was the perfect one – the girl her sorority sisters emulated and the one the boys desired. Back in school, Eva had wanted to win her approval so badly. And to Eva's surprise the years hadn't erased that need to please. For a moment, she wished now she'd run a brush through her hair and picked her best shirt. And then Eva caught herself. 'I want to talk about Sara Miller.'

Kristen huffed her impatience. 'What about her?'

'Sara is dead too.'

Kristen folded her arms. 'What?'

'Killed. Murdered. I've seen pictures of her body.'

Color drained from Kristen's already-pale features. 'Why are you telling me this?'

'I thought you might know what happened to her. Or who might have killed her.'

'Why would I know something like that?' The disgust in her voice sounded genuine.

'Let's face it, Kristen, you had your pretty little fingers in everyone's business in college and I'll bet nothing's changed.'

Kristen shook her head. 'You hated us.'

'What?'

'You hated Sara, Lisa and me. We had money, whereas you had to scrape to get money from a vending machine.'

'You three were my friends until the trial.'

'You mean until we saw you kill Josiah,' she hissed. 'What do you expect? That we'd all remain friends?'

'Where were you standing when you saw me kill Josiah?'

'What?'

'Where were you standing?' Eva wanted those missing minutes broken down into minute detail, and Kristen was the only one who could do it for her.

'How am I supposed to remember something like that?'

'You'd think a moment like that would be burned in your brain.'

'This is an insane conversation. And if you don't leave now I'm going to call the cops.'

The threat didn't carry the weight it would have a few days ago. 'Go ahead. Call them. There are things I never discussed because I was protecting you. But now I'm wondering why I should keep quiet.'

The lines around Kristen's mouth and eyes hardened and for a moment she looked ready to call someone. 'What is this visit about?'

'I keep wondering about the night Josiah attacked me. The night you told us about the baby.'

'Shut up. I never told you anything like that.'

'A lot of details are hazy from that night. But that tidbit is crystal clear.'

'I don't have time for this.'

Eva glanced at Kristen's hand and the large ring on her engagement ring finger. 'You're getting married. That's nice.'

'So what if I am?'

'Your fiancé doesn't know about the baby.'

'There was no baby,' she said through gritted teeth.

Eva leaned in. 'I remember how you threw up every morning. How you cried to us about having Josiah's baby. You were terrified for the baby.'

Ice returned to her eyes. 'You've got the wrong girl, Eva. Maybe you were the one that was knocked up. Maybe in a drunken rage you killed Josiah when he threatened to tell your secret.'

The distortion unlocked something in her subconscious. 'I only had half a glass of wine that night.'

'I refilled your glass a half dozen times.'

'I kept pouring it out. I should have been sober but I felt groggy.'

'You drank more than you thought.'

Eva didn't have all the pieces but some tumbled into place enough for her to say, 'You set me up.'

Kristen's eyes narrowed. 'What are you talking about?'

'You knew Josiah was coming that night. You left me alone in the house because you knew what he'd do to me. Did you drug my wine?'

Her skin paled a fraction. 'Prison and time has made you insane.'

Eva didn't rise to the bait. 'Why would you set me up? I don't remember killing him. And over the years, as hard as I've tried to recall what happened, I can't. I'm starting to wonder now if I did kill him.'

'Get out of this building now!'

Kristen's voice rose higher than she intended and a neighbor opened his door. He was an old man, bald, dark, wearing a workout suit.

'Everything all right, Ms Hall?' he said.

Kristen chiseled a smile from her icy features. 'Just fine, Mr Gayton.'

His beady gaze darted between Kristen and Eva, and when it settled on Eva's tattered jeans and T-shirt, it hardened. 'I'm calling the cops.'

'No, don't!' Kristen said quickly. For the first time, Eva realized someone else feared the cops more than she. She'd struck at the heart of a nerve.

When the old man finally vanished, Kristen hissed, 'Get the hell out of my life. And if you breathe a word of any of this to anyone, I'll have my attorney bury you.'

'Someone is killing people we know. Someone is branding them with a four-pointed star.'

Kristen lifted a brow. 'Is that someone you?'

'Drugs and pain aren't clouding my memory or thoughts now. I see very clearly. The big question is am I looking at the killer?'

'Stay away from me or you will find out.'

Eva shook her head. 'Be careful, Kristen. Two of the three girls who testified against me are dead.'

The anger in her gaze wavered briefly. 'Is that a threat?'

'No. I'm just pointing out the pattern to you, like when we were in college. You remember how I could guess the test questions so well? I see a pattern and you and I are a part of it.'

'Stay away from me.' Kristen stormed back into her apartment.

Eva stood there a long moment, her grip on her knapsack strap so tight her hand ached. 'Don't count on it.'

Garrison parked at the Cross mansion an hour later. Built in the 1930s, the house's stone façade and heavy windows with overhangs gave it a gothic old-world look. A heavy front door with a wrought-iron door handle and knocker added to the heaviness.

When Garrison rang the bell he waited barely seconds before a maid opened the front door. He held out his badge. 'I'm Detective Garrison with the Alexandria Police Department. Is Mr Micah Cross available?'

Most people were taken aback when he showed up on their doorstep. People just didn't like talking to cops. But the maid didn't seem rattled. 'Please come inside. I'll see if he is available.'

Garrison was escorted into a living room furnished with Mission-style furniture, artwork that looked expensive and carpets that cost more than he made in a year. The room had a heavy feel that reminded him of a 1950s B movie.

Garrison moved toward the fireplace mantel. Above it hung a portrait of Darius Cross. His features were stern, his gaze hard. On the mantel sat a collection of photos.

Most of the pictures of Micah and Josiah appeared to have been taken at least twenty years ago. As he stared at the faces that were so identical, he realized the boys had been twins, something he'd not known.

Micah Cross appeared. Tall and slim, he had a pale complexion and dark brown hair. Glasses set off blue eyes and accentuated hollowed cheekbones. The pictures of Josiah in Eva's file had been of a young college kid, not a man in his early thirties. Still, even as a young man, Josiah's angry hardness made him appear older than Micah did now.

'Detective Garrison, is it?'

'Yes.' He pulled out his badge and held it out for Mr Cross to examine. 'Thank you for seeing me.'

Cross lifted his gaze from the badge. 'What can I do for you?'

'We're investigating the murder of Sara Miller. I believe you worked with Ms Miller on an ad campaign for Fairchild Advertising.'

He frowned. 'Ms Miller is dead?'

'Yes, sir.'

'How?' His voice sounded rough and drowning in emotion.

'I can't give any more details.'

'I had no idea.' His face tightened with grief.

Garrison stared at him, trying to gauge his genuineness. 'I'm sorry to be the one to tell you.'

Micah pushed a hand through his dark hair. 'She was such a lovely young woman. God, I'm really sorry to hear about Sara. I liked her. She was smart and very efficient.' He extended his hand toward the sofa, and when Garrison sat so did he. 'How can I help?'

'We're trying to piece together the last twenty-four to forty-eight hours leading up to her disappearance. According to her boss you two were scheduled to have dinner on Tuesday night.'

He steepled his fingers. 'Yes. Fairchild Advertising was making a big presentation to my board next week and she wanted to meet and make sure she'd covered all the creative bases.'

'Did she seem nervous or upset when you had dinner?'

'Not at all. It was business as usual.'

'Why the switch in advertising companies?'

'What made you ask that?'

'Mr Fairchild said that you contacted him about an ad campaign.'

'My father died eight months ago and now that I have complete control I've decided to change elements in the company. Father didn't embrace change and the company had grown very stagnant in the last five to ten years.'

'Since your brother died?'

'Basically. After Josiah died, Dad was never the same. In the ways of the old world, a son was everything to a man.'

'Where was he born?'

'Kentucky. In the mountains. He was raised by his aunt and uncle. Wasn't a happy home. He met my mother when they were young. Father did just about anything to make money. And he made a lot of it.'

'Where is your mother now?'

A hint of sadness darkened his eyes. 'She passed away when Josiah and I were thirteen.'

'Must have been hard.'

'We all had each other.'

'Illness?'

'A car accident.'

Garrison let a moment's pause settle between them. 'I've read a report on your brother's death.'

Cross arched a brow. 'Do you always dig so deeply into the lives of people you question during a homicide investigation?'

'Not generally. Can you tell me about what happened the night your brother died?'

'Why is this relevant?'

'Humor me. Please.'

Micah shrugged. 'I was still at school in Washington, D.C. Even to this day I know only what my father and the police reported to me.'

'You didn't go to Price.'

'No. Father believed it best that Josiah and I went to separate schools. Twins, especially identical twins, get lumped together a lot. He wanted us to be individuals.'

'You ever visit Price?'

'Sure. I even met the infamous Eva Rayburn.'

'Really? What was your impression of her?'

'A nice kid. Quiet. Hard-working. To make extra money she helped the sorority house's maid clean. The day I met her she and another girl were cleaning the house after a big party.'

'You two speak much?'

'Just the customary greeting. And I'll admit I was curious about her. Josiah had mentioned the fact that she'd beat him in a school-wide debate a couple of weeks earlier. He wasn't happy about it. Josiah hated to lose.'

238

'That wasn't mentioned in the file.' Garrison knew Micah was holding back.

'No, I doubt it was.'

Darius had been careful to sanitize anything that pointed to his son's temper. 'What did your father tell you about your brother's death?'

A furrow creased the smooth, pale skin of his forehead. 'Again, how does this relate to Ms Miller?'

'Bear with me.'

Cross shrugged. 'Father called me weeping the night Josiah died.' He drew in a breath. 'Dad didn't rest until justice was served.'

Garrison checked his notes, flipping pages and pretending to read. 'Eva Rayburn confessed to killing your brother after he attacked her.'

Cross nodded. 'I remember her testimony. But the rape was never proven. In fact, my father's attorney uncovered evidence that they were having an affair.'

'Were they?'

'I don't know.'

'You were at the trial?'

'No. My father sent me to Europe during the trial.' He sighed. 'I do know she's out of jail and back in Alexandria.'

'How do you know that?'

'Father had put in a request with the bureau of prisons to notify us when she was released. As the victim's family we had a right to know. They told me she had moved back to town.'

'How long have you known?'

'They told me days after she returned.'

'You must know that Ms Miller was one of the girls that testified against Eva.'

He raised a brow. 'She never said a word about that to me.'

'You don't remember her at the trial?'

'I barely remember the trial at all. I was in Europe at the time, remember?' Micah Cross was either a good actor or a great liar.

'Did you know Sara went to Price with your brother?'

'I did not. We never discussed colleges.'

'You know Ms Rayburn is in Alexandria but you didn't know Sara Miller went to Price?'

'That's right.'

'What did you talk to Ms Miller about?'

'Business. And the fact that she was leaving for Fairchild's New York offices in a day or two and wouldn't be back for a few weeks.'

'Did your brother have a history of violence?'

'He did. Father was good about hushing it up, but other girls made claims against Josiah. The judge didn't have access to that information, but just looking at the list of Ms Rayburn's injuries, it was clear Josiah had lost his temper with her.'

'He ever lose his temper with you?'

Darkness settled in his gaze. 'Again, what does any of this have to do with Sara Miller's death?'

'Where were you two nights ago?'

'At a fund-raiser. Surrounded by fifty of my closest friends. Would you like a list?'

'I'd appreciate that.'

'I'll have my secretary e-mail you a list.'

'Thanks.'

'My brother was murdered, as was a colleague of mine. Why do I feel like a suspect?'

Garrison grinned. 'I don't know.'

Humming, Lou sat in the darkened basement in front of the fire that crackled and spit in the hearth. The flames danced and swayed, creating a hypnotic spell too hard to resist. By the firelight, Lou glanced down at the photo of the infant boy, so red-faced and prunelike in his first hours of life.

Stroking the image, Lou remembered the faint scent of milk that had clung to the boy and the way he gurgled when he'd eaten his fill and was ready for a nap.

'I lost you too young. Too young. And I hate them for taking you from me. My sweet, sweet boy.'

Lou's weary eyes glistened with tears that pooled and spilled down cheeks made ruddy by the hot fire. 'But we're going to show them all they should have left us alone. They shouldn't have taken you from me.'

Lou glanced up at the flames. The schedule was moving much faster than originally anticipated. The hope had been to draw out this process so that those that remained had time to worry and wonder if they were next. But the schedule had had to be changed because that other woman had planned an extended trip. Selfish bitch. So like all those sorority girls to do what they pleased even if it meant stepping on someone else's toes.

Two had died. But there were more that needed to pay. More that had to suffer the pain of the brand and feel the sharp tip of the knife.

Perhaps if they all suffered and died, perhaps then Lou

could finally release the pain that had haunted her for far too many years. Perhaps . . .

Garrison found Macy LaPorta behind her desk at Firehouse 20. She'd long since been promoted to administration and could have left behind the shift work, but she'd chosen to work ten hours a week in one of the station houses in her district. She liked keeping current, liked remembering what it felt like to battle the blaze head-on.

He knocked on her door and she glanced up from a pile of paperwork. The frown creasing her brow deepened. 'What can I do for you?'

Garrison moved toward her desk and dropped a file square in the center. 'I'd like you to have a look at pictures taken of a fire.'

She arched a brow, studying him a beat before she dropped her gaze to the file. 'This fire happened almost ten years ago.'

'I know.' He gave her a recap of the case.

'I'm not sure what you want from me on this one.'

'I honestly don't know either. It's just the more I read the case file, the more I question the results.'

She pursed her lips as she flipped the pages. 'Point of origin was near the fireplace.'

'That's what the report says. I want to know your thoughts after you've had a chance to read the file.'

'Do you think this fire is linked to the one on Monday night?'

'I don't know.' He'd been going nonstop since Monday and, despite a few extra hours of sleep, fatigue nipped at him like a hungry animal. 'Just have a look.'

'I'll see what I can do.'

Garrison nodded his thanks and headed out of the station house. As he slid into the driver's seat his cell rang. 'Garrison.'

'It's Vic Jones, with the Bureau of Prisons. You called about Eva Rayburn.'

'I did.' Garrison closed his door and loosened his tie. 'She's moved into my city. And we've had a couple of murders that I think might be linked to her.'

A chair squeaked as the man seemed to lean forward. 'She a suspect?'

'Not now. Two of the women who testified against her are dead. What can you tell me about her time in prison?'

'She was a model prisoner. Took every class she could and read every book she could get her hands on. Worked in the prison library and tutored other inmates in reading and math. Kept to herself.'

'Did she have any visitors?'

'None. Which is unusual. Most of our inmates have someone that visits.'

'Letters?'

'None sent to her, but in the beginning she wrote her share of letters.'

'To whom?'

Papers rustled in the background. 'To the same three women: Lisa Black, Sara Miller and Kristen Hall.'

Grim tension fisted in his gut. 'I assume they never responded.'

'Not one word.'

'What did she write them about?'

'She kept asking for more details about the night Josiah

243

Cross died. She wanted to remember killing him but she couldn't.'

The lunch crowd had slowed. Eva had maybe three tables left, which she expected would clear out in the next fifteen or twenty minutes. As she loaded the chocolate dessert on a tray, she checked her watch. By three she and King could take a break before the dinner rush.

She hefted the tray and moved to the table of four women. They'd ordered a couple of rounds of drinks and no one at the table felt any pain. She'd overheard one say it was a divorce party for the tall brunette on the inside left side of the booth.

But like all women, they wanted just a bite of dessert. Hence, the one piece of cake and four spoons. She moved toward the table, which suddenly erupted in laughter. Eva set the cake in the table's center and laid out clean spoons and napkins in front of each woman.

Smiling, she turned. A quick check on table six and she'd take a break. But as she turned, she noted a man had been seated at table eight. Crap.

Moving toward her newest customer, she raised her gaze. Her greeting died on her lips when their gazes connected. For a moment she imagined a ghost stood in front of her. Time had leaned out his face. His hair was shorter and dark horn-rimmed glasses covered sharp blue eyes. The startling familiar features jerked her breath away and when she did claw in air, she spoke before she thought. 'Josiah.'

'Micah,' he said.

Her mind tripped, stumbled and then righted. She

realized the sharp blue eyes held curiosity and sadness, not hate and anger. 'Sorry. You caught me by surprise.'

A shy smile lifted the edge of his lips. 'Sorry, Eva.'

'It's been a long time.'

His gaze traveled briefly over her frame. 'You look great.'

That made her laugh. Micah had been as kind as Josiah was cruel. 'I smell like the day's special and I think I'm actually wearing some of it.'

Absently, he picked up the salt shaker and set it back down with precision next to the pepper. 'You wear both well.'

An unexpected softening left her feeling exposed. His family had brutalized her and stolen so much of her life. Only a fool felt anything more than fear for this family. 'So what brings you here?'

'The cops told me about Lisa and Sara.'

'Very sad.'

He knitted his long fingers together and rested them on the table. 'I'd think you'd still hate them both.'

'I carried the hate for a long time, but it just got to be too heavy.' She glanced around, not comfortable discussing any of her past, especially here, where no one knew about her. 'I've been back about six months.'

'I wished you'd called me and told me.'

That caught her short. 'Would have been kind of weird, don't you think? Considering the history.'

His expression darkened. 'I always wanted to tell you how sorry I was. I never realized Josiah would ever go so far.' The last word held an edge of anger that she'd never heard from him before. 'I should have seen it coming. I should have known he was up to something.'

There'd been a million warning signs of Josiah's behavior and they'd been ignored or covered every step of the way.

He tapped his fingertips together. 'I was his twin. At times, I could just about read his mind. I knew he had a thing for you.'

She remembered how Josiah stared at her when he visited the house. His gaze would linger so long her skin would itch. She glanced around and, realizing none of her customers needed her, she sat across from Micah. 'Why me?'

'You were smart, strong and you were helping Kristen succeed. The stronger she became, the less she needed Josiah. He resented that.'

Anger cut through her. 'Why didn't you ever say anything?'

'Father sent me away during the trial.'

'What about before or after? Your father's lawyers made it look like I provoked the whole thing.'

'My silence is what I feel worst about. That's why I'm here. To say I'm sorry.'

She shook her head. 'Micah, "sorry" sounds slim and meager.'

'I know, but I'm truly sorry. I'd do anything to make it up to you.'

Bobby rushed down the stairs and bolted into the room. For the first time the kid seemed filled with pure joy. For an instant she marveled. He was acting like a kid. A strong urge to protect Bobby welled inside her. She would safeguard what she could of his childhood.

His close proximity to Micah sent tension coiling

around her chest. Micah had done nothing to her, but he was a Cross and as her mother used to say, 'The apple doesn't fall far from the tree.'

When the boy darted into the safety of the kitchen she finally could say, 'The best thing you can do for me is just leave King's and never come back.'

'I want to make it up to you.'

'That's impossible.' A customer yelled 'Waitress' and she gratefully glanced toward the group of women who now looked anxious to pay and leave. 'Micah, I've got to get back to work.'

Before he could respond, she moved to the table of women. She barely registered what they said. Instead, she was aware of Micah's gaze on her. It seemed to bore into her and leave her skin tingling with worry and fear.

Mindlessly, she handed the women the check and waited as they argued over who was going to pay. When one woman finally pressed a credit card into her hand, she smiled and turned.

Micah had left.

She prayed she never saw him again, but deep in her heart she sensed the Cross family wasn't finished with her.

Chapter 13

Angie was running late when she arrived at Branford's Coffee Shop. Another late night. A little too much wine to block out feelings that haunted her. And she ended up with another morning that was too short on time. She'd not had breakfast and now that she was out of court she was starving.

Bells jingled above her head as she dashed through the front entrance past packed tables to the front counter. A tall, slim man with blond hair, ice-blue eyes and pale pock-marked skin smiled at her. 'Do you suppose you can cut your day any closer?'

'Brad.' She dug in her huge Prada purse and fished until she found her wallet. She slapped a ten on the counter. 'I'll get the usual.'

'Afternoon, Ms Carlson.' He lifted a coffeepot, filled a to-go cup and then dumped two sugars into the hot brew. 'So what got you this time?'

'Don't ask. And instead of a ham sandwich, just make it a plain bagel and toss in a ginger ale.'

'Ginger ale? You mock cola drinkers.'

'Today, I take back every smart-ass comment I've ever uttered about cola drinkers.' Just the smell of the coffee sent her stomach tumbling. She'd not have bought a coffee at all if he'd not poured it.

248

He nested the lid on top of the cup. 'You feeling all right?'

Angie wrinkled her nose. 'Just got a bug. I'll live.'

Brad nodded. 'I hear there's one going around.'

She smiled. 'I heard that too.'

'I'll set you right up. My mom says extra ice and the carbonation are a sure cure for a bad stomach.'

'Bless you.'

He turned to fill her soda. She checked her watch and cursed that she'd overslept. What the hell ate at her lately? Control seemed to be slipping from her fingers at every corner.

Brad glanced back and set her soda on the counter. 'Fresh bagels are in the back. Be right back.'

'You're a god.' Angie slumped down on an empty counter stool and took a sip of the soda. Her stomach protested then eased a fraction.

'Maybe it's the hair of the dog that you need. Sodas are for kids.' The comment came from the man sitting on the stool beside her.

Surprised, she glanced up, feeling defensive and ready to tell him to back off. But the sheepish smile on his face stopped her short. He was cute. Shoulder-length brown hair with auburn highlights, an open-collared button-down and long slim hands that wrapped around a coffee mug. 'Thanks for the advice.'

He shrugged. 'I'm not one to throw stones. I've been there a lot myself lately.'

She sipped her soda. 'What do you mean?'

He winked and dropped his voice a notch. 'Hung over.'

Angie faced him, trying to ignore the way her stomach

groaned at the slightest movement. 'I'm not hung over. I've got a bug.'

'Right. Right. What's it called? The vodka virus?' He pretended to study her. 'Or the white wine syndrome.'

She glanced back toward the kitchen door hoping Brad would bring her bagel so she could leave. She wasn't sure why she should care what a stranger thought about her, but she did. 'Very funny.'

'It's no crime to drink a little too much now and again.'

'You're wrong about me.'

It troubled her that he had cut right to her darkest secret. *Secret*. The word put such a torrid spin on everything. She didn't have anything as tawdry as a *secret*. It wasn't like she was an alcoholic. She'd had a few too many glasses of wine last night. And maybe the night before.

The man sipped his coffee. 'I do that too.'

Brad appeared at the dinner bar with a paper bag. 'Here ya go.'

Angie glanced at the ten on the counter, no longer willing to wait for change. 'Thanks, Brad. See you tomorrow.'

'I'll be here.'

The stranger held up his cup to her. Small lines creased the corners of his eyes as he smiled. 'You have a good day. Remember what I said about the hair of the dog.'

Angie snatched up the bag and started to leave. She walked two steps before the need to defend her actions took over. 'Just for the record, Mr . . .'

He set his cup down. 'Walters. Jim Walters.'

The guy didn't look like a Jim Walters. The name sounded too plain for him, but who was she to question a decision his parents made well over thirty years ago. 'Well,

Mr Walters, I do not have an issue.' She lowered her voice. 'I am not hung over. I have a bug.'

'I hear ya.' His eyes twinkled in a way that charmed and irritated. It had been a very long time since someone had looked past the tailored suits and the schoolteacher bun to see her as a woman. Feminine pride rose up. Just her luck it would happen on a day when she felt like crap. 'It's okay. Really.'

She leaned toward him, ready to argue her point again, when she realized she must look like the biggest fool. 'Okay, fine. I had a little wine last night.' The truth sounded too harsh so she softened it with an innocent lie. 'I settled a big case last night and I did have a few too many with my partners.' That was a lie. She drank almost the entire bottle alone in her house.

Walters winked. 'Like I said, the hair of the dog will fix what's ailing you.'

For a brief second the walls dropped. She was so tired of pretense and arguing shaky cases. 'Honestly, hemlock sounds better.'

He chuckled. 'Aspirin and ginger ale. Pain relief and hydrate. You'll be as good as new by dinner.'

A faint smile curved the edge of her lips. 'If I live that long.'

He picked up his cup, pausing by his lips. 'If you do live until dinner, would you like to break bread with me?' He sipped his coffee, so relaxed and confident.

'Did you ask me out on a date?' Angie didn't hide her shock.

Walters set his cup down softly on the saucer. 'Yeah, why not?'

Automatically, she shuffled through her brain trying to remember the last time she'd been asked out, couldn't remember and then immediately came up with six reasons why she didn't want to go out with him.

'Let me guess,' he said easily. 'You're a lawyer.'

'You can hear the debate in my head right now, can't you?'

'Loud and clear.'

'Sorry. I'm just out of practice.' But before one more objection could rear its head, she heard herself saying, 'Sure. Dinner sounds good.'

His impish grin managed to ease her hangover. He rose. 'Great. Seven?'

She tipped her head back so that she could maintain eye contact. 'Perfect.'

'Now are you going to tell me your name?'

Laughter bubbled inside her, clanging against the insides of her throbbing head. 'Angie Carlson.' She pulled a business card from her pocket and handed it to him. 'You can text me later with a place.'

He studied the card, flicking the edge with his index finger. 'I'll text you later, Ms Angelina R. Carlson, Esquire.'

'Great.'

Beer sloshed all over Eva's hand, making her curse and snap the tap closed. Annoyed she'd zoned out, she set two overflowing beers in front of a couple of customers, so hard the beer again sloshed on her hands.

'Whoa,' a guy said. He was a regular named Doug. He looked like a thinner version of John Belushi. 'What's eating you?'

His buddy Pete grinned. 'Must be that time of the month.'

The look Eva shot Pete and Doug wiped the smiles from their lips, however the twinkle in their eyes remained.

'Ah, come on, Eva, don't be such a sourpuss. We got wives. We get it.'

Doug and Pete were basically good guys and they tipped well. She sure wasn't going to get into it with them. 'Right, I'm the Wicked Witch. I get it. Better I retreat now before I explode or something.' To soften her entire demeanor, she gave each a fresh beer. 'On the house.'

Without a word she turned her attention to the crate of clean glasses waiting to be restocked. She started pulling glasses from the dishwasher and stacking them on the glass shelf behind the bar.

Lisa and Sara's deaths. Micah's visit. Seeing Kristen. Life kept dragging her back to those missing moments when Josiah died. Two weeks ago, she would have fought the journey back to the past as she chanted 'Eyes forward.' But she now believed that unless she sketched in those missing minutes, the future was in peril.

'So what's a gal got to do to get a beer around here?' Sally's gravelly voice had Eva turning back toward the bar.

Despite her mood, Eva smiled. 'For you, anything. How's it going?'

Silver bracelets dangled from Sally's slim wrist as she brushed a strand of hair from her face. 'Hanging tough. But you don't look so good.'

Eva set a soda in front of Sally. 'Long day. You want the regular?'

'Thanks, doll.' Sally sipped her cola. 'Tell Mama Sally about it.'

The edge of Eva's mouth tipped into a smile. She could count on one hand the number of people she liked. Sally numbered among them. She punched the order into the computer. 'I'm doing fine.'

The sun had etched deep lines into Sally's face, giving it a sagelike quality. 'Yeah, and I'm a rock star diva. Where's my guitar?'

Eva smiled wearily, so tired of not trusting and of keeping her past hidden. She'd wanted to push it aside, but the old wounds had been clawed open and wouldn't be ignored. 'I saw a friend from college today as well as a guy I knew back then.'

Sally cocked a brow. 'Ah, college. I'm still not too old to have forgotten that. That's the kind of encounter that can go either way. Good or bad?'

'Not well.' She picked up a rag and started to wipe the counter. She wished she could wipe the past as easily as a spill. 'Real bad.'

Sally pushed her drink aside and leaned in. 'Want to tell me about it?'

The words danced on the edge of Eva's tongue. 'It's a can of nasty worms.'

'I've never run from nasty. Really, kid, whatever you say ain't gonna scare me away.'

'I've heard that before.'

Sally's eyes hardened with startling intensity. 'Not from me.'

Eva stared into the sharp blue-gray eyes and knew Sally was no quitter. Eva sensed she could toss her worst secrets out on the table and Sally wouldn't flinch. 'I went to talk to this woman about something that happened in college.'

'That's old news, isn't it?'

'You'd think, but the past has a way of hanging on sometimes.'

'Tell me about it.'

'If I had a bit of common sense I'd have left well enough alone.'

'But you don't have any sense,' she said, teasing.

'I'm all out. Anyway, I tried to talk to her and discovered she's kind of rewritten history. She says what happened was all my fault.'

'Was it?'

Eva hesitated and then answered truthfully, 'I blamed myself for a long time but not anymore.' To this day she could still not remember killing Josiah, but she knew she must have acted in self-defense. 'I didn't ask for anything that happened to me.'

Sally's voice grew very soft. 'What happened?'

She'd never talked about the rape. There'd been one officer who'd been kind, but once Darius had heard about the kindness, he had the officer removed from the case. From then on she'd received no counseling. 'I was raped.'

Sally silently stared, her expression unreadable. 'I'm sorry.'

If Sally had shown pity, as her sister had, Eva would have completely lost it. Still, Sally's silence charged the air with emotions that without warning triggered tears she'd fought to control for so long. A tear spilled down her cheek and she swiped it. 'God, it's been over a decade. You'd think I'd be over it all by now.'

'It's a hard thing to let go of, honey.'

'I'd really believed that I'd stowed away the trauma of

that night. It wasn't my fault. I didn't ask for anything. But talking to Kristen today . . . I felt violated all over again.'

'How so?'

'She called me a liar. She said I asked for what happened.'

Sally's brows knotted. 'Why would she be so cruel?'

'I got a little too close to her own secrets.'

'Secrets?' Sally remained silent, but she leaned forward slightly as if waiting for a punch line. And as much as the whole story begged to be told, Eva couldn't.

'Hey, I shouldn't have mentioned anything.'

Sally shrugged. 'Don't get yourself in a twist, kid.'

Eva ran a shaky hand through her hair. 'I shouldn't have gone to see her.'

'Why did you?'

'Because college acquaintances of ours were murdered. I thought she might know something.'

'Did you learn anything?'

'Nothing I can prove. And she's about to leave for New York and make a whole new life for herself.'

Sally sipped her cola. 'Enough of the past. What have you done for Eva today?'

'What do you mean?'

'Have you heard from the scholarship committee?'

'They turned me down.'

'That makes no sense. You're as smart as a whip.'

'Smart isn't always enough.' Eva grabbed a nearly empty bowl of peanuts, dumped out the contents and refilled it.

Bobby pushed through the kitchen door and brought a box of napkins to Eva. Cleaned up, with fresh clothes that King had dug out of his attic, the boy looked like a different kid. 'King said to bring you napkins and to tell you I'm going to feed the kitten again.'

Eva smiled. 'Hey, I could use another bottle of olives. And there's open tuna in the fridge for the kitten.'

Bobby nodded. 'I'll get it right away.'

As he turned to go, Sally said, 'And who is this new guy?'

Bobby glanced back at Sally nervously, but instead of stopping to speak to her, he scurried back into the kitchen.

Eva frowned, suddenly remembering her mother's lessons on politeness. She felt as if she should bring Bobby back and have him speak to Sally, but he wasn't her child and she sure wasn't any kind of mother. And Sally was a social worker at heart and very likely to call Social Services if she knew about Eva's record. 'Sorry about that. He forgets his manners.'

Sally shrugged, her gaze still on the door through which the boy disappeared. 'No sweat. Whose is he?'

Eva liked Sally but didn't know her well enough to know how she'd react about Bobby. 'He's King's foster son.'

'He's cute. Reminds me of my son.'

That shocked her. 'You never told me you had a son.'

'Yeah, he's a great kid. All grown up. Maybe you can meet him sometime.'

The text from Jim Walters hit Angie's phone right at six P.M. She'd been knee-deep in briefs and still nursing a headache, but her stomach had eased and she felt human again. When she saw his name pop up on the phone she smiled.
Still on for dinner?

Angie texted back. Seeing as I survived, yes. Where?

O'Malley's.

Great. Time?

Seven.

Seven was early for her and she had too much work to knock off by seven. But O'Malley's was right around the corner and she reasoned she could have a quick bite with Jim and then head back to work. It would be a late night, but that beat sitting home alone.

It's a date. Smiling, she set the phone down and tried to concentrate on her brief. The words were a boring jumble and she ached to just toss the whole thing and get outside.

The hour ticked by slowly. Angie kept trying not to glance at the clock but she did. By ten minutes to seven she grabbed her coat and headed out the front door.

She reached O'Malley's right at seven and felt a little bit like a loser because of the excitement that swirled in her belly. She didn't want to care, didn't want to feel a tingle in her muscles. She wanted to be cool and uncaring because she knew in her bones that no matter how hard she tried, everyone always left her.

'Don't do this,' she muttered as she pushed through the front door of the restaurant. Music and laughter greeted her. 'All you got is right now.'

She glanced around the room and didn't see Jim. Pushing aside a stab of disappointment, she moved toward the bar. She chose a seat at the end, and setting her purse on the bar, she ordered a glass of white wine. What was she doing here? She should be back at the office getting her latest brief written. Yet here she sat. Alone waiting for a guy who very well might not show.

The bartender set her wineglass in front of her. Thanking him, she took a sip, refusing to look toward the door. A few minutes passed. Ten minutes passed. She neared the bottom of her glass, certain that she was a fool. Checking her watch, she noted he ran twenty minutes late – if she'd not been stood up. She pulled a ten from her purse, handed it to the bartender and stood.

Angie had stepped out in the street when she heard her name.

'Angie!' Jim's voice sounded rushed and breathless.

Her heart flipped and she turned, trying to play it cool. 'Hey!'

He jogged up to her. 'Sorry I'm late. I got caught up at work. Never fails if I want to get out early, all hell breaks loose.'

Relief washed over her. 'Hey, no problem.'

'Were you just leaving?'

'I thought we might have gotten our wires crossed.' Angie stared up into his eyes. He had nice eyes. Kind eyes. And he smelled of the faintest trace of aftershave. She'd not noticed it this morning and realized he'd slapped a little on before their date.

'No. And I'm glad you waited as long as you did. I'm not sure I'd have been so patient. I hate late people.'

'Why don't we just start over?'

'It's a deal.' He opened the door to O'Malley's. They bypassed the bar and chose a table in the corner. He held her chair out for her, which she found wonderfully old-fashioned and charming.

They ordered drinks and soon she found herself relaxing and chatting easily. The guy was so easy to be with. He asked questions, and when she answered he stared right into her eyes as if no one else in the world existed. Angie hadn't realized how starved she was of this.

'So do you have family in the area?'

Even that question didn't ruin her mood. 'My parents passed away a long time ago. My sister lives on the West Coast.' Truth be told, they'd not spoken in almost a decade. Angie had tried to find her sister, but all her searches had ended up empty-handed.

'Where on the West Coast?'

Angie was good at dodging – maybe that's why she'd chosen law. 'Oregon. Portland.'

'What does she do?'

'She's in computer science.' Angie had always pictured her sister writing intricate programs and solving the problems of the world.

'Sounds interesting.'

'More interesting than the law.'

He reached forward and pushed a stray blond strand out of her eyes. 'Hey, you want to get out of here? I know a great place for coffee.'

His touch sent bolts of energy shooting through her muscles. Screw the briefs. She'd work late tomorrow. 'Sounds good.'

Grinning in a way that caused her stomach to flutter, he kissed her. Before she knew it, she followed him willingly into the night.

Chapter 14

The short woman had dark hair peppered with white, and dark half glasses, which she now peered over. 'Can I help you?'

Garrison pulled out his badge and introduced them. 'I called ahead and the Dean of Admissions agreed to see me.'

'He's in his office. I'll let him know you are here. Must be something to bring him in on a Saturday.' She vanished down a cinder block hallway and reappeared seconds later with a short balding man in tow. The dean buttoned his jacket as he came toward the front desk. 'Detectives. I'm David Potts. Please come back.'

They followed and soon found themselves in an office.

Potts motioned for them to sit in the twin chairs in front of his desk. 'I pulled the school records for Lisa, Sara and Eva as you requested and was reviewing them. Lisa and Sara came from good families and both earned good grades. Smart kids.'

Garrison flipped through Lisa's file. Her record appeared impressive. 'Played tennis in addition to her sorority responsibilities.'

'And played tennis like a pro. I remember her. She was a sweet girl. Naïve and silly at times but a good kid.'

'And Sara?'

'Another smart one,' the dean said, handing her file to Garrison. 'She liked to ride horses.' He pulled off his glasses. 'I just don't understand why anyone would want to kill either woman. Both went on to live very successful lives.'

Garrison sat back in his chair studying Lisa's young face. She'd been much heavier in college. And her hair was dark and curly. She'd been a far cry from the woman she'd become.

'I've met Eva Rayburn.' Garrison didn't offer an opinion. He wanted Potts's perspective on her.

'Yes, I imagine as a policeman you would know of her.' Potts didn't hide his disgust. 'She caused quite a scandal. Fund-raising and admissions turned into a nightmare for several years.'

'What can you tell me about her?' Garrison was very curious about Eva. He wanted to know who she'd been before Josiah had raped her.

'Eva Rayburn scored off the charts and those scores earned her a full scholarship. In fact, the school paid Eva a stipend just so she would come to Price.' He opened the yearbook to a photo collage page and pointed to a page with four girls. Arm-in-arm, they all smiled into the camera. 'I remember she was a bit of a crusader. Once she joined the sorority house, she got them to volunteer at an animal shelter and a day care center.'

'Anything else?'

'The schoolwork came very easy for her and she skated through her courses. The girl could have done anything. If she'd stayed on track she'd have graduated in a couple of years.'

'Who's in this picture?' He pointed to the fourth

woman. She wore a bright smile and had wrapped her arm around Eva.

'Kristen Hall.'

'She appears to be good friends with Eva.'

'I suppose.'

'What's that mean? They'd have been unlikely friends? Do you have contact information for Kristen?'

Potts turned to his computer. 'I should. She's a generous donor.' He tapped a few keys. 'Here it is. Kristen Hall.' He wrote down her address and phone number and pushed the paper across the desk to Garrison.

Garrison glanced at the note then folded the paper in half, making the crease extra sharp. 'Lisa, Sara and Kristen were from the same world. You consider it odd they'd pull Eva into their circle?'

'At the time I didn't give it much consideration, but after your call yesterday I did a little digging. I'd forgotten that Kristen was on academic probation. And Lisa's grades had slipped the end of her junior year. After Eva joined the sorority their grades shot up.'

'How much?'

'A lot. Kristen wanted into a top graduate school and if her grades didn't skyrocket her senior year, her chances would have been nil. Suddenly, she befriends the smartest girl in the school. And her grades rise.'

'Were they cheating?' Garrison said.

'*Cheat*'s a strong word. Nothing was ever proven. I like to think Eva tutored them a great deal. But after the murder and the fire, who can say?'

'What about Josiah Cross?'

Potts frowned. 'Smart. Ambitious. Competitive. He

ranked top in the school academically until Eva arrived. He dated Kristen.'

'Was he capable of rape?'

Potts pulled off his glasses. For a moment he didn't answer. 'Before his father died, I'd have avoided that question. Now I can say freely that Josiah proved to be a handful. Other girls complained, but the problems always went away. We were very glad to see him graduating in the spring.'

'Any girls you remember who filed complaints against Josiah?'

'Price purges our security records as soon as a student graduates.'

Garrison held on to his temper with a white-knuckled grip. The school knew they'd had a problem with Cross and had chosen to look the other way. 'You know guys like Cross don't stop. They just get meaner and smarter and keep hurting.'

Potts straightened. 'Once they leave the campus they are not my problem.'

'No, they become mine.'

The detectives left the school. Once they were in their car, Malcolm said, 'So Eva, the brain child, gets raped and convicted of manslaughter. Her friends abandon her. She gets out of jail then decides to return to Alexandria. Within months of her arrival, Lisa and Sara are dead. She'd be smart enough to pull off and cover up a few murders.'

Garrison frowned, knowing Malcolm made sense. But he didn't believe Eva had killed those women. 'I want to talk to Kristen Hall.'

*

Micah Cross chose Torpedo Factory Art Center on Union Street in Old Town Alexandria for their meeting place. The Torpedo Factory had been a bomb factory years ago and now had been subdivided into over eight tiny glass cubicles that housed artists from all around the region.

Though the aisleways bustled this time of day, almost all of the visitors were tourists. Most were tired, hungry and didn't care about a single man studying the art in the individual shop windows. If perchance someone recognized him, he could simply say he was shopping for art. He loved art and no one would doubt the explanation.

Micah always thought about the angles, options and scenarios. Like a chess player, he tried to stay one step ahead, a trait he'd learned in his father's house. To avoid the wrath of Darius or Josiah's cruelty, he had to plan ahead. Habits died hard.

He stood in front of a crystal sculptor's booth staring at the vases, paperweights and plates. The pieces were all molded out of highly polished glass and caught the midday light, refracting it into a rainbow of colors. The artisan glanced up several times from her register, noting that he was studying her work. Finally, the third time she looked up, she moved around her small counter toward him.

That was his cue to smile and move on to the next vendor.

He wandered from booth to booth until he came across one with an OUT TO LUNCH sign on the door. The vendor's sign promised the store would reopen at two, in fifteen minutes. That gave him the time he needed.

'Lovely, isn't it?' The familiar voice behind him had him stiffening but he didn't turn.

He leaned deeper over the display case, not moving a fraction toward the speaker. Anger dripped from his words. 'I told you to be careful.'

'I am being careful. No one knows anything.'

'I don't like being questioned in a murder investigation.' That was a lie. His body had hummed with excitement as he'd talked to Garrison; he'd run scenarios wondering how he'd have done the deed and then covered it up.

Soft laughter followed. 'You like all this, don't you?'

'No.'

'Of course you do. I can see the way your hands tremble even now. Why did you visit King's? Did you apologize for the sins of your father and brother or did you go to see her because it gave you a secret thrill?'

'That's not —'

'Spare me. I know the real you.'

Micah tried to keep his gaze on the crystal, tried to be discreet, but he found he had to turn and look this monster in the eyes.

Only, when he turned, he discovered he was alone again.

Garrison and Malcolm arrived at Kristen's condo located on the top floor of a chic building constructed of sleek glass and steel and complicated by all the amenities a young wealthy professional expected. Garrison pressed the ringer.

High heels clicked across as a stone floor and seconds later she snapped open the front door. Her entire demeanor reflected impatience and anger. 'My bags are in the front hall. You can carry them to the car and I'll be down in a few minutes.'

Garrison stood for a split second and stared. The

woman was tall and her black slim-cut dress accentuated a narrow waist and full breasts. Red hair was styled into a flawless chignon and large diamonds winked from her ears and from the brooch on her shoulder.

He pulled out his badge. 'We're not with the limo service. We're from the Alexandria Police Department. I'm Detective Garrison and this is my partner, Detective Kier.'

For a moment she stared at them as if they'd lost their minds. 'Police? I didn't call the police.'

'No, ma'am. We've come to ask you a couple of questions.'

'What kind of questions?' The more he stared at her the more flaws he saw. The icy green of her eyes had a brittle edge and her manicured fingers were a bit too sharp for his tastes. 'We'd like to talk to you about Lisa Black and Sara Miller.'

She stared at them again as if gauging her words carefully before she spoke. 'I don't have much time. I'm catching a plane.'

'It shouldn't take too long.' Garrison's hackles rose.

'Fine. Sure. Come in.' She stepped aside.

The room projected style. Whitewashed wood, blues and yellows and too many ruffles. It all looked French, but Garrison wouldn't swear to it.

Kristen closed the front door and folded her arms over her chest. A neatly manicured finger tapped her arm. 'What do you need?'

Garrison didn't rush. She could miss her damn plane for all he cared. 'When did you speak to Lisa last?'

She raised a plucked brow but showed no signs of sadness. 'I read about her in the paper. Tragic. I haven't seen her lately. I did see her at our five-year reunion a few years ago. But not since.'

'You haven't spoken or communicated in any way?'

'No. I'm not sure what this has to do with anything. Just because a couple of my friends from college died doesn't mean it connects to me.'

'A couple of friends? I mentioned Lisa Black had died but not Sara Miller.'

'Well, I know about Sara Miller.'

'From?'

'Eva Rayburn came by yesterday. She went to school with us and served time in jail for killing her boyfriend. Very unpleasant visit.'

Garrison stiffened. 'Really?'

'I didn't listen to her ranting. In her own twisted way she's trying to pin what happened a decade ago on me.'

'In what way?'

'She's turning the facts all around to suit her. She likely feels guilty for taking a life.'

Garrison tamped down a surge of temper. 'I thought you two were friends in college.'

A hint of laughter twinkled in her eyes. 'That's a bit of a stretch. She served a purpose.'

'Which was?'

'She's some kind of genius. She was a few years younger than us, but kept up with the schoolwork so easily. She had a knack for outguessing the teachers and what would be in the tests. She was into probabilities and ratios and said she could predict patterns based on that kind of stuff. I don't know exactly how it worked, but it wasn't cheating and it was very useful.'

'So she was not a friend?'

'I let her hang out with our group. But she wasn't really a friend.'

Malcolm shifted his stance. He said nothing, but the slight movement telegraphed his annoyance toward this woman. 'What happened the night of the fire?'

'Lisa, Sara and I went to get more wine. It was our last night on campus. Eva was still on the pledge so she had to stay behind and clean up. She was glad to stay and it wasn't until later that I understood why.'

'Why?'

'Josiah Cross. My boyfriend. They were having an affair.'

'That came out at the trial.' Garrison kept his tone neutral.

'Don't be fooled by her. She's very clever and gets what she wants. She wanted Josiah and she got him.'

'Did you know about the affair?'

'I did. And I told Josiah to break it off. He agreed. I think he came to the house so that he could beg me to come back to him. When he got to the cottage, just Eva was there. Clearly she still had her hooks in him.' Convenient tears welled in her eyes. 'Eva must have been furious when he told her to back off. I can just imagine what happened.'

'Please share.'

'She pushed him. Probably demanded he get back with her. What she probably didn't realize was that Josiah had a bad temper.'

'He ever hit you?' Malcolm said.

'I'd never allow a man to do something like that to me.' The stiffness in her posture said otherwise.

'So what happened after Eva threw herself at Josiah?' The words rang hollow as Garrison spoke them.

'They made love.'

'I read the reports. The sex between them appeared forced and she had a star-shaped burn on her shoulder.'

'We had pendants.' She skidded completely around the rape question. 'I gave one to all the girls as a thank you for helping me get into Boston University's masters program.'

'Do you still have your star?'

'No. I lost it years ago. It was junk jewelry.'

'Lisa kept hers?'

'She always found it hard to let go of the past.'

'Anyone else that might have had a grudge against Lisa and Sara?'

'I wouldn't know.'

'You said you are going out of town?'

'To New York for a few weeks. I've a wedding to plan.'

'Where can you be reached?'

She moved to a desk and scribbled numbers on a piece of paper. 'This is my cell. You can reach me anytime.'

'Great.'

'I know Eva looks like a sad little creature. But she's not. She's smart and cunning. You might want to find out where she was when those poor girls were murdered. I'd bet my trust fund she had something to do with it.'

'I'll keep that in mind.'

Garrison arrived at King's just after ten at night. He should have just called it a day, but he couldn't shake the things Kristen said about Eva. Probably because the image he had of her was just as Kristen had described: a sad little creature. There was something about her that made him want to protect her. And that reaction bothered him as a cop and a man. He'd tried to protect his sister and his wife. He'd tried to be their knight and both times it had ended badly.

He took a seat at the bar and watched as she served a customer a beer. She wore her long hair in a high ponytail that accentuated her fresh-scrubbed face. She wore jeans that hung from narrow hips and a form-fitting Redskins T-shirt that fit her frame just right. He grabbed a handful of nuts and popped them in his mouth as he waited for her to notice him. He didn't have to wait long.

Eva moved toward him, drying her hands on a white towel. An aura of challenge wrapped her small frame, making her seem more like a late twenty-something than a teen. He welcomed the distinction.

'So, Detective, what can I get you?'

'How about a beer?'

She filled a mug from the tap and set it in front of him. 'Grill's open for another half hour. Hungry?'

He hadn't planned on eating here but the idea made good sense. 'Sure.'

'Would you the like the rare roast beef on toasted rye like you had before?'

'Do you ever forget anything?'

'Not generally.'

'Roast beef would do.' He turned the mug handle toward him. 'So if I rattled off a couple of dozen numbers you'd remember them?'

'Yes.'

No bravado. Just a statement of fact. 'Care to try?'

She shrugged. 'Is this some kind of parlor trick?'

'Just curious.'

'Sure. Shoot.'

He pulled his notebook and pen from his pocket. 'I'll have to write down what I rattle off or I won't remember.'

'Sure.'

'Ready.'

'Sure.'

He recited dozens of numbers, taking note of each as he did. 'Too much?'

She rested her hand on her hip. 'That the best you got?'

He liked seeing her confidence shine through. 'Let's hear the numbers.'

Eva recited the exact same numbers back to him. 'How's that for a show?'

He glanced at his notebook. She'd not missed one. 'Photographic memory.'

'So I'm told.' She leaned over and punched his order into the computer.

He loosened his tie. 'Why are you working behind a bar?'

'I like it here. King is a good man and the customers for the most part are good folk.'

'Eva, you have a photographic memory. And I've read your school file. Your IQ is off the charts.'

'You went to Price.' A bit of the teasing light in her eyes died and he was sorry for it.

It hit him then that she was afraid to show the world just how brilliant her mind was. After all, the last time she did, at Price, she'd ended up used, raped and convicted of manslaughter.

'I paid a visit to Kristen today.' He popped a nut in his mouth as he watched for her reaction.

'Did she tell you I came by?'

'Yes.'

She shoved out a sigh. 'Before you ask, I went to see her because I had questions about the night Josiah died. Long story short, she offered no help.'

'That's it?'

'What other reason would I have, Detective?' She leaned forward. 'Think I went to kill her?'

'That's what I'm trying to figure out. People you know have a habit of dying.'

'I'm bad luck. I know that.'

'Kristen said you were having an affair with Cross.'

A flash of anger popped in her eyes before she hid it. 'A lot of details are hazy, but that one is not. I never, ever slept with that guy. I saw the way he treated Kristen.'

'You sure?'

'She was the one that liked the slimy bastard. Not me. She's the one that hid the bruises he gave her and made excuses for his temper outbursts.'

'Why would she lie about the affair?'

She hesitated, her hands trembling just a little. 'Kristen does two things well in life. She uses people and she lies.'

King pushed through the door behind the bar. 'Eva. Need a hand.'

'Be right there. I'll check on your order.'

'Sure.'

Garrison sipped his beer as he watched her walk away. He found that he enjoyed the sway of her hips.

*

273

Eva's heart slammed her chest as she moved through the door. Sheltered by the kitchen, she let her shoulders slump forward. Shit. Cops in general rattled her, but it seemed this guy could get under her skin like no other. 'What do you need, King?'

King looked up from the grill. 'Nothing. You just looked like you could use a break.'

She rubbed the back of her neck with her hand. 'You saw us?'

'King sees all.'

She smiled. 'Thanks.'

King arched a brow. 'Want me to toss him out?'

'He's a cop.'

He flipped a burger on the grill and then lowered a basket of string potatoes into the fryer. 'I'm not so partial to cops. In fact, I'd enjoy tossing him out.'

'I can handle him. But thanks.'

'Sure thing, doll.'

'Where's Bobby?'

'Just ran upstairs to get another pen. Those pens and pencils you bought the kid have kept him busy for hours.'

'He's very smart. Given a little time and attention he'd rise to the top of his class.'

'Yeah,' King said. 'He's a good boy.'

She noted the full trash can and grabbed the excuse not to return back to the bar right away. 'While I'm here I'll haul the trash out.'

'Thanks, kid. I hate that job.'

She pulled the plastic bag from the can, grunting a little as she wrestled with the weight. 'Do you toss bricks away?'

He chuckled as he flipped a burger. 'Cinder blocks.'

She pulled the bag free, sealed the top and hauled it out the back door toward the dented green Dumpster. She hated the alley, especially at night, but she never shied from the task because fear did not rule her.

She half dragged and half carried the bag. Despite the cool air and the musty smells of the alley, it felt good to be outside and away from the stuffy bar. She opened the Dumpster and tossed in the trash. In no rush to go back inside, she moved slowly down the alley taking time to look at the stars above.

She was nearly at the back door when she saw a flicker of movement from the shadows. Tensing, she paused. She thought about Lisa and Sara. Stabbed. Mutilated. God, why had she come out here alone?

'Who is that?' she said in a clear loud voice. Her answer amounted to the sounds of scraping. Something scurried along the edge of the alley. 'I sure hope that's you, little kitten, and not a big rat. Here, kitty-kitty?'

She glanced at the bowl Bobby had left out for the kitten. Empty. 'Kitty?'

A soft meowing from behind the Dumpster had her smiling in relief. 'Kitty, I'll get you more kibbles.'

As she scooped up his bowl and turned, she found herself face-to-face with Bruce Radford when he stepped out of the shadows. The guy looked twice as big as he had the other night.

Eva started to back up, her hands up in surrender. 'I don't want any trouble. I was just doing my job, Mr Radford.'

He clenched large fists. 'You should have minded your own business. You and that bitch wife of mine can't leave well enough alone.'

'Hey, that was just business and nothing personal. In fact, I'm sorry for your marital troubles.' She clutched the cat bowl, wondering if she threw it just right if it would hit him.

He stepped toward her. 'It was damn personal to me. You should have stayed the hell away.'

She glanced from side to side, wondering if anyone would hear her scream out here. The music in the pub would drown out her screams, and outrunning this guy down a darkened alley didn't appear feasible. Still, running was the only option.

As she turned, he reached out and grabbed her, jerking her around and slamming her into the wall.

Images of Josiah slamming her against the floor exploded in her head. Josiah had told her not to scream or he'd kill her so she'd mutely taken his cruelty. But this time was different. She was different. This time she'd fight even if it meant dying.

Eva raised the cat bowl and slammed it against his head as hard as she could. He groaned in pain as she screamed until her throat burned.

He clamped a hand over her mouth and sneered. 'Shut the fuck up, bitch.' To add weight to his words he slammed her against the wall again. The second impact knocked the breath out of her lungs and her knees buckled. He snatched the cat bowl from her hand and tossed it aside. His erection pushed against her belly. 'When you fight, it excites me more because I know you're afraid and I will do whatever I want to you.'

'I'm not afraid.'

He laughed. 'When I'm finished with you you're gonna

look like hamburger. The cops won't know which piece to pick up first.' He pulled his hand away to kiss her mouth.

'Fuck you,' she managed. When Cross had attacked her, she'd begged him to stop. No begging tonight. She jabbed her knee into his groin. His painful grunt sounded sweet.

But she didn't have time to gloat. He shoved his forearm into her neck and started to choke the breath from her lungs. 'I'm gonna drag you far away from here and tear you apart bit by bit.'

She started to see spots and feared her last conscious image would be his ugly face. Desperation clawing at her, she grabbed a handful of his hair and yanked as hard as she could. When he recoiled, she drove her foot down his shin. Prison had taught her a few valuable lessons.

In the distance, she heard a door open and close, but she didn't dare remove her gaze from Radford. He growled with pain and reached for her T-shirt, jerking her hard against him. Fabric ripped as he grabbed her ponytail and jerked her head back so hard her neck hurt.

He reached for the snap of her pants and jerked it open. Smiling, his gaze bore into her. 'This is gonna be fun.'

He forced her zipper down and his hand into her panties. Sweat pooled on her back as she tried to jab her knee into his groin, but he easily blocked her moves. The muscles in her body tensed. During those terrifying moments when Cross had held her prisoner and brutalized her, she'd been too terrified to bargain with God. This time she'd deal with Satan to stop a second rape.

Think, Eva. Think. You can stop him!

She curled her fingers into fists and rammed them into his Adam's apple. He drew back and sputtered. This time he drew back his fist ready to slam her in the face. She braced for pain.

Before she could frame the next thought, his weight lifted. Without him supporting her, she dropped to her knees and started to gasp for air. Her hand clutched at the base of her throat, she looked up, trying to figure out what had happened.

Garrison slammed Radford face first against the wall and hooked the guy's arm behind him, wrenching it so hard she heard joints crack.

'That bitch isn't worth your trouble.'

Garrison twisted harder and shoved Radford's face harder against the brick wall. 'Don't you move a damn inch,' Garrison growled, 'or I swear I'll rip your arm off.'

Eva held her hand to her throat, which still burned with the heat of Radford's fingers. Her heart pounded as long-buried fears rose to life.

She zipped up and fastened her pants, her hands trembling so badly it took a couple of tries to get the snap fastened. Garrison had saved her.

'Let me go,' Radford said.

'Shut up.' Garrison's powerful muscles strained against his pants. 'Eva, are you all right?'

'Yes. Yes. I'm fine.'

'Did he hurt you?' The note of concern in his voice surprised her.

'No. Nothing permanent.'

'I didn't hurt her,' Radford said. 'I just wanted to scare her.'

Eva willed her legs to move forward. 'He would've killed me.'

Radford tried to twist his head so he could look at her. 'That's a lie.'

Garrison shoved him back against the wall. 'If you know what's good for you, you will keep your mouth shut.' His gaze didn't flicker off Radford. 'Who is this guy?'

'I served him with a subpoena a few days ago. His wife is divorcing him. I was waiting for him at his house the night of the fire.'

'Is that true, Radford? She served you with papers?' Garrison said.

'She sure did. Monday night. Bitch hid the papers in flowers. Pretended to be a delivery person. Shit. It's people like that bitch who drove her away from me,' the guy said.

'How'd you find me?' Eva said.

Radford grinned. 'Friend at DMV ran your plates.'

Garrison frowned. 'I'm gonna need that friend's name.'

'I'll call 911,' Eva said. The terror had faded for now, leaving a rush of adrenaline that left her mind jazzed and hungry for something to do.

'King already did,' Garrison said.

King burst through the back alley door, a meat cleaver in his hand. 'Cops are on the way.'

Eva had to smile as she looked at her knight. 'It's okay, King. No knives necessary.'

King's gaze narrowed. 'Why not? I wouldn't mind carving him up.'

Garrison kept his gaze on Radford. 'Thanks for the offer, but for now stand down.'

Garrison's feet remained braced and she noted his gun

holster. Seconds later the bright lights of two cars arrived at the lips of the alley. Two uniformed cops ran down the alley, guns drawn. When they saw Garrison had Radford restrained, one holstered his weapon while the other kept his trained on the man.

Garrison gave the cops a rundown of what happened and stood beside Eva as she told her story. After she signed a statement, they dragged Radford to the back of the squad car and took him away.

Eva stood silent and stunned as the cop lights retreated and faded. 'Well, that's that.'

She took one step and faltered, her ruined nerves belying her nonchalance. She tripped and had to stop and gather her thoughts before she could move forward.

'You're not okay,' Garrison said.

'I'm fine. Just shaken.'

He captured her elbow in his large hand. 'Let's get you back inside.'

The top of her head barely reached his shoulders and she suspected his weight doubled hers. This close she could see that not an ounce of fat clung to Garrison's frame. All muscle. Power. Normally, she stayed clear of men like him. Too risky. Dangerous. He could overpower her with less effort than Radford had used, but possessed a steady calmness that eased her nerves. He smelled of male earthiness and the faintest hint of aftershave. 'Thank you.'

He looked at her for the first time since he'd charged into the alley. Concern tempered the anger in his gaze. 'Your neck is red. You should see a doctor.'

'I've survived worse. This is nothing.'

'That doesn't mean you shouldn't see a doctor.'

'I'm good.' She didn't have insurance and cringed at the expense of an emergency room trip.

King clenched his bat. 'I'm grateful you were here, Detective. I can swing a bat if need be, but I don't move so fast.'

Garrison nodded. 'If you hadn't started yelling, I'd not have known what was happening until it was too late.'

Too late. Eva understood too late. No one had saved her from Cross.

'I'm fine. I've a shift to finish.'

King shook his head. 'You'll sit on that fanny of yours and ease up. That's an order.'

'I've dishes to wash, a register to cash out and' – her head spun – 'stuff to do.'

Garrison applied firm steady pressure, gently guiding her back through the kitchen into the bar. He sat her at a booth. 'Don't move.'

She'd have argued if she'd had the energy. But her head spun and her neck still burned. A swell of emotions triggered by the attack rose up in her, clawing at her insides. Damn Radford. Damn him!

Garrison set a soda in front of her and took the seat across from her. 'Drink.'

Hearing Garrison's voice steadied her emotions and she was grateful to have the soda to sip. Her cola eased the soreness in her throat, now raw from screaming. 'Thanks again.'

King arrived at the table and set two menus down. 'Order dinner. It's on me.'

'I ordered roast beef at the bar,' Garrison said. 'And I'll pay.'

'I'll make you a fresh one,' King said. 'It's cold by now. And you won't pay. Eva, what are you gonna eat?'

'I'm okay.'

'Stop your yapping and pick something,' King said.

Eva didn't bother with the menu. 'Burger.'

'Don't you move,' King said to Eva. 'No work. Sit. Rest.'

'Okay.'

'She won't go anywhere,' Garrison said. When King had left, he said again, 'You sure you're okay?'

'Why do you keep asking?'

'I read your police file from ten years ago, Eva. That kind of trauma doesn't evaporate.'

Embarrassment washed over her. 'I know.'

'You've nothing to be ashamed of.'

'I know that. I did nothing wrong.' She'd told herself that so many times, she just about believed it now.

'Reading your police files made me cringe. You must have been terrified.'

'I didn't know fear could be so intense that you could actually get sick to your stomach.' She rubbed her eyes.

'You ever get counseling?'

'Some in prison. It helped to know I wasn't alone.'

King arrived with their plates and set them on the table. 'Detective, be sure she eats her dinner. She's bad about eating.'

Garrison kept his gaze on Eva. 'Understood.'

Eva squirmed under his gaze. A sudden wave of desire moved through her body, making her wonder if she had lost her mind. 'I eat enough, King.'

King rolled his eyes. 'Don't believe her. She works too hard. Burns the candle at both ends.'

Garrison nodded. 'I'll keep that in mind.'

Eva dropped her gaze to her plate, taking a sudden interest in the ruffled potato chips.

Garrison studied her. He seemed to sense a raw nerve, but instead of pressing, he said, 'So who is that kid I saw here the other night? He your son?'

That surprised her. 'He's not my son. He's King's foster son.'

'Who's his mom?'

'King hasn't said much about the boy's past.'

Dark eyes assessed so very carefully. 'You're always on pins and needles around me.' He rested his elbows on the table and leaned forward. 'I'm not out to get you, Eva.'

'I'm not so sure about that.' She met his gaze. 'You're a cop. You're investigating two murders. I knew both the victims. I'm an ex-con. And I've learned the hard way that the less said to cops the better.' She started to rise.

'King told you to take a break. So prove to me you're not nervous and sit and eat.' A grin softened his face in ways that made trust tempting. 'We'll talk about the weather. That should be safe enough.'

'The weather?'

'Maybe basketball.'

The tension in her gut didn't ease, but she sat back in her seat. 'You use that smile of yours like a weapon.'

'How so?'

'To throw people off guard.'

The smile widened. 'Is it working?'

She ate a chip. 'Unfortunately.'

'Good.' He took a few bites of his roast beef sandwich. 'So when you go to school, what do you plan to study?'

'I don't want to talk about me. Let's talk about you.'

His defenses rose. 'Sure.'

'I see no wedding ring. Is there a Mrs Cop at home?'

'No.'

She studied him. 'Terse and to the point, which tells me there was a Mrs.'

'You're sharp. Yeah, there was a Mrs She died.'

Her brow knotted. 'I'm sorry.'

'It happens.'

'How?'

He set his sandwich down and wiped his hands with his napkin. 'For someone who doesn't worry about the past, you sure are interested in mine.'

She shrugged, no hint of an apology. 'You got to read files on me and I'll bet you called the prison.'

He'd never talked to Macy about his wife or his sister and yet he heard himself saying, 'My sister died of cystic fibrosis in high school. She was fifteen. My wife was a lost soul and I thought I could save her. I couldn't.'

'I'm sorry.'

'I was young and determined to fix the world.'

'Which isn't possible.'

'I've settled for saving little pieces at a time.'

For the first time she presented him with a warm smile. The look transformed her face, adding a glow that appealed to him far too much. Then she seemed to catch herself.

'Where'd the smile go?' he said.

'It just hit me that I'm having too good a time.'

That pleased him. 'That's bad?'

'Trusting you is dangerous.'

'I'm a good guy. All I'm trying to do is enjoy a meal.'
She laughed out loud. 'Right.'

Lou sat in the basement room thumbing through the Price yearbook. The book spine had cracked at the pages containing images of Lisa, Sara, Kristen and Eva. Of course, there were the class pictures. They smiled so neatly and carefully into the camera lens. Seemingly so perfect and sweet. The world didn't know that beneath the smiles lurked such vile evil.

The formal portraits weren't nearly as revealing as the photo snapped in front of the sorority house. Lisa, Sara and Kristen stood in the center of the front row of girls while Eva stood in the back to the left. All the girls smiled, but in this image, all four girls looked boldly at the camera. They all mocked the world and sent the silent message that only they knew The Secret.

But Lou knew the dark secret the girls harbored.

And soon the entire world would know as well . . . .

Chapter 15

Garrison dropped a file on Malcolm's desk. 'Have a look at this.'

Malcolm glanced up from a stack of papers to the file. 'What's that?'

'It's a collection of articles written on the Cross murder trial.'

'From a decade ago?'

'Correct. I printed them off the Net yesterday.'

'You were busy. I'm guessing all you did yesterday was read?'

Garrison took the seat in front of Malcolm's desk. He'd been restless when he'd gotten home from King's and hadn't been able to sleep. Thoughts of Eva tugged at him. 'I read the articles several times and at first missed a key detail. Glance through the files and tell me if there's something that jumps out at you.'

Malcolm shrugged. 'Can't you just tell me?'

'Humor me, okay?'

'Sure, I'll bite.' He opened the file and started to thumb through the pages. 'What am I looking for?'

'Just study the pictures. Something jumped out at me and I want to be sure someone who's had a full night of sleep sees what I saw.'

'I didn't sleep much last night either.'

'Was it Sharon or Ellie this time?'

'Sadly, neither lady visited me last night.'

'Too bad.'

Malcolm continued to thumb through the pages. Nothing caught his eye until he paused and turned the page back. He leaned forward, frowning. 'This is the picture of the courthouse after the verdict.'

He'd found the picture Garrison had spotted. In this image, Darius Cross stood in front of the courthouse with a dozen reporters' microphones pointed toward him. Darius smiled grimly, his eyes sparkling with a chilling malevolence.

The woman who stood behind Cross stared at him with an intensity that telegraphed anger.

'The woman in the background. She's younger. Not more than twenty. And she looks like Angie Carlson.'

Garrison nodded. 'That's what I thought so I did some checking. Turns out Eva Rayburn had an older half sister, Angelina. When their mother died, Eva was fifteen so she went into foster care. Angie stayed with her father.'

Malcolm whistled as he sat back in his chair. 'Well, ain't this a small, small world.'

'Isn't it?'

'Did Eva Rayburn ever mention that she had a sister?'

'I didn't ask directly about siblings but it was the kind of thing that should have come up.'

'She has a talent for omitting critical details.'

'Or maybe she was protecting her sister.'

'Do you think Angie knows Eva's back in Alexandria?'

'That I don't know. But I'd like to find out.'

'All comes back to Eva. She moved back to town six months ago and victims start showing up.'

'Let's have a chat with Angie Carlson and see what she knows about Eva.'

Malcolm rose. 'Let me do the honors on this interview. Ms Carlson led me by the nose during the Dixon trial cross-examination and nothing would give me greater pleasure than to drop a bomb like that on her.'

'She was doing her job during that trial. She broke no laws when she defended her client.'

'Legal doesn't always mean moral. And as far as I'm concerned, she's slime. My first priority is to get information for the case, and if I happen to make Ms Carlson squirm, then all the better.'

Angie pushed through the front doors of Wellington and James and for the first time in as long as she could remember, she felt good. Happy. Oddly content. She could thank Jim for the smile. They'd spent last night together and it had been pure bliss.

She tossed an unexpected smile to the receptionist.

'Don't tell me the world has come to an end?' The receptionist peered over glasses.

'What?'

'You're smiling.'

'Why not? It's a great day.' Having a connection with someone was something she'd not had in a very long time.

'Well, climb down off of cloud nine,' Iris quipped.

'Why?'

'Two cops are waiting for you in the conference room.'

She clung to her newfound happiness. 'Did they say what they wanted?'

'You know cops. They never come clean.'

'Point taken. So who's here?'

'Garrison and Kier.'

'Great.'

Angie squared her shoulders as she moved down the carpeted hallway. She found Garrison and Kier sitting in the chairs at the head of the polished table. They looked relaxed, as if they owned the place. 'Gentlemen, to what do I owe the pleasure? Do you have questions about Danvers?'

Garrison rose first. Kier took his time coming to his feet.

Kier looked annoyed, but he always did. And she'd pissed him off big time during the trial a few months back. She guessed her attempt to bring Danvers in hadn't counted for much. So be it. 'Ms Carlson, we have something else we'd like to discuss.'

'Sure.' *Jerk.* She closed the conference-room door and took a seat on the opposite side of the table.

She folded her arms over her chest and leaned back in her chair, expecting to do battle. 'Let's have it.'

Both sat. Kier pulled out a file, opened it and glanced down as if he had all the time in the world. 'What can you tell me about your sister?'

If he'd sucker punched her in the gut, he couldn't have knocked the wind out of her better. 'What does my sister have to do with anything?'

Kier glanced at the file but she suspected he knew all the details by heart. 'Her name is Eva.'

'That's correct.'

'She was convicted of manslaughter?'

'I'm sure your little file has already told you that she was convicted ten years ago. She's been out of jail over six months.'

'When is the last time you saw her?'

In her office, she asked the questions. 'What's this about? I can't imagine my family dramas would be of any interest to you.'

Malcolm rubbed his hand over his chin, already dark with stubble. 'It just might. Have you seen your sister lately?'

She wasn't about to dig into a wound for their pleasure or curiosity. 'Is this payback for the Dixon case?'

Kier's eyes darkened. 'No, ma'am. You've got every right to set bad guys free.'

'I did my job, Detective. If this is some kind of harassment, then you can get the hell out of here.'

'We all got our jobs to do. Isn't that what you said?'

She pushed away from the table. 'I don't know what this is about, but I'm in no mood for games, Detective Kier.'

'We've an active murder investigation,' Garrison said. 'Your sister's name came up.'

Angie sat down. 'A local murder investigation?'

'That's right,' Kier said.

'Then you have the wrong person. Eva hasn't been back to Alexandria since her conviction. No doubt because she didn't trust the cops in this area.'

Angie had arranged a homecoming party for her sister the day of her release. She had decorated her apartment with yellow balloons. On the day of Eva's release, she'd driven to Richmond only to discover Eva had already left prison a few days before.

'Your sister is back in Alexandria,' Garrison said.

And the second punch landed in her gut with as much force as the first. 'What?' Her voice barely rose above a strained whisper.

'She's living in Old Town. She's been back for six months.'

Angie's stomach churned. Betrayed. Even embarrassed that she had to find out this way.

Kier studied her face. 'You didn't know?'

It shamed her to have to admit to such a thing. 'No, no, I did not.'

'When's the last time you spoke to her?' His voice almost sounded softer, as if he pitied her.

Angie lifted her chin. 'Ten years. It was after her sentencing. She told me she didn't want anything to do with me again.'

'Why not?' Garrison said.

Angie tipped her head back, swearing she would not cry over this. 'She said she couldn't survive in jail knowing the outside world moved forward without her.'

'You never saw her again?'

'No.'

She pressed trembling fingertips to her brow. 'How long did you say she'd been back?'

'About six months,' Kier said.

Six months. Back in town and living so close they could walk to see each other. And they'd never met. 'You said something about a murder investigation?'

'We've had two women murdered,' Garrison said. 'Both

stabbed to death. And coincidentally the same case Danvers was associated with.'

'Interesting, isn't it?' Kier said. 'By the way, your client we mentioned is dead. Stabbed.'

Shoving aside her shock, she forced herself to think like an attorney. 'What could Eva possibly have to do with your case?'

'We believe the killer is connected to her,' Garrison said.

'How?'

Kier leaned forward and laid a photograph of a four-pointed star on her desk. 'Stars like this were burned into each victim.' He pulled out a second picture and laid it on her desk. 'This is the brand Cross burned into your sister.'

She picked up the picture of Eva and this time sudden tears welled in her eyes. 'Josiah Cross died in the fire. He can't be connected to this.'

'The two victims were Sara Miller and Lisa Black. Do you remember them?'

'Yeah, they went to Price with Eva. They testified against her.'

'Did you hate them?' Kier said.

Hysterical laughter rumbled in her chest. '*Hate*'s a strong word.' She leaned forward, threading her fingers together. 'Did you read Eva's file closely? Did you read the evidence of her rape? Did you read that before Cross burned my sister, he not only raped her, but he bit her at the top of her breast and he hit her so hard in the head that he shattered her eardrum?'

Kier's jaw tightened and Garrison stiffened. They had

read it. It gave her a measure of satisfaction to know that it bothered them.

'Revenge is the best motive for murder,' Kier said.

'Why would I or Eva entertain the idea of killing Lisa and Sara?'

'They testified against her. They said they saw your sister kill him.'

She stared at them, refusing to make a comment.

'You think Eva killed Cross?' Garrison said.

'Eva certainly had reason to kill him after what he did to her,' Malcolm offered.

Angie raised her chin. 'I don't think she did it.'

'Why?' Garrison challenged. 'Did she tell you she didn't?'

'She said she didn't remember what happened after she passed out.'

'She pled to manslaughter,' Kier countered.

'Under pressure from Darius Cross who wanted a pound of flesh. He wanted his son painted as the victim and he moved heaven and earth to get it. His political reach was huge and he used every bit of it against her.'

'Sounds like you went back and studied the case,' Garrison said.

'You bet your ass I did. Her defense was abysmal.'

'Why do you think she came back?' Garrison said.

Angie shrugged. 'It's clear I don't know my sister very well, otherwise she'd have called me by now. You'll have to ask her that question.' She reached for her purse. 'Better yet, Detective. It's a question I need to ask her myself.'

*

Radford's beating had left Eva's muscles stiff and sore. He'd only landed a punch or two before Garrison had stopped him, but those connection points were black and blue. She only hoped that she'd done damage to him when she'd shoved her knee into his crotch.

She'd not slept well Saturday night or last night. The explosion of violence had left her shaken and she'd found it very hard to unwind. She'd only drifted off sometime around two A.M.

She yawned as she replaced the napkins in the dispensers at the tables. She filled all the salt and pepper shakers and had mopped the floor when she heard the front door to the pub open. She cringed. She was irritated that she'd not relocked it after she'd accepted the order of tomatoes. She should have sent the delivery guy around to the back but he'd been in a rush. Damn.

'Sorry, we're closed until eleven.'

'Hello, Eva.'

Her sister's familiar voice sent a jolt of electricity shooting through her body and shattering her calm. Hauling in a deep breath, she slowly turned. Her sister, Angie, stood in the doorway. Morning light filtered in from the street, silhouetting her tall lean frame. She wore a sleek business suit, white silk blouse and high heels. As always, she looked perfect. Ladylike to Eva's awkwardness.

Eva set the napkin dispenser down and smoothed her fingers over her jeans and moved toward her sister. 'Angie.'

Angie moved forward, her expression unreadable. 'I'm surprised you remembered.'

The bite behind the words snapped. 'I remember.'

Angie glanced around the place, as if cataloging each

detail. 'You could have fooled me. I hear you've been back in town a while.'

'Six months.'

Angie nodded, tapped her flat purse against her thigh. 'You could have called me.'

She could have. But she couldn't bring herself to say that she didn't feel worthy. Out of prison or not, she remained branded a murderer.

The silence deepened Angie's frown. 'Why come back now? You've been gone for so long. Why come back now?'

'I've asked myself that question a lot lately.' She tried to keep her tone light but it fell flat.

'Why are you here, Eva?'

To find out why my best friends turned against me and sent me to prison. 'I guess home has a bigger pull than I imagined.' She sighed. 'I'm sorry I haven't called.'

'Why should you be sorry? The last time we saw each other you said you didn't want anything to do with me.'

'At the time it was better that way.'

'Better for you?'

'For you.'

'Did it occur to you that I might have needed you to come home? Mom is dead. Dad is gone. Maybe I needed family.'

Tears clogged Eva's throat. She slid her hand into her pocket. 'I've picked up the phone a thousand times, but I never could finish dialing. I guess I just didn't feel like I had the right to come back into your life.'

Some of the bluster and tension faded from Angie's shoulders. 'You should have called me.'

'I know.'

An awkward silence descended between them. Neither seemed to want to breach the quiet so pregnant with raw emotions.

Eva shifted attention from the painful to the mundane. 'I hear you're an attorney.'

Angie nodded, seemingly grateful for the shift. 'Yes. I practice defense.'

'I read about you in the paper. You won a big case.'

Angie stiffened. 'Big victory.'

'You were happy about the win. According to the paper, no one had expected Dixon to walk.' Angie had poked holes in the prosecution's logic, creating enough reasonable doubt to get her client off.

'I know.'

'I sense you're not happy about the win.'

Angie arched a brow. 'Don't try to get into my head, Eva.'

'Just asking.' They'd not seen each other in so long and already they'd slipped into the old scenario of Eva niggling at her sister.

Angie pursed her lips just as she'd done as a teen. 'Have you been by Mom's grave?'

The familiar imperious tone grated. 'Once. I didn't leave flowers.'

Angie let her gaze roam around the pub. 'You work here?'

'Yes,' she said without shame. 'The owner's good to me. Lets me rent a room on the top floor cheap. I'm saving for school.'

'School?'

'I've applied for scholarship money.' Pride wouldn't let her admit that she'd been rejected because of her record.

'Look, if you need money . . .'

'I don't. I'm good. I've got most of what I need saved.' She'd cut off a limb before taking money from her sister. 'How'd you find out about me?'

'The cops.'

'Which ones?'

'Garrison and Kier.'

Betrayal dug deep into Eva's heart. 'Detective Garrison never told me he'd put the pieces together about us. He should have come to me first.'

'It came to him late last night. He saw an old newspaper clip with a photo of me on the courthouse steps.'

She'd let herself forget how sneaky cops could be. She'd not forget again. 'He should have come to me.'

'I'm glad he didn't. Otherwise, I might not ever have known you were back.'

She slid her hands into her front pocket. 'I would have told you.'

'When, Eva? You've been back six months.'

Eva wanted to be able to give her sister a date and time. 'I don't know.'

Angie stiffened. 'Would you have ever told me?'

'I'd like to think so.'

'That about says it all.'

'No, it doesn't.'

'Look, Eva, Darius Cross is dead. His surviving son could care less about you. The only thing keeping you from calling me is you.'

'Working up the courage, I suppose.'

'To see me?'

'We didn't end on the best terms.'

Again more silence settled. What else could Eva say? Angie was right. She could have mended fences a long time ago and she hadn't.

'The cops think a couple of killings might have to do with my past.'

Angie's voice shifted to attorney mode. 'Who's killing those women?'

'I don't know. I really don't know.'

Angie frowned, an old sign her mind turned over all the variables. 'Be careful.'

The gruff warning triggered a stab of emotion she'd not expected. 'I can take care of myself. Don't worry about me.'

'I do.' Angie stared at her, her expression as solid as stone. She handed Eva a card. 'If you need anything, call me.'

Eva took the card, letting her thumb trace the gold embossed letters. 'Thanks.'

Angie pulled out her cell phone and prepared to type. 'Do you have a cell in case I need you?'

Eva shook her head. 'You can reach me here.' She rattled off the number.

She typed in the number. 'What's your cell?'

'I don't have one.'

Angie looked at her as if she'd just grown a third eye. 'Why not? You need to have a phone. Everybody has a phone.'

'Not everybody. And I've always been able to get my hands on a phone when I really needed one.'

'You should have a cell.'

'People have survived for thousands of years without one.'

Angie hesitated, clearly wanting to argue but deciding against it. She put her phone away. Eva shoved her hands into her pockets.

They stared at each other, both uncertain of how to end this meeting. A handshake, hug, even a *Have a Great Life* didn't suit them. What should have been natural didn't come easy to either one of them.

Finally, Angie nodded. 'Okay.'

'Right.'

'I'll call you.'

'Sure.'

Angie nodded, turned and left.

Eva stood in the center of the pub, the crushing weight of abrupt solitude squeezing her chest. Angie was hurt. Damn. Eva couldn't have messed things up better if she'd tried.

Eva's thoughts turned to Deacon Garrison. He'd meddled where he shouldn't have. 'Asshole.'

Shoving out a breath, Eva moved into the kitchen. The smells of chili mingled with the scent of the apple pies in the oven. Bobby sat on a stool wearing an oversized apron. He peeled potatoes. King stood to his right, doing the same. Whereas the boy had a small paring knife, King wielded a large knife that had a seven-inch blade on it.

'Why isn't he in school?' Eva said.

'Teacher workday or something,' King said.

'Look, Eva,' Bobby said. 'I've almost got the peel off this one.'

The potato looked as if it had gone through a meat grinder. Half the peel remained on, and what he'd managed to get off lay in thick uneven chunks on the counter. But none of that really mattered. The pride shining in the kid's eyes got to her.

She smiled and winked. 'I bet you could run this place in a few weeks if King gave the okay.'

King expertly carved away the potato skin. 'The boy can do just about anything. He helped me bake pies yesterday.'

'He's a smart guy.' Eva began peeling a potato.

'So who was that I heard you talking to?' King said. No missing the keen interest in his voice.

She hesitated. 'Nobody.'

'It was somebody.'

Eva glanced at Bobby, and winked but her comment was directed to King. 'Don't worry about it.'

'I worry.' King glanced down at Bobby. 'Eva is a lot like you, kid. She doesn't like to talk about her family or her past.'

Bobby glanced up at Eva, his face a solemn mask.

Eva frowned. 'That's not true. I'd talk about my family if I had something to say.'

'That expression,' King said to the kid. 'She gets that expression just like you. It's a don't-ask-me-no-more-questions look.'

Both Eva and Bobby suddenly became very interested in the potato they were peeling.

'Two peas in a pod,' King said.

Eva concentrated on the way her knife sliced under the potato peel. Up until this moment, her silence hadn't hurt anyone but herself. And that had been an acceptable trade-off. Now her silence not only hurt her, but Angie,

Bobby and Garrison's investigation. As comforting and safe as the silence had been, she could no longer afford it.

She tossed her potato into a pot of water. 'That woman you just heard me talking to is my sister.' She glanced from Bobby to King. 'Her name is Angie Carlson and she's an attorney in town.'

King grunted. 'She looked mad.'

Eva arched a brow. 'You were watching us?'

'Bobby and I peeked through the kitchen door. But we couldn't hear anything.'

'You were spying on me?'

King showed no repentance. 'We're nosy because we care. Right, Bobby?'

Bobby nodded. 'Yeah.'

Slowly, she picked up another potato and started to peel it. She could feel Bobby's gaze on her. 'I've been back in town six months and I never told Angie I was back. I should have told her. It's not good to keep secrets from family.'

'How'd she find out you were here?'

'Detective Garrison put the pieces together. He told her.'

'Why would he do that?'

Because he thinks I'm key to a murder investigation. 'I don't know.'

King glanced at her as if to say *You know.* 'So how'd it go out there?'

'Better than expected, I guess. But awkward. Real awkward.'

King walked around the counter and wrapped his big arm around Eva. 'I learned one thing about growing up with a houseful of sisters.'

Tears welled in her eyes and one rushed down her cheek. 'What's that?'

'They fight like cats and dogs, but they always forgive each other.'

God, how much she wanted to believe King. 'This isn't a fight over clothes, King. The hurt runs deep.'

He turned her to face him. 'Give it time. You'll both find a way back.'

She wanted to melt into his arms and press her face against his chest. She wanted him to hold her like her father did when she was a little girl, and chase away the demons. But her father's love had faded when the pressures of home life became too much and he'd left. His abandonment had taught her at a young age that she had to rely on herself.

Eva swiped away a tear. 'Thanks.'

'She doesn't believe me, Bobby,' King said. 'But she'll see that I'm right. And you, boy, will see that I'm right too. It's always better to trust someone.'

Bobby's gaze darted between Eva and King. He didn't speak, but the hard line that always seemed to furrow his brow had eased. 'My mom died,' he said quietly.

For a moment Eva didn't dare breathe for fear he'd shut down.

'I miss her,' he said.

'How long has she been dead?'

'A long time.'

'How did she die?'

'She got sick.'

'What was her name?' Eva said.

'It doesn't matter.' His shoulders crumpled forward

and she had the sense that the window he'd just barely cracked open had closed. 'I can't bring her back and I want to stay here.'

'We want to protect you,' Eva said softly.

Bobby looked at her, his eyes watery.

'I know you're scared,' she persisted. 'But you've got to tell us about your family.'

Bobby looked like the secret inside of him clawed to get out. Just a few more minutes and she might actually get some information out of him.

Then King smoothed his hand over the boy's head. 'We'll figure something out, kid. Don't sweat it.'

Bobby grabbed the out King had just given him. 'I don't have to tell.'

'Not until you're ready, pal.'

Eva glanced at King as if he'd lost his mind.

King puffed out his chest, defensive. 'No sense making it a big thing.'

Eva kept her tone light for Bobby's sake but right now she'd gladly have throttled King. 'Kinda is a big thing.'

'A problem for tomorrow.'

Eva could see what was happening. King had fallen into the role of father and he didn't want out. And arguing with him right now would be pointless. She'd catch him later and chew his ear.

Hanging around here would drive her a little insane. 'I gotta get going,' Eva said.

King arched a brow. 'Where you going?'

'I'm not making headway here now so I can at least track down that rat-bastard Garrison.'

Chapter 16

Monday, April 10, 12 Noon

The rented Lexus parked in front of Angie's office and the driver immediately reached for his cell. He typed: I'm outside. Got a minute?

They'd shared a couple of dates over the last few days. It had been fun enough. Yes.

A few minutes later Angie came outside. She wore her hair in a high ponytail but the wind caught the loose wisps around her face. Her eyes looked red and her skin pale, but she smiled at him.

He'd enjoyed her in bed last night and knew that she'd enjoyed him. Despite the reasons that drove him to her, he liked her. He kissed her lightly on the lips. 'You okay? You look upset.'

She kissed him again on the lips. 'I'll live.'

'What's wrong? It's nothing about last night, is it?'

'No. Last night was one of the very bright moments in my life.'

He rubbed her jawline with his thumb. 'Is it a case?'

She squeezed his forearm. 'It's a family thing. My sister is back in town. I'll handle it.'

'Sounds ominous. Want to grab a cup of coffee?'

'I can't. I've got more work than I can handle. But thanks. Rain check?'

'Sure, babe. No worries.' He took her hand in his. He tugged at her arm. 'You know there's a hotel only blocks from here. I bet you could slip away for an hour.'

'Very tempting, but the work . . .'

'Will be waiting for you when you get back. I'll even throw in a foot rub.'

Angie laughed. 'You are as tempting as the Devil.'

His laugh rang genuine. 'I hope so. I'd hate to think my best moves are being wasted.'

A smile tugged the edge of her lips. 'I've only got an hour.'

'Then let's get going.'

'You're bad.'

'I know.'

She took his hand and they walked to the hotel. They were kissing when he unlocked the door to their room and pushed her inside.

Angie could barely keep her hands off this man. She barely knew him but already she craved the release his lovemaking promised. She just needed to forget about all her problems. About Eva. Broken families. So much guilt. If only for a brief time.

He closed the door behind them and immediately kissed her again. The kiss was passionate. Full of promise. Each shrugged their clothes off as they groped their way to the bed.

A half hour later they both lay entwined in the sheets. Angie felt boneless and for the moment content.

He drew circles on her shoulder with his fingertip. 'So what's the deal with your sister? I can feel the tension in your body.'

She shoved out a sigh, trying to push the tension out with the stale air. 'She and I have been estranged for a while. She moved back to town six months ago and never told me.' She closed her eyes. 'She's working at a place called King's. Not a mile from my office.'

'I'm sorry. Is there anything I can do?'

She didn't want to say any more. She sat up, pushing the twisted sheets away from her body. 'I've got to go.'

He traced lazy circles on her back. 'Do you have to?'

'Duty calls.'

He sighed, sat up and moved his feet over the side of the bed. 'I hate duty.'

'Sometimes I do too.'

'I'm going to grab a quick shower,' he said. 'Join me.'

'Thanks, but I'll never get back if I get in that shower.'

He waggled his eyebrows. 'All part of my evil plan.'

She kissed him again, and as he walked naked into the bathroom she couldn't help but admire his lean form. Sighing, she glanced to the side and caught her reflection in the mirror. Her sleek ponytail was almost nonexistent and what remained had shifted to the side. Her lipstick had been smudged away and a definite hickey marked her neck. Angie didn't recognize herself. This was the first dangerous thing she'd done ever, and frankly it felt very, very good.

She got up, let the sheet drop and started to gather her clothes. She slipped on her panties, panty hose and bra and had started to untangle her blouse as she listened to the sound of the shower click on. As she put on her blouse she paced. Her gaze caught Jim's briefcase. She shouldn't peek inside. They were the man's private papers. But she'd slept with him twice and knew nothing about him. She'd never been this reckless and that bothered her.

Angie clicked open the briefcase. Inside was a file marked SORORITY HOUSE MURDER.

Sorority House Murder. That's what the press had called her sister's case ten years ago.

Frowning, she glanced back toward the bathroom. Jim sang in the shower as if he didn't have a care in the world. She picked up the file and found an old picture of Eva.

Angie started to sift through the file. There were more pictures of Eva. Handwritten notes that he'd made during a conversation with a private detective. Jim was trying to find Eva. But why?

She could feel all the blood drain from her face. Her hands started to tremble.

She'd been so intent on reading the file that she didn't hear the shower shut off or the bathroom door open.

'Find anything interesting?'

Angie started at the sound of his voice but she turned and faced him, feeling no hint of shame for having snooped. 'Why do you have a file on my sister?'

He had wrapped a towel around his waist and dried his hair with another. 'I'm trying to find her.'

The earth shifted under Angie's feet. Clutching her blouse to her chest, she suddenly felt dirty and used. 'Why?'

'I want to write about her.'

She glanced at the face that had filled her with such desire less than an hour ago. Now he repulsed her. 'How'd you find out she was my sister?'

'Private detective. You were easy to find, but she's fallen off the radar.'

Her chest tightened. She'd told him where Eva worked. 'Who are you?'

'Connor Donovan.'

'The reporter.'

'That's right.'

A sudden wave of nausea hit her. 'You were using me.'

'Hey, Angie, it wasn't that cold-blooded. I enjoyed this. So did you.'

She couldn't even summon tears. 'Christ, I was such a fool.'

'Hey, darling,' he said, taking a step toward her. 'I'm just doing my job.'

She clenched her fingers into tight fists. 'I swear, if you come a step closer I will kill you.'

He stopped midstride, his smile faltering. 'Like your sister killed her lover?'

'Go to hell.'

'I would, but I've got a story to write. Care to comment on this latest string of murders and your sister's association to them?'

She grabbed her pants, pulled them on and with trembling hands fastened the buttons of her blouse. 'Fuck you.'

'You just did, as I remember.'

She glared at him as she zipped up her pants. 'Come near me again, or my sister, and I'll sue you for every dime you're worth.'

'You can't stop me.'

She grabbed her purse. 'Just watch me.'

She stumbled out into the hallway and slammed the door behind her. She tucked in her blouse and pulled the clip from her hair, running fingers through her messy hair. The elevator dinged open and she dug her cell phone out of her purse. She called King's.

An old man picked up the phone. 'King's.'

'Eva Rayburn.'

He hesitated a moment. 'She ain't here.'

'Is this King?'

'One and only.'

'This is her sister, Angie Carlson.' Angie swallowed a lump in her throat. 'Tell her to call me ASAP.'

Angie closed the phone, stumbled out of the elevator and hurried through the lobby. She winced when she stepped into the bright noonday sun. 'What have I done?'

The hairs on the back of Eva's neck rose, as if someone stood close by and watched her. But when she turned, she saw only police officers heading to and from the station. Reasonable she'd feel nervous here. She'd sworn years ago she'd never again step foot in a police station and yet here she stood. Nerves. Feeling watched. It made sense.

Drawing in a breath, she pushed through the front door of the Alexandria police station on Mill Street. The fire in her belly that had driven her here cooled to smoldering embers. She'd come this far and hoped she had enough steam to confront Garrison.

Eva's fingers tightened around her backpack's strap as she approached the reception desk. An officer with graying hair looked up at her with no hint of welcome in his gray eyes.

'Yes, ma'am?' The 'ma'am' sounded forced, as if he believed she wasn't old enough for the title.

Not in the mood for judgments, she straightened. 'I'm here to see Detective Deacon Garrison.'

The officer knitted his fingers together. 'He's in a meeting.'

'Tell him Eva Rayburn is here to see him.' Her cool voice belied the butterflies chewing at her gut.

He stared at her a long moment.

'He'll be upset if you don't.'

The officer sighed and picked up the phone. He punched some numbers, waited a couple of seconds and then said, 'There's an Eva Rayburn down here.'

Eva's stomach churned with the temptation to leave. Forget this whole mess. Right. She'd spent the last decade trying to forget, and where had it landed her? Exactly where she'd started, facing the same set of demons.

The officer hung up. 'He'll be right here.'

'Great.' She glanced around the lobby, not sure if she should sit or if she should pace. She opted to stand, but not to pace. Pacing suggested desperate and she was not desperate. She was angry.

A side door off the lobby opened and Garrison appeared. He wore dark slacks, a white shirt and a sports jacket that accentuated his broad shoulders. A clean-shaven jaw sharpened the angles on his lean face, which now seemed more raw-boned, as if stress kept him awake. At least she wasn't the only one not sleeping.

Garrison crossed the lobby and reached her in a few long strides. 'Eva.'

She adjusted her backpack on her shoulder, more out of nerves than necessity. 'I'd like to talk to you.'

'Sure.' No hesitation, yet no pressure, much like a fisherman reeling in the big fish.

'Okay.'

'Follow me to my office.'

'Right.'

The last time she'd been in a police station it had been the morning after the rape and the fire. She'd been numb and scared and alone. The cops had stuck her in a plain room – one desk, two chairs – and they'd left her to stew and worry for hours. By the time the sheriff had come in to question her, her nerves had been jumping with fear.

Garrison led her through the door he'd just emerged from and up a single flight of stairs. 'I usually don't take the elevator. It's quicker this way.'

'That's fine. I'm used to stairs.'

He opened the second-floor door and waited for her to enter. A collection of cubicles, the hum of voices and the sound of random phones ringing greeted her. No one seemed to look up or take notice. Just another woman. Just another day. Not the prime murder suspect the entire station had been discussing.

'This way,' Garrison said.

She followed his outstretched hand down a hallway to a corner office. She stepped inside and glanced around the room. Shelves along one wall were packed with books and files. A desk in the center had more books and papers. Two chairs were nested in front of the desk and diplomas on the wall: Air Force Academy. A double frame on a window shelf featured two young girls – one appeared to have been taken recently, but the other years ago. The place looked a breath away from chaos.

'Have a seat.'

'Thanks.'

'Can I get you a coffee or water?'

'No. No. I'm good.'

Instead of taking the seat behind the desk, he chose the one opposite. This close she could feel the energy radiating off him and half wished he'd sit behind the desk. She could have used a barrier between them.

'What can I do for you, Eva?'

The gentleness in his voice almost, almost made her forget why she'd come. 'You told my sister about me.'

Garrison nodded, no hint of apology in his eyes. 'I did.'

'Why? Why did you go to her and not come to me?'

'I'm trying to solve a couple of murders, Eva. Like it or not, you are linked to the victims. And since you've not been the most forthcoming, I decided on a different tack. I'd hoped Angie could tell me something about Josiah Cross.'

'She doesn't know anything about him. She never met him. She never had a chance to visit Price.'

'I know.'

'I really wish you'd not gone to see her. You stirred up things I just wasn't ready to deal with.'

Garrison sat back in his chair. 'If you didn't want to see her, why'd you come back to Alexandria, Eva?'

'You had no right to meddle with my family.'

'Murder changes all the rules, Eva.'

'So what were you after when you went to see her?'

'Like I said, I wanted her perspective on you and Cross's death.'

Frustration chewed at her insides. 'She came to see me today at King's. I wasn't ready.'

'When do you think you would have been ready?'

'I don't know. But that was for me to decide.' She patted her flat hand against her chest. 'Her visit churned up a lot of memories.'

'Maybe that's good. There are moments in the night Josiah died that you've been unable to remember.'

His tone rang so genuine, and for a moment the walls around her crumbled. 'She had nothing to do with those missing moments.'

'You never know what will jog loose.'

'Two of the three women who could have helped me are dead and the third won't give me the time of day.'

'Do you think the three girls lied about seeing you hit Josiah?'

She stared into his dark eyes that focused on her as if she were the only person in the world. 'You almost sound like you give a crap.'

'I do care what happens to you. I believe you got a bad deal ten years ago. But like it or not, that night connects with today's murders. And you remembering those missing minutes is just as important to my case as it is to your peace of mind.'

'How could it? Josiah is dead. His father is dead. And Micah was never the kind of guy who would risk his security for murder.'

'What do you know about Micah?'

'He didn't go to Price. His father wanted the boys to

have separate lives. But I saw him at the school from time to time. He came by the house with his brother. He and Josiah might have been twins, but Micah was as docile as Josiah was violent.'

'What aren't you telling about that night?'

Eva's stomach churned and her muscles twitched with the desire to flee. For an instant, she even pictured the door behind her and tried to calculate the steps to the elevator.

She tugged at a loose thread where the fabric of her jeans had worn just above her knee. 'Kristen confessed that she was pregnant with Josiah's baby.'

'Pregnant. You sure about that?'

'Very. I'd not had much to drink. The wine made me sick to my stomach so I'd been nursing it most of the evening. I kept pouring it down the sink when no one was looking. Kristen kept pushing the wine on me, but I was sober and I know what I heard.'

'Okay.'

'Kristen had broken up with Josiah. We were glad because we knew he wasn't good to her. We'd all seen bruises. I'd spotted him standing outside her window at night. The guy was dangerous.'

'Okay.'

'Anyway, we all swore we wouldn't tell. And then the wine was gone and Kristen decided it was time to get more booze. The other girls said they'd make a run to the store and I was told to stay behind. I was still the junior member of the sorority so I had to do what I was told.' She shook her head. 'Rules of a sorority house seem so pointless now.'

'You were trying to fit in and play by the rules. Don't apologize for that.'

'I just tried so hard with those three but I was always the odd man out. They always had secrets. I'd come into the room and they'd stop talking. That happened a lot that last week. Once, Lisa appeared so upset after one of their meetings. I asked her what was wrong but she'd never say. But that last night they included me and I felt like an insider for once.'

Garrison nodded. 'Are you sure Kristen was pregnant?'

'Yes.' She tapped her fingers on her thigh. 'And I think Josiah knew about the baby. When he showed up at the front door, he was all smiles and had a bouquet of flowers in his hands. I told him Kristen had gone and he asked if he could come in and wait.' God, why hadn't she just done what instinct had demanded and slammed the door in his face? 'I let him in.'

'What happened?'

'He kept asking me about Kristen. I kept avoiding his questions and he got mad very quickly. He told me Kristen was a fool if she thought she could keep secrets.'

'But you never told him about the baby?'

'No. The crueler he was, the more determined I became to keep the secret. He was a monster. And I never told during the trial.'

'Why didn't you? It could have helped your case.'

'I saw firsthand how evil Josiah could really be. And his father wasn't much better. I kept thinking about that baby and how they'd ruin its life. A life sentence even before it was born.'

'After the attack, what's the next thing you remember?'

'Being dragged out by the fireman.'

She closed her eyes and squeezed the bridge of her nose. Even to this day, she could still smell the smoke and feel the heat of the flames. 'When he burned me, the pain flipped a switch in me. Everything just went blank and I blacked out. I don't know how much time passed or how the fire got started. But I never, ever remember hitting him. I've tried to remember that but I can't.'

He rose and moved to his desk where he dug out a file. He opened it, carefully searching for the right image. He came around the side of the desk and sat again. 'These are photos of the victims' stomachs.'

Her gaze held his for a moment. She didn't want to look but found her gaze dropping. The image was of a red, raw scar with a backdrop of the dead woman's pale white skin. For a moment she couldn't breathe and then she pushed aside her fears and studied the image.

She shrugged off her jacket and exposed her shoulder and her scar.

His gaze darkened as he stared at it. 'Think hard, Eva,' Garrison said softly. 'Who would want to do this to them?'

'I don't know. I really don't know.'

'What about Micah Cross?'

'This just doesn't seem like Micah. It just doesn't.'

'Do you think Kristen is doing this? You, Lisa and Sara all knew about the baby. Maybe that's too much of a secret for her to have now that she's got this big fancy wedding planned.'

'Kind of medieval, don't you think? Birth mothers go on to have normal lives all the time.'

'I did some checking on Kristen. Her family is in tough

financial straits. They lost a lot last year. This marriage will fix a lot of problems. A baby might tarnish her image.'

'Kristen always got what she wanted.' Her gaze dropped to the date marked digitally on the bottom of victim one's photo. 'She didn't care who she hurt in the process.'

'It's time I had another talk with Kristen.'

'You believe me?' Surprise coated the words.

'Yes.' He wasn't her friend or enemy. He was an impartial cop looking for a killer. But she sensed she could trust him.

Eva trusting a cop. The thought almost made her laugh. 'Fair enough.' She rose.

He straightened. 'Eva, we found a journal in Lisa's condo. It was written in code.'

And it seemed he trusted her a bit as well. That felt really good. 'Lisa loved the idea of codes and keeping her thoughts very private. I taught her the ROT13 code at school.' She explained the system.

'Thanks.' He studied her. 'Have you been back to Price?'

'No.'

'Have you considered it?'

'I've thought about it, but I just haven't found the time.' She shook her head. 'Who am I kidding? I've avoided it like the plague.'

He leaned toward her. 'Would you be willing to go back now?'

'You think it'll jog my memory?'

'It could.'

The thought of walking the grounds that had been the source of so much pain robbed her of breath. Yet the running in fear from Josiah bothered her more. 'Sure, I'll go.'

'How about right now? How about I drive you now?'

The challenge in his voice goaded even more than the fear. 'Yeah, sure, why not?'

He grinned. 'I'll get my keys.'

The drive to Price University took Garrison less than forty minutes. She sat in the front seat, her hands folded in her lap as she watched the city pass by and then slowly thin until only countryside passed by her window.

'You doing okay?' he said.

She shrugged, determined to keep her nerves in check. 'Last time I was in a police car I was being carted off to jail.' She tossed one of his grins back at him but sensed hers looked a little strained. 'Not one of my brighter moments.'

His fingers tightened on the wheel. 'You got a raw deal.'

'Yeah, tell me about it.' She flexed her fingers, not willing to dig into bitterness now. 'So you really think a trip down memory lane is going to help?'

'It might jog something loose.'

'I hope it does. For a long time I didn't want to remember any more than I had. Now I want to know what happened every second of that day.'

Eva wasn't sure if she'd have made this trip alone. But having Garrison so close eased her fears. She'd like to have filled the silence with conversation, but she didn't know how to make small talk with him. With the bar patrons all she needed was a bit of sports information or a tidbit from the entertainment section of the paper, but with him, all that just felt flat and foolish.

'So what makes a guy chase murderers?'

'Someone has to.'

'But why you?'

He shrugged. 'After I got out of the air force, it made sense. My dad had been a cop for thirty years.'

She'd noted before that the academy class ring was the only jewelry he wore. 'How'd your wife die?'

'That's an odd question.'

'Sorry. Curious, I suppose.'

For a moment he kept his eyes forward on the road. A muscle in the side of his cheek pulsed as if he'd not answer. 'Suicide.'

The word sounded wrenched from his chest, as if he'd confessed a terrible secret. 'Why?'

Again another pause, as she sensed she'd just shined a light into the darkest of corners. 'She'd been ill for some time.'

'My mother killed herself. She didn't like living without my dad. And then she got sick. I guess living was just too much work.'

'She had you.'

'And your wife had you. Sometimes we just aren't good enough to save them.'

He shot her a glance. And in that moment she saw a lifetime of pain and anger. 'Sounds like you've thought about that a lot.'

'That's one advantage to going to prison. You've got time to think.'

This big strong man who looked nearly bulletproof carried a wound that, judging by the added tension in his shoulders, hadn't really healed. And for the oddest reason she didn't feel so alone knowing she wasn't the only damaged person in this car.

Garrison slowed as they neared the white columns that marked the university's entrance and wound down the main entrance road toward the first parking lot. It had been paved since she was last here and more bike racks and even security panic buttons had been added.

Price was nestled in the rolling hillside; its old brick buildings with white columns dated back to the early 1900s. Lush green lawns, thick and well manicured, covered the ground around meandering paths.

Clean, neat students walked toward the main quadrangle where the school's oldest four buildings bracketed the main common area. They smiled and one laughed, tossing back her hair.

For a moment she sat and wondered what good could possibly come of this visit.

Her backpack slung on her shoulder, she stepped from the car and moved with her back ramrod straight and her eyes focused ahead. On the path to the main buildings, gravel crunched under her feet. 'There'd been a time when I was that girl.'

'You, carefree?' The teasing tone made her smile.

'Well, not exactly like them.' And before she thought to censor herself, she said, 'For the one brief year I was here, I believed in possibilities and building a new shining life.'

He stood nearly a foot taller than her and his frame blocked the sun and covered her with his shadow. 'You can still have that.'

'I know. I will.'

The scent of boxwoods greeted them as she passed an old building they'd called East Wing and moved across the green quad toward the road that led to sorority row.

As they moved along, she gave him a brief history of the school, surprised she remembered so much. Her house had been the third on the right, but she wasn't sure what she'd find now, knowing the house that had been hers had been ravaged by fire.

When they topped the little hill, she was surprised to see that the building had been replaced with a new house. A bright shining white house, with a wide front porch complete with rockers and lush planters filled with winter pansies. By the main entrance a brass plaque read CROSS HOUSE.

'Cross House.' Bitterness twisted inside her. This was no doubt Darius's handiwork.

'His father rebuilt the house in his son's honor.'

'How nice.'

They climbed the front steps, listening as music drifted out of the wide-open front door. The singer crooned on and on about second chances. Fitting, she thought as she pushed through the open front door.

She paused by the threshold.

'You okay?'

His quiet and unyielding presence shored up shaky nerves. 'Great.'

They moved inside the house. The foyer was carpeted and the walls a soft beige. A creak from a top center staircase had her looking up. A slim girl wearing sweats and a Price T-shirt and her dark hair up in a ponytail came down the stairs. The girl glanced from Eva to Garrison and back, trying to figure out their relationship. 'You planning on going here?'

Before Garrison could pull out his badge, Eva grabbed on to the opening and took advantage of her youthful appearance. 'I am. The college keeps sending me a bunch of brochures and so my brother and I thought we'd have a look around.'

The girl's attention flickered back up to Garrison whose amused expression nearly made Eva laugh.

The slight tension in the girl's shoulders eased. 'So you a transfer student?'

'What makes you say that?'

'You don't have the wide-eyed look of the high school girls.'

'Thanks for noticing. Most people think I'm just a kid.'

Garrison cleared his throat. 'That's not entirely true.'

Eva glanced up at him, and for the briefest moment she saw raw desire flash in his eyes. Instead of scaring her, it sent a reciprocal thrill shooting through her limbs.

'Would you like a tour of the ground floor of the house? Upstairs is limited to sisters only.'

'That would be great,' Eva said. 'The house looks so new.'

'Only nine years old.'

They followed her into a side parlor, but the instant Eva stepped inside, she regretted it. A huge portrait of Josiah Cross greeted her. He stood by a black stallion, holding the bridle and staring boldly at the artist and the world. A smug smile tipped the edge of his mouth as it had done that night he'd backed her up against a wall and held his hand to her throat. She'd been afraid and he'd drunk in her fear like a tonic.

'You little upstart, bitch. Where the hell is Kristen?' His breath smelled of beer and cigarettes.

'I don't know,' she lied.

He'd reached for the waistband of her pants. She'd flinched and he'd laughed and grown bolder.

'You don't have to be so cruel.'

'I drank cruelty from my mother's breast. It's like honey to me.'

'You okay?' Garrison said.

Eva started and turned. It took a second for the emotions to clear and for her to see Garrison and the young coed standing by the door. 'I'm fine.'

The girl pretended to shiver. 'Don't let Mr Creepy put you off.'

A laugh bubbled inside Eva. 'Mr Creepy?'

'Yeah, he came with the house. None of the girls like him, but he's a condition of the house. We tolerate him for state-of-the-art wireless and flat-panel televisions.'

Eva leaned forward and pretended to read the plaque, 'Josiah Louis Cross?'

'Some guy that was murdered. I know, weird. But, like I said, his old man wanted to build a house in his honor. We call him Mr Creepy but I guess he's not that bad. Besides it's just a painting.'

It was a painting of the Devil. 'Right.'

Pain all but dulled her mind to any clear thought as she looked up and saw Josiah standing over her. He was smiling. And then just as quickly, he staggered forward as blood rushed from his head.

Eva's fingers tensed around the strap of her backpack. She tried to hold on to the flash of memory, but it vanished as quickly as it came.

'I got to say, Mr Creepy has had his share of visitors this week.'

'Who else has been here?' Garrison said.

'Well, there was that guy just the other day. He was asking questions about the girl that killed Mr Creepy. He kept asking if we knew were she lived now. Very weird. I called Security on him.'

'He leave?'

'Oh, yeah. Ran out of here quick.'

'You said there was someone else?' Garrison prompted.

'Yeah. A weird old guy. Our week for weird guys, I guess. I didn't see him but Missy down the hallway did. This guy kept talking about how sinners must atone. Again, we called Security, but he ran off.'

'What did she say about him?' Garrison said.

'Hey, I don't want to creep your sister out with tales of creepy guys. Price is really a nice school. People care about you here.'

Garrison pulled out his badge. 'She's not my sister and I'd like to talk to Missy.'

Chapter 17

Eva and Garrison drove back to Alexandria. On the way, he called his partner and told him to meet with Missy and a police sketch artist.

They drove to the police station where Eva's truck was parked. Garrison got out with her and walked her to her truck. She unlocked it and opened the front door, pausing as he stood by her. Heat and energy radiated from him and the urge to touch him toyed with her. What would those arms feel like wrapped around her?

Dark sunglasses tossed back her reflection as she stared up at him. 'Thanks.'

'Thank you.' He leaned forward a fraction, one hand resting on the open door and the other on the roof of the truck. 'I want you to be careful, Eva. I'm going to put a patrol car out in front of King's, but I want you to be cautious.'

'Hey, I'll be fine. I'm an ex-con and I've got eyes in the back of my head.'

His jaw tensed. 'I'll be by to see you as soon as we get a sketch. I want you to look at it.'

'Okay.' She wanted to lean forward and kiss him. Not a chaste simple kiss but a full on-the-mouth kiss. She wanted to know what he felt and tasted like. Instead, she nodded

325

and slipped behind the wheel of her truck. He closed her door and watched and waited as she drove away.

Garrison standing in the parking lot was the last image she had in the rearview mirror before she rounded the corner.

Eva arrived back at the pub just after four and was behind the bar and ready to work fifteen minutes after that. As much as she tried to immerse herself in the work, her mind kept drifting back to Price. Who was so interested in her and Josiah?

When she heard the bells above the threshold jingle, she glanced up and tossed the customer a smile as King always asked: *Greet 'em. They won't forget you when you do.*

The tall, lean man entered the pub, scanning the crowd until his gaze settled on her. She raised a hand, signaling she'd be right over.

He nodded and waited, cool and relaxed as he surveyed the room. When she'd refilled drinks at table six and given change to table five, she hurried up to him. 'Here for dinner?'

'I am.'

'How many?'

'Just one.'

'Follow me.' She grabbed a menu and guided him to a corner booth. When he'd sat, she took his drink order and promised to return. When she set his drink down in front of him, she pulled out her pad. 'So what can I get you?'

'Reuben on rye will do it.' He closed the menu and looked up at her, his gaze skimming her name tag. 'Doris. You don't look like a Doris.'

'I get that a lot.'

'No seriously, I know people and names and you are not a Doris.'

'Blame it on my folks.' Chatty customers were fine on slow days but the late evening crowd had grown and she didn't have time for small talk. 'Be right back with that Reuben.'

She moved around the pub, filling drink orders, collecting tabs and wiping up spills. Nonstop motion didn't ease the feeling that the corner booth's customer's gaze was on her.

Be careful.

Garrison's words rattled in her head. When his order was up she moved toward him more carefully and mindfully this time. He was attractive. Button-down rolled up to his forearm. Smooth fingers. She'd never seen him before.

When she set the plate in front of him, she paused. 'Do I know you?'

'I don't think so.' His eyes danced with a good humor that undermined her suspicion. 'Maybe I just have one of those faces.'

'Yeah, maybe. Can I get you anything else? More beer? Mustard?'

'No thanks, Eva.' His gaze pinned hers as if waiting for a reaction.

Energy bolted through her limbs. 'What did you call me?'

'Eva.' His grin widened. 'It's your name.'

'I never told you my name.'

'I know.' He picked up a chip and popped it in his mouth.

'Were you at Price asking questions about me?'

He nodded, pleased with himself. 'I do get around.'

She clutched her round serving tray close to her chest. 'Who told you about me?'

'Your sister, Angie. She told me all about you.' He winked and glanced down at the plate. 'Looks delicious.'

A sudden chill cooled her body. 'Who are you?'

'I'm Connor Donovan. I'm a writer. I wrote a lot of articles about you a decade ago.'

She took a step back. 'I don't talk to reporters.'

'I know. You refused all my interview requests when you were in jail.'

The earth seemed to shift under her feet.

'Did you kill those two women because they fingered you as Josiah's killer?'

Pain squeezed her heart and for a moment she couldn't breathe. Angie wouldn't do this to her. Would she? 'I don't have anything to say.'

He stood abruptly and blocked her retreat. 'Come on, Eva, help me write a follow-up. You were a hot item back in the day. This is your chance to tell your side of the story. I've read the transcript of the trial and all the old articles. I can see that you were railroaded.'

The bait dangled on the tip of his hook and she knew if she bit, she'd suffer. 'Go to hell, Mr Donovan. Leave now or I'm calling the cops.'

'I'm not breaking any laws.'

'You are now a trespasser. King's reserves the right to refuse service and we are refusing you service. Leave.' Her hands trembled as she grabbed his plate from the table and marched across the room to the bar. Unmindful of the customers trying to catch her eye, she pushed through the swinging door that led into the kitchen. 'King!'

He glanced up from a pot of stew. She recapped what had happened. 'You say he's got to go, then he's got to go.'

She dumped the sandwich in the trash. 'Deduct the cost out of my paycheck.'

'No need for that, kid.'

'God, I can't believe she'd do this to me.'

'Who?'

'My sister, Angie. She told that Connor guy all about me and where to find me.'

King looked startled, and as if remembering pulled a crumpled slip of paper from his pocket. 'You got a call today. From your sister.'

She glanced at the scrawled words. 'Angie. Shit.' No time on the note. 'What time did she call?'

'About one. Sorry, I just forgot.'

Some of her anger vanished. 'I can't read your handwriting, King. Is the last digit of her phone number a seven or a five?'

He shrugged. 'I've no idea.'

She groaned. 'King.'

'Baby, I got alligators biting on my ass right now. I don't know. And I got three orders you need to serve before they get cold.'

Frustrated, she shoved the slip of paper in her pocket. Bobby came down the backstairs, a new book in hand. 'Eva, what is this word?'

Her head spun and she glanced at the word marked by his pudgy fingertip. 'Sound it out like I showed you.'

'Te. Te. Technology.'

'That's right.'

He smiled up at her, such trust in his eyes. And again,

she feared for Bobby. With someone like Connor Dono-van snooping around, there was no telling how long she could keep the boy safe.

King barely noticed the heat from his stove, the noise of the exhaust fan or the rumble of the crowd in his restaur-ant. For a moment, he stood as still as stone, replaying what Eva had just told him. A reporter had tracked Eva down to his restaurant. Reporters meant attention and attention often led to trouble.

Slowly, he stirred the stew. He'd spent a lot of time and resources pulling events together and now that shithead Donovan was going to muck it up. His first inclination was to track the guy down and beat the piss out of him.

Which might provide King with a moment's satisfac-tion but in the long run would only cause him trouble.

King shoved out a breath. He'd weathered a lot of shit in his life. So had Eva. So had Bobby. They all could sur-vive an article or two. And then when the chaos died down again, people would forget about them and he could fol-low through with the next step.

Kristen sat in the park by the river staring at the slow, meandering waters of the Potomac. A gentle spring breeze flowed past. Couples strolled the path. Kids on bikes rolled past. Laughter swirled around her head.

She'd been thrown off by Eva Rayburn's visit but had planned to fly to New York, more determined than ever to get out of town and forget all about Alexandria. But a few hours ago, she'd gotten a call on her private cell.

*

'Do you want to see your baby?' the caller had said.

Your baby.

'How'd you get this number?'

Laughter crackled. 'Friends. Do you want to know about the baby?'

'I don't have a baby,' she'd said.

'Yes, you do. Only, he's not a baby now, is he?'

She'd gripped the phone, silent, unable to speak and unable to hang up.

'He'll be in the Riverside Park tomorrow about two if you want to see him.'

The caller had hung up, leaving her dazed and rattled. As much as she'd wanted to leave town, she'd been unable to get on that plane.

Now, here she sat on a park bench staring at the old worn photo in her hand. She'd carried the picture tucked deep inside her wallet for over a decade and the frayed edges reflected the wear and tear.

She traced the lines of the newborn's face.

Kristen would have been so much better off if she'd never met Josiah Cross.

During that year she'd made a series of bad decisions, starting with pursuing Josiah Cross. He'd been considered the catch and she'd wanted what she'd perceived as the best. 'Be careful what you wish for,' her mother used to say. They'd been dating four months when she'd found out she was pregnant. She'd hated and resented a lot of things in her life, but she'd loved her son from the moment she'd known he was inside her. She'd have dealt with the Devil to save him.

*

'Sign the paper, Kristen.' Her mother's urgent whisper still echoed in her head. 'Sign it!'

'Mom, he's my son,' she'd said, crying.

'That baby is going to ruin your life, Kristen. Honey, we want you to go to graduate school, to marry well and to have a promising career.'

'A lot of women have babies out of wedlock and raise them.' And with Josiah dead, she'd be free to raise her son.

Her mother gently stroked her hair. 'That's not an option for people like us. More is expected of us.'

Through watery eyes she looked up at her mother, feeling her father's intense stare from across the room. 'He's your grandson.'

'I'll cut you off completely if you keep him,' her father said. 'Sign the papers.'

Her mother smiled weakly. 'He'll be better off. You're making the right decision.'

Better off.

Tears rolled down her cheeks.

'Kristen.' The voice came from behind her.

Swiping away the tears, she turned. 'You're the one that called me.'

'I have news of your son.'

Kristen rose. 'Tell me.'

'He's over here. Follow me.'

'You found him?'

'Yes. I've got to take him to his parents, but you can see him before I do.'

Oh, God, but she wanted to just see him. How many nights had she lain awake wondering what he looked like? Did he have her nose? How much of Josiah was in him?

She'd moved heaven and earth to see that Josiah would never be in the child's life.

Kristen had done so much to keep her son safe.

Since Eva's visit, she'd been plagued with worries that Eva would remember the details of the fire.

Had Eva figured it out?

Kristen stood, her legs unsteady and her heart pounding in her chest. Her hands trembled with a heady excitement. Worries about her secret, the murders, even her upcoming marriage all faded as she thought about her son.

'He's in the van by the playground,' the caller said, pointing.

Kristen looked ahead to the black van. 'What's his name?'

The van door automatically opened. 'Ask him yourself.'

Kristen moved toward the van and leaned into it, searching the seats for her son. At first she thought she might be missing something, and then she realized he wasn't there. Anger burned through her. 'What kind of game are you playing?'

A sharp needle jabbed into her back and she could feel the hot rush of fluid into her body. In a matter of seconds, her mind slipped into blackness.

Chapter 18

Tuesday, April 11, 8:00 A.M.

Eva arrived at the law offices of Wellington and James just after eight. She'd opted to walk the ten blocks, hoping she'd have time to soothe her temper. She buzzed the front bell.

The receptionist looked at her on the video monitor. 'What can I do for you?'

'I'm delivering a subpoena for Luke Fraser, LTF Processing.' The white lie would get her inside.

'Sure.'

The door buzzed once and Eva yanked open the front door. In the reception area, she immediately felt out of her depth. Rich carpets, old world paintings on the wall and crystal lamps created the impression of money.

'What do I need to sign?' the receptionist said.

Eva lifted her chin, not bothering to slow her pace. 'I'm actually here to see Angie Carlson.'

The woman shook her head. 'I'll sign for her.'

'No worries. I'm her sister.' She moved toward the hallway that led to the back. 'Which office is hers?'

The woman arched a brow. 'Angie doesn't have a sister. And if you don't stop right now I'm calling the cops.'

'You do that.' She glanced in an office on her left.

'Look, I've known Angie for a year and she's never mentioned a sister.'

'She's got one and she's just about ready to find out how pissed she really is.'

'That's it,' the woman said, bustling ahead of Eva. 'Get out.'

'Nope. Angie!'

The older woman hustled into a side office and picked up a phone. The cops would no doubt be here in minutes.

'Angie!'

Seconds later Angie emerged from the office at the back of the hallway. Hope and confusion flickered in her eyes. 'Eva.'

'You might want to talk to your receptionist. She's calling the cops on me.'

Angie rolled her eyes. 'Iris! Don't call the cops.'

Iris hung up her phone and appeared at the end of the hallway. 'Are you sure?'

'Yes.'

'She says she's your sister.'

Angie nodded. 'She is.'

Iris arched a brow as her gaze shifted to Eva and then back to Angie. She didn't say anything but Eva guessed that Angie had some explaining to do.

Angie motioned Eva toward her office. 'Come in here.'

Eva moved inside the office, clutching the strap of her backpack. Angie's office was just as elegant as the front office. 'I know you're pissed about me not calling you, but did you have to dish dirt to your writer boyfriend?'

Angie folded her arms over her chest. 'I called you yesterday. Didn't you get my message?'

'King didn't give me the message until late. After your boyfriend paid me a visit.'

Angie frowned. 'Connor came by?'

'Oh, yeah, and he was full of questions. Why'd you rat me out to him?'

'I didn't. I didn't know who he was at first. He said he was in town on business.'

'Yeah, he was in town on business, all right. The business of writing a story on the Cross family.'

Angie's face tightened with hurt and anger. 'Like I said, he lied to me. We'd just seen each other and I was hurt. I said my sister and I had had a fight. That's all I said.'

The tightness in Angie's voice said more than her words. Donovan had hurt and humiliated her. And in that moment the bluster she'd been chewing on since last night vanished. 'Did you tell him where I worked?'

Angie thought for a moment. 'Yes. Shit. Eva, I am sorry. I wouldn't have said anything to him if I'd known what he was after.'

An awkward silence hung between them but neither could cut through their own emotions to speak for a moment.

Eva shifted her stance. 'Donovan came by the pub last night. He pretended to be a customer.'

'He's a dick.'

That nearly coaxed a smile. 'Why'd you get tangled up with him?'

Dark circles hung under Angie's eyes. 'Momentary lapse in judgment.'

'You didn't sleep with him, did you?'

'Like I said. Bad judgment, all around. Won't happen again.'

Eva suddenly felt angry for her sister who'd been betrayed by a man she'd taken to her bed. 'We've all had those moments. The trick is to get smarter and savvier so it doesn't happen again.'

'Let's hope.' Angie frowned. 'Getting a hold of you yesterday was a bear. You should carry a cell.'

'I promise to get around to it.'

Angie moved toward her desk. 'I have an extra one.'

'Thanks, but no. I've managed just fine so far.'

Angie opened the top desk drawer and pulled out a cell. 'It's a little large and clunky but it still works.'

'I don't want your charity.'

'It's not charity.'

'It's free. You feel sorry for me.'

Angie crossed the room and held out the phone. 'Eva, two women are dead. Two of those women you once knew. Take the damn phone until this nutcase is caught.'

Eva didn't budge. 'I don't need anyone to look after me.'

'We're sisters,' Angie said softly. 'I couldn't help ten years ago, but I can help with this small thing now. The phone. Please.'

The 'Please' is what got her. Eva reached out and took the phone. 'Only until the killer is caught. And I'll pay you for any calls.'

'You can try, but I won't take your money. Just say thank you, and shut up.' She rattled off the phone's number.

Ignoring the jab of emotion, Eva tried to inject a bit of smartass into her voice. 'I can see you're still as bossy as you used to be.'

'And you're still as distrustful as you ever were.'

Eva smiled. 'Maybe.' She held up the phone. 'Thanks.'

'No sweat.'

'I've got to go.'

'Call me sometime. We can have lunch.'

'Let's do lunch?'

'I mean that. I want us to at least try to be friends.'

'Okay.' No tearful reunion, but a start.

When Eva got back to the pub, King sat in the kitchen drinking a cup of coffee. He leaned over the morning paper, his brow furrowed. 'You're not going to like this.'

'What am I not going to like?'

'This article on page two of the *Post*.'

'Please tell me that the byline is not by Connor Donovan.'

'How'd you know?'

'Remember, he was here last night.' She peered over his shoulder and read the headline. SERIAL KILLER LINKED TO SORORITY HOUSE MURDER. 'Oh, God.'

'I knew what I was getting into when I hired you.' King glanced up at her. She braced for anger or recrimination. But she saw no traces of either. 'Luke Fraser called. He says you're fired.'

'Right.' Luke didn't like attention, and now for her next Fifteen Minutes of Fame she'd be an attention magnet. 'Are you canning me, too?'

'No. No, I'm not.'

'Why not?'

He shrugged. 'I like you. You're a good kid. Knew it from the minute I saw you at that halfway house arguing with the attendant about clean water. Besides, how the hell am I gonna run that fancy computer system you installed if you don't stay?' His voice had softened and lost a good bit of bluster.

'You'd figure it out.'

'Maybe, but I don't want to.'

Her throat tightened with the sting of emotion. Twice today people had reached out to her. 'But we have a bigger problem.'

King cleared his throat. 'Bobby.'

'Social Services might have an issue with my background.'

'You served your time, Eva. You're free and clear as far as the law is concerned.'

'Still, they can be funny about that kind of thing.'

'I'll handle them.'

She nodded. 'Reporters will be snooping around. My story was huge back in the day.' A heavy weight settled on her shoulders. 'I can call Social Services.'

'No. Let them call us. I like the kid and won't give him up without a fight.'

Macy sauntered into Garrison's office and tossed a file on his desk. 'Whoever did the investigation on your fire was an idiot.'

He lifted his gaze, immediately intrigued. 'Tell me.'

She sat in the chair across from his desk. 'It makes no sense to me.'

'Explain.'

'I looked at the pictures and I read the report. They don't match.' She leaned forward and opened the file and pointed to an image of a burned-out structure. All that remained was a charred brick foundation. 'See that black smudge in the corner of the foundation?'

'Sure.'

'That's the fire's point of origin.'

He studied the image. 'The investigator said the point of origin was the fireplace on the ground floor.'

'No. This fire started in the back of the house by the back door. Those black scorch marks indicate intense flames.'

'Like the shelter fire.'

'Exactly. Someone tossed accelerant by the back door and set the place on fire.'

'Witnesses said that Eva hit Josiah and then used the burning logs in the fireplace to set the blaze.'

Macy shrugged. 'Unless she ran outside, set the blaze and then ran back inside, she did not set that fire.'

'Which means she may not have killed Josiah.'

'That, my friend, is for you to figure out.'

The homicide team assembled less than a half hour later in the conference room. Garrison sat at the head of the table. Malcolm sat on his right, Rokov on his left. Sinclair had been summoned and promised to show as soon as she could.

Rokov folded large arms over his chest. 'I get why Danvers is up there. He likely saw the killer, but why the other stabbing victim? She had no brand or apparent connection to the other cases.'

Garrison sat back in his chair studying the image of Eliza Martinez. 'Her wounds are too similar to Danvers's. Four stab wounds to the chest.'

'So why no brands?' Malcolm said.

'Like Danvers, Eliza Martinez was in the way. Her killing, in the killer's mind, wasn't personal,' Garrison said.

Malcolm snorted. 'We did a full background check on Martinez after she died. Nothing came up.'

The door to the conference room opened and Sinclair entered. Her cheeks looked flushed and her eyes bright with excitement. She held Lisa's journal in her hand. 'Sorry I'm late. I've been working on Lisa Black's journal, based on the theory that it's a ROT13 code.'

'And?' Garrison said.

'You were right. That was the code.'

'Good.'

'You won't believe who she hooked up with last spring.' Garrison leaned back in his chair, his body tense.

Sinclair grinned like a contented cat. 'Darius Cross. They were lovers. Here is her March 7 entry from last year.

I had too much to drink and told Darius who I really was. He went ballistic and hit me because I'd lied to him. When I thought he'd hit me a second time I told him The Secret. His face paled. He dressed and left and I know I'll never see him again.

'The Secret. Could it be Kristen's pregnancy?' Malcolm said.

'Macy said she didn't think the sorority house fire started by the fireplace,' Garrison said. 'Maybe The Secret was bigger than that. Maybe Lisa or one of the other girls set the fire. Maybe Eva Rayburn doesn't remember killing Josiah because she didn't.'

'Have a look at the sketch artist's work,' Malcolm said.

341

He opened a file and slid the sketches across the desk. 'The first visitor is clearly Connor Donovan. He was doing a little research on his story.'

Garrison studied the very accurate sketch. 'Let's hope the other sketch is as accurate.'

Malcolm pushed it toward Garrison. 'Hard to say.'

This guy had a beard and glasses but his face was small, even delicate. 'I feel like I've seen this picture before, but I can't place him.'

Malcolm nodded. 'I had the same feeling.'

Garrison's mind flipped through the facts of the case. 'Remember the bartender at Moments mentioned that Lisa's older boyfriend had a driver?'

Malcolm nodded. 'Sure.'

'Let's assume the older boyfriend was Darius and the driver was his.'

Malcolm snapped his fingers. 'Drivers hear a lot.'

Garrison rubbed the back of his neck. 'Rokov, see if you can track down this driver. Let's see what light he can shed on this family.'

Kristen woke in stages. At first she thought she'd had another bad dream about her baby. She dreamed about him a lot lately. His cries filled her nightmares and she always found herself searching the darkness for him. But no matter how much she called out to him or how many bargains she made with God, she never found the boy.

But as she opened her eyes, she knew immediately that something was terribly wrong. She lay on a concrete floor and thick chains held her hands and feet to the ground. In

342

the far corner a darkened figure sat next to a hearth where a fire blazed.

Panic burned through her body. She tugged at her chains, testing, hoping she'd be free and discover this wasn't real. The rattle of the metal links echoed in the room.

The figure didn't turn but stoked the embers of the fire. 'Good, you're awake. And just in time.'

Chapter 19

The sketch Garrison faxed to the pub last night still niggled Eva's mind as she flipped the sign from CLOSED to OPEN. She'd not recognized the man but sensed he was no stranger either.

Damn. She rubbed her eyes as the first customer of the day sauntered through the front door. She recognized him. Stan. A regular, he always showed up for lunch before eleven-thirty. And each day he ordered the same thing: turkey, with white American cheese on white bread, chips on the side, soda with no ice.

Stan nodded and came into the pub, taking his regular seat. According to King he'd been coming here for over a decade. Since she'd been serving him, he sat in the same booth.

Eva filled a glass with soda and set it in front of him. 'Morning, Stan. You want the usual?'

'Morning, Doris.' He stared at his cola. 'Yep. I'll have the regular.'

'Great.' Relief washed over her at the normalcy of the moment. He treated her today just like he had yesterday. Nothing had changed.

She put in his order, and then seated a few more customers. No one said anything about the article and she started to believe that maybe, just maybe, she could stay under the radar. Maybe no one cared about her past.

Eva set Stan's turkey sandwich in front of him and refilled his glass with cola from a pitcher.

Instead of diving into the meal as he always had, he stared at it and his brow furrowed.

'Something wrong, Stan? Did I put the chips in the wrong place?'

He continued to stare at his plate. 'So is what the papers say true?'

And so it began. She'd resolved this morning when she'd read the article that she'd not lie about her past. 'Some of it.'

'What was it like in jail?'

She kept her shoulders relaxed. 'Not the kind of place I ever want to go back to.'

He rotated his plate so that the chips shifted from four o'clock to seven o'clock. 'How do I know you haven't slipped poison into my food?'

She laughed. 'You're kidding, right?'

His lips flattened. 'Serious as a heart attack.'

She stared at him, waiting for him to crack a smile or show her this was a joke. But when he only projected seriousness, her anger rose. 'Look, if you don't want to eat,' she said as she reached for his plate.

'I didn't say that.'

'Then what are you saying?' Anger now tugged at her insides.

'I'm just saying, I got to be careful if I'm dealing with an ex-con. That is what they call you people, right? Ex-cons?'

'There a problem here?' King said as he dried his hands on his apron.

'There's no problem,' Eva said.

Stan shrugged. 'I just asked about this morning's article. Didn't expect her to get so prickly about it.'

King planted a meaty fist on his hip. 'You got a point to make, Stan?'

Stan arched a thin eyebrow. 'You know you have a murderer working for you.'

King's expression turned fierce. 'Stan, you aren't one to hold someone's past against them, are you? Yours is a bit colorful.'

Stan stood, his thin body stiff and awkward. 'I may not be perfect, but I ain't no murderer. And I don't like the fact that a murderer is serving me.'

Eva could see King's temper rising. 'Stan, if I were going to poison you, don't you think I'd have done it by now?'

King's eyes flashed with outrage. 'Poison!'

Stan shrugged. 'Maybe, maybe not.'

Eva smiled. 'I'm not going to poison you or anyone else. I do need to take orders at table six and seven. Now, if you don't need anything else, I've got to get moving.'

As Eva moved away, Stan said, 'I don't know if I trust that girl.'

King waved Stan away as he scooped up his plate and headed back to the kitchen. 'Shut up, Stan. And get the hell out of my place.'

Fifteen minutes later after Eva had taken orders and refilled drinks, she pushed through the kitchen door and moved over toward King as he dropped the basket of fries into the hot oil. 'There are a lot of people like Stan, King. And most won't be as up-front as Stan is. They might want to get another morbid look at That Waitress at King's but they'll stop coming.'

'Screw 'em.'

'Easier said than done.' Suddenly a deep weariness settled in her bones. Would this follow her all her life or would the day come when no one cared? 'I'm worried about Bobby. This is going to draw the attention of Social Services.'

King pulled out a chef's knife and started to carve a turkey. 'I'm his foster parent, not you. It shouldn't be a problem.'

'If Connor Donovan keeps writing his articles, then it could be a huge problem. Ten years ago, he built a career on my case.'

'It will blow over.'

King sounded so confident, as if he could weather any storm. But she wasn't so certain. His profit and loss margins on the restaurant were slim and if he lost even a handful of regulars he'd soon be in the red. 'Maybe I should move out for a while. Until the media stuff blows over.'

King glared at her. 'No. This is your home. We will get through this.'

We will get through this. That was the last thing Angie had said to her a decade ago. Angie had underestimated how much damage Donovan could do.

A horn blared outside. Eva pushed open the swinging door and through the front window saw a news van trying to find parking. Her thoughts turned to Deacon. For reasons she couldn't explain, she trusted him and sensed he might be able to help in some way.

'This will not turn into the nightmare it did a decade ago.'

Donovan's article had generated a great buzz. Already, he spun ideas for the follow-up piece, which his editor had scheduled for the Sunday edition. If he played it right, this story would grab the attention of national television news, which could very well lead to a book deal. Eva Rayburn had launched his career and now she was going to save it. She was the gift that kept on giving.

Like the series a decade ago, he'd portrayed Eva as a femme fatale, a woman who'd do anything to break free of her foster care roots. Now he'd suggested that she might have returned to the area to get the revenge on the women who'd testified against her.

As he sipped his coffee, he contemplated getting an agent and a book deal. Fans already wanted to know more about Eva, and if Connor didn't get her story, another reporter would. But so far, he'd had no luck getting her on the phone at King's and King had threatened to break his kneecaps if he showed his face again at the pub. There had to be another place he could ambush her. He was a fast talker, he could be charming and he just needed to get her alone when she didn't have her defenses in place.

His phone rang and he picked it up on the second ring. 'Donovan.'

'This is Eva.' Her voice sounded soft, barely a hoarse whisper.

He sat forward in his chair, his heart pounding furiously.

'You've been trying to call me.'

'I sure have. I really want to interview you. And I'm sorry about the other night. I had no right to ambush you like that.'

'I'm ready to talk now.'

He scrambled through his papers for a pen. 'You name the time and place.'

'There's a house I know. In an hour.'

Donovan scribbled the address on the edge of the morning newspaper. 'I'll be there.'

He hung up the phone and let out a whoop.

Since he'd read the article, Garrison had been thinking about Eva all morning. He'd called the pub but the line was always busy. That son of a bitch Donovan had opened the door for every nut-job and copycat to come after Eva. He feared this kind of media glare would send her running to the next town.

His phone buzzed and he snapped it up. 'Garrison.'

'There's a Ms Rayburn down here to see you,' the officer at the front desk said.

'I'll be right down.'

He pulled on his jacket and hurried down the stairs to find her standing in the lobby, clutching her backpack. Her back was rigid with tension. 'Ms Rayburn.'

'Detective Garrison.' She moved toward him in quick efficient strides.

'How are you holding up after Donovan's article?'

'We closed at one today. A television news reporter made the day miserable.'

'I'm sorry.'

'I'll survive. But I'm worried about Bobby and King. They shouldn't have been dragged into my mess.'

This would all blow over eventually, but the interim could be miserable and destructive. 'I've not been able to remember anything about the other man in the sketch. But I want to help you find this guy.'

'Come up to my office. I want to show you something.'

'Sure.'

He opened the door for her and followed her up the stairs to his office. 'Another woman was murdered six weeks ago. She wasn't branded but her wounds make me think she's connected to the other killings.' He reached in the file and pulled out a picture. 'This is her DMV photo.'

'Okay.' She slid slender fingers into her pockets.

He laid the picture on his desk.

Eva studied the image for a little more than a second before she said, 'Eliza Martinez.'

Unexpected excitement rushed through him. 'You know her?'

'She cleaned the sorority house.' She picked up the picture. 'Her hair is grayer, but she looks almost exactly the same. How did she die?'

'She was stabbed. Four times.'

'The number four again.' She traced Eliza's face with her fingertip. 'Why would anyone want to kill her?'

'I'm hoping you can tell me.'

'She was a nice lady. She even taught me her empanada recipe.'

'Where was she the day Josiah died?'

'She'd been at the house cleaning all day. There was a lot to do since most of the girls had moved out for the summer. I remember she left early because her daughter was ill.'

'No one made threats? No run-ins with Josiah?'

'I never saw anything. But I wasn't always in the house. I do remember her daughter had a little crush on Josiah at the beginning of the school year.' Memories flickered on the edge of her mind. 'Josiah liked Eliza. He called her his little mother.'

'Little mother.'

'Said she reminded him of his mother.'

Garrison rubbed the back of his neck with his hand. 'Micah Cross said their mother died when they were about thirteen.'

'That would be about right. I saw her gravestone a few days ago.'

'You went to her grave?'

She shrugged. 'I wanted to see Josiah's grave. Both his parents' graves were beside it. I don't know anything about her.'

Tension tightened around his spine – a sign he was missing something. But nothing flickered. 'You shouldn't go back to the pub for the next few days. It's not safe. Is there anywhere else you can stay?'

'No.'

'What about Angie's house?'

'I don't know.'

'She's your sister.'

'Yeah.'

'Call her, Eva. She wasn't mentioned in the article, and staying with her will be safest for you, King and Bobby.'

*

Detective Deacon Garrison's presence consumed the front seat as he drove Eva to her sister's. Energy radiated from him. However, instead of intimidating Eva, his closeness left her a little breathless. She realized she liked having him close.

She smoothed her hands over her worn jeans. 'Thanks for doing this, Detective.'

'It's no problem. And you can call me Deacon, if you want.'

'Okay.' A hint of a smile tugged at her lips.

'Right.' He maneuvered the car easily in and out of traffic. 'Angie said she'd meet us at her house?'

'Yes. She was really sweet about it.' The concern in her sister's voice still humbled her. 'She's got to get back to court, but said I could stay as long as I wanted.'

'Good.'

He drove down the tree-lined street and within minutes they spotted the one-level brick house. The lawn was well manicured, but no flowers filled the beds and the table under the big oak tree was blanketed with leaves. When Garrison pulled into the gravel drive, Angie came out the front door. Her hair was pulled back in a tight bun and she wore a dark business suit.

As Eva got out of the car, Angie smiled and crossed the lawn toward her. She hugged Eva. 'I'm so glad you called.'

Eva studied her sister's face. 'Are you sure? If this doesn't work . . .'

Angie squeezed Eva's shoulder. 'Don't say it. I want to help.'

Tears tightened Eva's throat. 'Thanks.'

'I wish I could give you the grand tour, but I've got to be in court in a half hour. The second bedroom on the right is yours and the refrigerator has got the basics.'

Garrison moved behind Eva. 'Thank you.'

Angie glanced up at him, no hint of the defense attorney in her gaze. 'Thank you for making her call me. I'll be back late.' She kissed Eva on the cheek and headed toward her BMW parked in the street.

Garrison lingered and Eva was glad for it. 'Want me to stick around a few minutes?'

She released a sigh. 'That would be great. This is all a little weird for me.'

'I'll make you coffee, provided your sister has it.'

She nodded and they moved inside the house. Only one area rug warmed the hardwood floor in the living room but it anchored the sofa, coffee table and two end chairs. Above the simple hearth hung a gilded mirror that caught the light from French doors that overlooked the backyard.

'Simple, tasteful and very Angie,' Eva said. 'Her father's family always seemed a cut above.'

'You're half sisters.'

'Yes. Angie lived with her dad most of the time. She visited Mom and me occasionally. When Mom died, I went to foster care. Angie was in college on the West Coast.'

'Angie's father didn't consider taking you?'

'No. I'm not sure of the details, but I think my mom left him for my dad. I look like my dad so I guess having me around was a bad reminder.' She set her backpack beside the sofa and moved into the kitchen. Angie had left the lights on. The granite countertop was polished to sparkling and cluttered with only a microwave and a coffeemaker.

Eva opened a cabinet door and found coffee and filters. 'Looks like we're in business.'

Garrison shrugged off his jacket and draped it over a chrome chair, which was part of the dinette set. 'Coffee is a specialty of mine.'

'Great.' She moved to the refrigerator. 'She's got cold cuts. Want a sandwich?'

'Sounds good.'

They both worked silently at their tasks and soon sat at the dinette set. For a moment neither spoke but ate, understanding that opportunities to fuel up shouldn't be bypassed.

'You were right about Lisa's book. It was a simple code and we broke it easily.' He carefully and deliberately set down his sandwich half. 'She says that she met Darius Cross last year.'

'Really?'

'She said they were lovers.'

'I don't know what to say to that.'

'He didn't recognize her at first. When she told him he felt duped and got angry. She told him about The Secret.'

'You mean Kristen's baby?'

'I don't think so. I'm willing to bet if he knew about the baby, he'd have moved heaven and earth to find it.'

'He put a great deal of stock in blood relations. Blood is thicker than water. Josiah said that several times.' She picked at the crust. 'So if not the baby, what secret?'

'I don't know.' He shoved out a breath. 'I also had a fire investigator look at the photos of the sorority house. She doesn't think the fire started by the hearth but by the back door.'

'I don't remember the fire starting. I just remember the flames.' She closed her eyes, willing the haze to fade from her mind so that she could remember. 'I can't tell you how many hours I've tried to relive those moments. But I always come up blank. Have you talked to Kristen about any of this?'

'Her cell went to voice mail. She's in New York.'

'She's got a wedding to plan.'

Garrison let the comment hang in the air. 'What kind of relationship did Micah and Josiah have?'

'I happened by a chemistry lab and heard fighting. I poked my head in and saw the two of them going at it. Micah said he wished Josiah had never been born.' She shook her head. 'When Josiah lunged for Micah, I screamed and the two brothers saw me. They were furious and told me to leave.'

'When did that happen?'

'A couple of weeks before the end of the semester.'

'You see Micah after that?'

'He caught up to me on campus a couple of days later. He wanted to apologize. He seemed concerned that I not share what had happened with anyone.'

'Did you?'

'No. What does Micah have to do with any of this?'

'I don't know. But I can't seem to get the guy out of my head. He's not what he seems.'

'That should have been the motto of the Cross family.'

'What about the kids on campus? Any like or dislike Josiah?'

'Some hung around because of his connections, but I doubt any had great loyalty for Josiah.'

'Can you remember any of them?'

She nibbled on the edge of the sandwich bread crust. 'Brad Morgan. He was on the football team with Josiah. Mike Wells. Joe St John. Those are the faces I remember seeing in the crowd when I sat in the back of the ambulance after the fire. There could be more but I don't remember.'

'They'd be worth talking to.'

'Why are you digging this up?'

'The killings are all connected to that night of the sorority house fire. The killer has chosen the star for a very specific reason.'

'But Kristen and I are still walking around.'

'Maybe your time hasn't come yet.'

Kristen was still alive. Lisa had talked about The Secret. Theories that had been brewing inside her begged to be voiced. 'I'm starting to think Kristen set me up.'

He leaned back in his chair, studying her. 'Why do you say that?'

'I was always a means to an end to her. I know now she was never my friend. She used me to improve her grades and to get into graduate school. Maybe she used me to get rid of Josiah.'

'There's no evidence of that.'

'I know. But then she'd have been careful.'

'It's worth investigating.'

She searched his gaze. 'You believe me?'

'Yes.'

He'd spoken his answer clearly and without hesitation. Having him believe in her meant more than she realized.

Nervous and anxious to move, she raised her plate. 'I'll clean this.'

He reached out and took the plate from her. His fingers brushed hers and for a minute electricity shot through his body. He stared down at her and for an instant the sudden urge to touch her hit him like bricks.

She released the plate but didn't move to step away from him or avert her gaze. This close he could feel the heat from her body. Christ, he needed to get a hold of himself. As much as he wanted to touch her right now, he wouldn't. Couldn't. Too many had taken from her and he'd be damned if he'd join the list.

'I'm not made of china,' Eva said. 'I'm pretty tough.'

'I've no doubt.'

'You want to kiss me.'

'I do.'

And she wanted to kiss him. *He believed her.* She took the plate from him and set it on the counter. 'Then kiss me.'

'Not a good idea.'

Her face impassive, she rose on tiptoe and cupped the back of his head with her hand. 'Unless you have a step-ladder, you'll have to meet me halfway.'

Garrison didn't lean forward but he didn't move away either. The desire that had been rattling around roared inside him. 'Eva. This isn't the time or the place.'

'It's a good time.'

'You know it's not.'

'You don't want me?'

He laid his hand on her shoulders. 'I do. But not now. Not with all this hanging over our heads.'

She stared at him a long moment and then wrapped her

hands around his neck. 'Once thing I've learned, Garrison, you can't count on tomorrow.'

Rising on tiptoe, she kissed him on the lips, savoring the salty taste. He wrapped his arms around her, pulling her close to him. His erection pushed against her belly, setting every nerve ending in her body on fire. She wanted this. She wanted him.

Kristen lay on her back, her hands and feet shackled to the cold brick floor. The acrid scents of smoke, urine and blood assailed her nose as her unfocused gaze stared up at the ceiling's roughly hewn beams. Four stars burned the flesh around her navel and even the slightest breeze had her quivering in pain.

She closed her eyes and for a moment let her mind float back to the first and only time she'd held her son in her arms. His little body had been neatly nestled in the crook of her arm. His surprisingly strong mouth had suckled her breast. She'd stroked the soft downy hair on his head. It had been pure bliss.

She'd replayed that moment so many times in the last decade. She'd sacrificed so much for that moment. And she knew now, what she'd done for her son years ago had brought her to this moment.

'I need you do something for me, Kristen.' The voice brought her mind back to the present, like a string jerked a kite from the air.

Her eyes remained closed, her last rebellion.

'You'll do me a favor, won't you? Just one more phone call.' And when she didn't move, 'I know where your son lives.'

Her eyes opened. 'Where?'

'Ah, there's a good girl.'

'Where is he?' She didn't beg for release.

'I'll tell as soon as you call.'

'You swear?'

'Yes.'

Donovan arrived at the brick house as Eva had instructed. The house looked as if it had been built in the 1920s. The overgrown bushes blocked most of the ground-floor windows. The front sidewalk had cracked and splintered in several places and the front handrail had fallen over.

'You sure can pick locations, Eva.'

The phone in his pocket buzzed; he reached for it and flipped it open. 'Donovan.'

'It's Eva. I'm inside. The door is unlocked.'

The woman's voice was faint and it sounded enough like Eva for him to open the door and enter the darkened foyer. Floorboards creaked under his feet. Thanks to light streaming in through a side window, he could see the house was deserted, the furniture long cleared out. He hung up his phone. 'Eva.'

'Over here.' The voice sounded older, not like Eva at all.

He took two uncertain steps before he felt a blinding pain in the back of his skull. He dropped to his knees, trying to stay conscious even as he realized the battle was futile.

He fell forward and passed out.

Eva took Deacon by the hand and led him down the hallway to the spare room. She pulled him over the threshold, amazed at how calm and sure she felt until she looked at the bed.

And then the uncertainty rose up inside her. She had no experience with men. And she didn't want to mess this up. 'I've never seduced a man,' she said. 'I'm not sure what to do next.'

He laid his hands on her shoulders. 'You don't have to do anything. None of this has to happen now.' His voice sounded ragged, even a bit nervous.

She turned and faced him. 'But I want this. I want you.'

He cupped her face, his expression a hard unreadable mask. She thought for a moment he'd reject her. She wondered if she could bear the rejection. It had taken so much for her to get to this moment.

And then he leaned forward and kissed her on the lips. The first kiss was gentle, more like exploration than grand passion. But it boosted her confidence and the courage to wrap her arms around his neck. She pressed her breasts against his chest. Her nipples hardened.

Tensing, he brushed her hair off her face and away from her neck, exposing the tender flesh. He kissed the hollow of her throat, her collarbone and then her ear. Heat bubbled inside her and she tightened her hold on his shoulders.

He backed her up toward the bed until her legs bumped the mattress. She braced, expecting fear, but none came and that gave her the courage to grab the hem of her T-shirt and pull it over her head.

Garrison's gaze darkened as he stared at her breasts. He leaned down and kissed each soft mound and then slipped his fingers under her bra and teased the tips of her nipples until they hardened more. Eva closed her eyes, moaning her pleasure.

She fumbled with the buckle of his pants but he pushed her hands away.

'Slow.' He eased her back against the mattress and straddled her body. He ran his hands up her thighs and over her flat belly. He was in no rush.

'I like it when you touch me,' she said.

'Good.'

He reached for the bra clasp between her breasts and undid the delicate snap. He cupped her breasts as he leaned forward and kissed her.

The weight of him didn't scare her nor did it make her want to scream. She'd always feared her first real sexual encounter would be difficult because of the rape, but this felt so different from the last time. Deacon's touch was as gentle as Josiah's had been violent.

Garrison suckled her breast. She arched into him.

Her response encouraged him to reach for the snap of her jeans. He unfastened it and stroked the pink fabric of her panties. She grew wet.

With her help, he pulled off her pants and tossed them on the floor. Raw sexual need darkened his eyes as he kissed the panties and pushed his finger under the elastic. He teased her most intimate center, stoking a desire in her she'd never felt before. 'Please,' she whispered.

He pressed his lips to her ear and kissed her gently. 'Please what?'

'More.'

'You're sure?'

This time his voice sounded strained, as if backing off

wouldn't be nearly as easy, but she trusted that he would if she asked. And that made her want him more.

'Yes.' This time when she reached for his belt buckle, he didn't push her hands away. Instead he watched as she undid the pants and pushed them down over his hips.

When she touched his hardness, Garrison swallowed and a vein in the side of his neck pulsed. He quickly reached in his pocket and pulled a condom from his wallet. He slid it expertly over his erection and then came down on top of her. As he kissed her, he pulled at her panties. Fabric ripped but neither cared.

She opened her legs and he straddled above her. He hesitated, poised at the edge of her, and when she raised her hips, he pushed into her.

He filled her so completely. She tensed, expecting pain, as her body stretched and molded to him. He held steady, kissing her on the lips but not yet moving inside of her. When the tightness eased, he started to move slowly and steadily.

Sensations built inside of her, and when he reached down to touch her again and stroke her softness, her desire bubbled over. She wrapped her legs around him and took all of him. He stroked faster, and in the next second she arched and welcomed his release.

He collapsed against her and rested his face in the crook of her neck. A fine sheen of sweat glistened on their bodies. Their racing heartbeats mingled.

Finally, he rolled on his side and pulled her against him. He cupped his hand over her breast and she nestled her bottom against him. Neither spoke, savoring the union they just shared.

Finally, his hand moved from her breast to the star-shaped scar on her shoulder. He traced it. Kissed it.

'I'll never let anyone hurt you again,' he whispered.

Giddiness bubbled in Lou. The plan was coming together. Soon all those who'd needed to be punished would be dead. And Donovan, well, he was about to get the story of his life.

The deadweight of Donovan's body proved a bit of a struggle but finally Lou dragged him from the house to the waiting van. No doubt the embers in the basement haven had dimmed by now, but it would take little effort to stoke them and get them burning hot once again.

When the haze cleared from Donovan's brain, his head snapped up in a quick jerky movement. A dry mouth and a pounding headache had him instantly craving a soda and aspirin. 'Shit.'

He opened his eyes to a near-dark room. He sat in a chair, his hands tied to the arms. A swell of panic rose up through him and threatened to chase away rational thought. He'd been in bad spots before, like when the drug dealer he'd interviewed had decided he didn't like the tone of his questions and had tried to jam a knife in his gut, or when a killer-for-hire had threatened to shoot him. Each of those times, he'd been able to talk his way out of trouble.

And he'd do it now.

Donovan glanced down and realized he'd pissed on himself. The ropes that held him to the chair arms had rubbed raw red rings.

Again the panic seared. He cleared his throat. 'Hey.' His voice sounded like sandpaper against metal. He sniffed and raised his chin. 'Is anyone there?'

His only answer was the drip, drip of a leaking pipe.

'Hey, I know you're there. I can hear you!' He couldn't hear but he could bluff. 'Talk to me.' *Talk to me. I can reason my way out of anything but you've got to talk to me.*

A soft moan rose from a shadowed corner.

'Hello!' A thrill of excitement snapped against his nerve endings, making him sit just a little straighter. 'Who is it?'

This time the moan was louder and more desperate. The sound reminded him of an animal dying in a trap.

'He's going to kill us,' a woman said.

A chill scraped down Donovan's back. 'Who? Who?'

'I don't know. I don't know.' She started to sob softly.

Donovan jerked at his ropes. 'Stop crying. It's not going to help.'

'You don't know what he's going to do to you.' Her words sounded like a whimper.

'What do you mean?'

'He's going to burn you.'

Donovan's pulse thrummed in his neck. 'What?'

'Just like he did me. He's going to burn you.'

Shit. Terror scratched at his insides, leaving him feeling more helpless. He didn't want to be afraid. He wanted to be the tough-as-nails-reporter he'd led the world to believe he was. Digging below the fear, he searched for a shred of anger that he could cling to – anger that would give him the power to get out of this. At least angry, he could hang on to a semblance of control.

It frustrated him that he couldn't see her. 'Who are you?'

For a long moment, she didn't answer. 'Kristen Hall.'

'Kristen Hall? You were one of the girls who testified against Eva Rayburn.'

Her laugh was weak, half hysterical. 'He said you'd be asking me questions. I'm supposed to give you the story of your life.'

Donovan let his head fall forward. 'Yesterday, I'd have been thrilled to talk to you.'

'I'm supposed to tell you everything.'

'And then what?'

'He's going to kill us.'

Donovan jerked against his bindings. 'I don't want to hear what you have to say.'

'I have to tell. I have to tell or it will be worse.'

He'd spent his professional career looking under rocks and trying to get to the next story. Every time he'd been hungry for more information. He needed to know. Now, he was too afraid to ask. And yet, a lifetime of habits wouldn't let go. 'What are you supposed to tell me?'

'I killed Josiah Cross.'

'What?'

'I was pregnant with his child. I was afraid of what he'd do when he found out.' She paused. 'He was a monster. I couldn't spend my life shackled to him.'

'Why not just get an abortion?'

'I couldn't.' Emotion choked her voice. 'But I could kill Josiah. I let it slip that Eva would be alone at the house. I knew he'd come. He hated her.' A soft bitter laugh rumbled in her throat. 'He often talked about bringing her down a peg.'

How many times had Donovan set someone up for a story? Still, what Josiah had done to Eva . . . he couldn't have done that, could he? 'She was bait?'

'Yes.'

'He raped her. Brutalized her.'

She didn't respond for a long time and he thought she might have passed out.

'Tell me!' Connor shouted.

'I saw her lying on the floor,' Kristen continued finally. 'She'd passed out, but I thought she was dead. Josiah looked worried. He always panicked when he went too far with someone. I knew I had a few minutes so I slipped in through the side door and hit him with the poker. He died right away.'

'And you set the fire?'

'I freaked when I saw all the blood. I ran out back where Lisa and Sara were waiting. I stripped to my underwear while Sara got gasoline from the shed and dumped it on my clothes. Lisa got spare clothes from her car. As Sara dumped gasoline on my clothes I struck a match and tossed it on the heap. It caught immediately and spread to the house so fast. The place was in flames in seconds.'

'Christ. You lied about it all.'

'Yes.'

'Where's the kid?'

'My mother took him. Gave him away.'

In that moment, floodlights flipped on, bright and harsh. Donovan winched, closing his eyes and ducking his head from the glare. Seconds passed before he lifted a lid and let in a bit of light. Slowly, he opened his eyes more until he became accustomed to it.

In an instant he regretted the light.

Directly in front of him was the woman, Kristen, shackled to an ancient brick wall, her arms above her head and her legs anchored to the floor. She wore no shirt, only a lace black bra and designer jeans. No shoes and toes that looked like they'd been manicured were chipped and covered in dirt. Above the waistband of her jeans were four clear burns. Stars. All circling her navel.

Tears had pulled the mascara down her pale cheeks in black streaks and her red hair was a wild, knotted mess. She stared at him with green eyes that registered resignation.

Donovan swallowed, at a loss for words. He could barely look at her. She disgusted and scared him.

Tears streamed down Kristen's face. 'I didn't want anyone to know about the baby. The Cross family would have turned him into a monster.'

Donovan shook his head. 'Who is doing this to us?'

'I don't know.'

'Is it Eva?'

'I don't know.' For a moment her knees buckled and her legs folded. Only the manacles that bound her hands held her up.

She'd passed out or, worse, died. Fear exploded inside of Donovan. He didn't want to be left here alone. 'Kristen! Kristen! Wake up. Wake up.'

For a long moment Kristen didn't move. Her breathing was so imperceptible that he thought she might have died. She hung lifeless like a puppet on strings. And then she raised her head and looked at him.

'Kristen! Kristen! Wake up! Why am I here?' He jerked

at the ropes, unmindful of the pain the twine caused his raw skin.

'The articles you wrote.' The words wheezed from her lips.

'The articles I've written?'

'Yes.'

His mind shuffled through the articles. 'I was harsh on Eva in the latest piece and a decade ago.'

Kristen nodded. 'I remember the old articles.'

'It has to be Eva. She has to be doing this.'

Kristen stared at him. 'She's punishing us for our sins.'

'I didn't do anything wrong. I was doing my job. I didn't sin!'

Kristen was silent for a moment. 'She thinks you did.'

The lights went out.

Chapter 20

After Garrison left Eva at Angie's house, he drove directly to Micah Cross's estate. A housekeeper greeted him and escorted him back into the main room where he and Cross had met before. Garrison moved toward the hearth, a Price yearbook tucked under his arm. A fire crackled inside.

'Detective,' Micah said from the doorway. 'Another visit?'

Garrison turned. 'Mr Cross. Thank you for seeing me.'

Cross's demeanor was cool, reserved to the point of withdrawn. 'What can I do to help you?'

Garrison smiled. 'I had a few more questions about your brother.'

The welcoming hint in Micah's eyes faded. 'Sure. What do you want to know?'

'Your brother was a pretty big deal in college.'

'He was. Played football. Did well academically.'

'I understand he dated a girl named Kristen Hall.'

'Maybe. He dated a lot of women. Girls like a good-looking guy.'

'Kristen would have been special. I understand they went out for several months.'

369

Micah pulled an imaginary thread from his pant leg. 'If you say so.'

'So you don't remember her?'

'The name escapes me. But if you have a picture, maybe I'd recognize her.'

Garrison opened the yearbook. 'As a matter of fact, I brought the yearbook from your brother's senior year.'

'Very efficient of you.'

Garrison opened the page to the picture featuring the Rising Stars. 'Any of these girls look familiar?'

'I know Eva Rayburn. Hard to forget her.' He seemed to study the other photos. 'I know the faces. And I recognize Sara. Which one is Kristen?'

'The redhead.'

'If you say so. Where is this leading? It's starting to sound like I need an attorney.'

Garrison wanted this interview to remain light and easy so Micah didn't marshal attorneys to shut down the questions. But keeping it light wasn't as easy as usual. A very primal part of him wanted to tell Micah to stay the hell away from Eva, who didn't need reminders of the man that had raped her. 'I'm just gathering background information, Mr Cross. Nothing to be concerned about.'

'I don't understand. My brother died over a decade ago. The case was solved. Closed.'

Garrison smiled. 'You've read about the murders in the paper?'

'Those women that were stabbed? Sure. Poor Sara. I still can't believe she's dead. But what does that killing and the other one have to do with me or Josiah?'

'Two of the women were in this picture. Lisa Black and Sara Miller.'

'You asked me about Kristen Hall. Is she dead?'

'She's not answering her cell.' Garrison shifted tactics. 'You went to see Eva. Why?'

'To let her know there were no hard feelings.'

'Just like that?'

'Yeah.' He sighed. 'Look, I want to put the past behind us. After Josiah died my father was never the same. But I got on with my life. I wanted her to know that.'

Garrison often learned more about people from the words left unspoken. 'Your brother's death must have been doubly hard seeing as you'd already lost your mother. Car accident, wasn't it?'

'Of course it was hard.' Micah tensed as if struggling with anger.

'Was your father upset about your mom's passing?'

'Of course. They were husband and wife.'

'According to many, he had many girlfriends not long after her death.'

'They didn't have the best marriage. And Dad deserved a life.'

'Tell me about the car accident.'

'It was out west in Colorado. She'd gone out there with friends. A spa getaway weekend, from what Dad told me. The car she and her friends were driving skidded off the road and into an embankment. Mom was killed instantly.'

'That would have been twenty years ago.'

'Nineteen years in May.'

'Her death must have been so hard on you and Josiah.'

'We managed to put our lives back together. Dad called us the Three Musketeers. But when Josiah died, Dad just couldn't rebound. He became obsessed with Josiah and honoring his memory.'

'I saw the Cross house at Price. And your brother's portrait.'

'Did you also see the Cross wing on the library? Or the additions to the football field made in my brother's honor?'

Was that jealousy woven around the words? 'Missed that. Have you been back to Price lately?'

'No. I'm not so fond of the place.' Micah slid his hand into his pocket. 'I don't see what all this has to do with these murdered women.'

'Just trying to piece it all together. Do you have a picture of your mother?'

'No. Dad burned them all.'

'He burned them?'

'Yes.'

'Says a lot about their marriage, don't you think?'

'They never shared the details of their marriage with me.'

Garrison sensed Micah was holding back. But what? 'Until this case is closed, would you do me a favor?'

'If I can.'

'Stay away from Eva Rayburn.'

Micah cocked an eyebrow. 'You sound overly protective of her, Detective.'

'Good.'

Donovan lost track of time in the dark. He didn't know if it was day or night and he didn't care. The woman had grown silent. He'd called out to her but she no longer answered him even with her pitiful moans. He feared she'd died.

'Kristen.' Donovan wanted her awake, wanted to know that he wasn't in this damn basement alone. He didn't want to die alone.

His bindings had rubbed his wrists raw and now each time he moved his skin burned and bled. So he'd learned to be still. However, hardest to ignore was the thirst. It had started off as annoying but with each passing minute it grew stronger until now that was all he could think about.

Water. Drinking something.

The lights came on and he found himself again wincing at the intense glare. He braced but didn't raise his head to see the woman on the other side of the room. Looking at her churned his gut.

A door opened and he cracked his lids so that he could finally see who did this to him. For several tense seconds, his vision blurred and he couldn't make out who stood in the doorway. Then slowly his pupils constricted.

A slim man stood before him and immediately it pissed off Donovan. Hell, he could have taken the guy in a fist-fight. To know such a weakling had taken him ramped up his anger and bitterness. Gotten the best of by a troll.

His bearded captor wore dark baggy jeans, a black hooded jacket, gloves, sunglasses and what looked like a gray wig. The lunacy of this whole situation triggered a second of hysteria. How could he have landed in such a bad dream?

Donovan moistened his dry lips. He could get anyone

to talk and he knew if he could get this son of a bitch to talk he'd find a way to get his ass out of here.

A smile would be forced but Donovan figured if he could just sound casual and relaxed that would be enough. 'Who are you? What do you want?'

'I'm the one who has been sent to see that you atone for your sins.'

The figure turned from him and moved toward Kristen. He pulled out a knife. The sharp blade caught a glint of the light as their jailer raised the knife over his head and plunged it into Kristen's body.

'Shit!' Donovan shouted. He jerked at his bindings and started to rock the chair back and forth. Blood ran from Kristen's body. 'Shit! Shit! Shit! Christ, someone help me!'

The man stabbed Kristen three more times before turning toward Donovan. 'No one is going to help you. No one can hear you. So be quiet and accept your medicine like a real man.'

Donovan's stomach lurched, and if there'd been any food in his stomach he'd have retched it up. 'Stay the fuck away from me.'

'What's wrong, Mr Donovan? No smooth words?'

Normally free-flowing sentences jumbled and tangled in a thicket of fear. 'What the hell do you want?'

'Atonement.'

He jerked raw wrists against his bindings. 'What does that mean?'

The man moved toward the hearth and started to build a small pile of sticks over balled-up paper. He pulled a lighter from his pocket and lit the paper. The fire caught immediately and the flames began to hiss and pop.

The killer started to whistle 'Happy Birthday.' The happy song took on the grotesque in this setting.

'Whose birthday is it?'

'His birthday was last Friday but I always extended the celebration a week.' Carefully stacked kindling fed the fire. 'The trick is to slowly build the embers. Overfeeding smothers it. And we don't want that, do we?'

Donovan yanked at his bindings, ignoring the pain and fresh stream of blood that trickled down his wrists and onto the floor. 'Let me go! Let me go!'

'Not just yet. You have to learn a few lessons first.' A larger stack of wood on the flames had it soon roaring to life. 'It'll be a few minutes before the iron gets nice and hot.'

Tears stung Donovan's eyes. He did not want to die.

It didn't take a genius to know what came next. He was going to burn.

Donovan screamed.

Chapter 21

Eva had a restless night. She'd been plagued by night-mares. The fire. Josiah. Bobby. Garrison. When she woke, exhaustion hovered around her shoulders like a cold, wet blanket.

She rolled on her side and inhaled Garrison's lingering scent on the pillow. She'd barely given the room any notice when she and Garrison had stumbled into it yesterday. There'd only been him. His smell. His touch. The sound of his voice whispering dark erotic words as they'd made love.

Eva swung her legs over the side of her bed and ran her hands through her hair. She glanced toward the door and realized it was wide open. Last night had been the first time in a decade that she'd slept with the door open. Instead of panic, she savored a real feeling of peace. So much chaos surrounded her now, but a small seed of peace had taken root.

The room's furnishings could be categorized as career-woman-with-no-time-to-decorate. The bed had no headboard, and the dresser looked as if it had been hur-riedly purchased at a box store and assembled with thoughts to storage not fashion. In the corner sat a wing-back chair in need of re-covering. Pinned to the chair was a note.

Eva padded across the floor and grabbed the note. In her sister's neat script, she read:

EARLY COURT APPEARANCE. I'LL BE HOME EARLY SO WE CAN HAVE DINNER.

Eva smiled and tucked the note into her pocket. She dressed and padded into the kitchen. She made coffee and as it dripped she called King. The line buzzed, signaling he still had the phone off the hook. She poured herself a cup, wondering how he and Bobby fared. They'd been her family these last few months, and hiding out here felt like a betrayal.

The more she thought about King and Bobby the more she paced and worried. He couldn't afford to stay closed forever and she worried he'd not be able to handle the crowds. King would tell her to stay hidden and safe, which only bolstered her need to check on him.

Perhaps if she snuck in the back alley, she could check on them without the media seeing her. She called a cab and, twenty minutes later, slipped down the back alley toward King's kitchen entrance. As she unlocked the door, Merlin meowed from behind the Dumpster.

She glanced over and saw a kitten peeking his head out. She moved toward him, hoping to catch him, but he vanished back behind the Dumpster. Merlin wasn't quite ready to join their patchwork family but it was only a matter of time. 'I'll get you some tuna, Merlin.'

The cat meowed.

Eva pushed open the door. 'King?'

He poked his head out of the storage cabinet. 'What are you doing here? You're supposed to be in hiding.'

377

'Couldn't do it. I was too worried about you and Bobby.' She went to the refrigerator and pulled out a half-open can of tuna. 'Merlin is hungry. Did you feed him this morning?'

'Twice. That damn kitten eats like a horse.'

She smiled. 'Bobby feeds him at least ten times a day. He's spoiled.'

She took the tuna outside and scraped it into the cat's bowl.

Back inside she washed her hands. 'We opening for lunch today?'

He frowned. 'What are you doing here?'

'Checking on you.'

'The reporters lost interest last night about midnight, but they'll be back.'

'I know. I'll leave soon. Did Bobby go to school?'

'He did. Didn't want to go, but I made him because he's got a big spelling test before lunch.'

'Good. It's doubtful anyone will connect him to me at school so it should be okay for him today.'

'I sent a cell phone in his backpack just in case.'

'You're a good dad, King.'

He looked at her, his gaze full of emotion she'd not expected. 'Thanks. That means a lot.'

'Are you going to adopt Bobby?'

He shrugged. 'I miss being a father.'

She'd never pried into King's past – a place she suspected was as dark as her own. But she was beginning to see that forgetting the past didn't solve as much as she'd have wished. 'Tell me about your son.'

'Before I do that, I need to tell you something you might not like.'

An uneasy quietness settled in her bones. 'Okay.'

'I didn't just happen on that halfway house where you were living. I have a friend in the parole system who told me where you were.'

'Why?'

He shoved out a breath. 'I followed your trial. It made me sick watching what the Cross family did to you. That Darius was like a damn steamroller. He got what he wanted no matter what.'

She wasn't sure how she felt about this. 'You came looking for me.'

'I know how it can be for parolees. Hand to mouth. I figured if you came back here I could help you get back on your feet.'

She studied King, not sure what to say. Finally, she whispered, 'Why didn't you tell me this at the beginning?'

'I figured you'd not take me up on the offer. Besides, the job offer wasn't totally out of the goodness of my heart. A big part of the offer had to do with revenge.'

She stared at him as if she'd never seen him before. 'I don't understand.'

'My son's name was Kyle. Great, great kid.' His voice lost its edge and grew softer. 'Died in a car accident when he was twelve. His mom was driving. A drunk driver broadsided them. Kyle died outright. Irene lived through the crash, but she never got over it. She blamed herself. A year to the day Kyle died, she killed herself.'

'King.' Her heart squeezed tight, choking off her breath and words for a moment. 'I'm so sorry.'

He sniffed and rubbed his eye. 'The accident was a long time ago. Nineteen years.'

'Time doesn't completely fix pain like that.'

'No, it doesn't. You know loss as well as anybody.'

'But it doesn't rule my life like it did.'

He nodded. 'I can think about Kyle and Irene and remember the good times.' He met her gaze. 'There's something else I need to tell you.'

'What?'

'That drunk driver that killed Kyle and my wife. It was Louise Cross.'

'Josiah's mother? She died in a car accident herself nineteen years ago. I saw her grave.'

'She's not dead.'

She felt as if the wind had been knocked out her. 'What?'

'That bitch is alive and well.'

'Where?'

'I don't know. Her husband swore she'd never walk free again if the cops didn't file charges. I argued but in the end his money and power won. Darius vowed he'd be his wife's jailer and she'd never see daylight again.'

'Darius is dead. Who's her jailer now?'

Garrison picked up his phone on the third ring. 'Yeah.'

'It's Eva.'

The tension in her voice had him leaning forward. 'Everything all right?'

'Yeah. Hey, did you know Josiah and Micah's mother is still alive?'

'That can't be right. Micah said she died. You saw her grave.'

She told him King's story. With each bit, his grip on the receiver tightened. 'Are you sure?'

'Yes.'

He shoved out a breath. 'We've been looking for a man all along.'

'Could Louise Cross be doing all this?'

'Anything is possible. Eva, be careful. Whoever is doing this is dangerous. No one has seen Kristen in thirty-six hours and I'm starting to think she's in real trouble and that you're next.'

'I'm at King's and I'm not going anywhere. I'm safer here surrounded by people.'

'Swear you won't leave King's.' His concern leaked into the statement.

'Promise.'

With her safe, he could think. 'I'll call you soon. Be careful.'

'I will.'

He hung up and called Dispatch. He ordered a patrol car to park in front of King's. When he hung up, he found Malcolm in his office. 'Where's that sketch artist?'

'Around. Why?'

'I want her to redraw the picture but without the beard. And give the person long hair like a woman.'

'Will do.'

His phone rang and he snatched it up. His irritation shone through when he barked, 'Garrison.'

'Madge Olsen. Social Services. You called about one of my kids?'

'Right.' He'd called yesterday to talk about Bobby's case because Eva had been worried. 'Bobby Torres. Foster son of Toby King.'

'Right. His full name is Robert Martinez Torres.'

'Did you say Martinez?' He dug through his files searching for Eliza Martinez's file.

'That's right. Middle name was his mother's maiden name. Bobby's mother died of cancer last year and he went to live with his grandmother for a while. She couldn't handle the day-to-day responsibility of a child so she allowed him to go into foster care.'

'His grandmother, Eliza Martinez, was murdered three months ago.' She'd been stabbed four times just like Lisa, Sara and Danvers.

'Yes. I know. And often it's hard to place a ten-year-old boy who's endured a trauma. But not this time.'

'Explain.'

'Toby King approached us just a day after the kid's grandmother died. He has friends in Social Services who pushed through his paperwork. His background check cleared so we awarded him custody fairly quickly.'

And now King housed Eva and Bobby, both of whom had a connection to the Cross family. Garrison's gut tightened. 'Thanks, Madge.'

He picked up the phone and called King's. The line was busy.

After that homicidal creep had killed Kristen he'd untied her body and carried her away, leaving Donovan alone to watch the hearth's flames dance and dwindle.

Panic had brewed inside his gut, and several times he screamed. But when no one came and no one heard him cry out, he'd known getting out of here alive rested on his shoulders.

This guy has got to have some sort of weakness, Donovan

thought as he tried to shove the fear away. Everybody has a weakness.

For him it was bourbon and too many women. Both vices had gotten him more than his share of trouble and both had nearly cost him his job. The trick now was to figure out his captor's weakness.

Atonement was his thing. And if Donovan could just figure out what had driven this guy to the brink, then maybe he could find the chink in his armor.

Think, Donovan. You're good at this. You're good at getting people to open up. He pictured Angie. She'd been a hard case, but he'd found just the right buttons to push and she'd opened up to him like a flower hungry for sunshine.

Just study the guy. You'll see the weakness.

The top door leading down to the basement opened. The killer flipped on the lights and moved down the stairs, slowly, deliberately.

Donovan stiffened. Shit. What the hell had this creepy bastard planned for him?

With a great effort, he chased the fear from his voice. 'So I'm here to atone?'

The hooded figure nodded. 'That's exactly right, Mr Donovan.'

Donovan sat straight up in his chair, tracking every footstep toward the fireplace. 'I've been trying to think what I did that ticked you off. All I can come up with is the article on Eva Rayburn.'

Just the sound of the woman's name brought tension to the figure.

'I got to say,' Donovan pressed. 'She's one hard case. A lot like her sister, Angie. I've been trying to figure out how you could know Eva? She's only been back in town six months.'

Crumpled pieces of newspaper were fitted between dried twigs and branches. And a flick of the lighter soon had a fire crackling.

'You must hate her.'

'I don't hate the sinner but the sin.'

'What could she have done to you? How did she hurt you?'

'You're clever, Mr Donovan, but if you believe getting me to talk is going to change things, then you are wrong.'

Donovan leaned forward. He had the story of a life-time but he needed to live to tell it. 'What did Eva do to you? Did she do something to you?'

'She stole the most important thing in the world from me!'

Donovan sensed a door had been cracked open to his kidnapper's soul. 'What did she steal?'

Silence followed and then soft laughter. 'You're so clever. Why don't you figure it out?'

'She was sent away a decade ago. It happened a long time ago.'

'Some wounds can never be forgotten.'

He moistened his lips, tried a half smile that, given a different set of circumstances, could have hidden his desperation better. 'Wounds, you speak about . . . She didn't take a thing from you, but a person?'

Tension rippled and suddenly his captor stoked the flames with angry thrusts.

'Who did she steal from you?'

'It doesn't matter now. What's done is done.'

'Tell me.' His words sounded like a gentle whisper of a lover.

'You are very clever. Is that how you got Angie Carlson into your bed? Did you whisper to her like that?'

'I needed to find Eva. Angie was my only link.'

'And so you used her.' The tip of the branding iron started to glow red. Steam rose from the metal tip. Soon it would be ready. 'Did she cry when she realized she'd been used?'

Donovan stared at the branding iron. Showing fear and begging wasn't going to save him now. 'I'm sure she did. She liked me. Liked me a lot.'

'You broke her heart?'

'Sure.' He'd say whatever this guy wanted him to say to get out of here.

'You're not a very nice man, Mr Donovan.'

'People get hurt. It happens. But I don't deserve to die. In fact, let me live and I will work to turn the public against Eva Rayburn.'

'Your last article caused her pain.'

'Then let me write more.' He watched the hooded figure heft the branding iron in small, gloved hands. The iron appeared to feel heavy. The tip glowed red now and was ready.

'That's not necessary. I can handle things from here.'

'Look,' Donovan said quickly, 'at least let me see your face. I should at least know who is doing this to me.'

'Sure, why not?' He removed the hood and glasses. Slowly, he peeled off the beard.

His jailer wasn't a man but a woman! Donovan searched the woman's face for any signs of familiarity. 'Do I know you?'

She laughed. 'I don't know. Do you?'

Donovan's next comment was silenced by the jab of the branding iron into his belly. He screamed so loud, the sound seemed to bounce off the walls forever.

He slumped forward in a sweaty, exhausted heap. 'You don't have to do this. I can help you.'

'Always the talker.'

The iron still glowed hot, enough to burn his skin a second time.

Donovan had never known such agony. His body vibrated with pain. His nostrils were filled with the scent of his own burning skin. As his captor jabbed the branding iron back into the flames, he knew he'd endure more pain. Only one brand on his belly meant three to come.

'Let me help you.' His voice sounded so hoarse.

'Thanks, but I've got this under control.'

'Let me go and I'll do whatever you want. I'll write whatever you want.'

'I bet you would write anything at this moment. But your meager attempt at atonement has little meaning now. You'd do anything now to stop the pain.'

'I would.'

She pressed the hot iron into his belly.

Donovan howled, arching his back and straining against his bindings. 'Stop! P-P-P-Please.'

'Okay, I'll stop the pain.'

Donovan forced his eyes open. He knew pathetic hope glistened in his eyes as he searched for a sign of mercy.

Mercy came in the shape of a sharp blade that glinted and caught the light from the fire. And before he could speak, the tip of the blade pierced his chest, sliced through flesh and grazed bone.

His body froze. And for one, two, three beats of his heart he believed life melted from his body.

Garrison called the patrol car stationed at King's to check on Eva. The officer had reported seeing her through the window of the pub waiting tables. He'd also ordered Rokov to do a complete background check on King.

For now Eva was safe and the patrol officer would keep tabs on her. But it bothered him that he wasn't there looking after her himself. In his core he believed only he could keep her alive. It was a foolish feeling rooted in the deaths of his sister and wife.

Tension snapped at him as he pulled up in front of the one-story rancher.

'I still don't see why we're here. We've talked to Dave Torres four or five times,' Malcolm said.

Dave Torres was the nephew of the first victim, Eliza Martinez. He'd been helpful and had answered all of Garrison's questions. 'We've missed something.'

'What? We went over Martinez's past. She came up clean.'

'She's Bobby's grandmother and King brought the boy to live with him and Eva. Too many coincidences.' Garrison rang the bell.

Seconds later the door snapped open. A tall, willowy man with downturned eyes and a thick stubble of beard stared back at them through the screened door. 'Mr Torres.'

Torres threaded bony fingers through his hair. 'Detective. Do you have word on my aunt's killer?'

'No, sir, but I hoped we could talk again.'

Torres shrugged and pushed open the screen door. 'Sure. If you think it will help.'

'Thank you, sir.'

The officers moved into the cramped living room filled with piles of old newspapers. Torres had admitted on their first visit that he had trouble parting with newspapers. All his spare rooms and most of his kitchen were filled with copies of the *Post* and *Journal*. Since their last visit, Torres had filled the extra chairs in the living room with paper, leaving no place to sit.

'I'm not sure what else I can add.'

Garrison pulled out his notebook. 'What can you tell me about your aunt's grandson?'

'Bobby?' Torres shrugged. 'Quiet kid. I never saw him much. He lived with his mom.'

Garrison checked his notes. 'Mrs Martinez's daughter died last year of cancer?'

'That's right. Tough for someone so young to die like that.'

'What happened to the boy?'

'Foster care. Eliza didn't have it in her to raise the kid. But she had him over for sleepovers often.'

'Did he have a sleepover with his grandmother the night she died?'

'No, thank God. He and I were at a concert in D.C. This rock band. My ears are still ringing. But the kid loved it. He spent the night with me. We found out about his grandmother the next day.'

'He switched foster homes after his grandmother's death.'

'The kid was hurt and angry when he found out Aunt Eliza was dead. His family didn't want to deal with an angry kid. But his new foster dad didn't mind that Bobby was a handful. Lucky for the kid.'

Garrison didn't think luck played into the scenario at all. 'Why didn't you take the boy?'

He shifted, uncomfortable. 'I'm good with the kid for a night here and there but not full-time.'

'And the boy's father?'

'Never in the picture. In fact, I'm not sure if Rebecca ever told him about the kid. She said the guy frightened her.'

'Did Rebecca go to Price?'

'No. She could never afford a private college. She went to a community college here in Alexandria. Dropped out her freshman year to have Bobby. Worked lots of jobs to keep food on the table. She did visit Price a couple of times. She'd help her mom cleaning up after those sorority girls had a party.'

'Rebecca say anything about her visits to Price?'

'The first couple of visits were a blast. She met a guy. But the last wasn't so great. Something happened, but she'd never say what.'

'That patrolman keeps watching the place,' King said. He set two hamburger orders on the bar for Eva to deliver.

Eva filled a mug with cold beer. 'Garrison is keeping an eye on me. He's worried.'

King grunted. 'Good. He should be.' He wiped his hands on his apron. 'Maybe I should take him some coffee.'

'I can do that,' Eva said.

'You, help a cop?'

She shrugged. 'Maybe they're not all bad.'

King laughed. 'You keep working. I'll run the coffee out. And do me a favor and call Betty. She's late.'

'Will do.'

Garrison slammed his phone down so hard the desk rattled.

Malcolm leaned forward in his chair. 'Still no Kristen?'

'She never boarded her return flight to New York.' He ran his hand through his hair. 'I want every cop in the city looking for Kristen Hall. We need to find her.'

Garrison called the patrolman watching the pub. 'You see Eva?'

'I did a few minutes ago.'

'What about now?'

'At the moment, I don't see her.'

'Go in and find her. And call me.' He hung up the phone.

Sinclair poked her head in the door. 'We've got another body.'

Garrison's heart stopped beating for a minute and he found himself bargaining with God for it not to be Eva. 'Who is it?'

'Cops on the scene don't have an ID.'

Chapter 22

When Eva realized King had taken the phone off the hook, she nested the receiver back in the cradle. She'd risk dealing with a reporter on the off chance that Garrison was trying to reach her.

Minutes later when the phone did ring, she'd filled a bucket with warm soapy water and dug the mop out of the storage closet. She sprinted across the pub and snapped up the phone on the third ring. 'King's.'

'Eva.' Bobby's frail voice echoed over the line.

'Bobby! What's wrong?' Sudden tears welled in her eyes.

'People at school are being mean. I want to come home.'

'Where are you?'

'I left school.'

'Where are you?' Even as she spoke she tore off her apron and moved toward her purse.

'I'm hiding in the park behind the school.'

'Honey, your teacher must be terrified.'

'She doesn't know I've gone yet. I left when we were switching from PE to Music.'

She thought about calling the school but feared an all-out search for Bobby would make him panic. 'I'll be there

391

in fifteen minutes. Don't move.' She glanced around for King and remembered he'd gone outside to check on the cop again. She'd be back before he knew she was gone.

Tears ran down her face as she thought about Bobby hiding in the wooded park, scared and alone. All this mess was because of her.

A fine cold mist left the air feeling wet and raw when Garrison and Malcolm arrived at the crime scene just after two. He and Malcolm got out of his car and crossed the parking lot of the high-rise apartment complex to the Dumpsters.

Already Forensics had secured the area with yellow crime scene tape and uniforms held the crowd at bay. He scanned the crowd, wondering if the killer stood among the dozens of people, half hoping to see Eva as he had at the first crime scene. But a quick glance revealed no signs of Eva or anyone else that seemed overly interested.

'I don't see Donovan,' Malcolm said. 'This is his kind of chaos.'

Garrison frowned.

They ducked under the tape and moved toward a uniformed officer who had already covered the body and tented another tarp above it to keep the rain off.

The officer was a petite woman in her twenties, but moved with the efficiency of a drill sergeant. She extended her hand. 'I'm Officer Brennan.'

Garrison accepted her hand, noting she had a strong grip. 'What do you have?'

'A woman killed like the others.'

'Who is it?'

'Based on the picture you've been circulating, it's Kristen Hall.' She moved under the tent, knelt by the blue tarp and lifted the edge.

Garrison stared down at Kristen's face. 'Damn.'

Brennan pulled back more tarp, exposing four knife wounds to her heart and then her flat naked belly, marked with four stars arranged in a circle.

'Shit.' Garrison planted his hands on his hips.

'She was hell-bent on getting out of town,' Malcolm said. He squatted by her body and studied the star burns on her belly. 'What could have brought her back?'

'I want to see all her phone records,' Garrison said. 'I want all surveillance tapes from her building. Check to see if her car had GPS and track it down. I want to know every damn step she took in the last thirty-six hours.'

Brennan carefully covered Kristen's body.

'Three women with connections to Price University and Eva Rayburn,' Malcolm said.

Garrison's phone rang. 'Yeah.'

It was the patrolman stationed outside of King's. 'Eva Rayburn is gone.'

Lou had left listening devices all around the pub and when she'd heard that Eva was going to get Bobby, the opportunity to strike was too perfect to resist. Standing near the school, Lou waited for Eva and tried to picture the latest crime scene.

By now the cops would have roped off the area around the bodies and marked patrol cars would have blocked off the streets to keep all onlookers away. The forensics van would have arrived. There'd be chaos.

Excitement burned. Killing had become a drug that Lou now craved. Each kill brought with it release, but the calm didn't last. In fact, it faded faster and faster with each death. Perhaps when Eva was dead the peace would finally come. Yes, maybe once the stars marked her belly and her eyes grew glassy with death everything would feel normal again.

Normal. It had been so long since a normal day. For so long, it had been necessary to hide and stay out of sight. Too long, the worry of being discovered hovered liked Damocles' sword.

'I just want the anger to go away,' she whispered. 'I want to be happy. I want to live.'

Maybe once Eva paid for her sins the clouds would be lifted.

Eva dug her phone out of her purse as she ran into the park looking for Bobby. She glanced at the phone and saw that she'd missed a call. *Angie Carlson.* She'd not heard the phone ring while she was driving and she realized she'd put it on silent mode.

Eva shoved out a breath and turned up the volume. She and Angie did need to talk. Hell, she and Garrison needed to talk. For so long she'd been alone. And now her life had filled with so many people. People she did not want to lose.

She stared at the swing set, watching the swings sway in the wind. Where was Bobby? He'd said the park by the school. 'Bobby!'

She checked her watch. Maybe it was time to call Garrison.

'Eva.'

The sound of Bobby's voice had her turning in a rush of excitement and relief. He stood on the other side of the park, waving at her.

She'd never been happier to see anyone than that kid. Without a thought she ran toward him, closing the gap between them in seconds. Breathless, she stopped in front of him. 'Thank God you're okay.'

His face was tight with tension.

'What's wrong, Bobby?' She knelt down in front of him and laid her hands on his shoulders. 'What's wrong?'

Tears welled in his eyes and flowed down his cheeks.

She gripped his shoulders. 'Honey, what's the problem?'

'I'm sorry. She told me she'd caught Merlin.'

'I don't understand. Merlin is back in the alley.'

In that moment, a bolt of electricity shot through her body. All her muscles collapsed, and before she realized what had happened, she lay on the ground, feeling consciousness slip away.

Garrison's phone rang as he strode into King's. 'Yeah.'

'I'm texting you a picture,' Malcolm said. 'It's the artist's latest sketch. Will you look at it now?'

'I'll have a look and call you right back.'

He flipped open the phone and looked at the image. The artist had taken away the man's glasses, the beard and added long hair. The few changes had transformed a stranger into someone he knew. Sally Walton.

'Shit.' He called Malcolm. 'I want Sally Walton in my office now.'

'I've already sent cars to her apartment and they just reported back that she's not there.'

'I want every uniform to have that sketch.'

'Right.'

Garrison strode through the pub past the customers and a harried waitress and pushed through the kitchen door. King stood at the stove, cursing as he pulled a burning pan from the oven.

'King. We need to talk,' Garrison said.

The older man looked up, his face a mixture of relief and anger.

'Where the hell is Eva?' Garrison asked.

'I don't know. I thought you would.' He dropped the pan on the stovetop and started toward the back door. 'I've got to go to the school. Bobby's teacher can't find him. He didn't come back from his music class.'

'Is he with Eva?'

'I don't know!' King shouted.

'King, I want to help you but you have got to tell me what the hell is going on.'

The old man looked frazzled and for the first time frail. 'I don't know what's happening.'

'You know a hell of a lot more. How did you know Louise Cross was alive?'

King paused by the back door. 'Eva told you?'

'Yes. What the hell have you been doing?'

'I've been trying to clean up some of the damn mess the Cross family made. Those bloodsuckers leave destruction everywhere they go.'

'That's why you brought Eva here?'

'Yes.'

'Why the boy?'

'His mother worked at Price. She was a maid. Josiah got her pregnant and then threatened to ruin her if she ever told anyone.'

'Josiah Cross is the kid's father?'

'I'm not certain. But if I had to bet I'd say yes.'

Garrison clenched his fingers around his car keys. 'How long since you last saw Eva?'

'I'm not sure. An hour. I even called her sister and she doesn't know where Eva is. Some shit is going down. And I'm scared.'

'What about Sally? Has she been around?'

'Sally? Why? What does she have to do with anything?'

'I think she's Louise Cross.'

'What? That can't be! That woman's face is burned into my brain.'

'Nineteen years changes a lot.'

King drew in a breath as if he'd been punched. 'No way. No way that bitch could be in my place and I'd not know it. She killed my family.'

'I'll bet she looks very different than the last time you saw her.'

'But I would know.'

'Not necessarily.'

'If she's Louise Cross then you've got to find her fast. That bitch is evil. Josiah got all his evil from her. She's got my boy and Eva. Please find her.'

'I will.' Garrison didn't wait to reach his car before he started dialing Angie's number. She answered immediately.

'What's the number of the phone you gave her?'

Without hesitating, Angie recited the numbers. 'Are you going to trace her phone?'

'I sure am.'

Malcolm met Garrison when he arrived at the office. 'I have information for you.'

'About?' He didn't stop to talk, but charged ahead to get the warrant he needed to trace Eva's phone.

'The Cross family. They're a real Addams Family, if you know what I mean.'

'I don't.'

'Old man Darius was a bit of a rebel back in the day. Bent his share of laws. He married Louise Winters while she was still in high school. A couple of years later Louise gave birth to twins.'

'Josiah and Micah.'

'Bingo. But from that moment on the marriage started to go downhill. Darius had lots of mistresses.'

'How do you know that?'

'Rokov tracked down Darius's former driver who worked for the family for thirty-plus years.'

Impatience wrapped around Garrison's chest. 'Okay. Bad marriage. What's the point?'

'King was right. Louise didn't die in a car accident as Darius told his sons and everyone else. Darius had his wife committed to a mental hospital up in western Maryland. And here's the pisser. Six months before he died, Darius checked his wife out of the hospital.'

'Lisa tells him about The Secret. He knows he was dying, so he turns Louise loose, and creates a new identity for her so she can go out to do what he couldn't.'

'Exactly. And here's another tidbit. Darius bought Louise a house.'

When Eva awoke and opened her eyes she thought for a moment that she might be dead. She was surrounded by darkness. She blinked, but the darkness remained.

Then she noticed the ache in her side still tender from the shock she'd received. God, she felt like a truck had hit her.

She shook her head and tried to raise her hands, only to discover they were tied to the arms of a chair. Her blood pressure rose like a rocket, sending her heartbeat and mind into overdrive.

Bobby. Where was Bobby? The boy had been standing right in front of her when she'd been shocked. Had he seen who'd done this? Had he run to safety? Or was he tied up in this room somewhere?

'Bobby?' she whispered. 'Bobby, are you in this room? Wake up, honey.'

No voice or sound came out of the darkness; only the silence.

Her cell phone started to vibrate somewhere. Her purse. It must be somewhere close. She strained against her bindings, trying to break free so that she could feel around the room for her purse. But her hands were tied so tight, her fingers tingled. Finally, the vibrating stopped and the phone sunk into the darkness.

A lifeline was so close to her and she couldn't reach it. She tried to rock her chair from side to side but found it was bolted. She was trapped.

Eva wasn't sure how much time passed before she

heard a door open and overhead lights snapped on bright and harsh.

She winced against the onslaught, hating that she had to close her eyes, but unable to bear the pain of the light. Footsteps moved down a staircase as she struggled to help her eyes adjust to the light. Finally, she was able to tolerate a blur of white as she begged her eyes to focus.

'I've been waiting for this for a long time, Eva.'

The voice was so familiar, she dismissed her initial thought immediately. It didn't make sense. And then her vision focused on the person standing in front of her.

The suit and wig were meant to mimic a man, but she knew instantly that no disguise could hide such familiar eyes.

'Sally.'

The older woman hesitated a moment and then smiled. 'Surprise.'

Confusion jumbled her thoughts. This made no sense. Sally was her friend. 'Why are you here? Why?'

Sally pulled off her wig and ran her fingers through her hair. 'Take a good look at me. Do I remind you of anyone?'

Eva stared at Sally's deep eyes and the slight downturn of her lips. The feature that stood out most now was her eyes. Not the color or the shape but the utter hollowness.

Eva felt a tightening in her chest similar to what she'd felt in the months and years after the night Josiah raped her. She'd forgotten many of the details of the rape but she'd never forgotten Josiah's eyes. Void of emotion, she felt as if she stared into the eyes of Satan.

Memories of that night started to crawl out from the

darkness. Josiah's dead lifeless eyes. The touch of his hands on her breasts. His peppermint-scented breath. 'You were Josiah's mother.'

She nodded. 'Very good.'

'Josiah and Micah thought you were dead.'

Sadness welled in her eyes. 'That's what their father told them. As you well know, Darius lied to get what he wanted.'

'Why?'

The slump in Sally's shoulders was almost imperceptible. 'Darius and I married when I was in high school. He was the older bad boy. I was seventeen, needing to leave a crappy home. We were each other's lifelines. In the heat of the moment, we ran off and got married. And for a while we did okay. Darius could make money like nobody I knew. Didn't worry about shortcuts. And then the twins came and it was good.' Tears welled in her eyes, as she seemed to live some faraway memory. 'But the more money Darius made, the more distant he grew. And when he realized I couldn't have more children, he started to treat me badly. Once we were having a party and he hit me because the glasses I'd set out didn't match. I became a reminder of what he couldn't have and he hated me for it.'

If she and Sally had had this conversation a week ago Eva would have wept with her. But now as she twisted her wrists under the rope and tried to ignore the growing pain of the rope burn, screams welled inside her. *You crazy bitch! Let me go!* But she'd learned to hide her fear very well in prison. 'I'm so sorry, Sally.'

Sally didn't seem to hear Eva. 'When the boys turned thirteen, I made an unfortunate mistake.'

'The car accident?'

'King told you about that.'

'Why would you come into his pub? He knew you.'

'I was looking for you, not him. When I saw him the first time I really thought I'd ruined it. But he didn't connect the pieces. Fool! I was cemented in his memory as a much younger and very different woman. No more dyed hair, no more designer suits, or manicured nails. Just old frumpy Sally with her peasant skirts.'

'You killed his family.'

She bristled. 'That dumb woman driver got in my way. She should have moved faster.'

Eva felt sick for King, who had lost so much to a woman who had no remorse. 'That's when Darius sent you away.'

'He had me locked up in a private home for the insane.' Tears fell down her cheeks. 'Bastard. He took almost twenty years of my life.' Anger seemed to rush through her like a wildfire. 'And then Darius came to see me last year. The cancer had whittled away his body and he looked so weak and tired. I almost didn't recognize him. But he'd learned from that whore Lisa about what had happened the night my boy died. He didn't have the strength to kill you all, so he asked me to do it. Of course I said yes.'

'Where is Bobby?'

'Upstairs. Safe. I bought a television and snacks. Kids like snacks and cartoons.'

'Why do you want Bobby?'

'I'm his grandmother.'

'His grandmother is dead.'

'You mean his *other* grandmother. Yes, I know. I killed her.'

'I remember Eliza's daughter.'

'She had a crush on my boy. And she managed to get herself pregnant. Darius didn't want a bastard grandchild and told her he'd ruin her family if she ever told anyone. When Darius came to me he told me about Bobby. I knew I had to see him.'

A tear rolled down her cheek. 'Why did you kill Eliza?'

'I drove by her house to see Bobby and she saw me. Believe it or not, she recognized me. She would have told everyone I was back and ruined all my plans. So I killed her.' She released a breath. 'Soon it will be just Bobby and me. . . .'

Garrison and three other police cars arrived at the residential house made of brick. This was the house Lenny had described. This was where he'd heard the woman scream. Where he'd smelled burning flesh. Garrison prayed they had arrived in time.

Sally smiled as the tip of the brand started to heat. Just one more minute and it should be ready.

'What are you going to do?'

'Mark you like those others. You want to be remembered as rising stars and you will be.'

'Your son already marked me once.'

'He should have finished you then. The delay is what killed him. He was having too much fun, I'll bet. Men are weak when it comes to women.'

'He raped me.'

'Please,' Sally said. 'I'll bet you waggled your cute little bottom in front of him, knowing the effect you had on him. The other girls did the same. They enticed him to take them.'

Upstairs, footsteps sounded and Eva glanced up the staircase. Bobby's voice sounded at the top of the stairs. 'Sally?'

Sally crossed quickly to Eva and shoved a rag in her mouth. 'I'm down here. Wait and I'll come get you.'

Sally secured the rag in Eva's mouth with a strip of duct tape. Satisfied Eva couldn't warn the boy, she headed up the stairs. Bolting the door behind her she led Bobby to the basement.

Eva stared in horror as Bobby moved down the stairs. When he reached the bottom he stopped and stared at her.

'Don't be fooled by her, son. She is the Devil.'

'You tied her up,' Bobby said.

'Yes. She's been bad and she needs to be punished.'

'What are you going to do to her?' A hitch in his voice betrayed fear and uncertainty.

Eva tried to scrape her chin against her shoulder and remove the tape but it didn't budge. She stared at Bobby, trying to will him to understand that she really did care.

Sally laid her hands on his shoulders and stared into Eva's eyes. 'I'm going to teach her what happens to bad girls. And I want you to take note. This is your first lesson on the step to manhood.'

Tears welled and ran down Bobby's face. He tried to pull away but she wouldn't release him. 'Don't hurt her!'

Sally dragged Bobby toward the fireplace and picked

up the red-hot branding iron. 'We need to teach Eva a lesson.'

'No!' Bobby shouted.

Eva didn't have hope that she would get out of the basement alive.

Garrison rang the bell. No answer. 'There's a basement. We need to get to the basement.'

He moved to a window by the front door and using the handle of his gun broke the glass. He wrapped his jacket around his arm and reached through the jagged glass for the latch. Glass cut through the back as he strained and finally reached the lock.

He pushed open the window, hoisted himself inside the house and then opened the front door for the other detectives. They rushed through the house, sweeping and searching as they went.

Rokov moved to a side parlor and slid open the door. 'I have something.'

'What?' He couldn't bring himself to ask if it was Eva or the boy.

'It's Donovan.' Rokov and Sinclair, guns drawn, carefully entered the room. While Rokov remained on alert, Sinclair checked Donovan's vitals.

'He's alive. But barely.'

Garrison moved to the kitchen and found the basement door. It was locked. Bolted from the inside. He was about to request the battering ram when Eva's scream tore through the house.

Through the burning pain that seared every nerve ending in her body, Eva heard Bobby weep.

'Stop!' the boy screamed.

Sally turned from Eva who had draped forward in a sweaty crumpled heap. 'I have to do this.'

Bobby raced to her, taking her hand in his. 'Eva, wake up. I'm sorry.'

Sally grabbed Bobby by the arm. 'You have to be strong. Like a real man. You can't be sniveling. Your uncle Micah snivels.'

Bobby tore away from Sally and gripped Eva's hands tighter. 'Eva, wake up!'

She raised her head. The pain of the burn had eased a fraction so that she could think a little more clearly.

The boy pulled the tape and gag from her mouth. 'Get out of here, Bobby. Get away.'

'He's not going anywhere. Are you, Bobby?' Sally said. 'He's going to watch me burn every inch of your body and then stab you in the heart when I'm done.'

Sally left Bobby at Eva's side as she returned to the hearth and jabbed the end of the branding iron into the embers.

Tears rolled down Bobby's face. 'I'm sorry.'

'Get out of here,' she said, adding as much force as she could muster.

Bobby glanced at Sally and then at the stairs. 'I'm going to save you, Eva.'

He turned and ran toward the stairs. But Sally was faster and cut him off at the staircase. 'Where are you going?'

'I hate you. I hate you!'

'One day you will thank me.'

'I hate you!'

Sally reared back her hand to slap the boy when the door at the top of the stairs exploded open. Garrison and three other men rushed down the stairs, guns pointed at Sally.

Sally grabbed Bobby by the arm, jerked him around and retreated to a corner. She pulled a knife from her pocket and thrust it against his neck. 'I'll kill him.'

Garrison didn't take his gaze off Sally. 'Eva!'

'I'm here.' Her voice sounded weak.

Garrison's expression hardened as he stared at Sally. 'Let the boy go.'

Bobby wept as he tried to twist free. 'Let me go.'

She nicked his neck until a droplet of blood rolled down his neck. 'Nope. Ain't gonna back away from this one, sport.'

The slightest movement aggravated Eva's burn and sent pain bolting through her body. 'Sally is Josiah's mother. She turned him into the monster he became.'

'My son was no monster. I taught him how to be strong.'

'You taught him how to be weak,' Eva said. The more she could worm her way under Sally's skin, the greater the chance Sally would get distracted, allowing Garrison to act.

'You turned him into a sniveling coward.' Eva raised her head. 'He cried like a baby after he hurt me. He begged for my forgiveness.'

Sally flinched. 'Liar.'

Eva moistened her lips. 'And then he wet his pants like a baby.'

Sally whirled around. But before she could speak, Garrison fired, hitting her in the chest. Sally fell to her knees and dropped forward, hitting the hard stone floor.

Bobby hugged his arms around his chest and Garrison pulled him into an embrace. 'Shh. It's over.'

'She hurt Eva.'

'An ambulance is on the way,' Kier said.

Garrison tensed and pulled the boy with him to Eva. 'Stand here, Bobby, while I check her out.'

He untied her hands and feet and then studied the brand on her shoulder. 'Eva.'

'I'll live,' she said.

'Christ, honey.' He picked her up, careful not to cause her more pain.

'I'm okay.'

Tears rolled down Bobby's face. 'I'm sorry, Eva. I'm sorry.'

'I'm fine, honey.'

'She burned you.'

'It will all heal.'

Garrison stared at her, his expression grim. The healing would take a long time.

Epilogue

Eva dumped her backpack loaded with books on the bar. The pub was quiet. The lunch crowd wouldn't arrive for another hour but already the smells of soups and fresh breads drifted out from the kitchen along with King's favorite Elvis song, 'Love Me Tender.'

She'd started school six weeks ago, with financial help from Angie. Her sister had called the money a gift, whereas Eva insisted it was a loan.

So far she was having the time of her life. She loved it all: the clueless freshmen; the bad food in the dining hall; the studying. Even today's quiz.

She'd considered living in the dorms, but the cinderblock walls had reminded her of prison. And since she couldn't afford to take out an apartment near campus, it just made sense to stay at King's. She still worked three lunch shifts a week and kept King's books. And she got to see Bobby each day when he came home from school.

Staying at King's also kept her closer to Angie. They'd been doing their best to make amends. It wasn't always easygoing but they were managing. With Angie's help, Eva had petitioned the governor to have her sentence overturned. He'd signed the decree just days ago.

Donovan had survived his injuries, and he told the

world what Kristen had confessed to him before she died. The story had gone national and the paper recently reported that he'd inked a book deal.

That had brought more reporters into Eva's life. She'd refused all interviews, but that hadn't stopped the chaos from spinning out of control for most of the summer. Finally, in late August, the world had started to forget about Eva.

She pushed through the swinging door and found King frosting cupcakes. Five trays covered the counter. 'So who's having a party?'

'Bobby's birthday is coming.'

She snuck a spoonful of icing. 'Not until next week.'

'But he wanted to have a party at school tomorrow. I told the teacher I'd bake some cupcakes.'

'King, there must be four hundred cupcakes here.'

King frowned down at the army of cakes. 'Do you think I made too many?'

She laughed. 'No. Believe me, they'll get eaten. And whatever is left over you can give to the teachers. They might help smooth out that situation Bobby had on the playground last week.'

Bobby had moved in with King in the spring and had started fourth grade in the fall. He was doing well for the most part. School required extra help from Eva and King, and sometimes the scrapper in Bobby emerged on the playground. As secure as the kid was now, he still got into fights when challenged about his past.

King had hoped when news of Bobby's paternity was settled, he could begin the adoption process. Maybe then Bobby would feel really at home and the altercations would stop.

Eva took another larger dollop of chocolate icing. Licking the spoon, she couldn't help but croon her praise. 'Wonderful!' She leaned in for another scoop.

'Get out of my icing, girl. I might run out.'

'Not unless you're planning on making two million more cupcakes.'

Bells on the front door had her pushing through the kitchen door to see who had arrived. It was Garrison. He strode into the room, moving with a swagger that still made her body tight with wanting when she saw him.

They'd been dating these last six months. They'd both sworn to go slow but hadn't had much luck with it. She crossed the room and let him fold his arms around her. He kissed her on the lips.

'You taste good,' he said. 'Like chocolate.'

She laughed. 'You taste good too.'

He kissed her again, letting his lips linger the second time. Slowly, he pulled back. 'I received news from Madge this morning about Bobby.'

It took a moment to shake the fog from her brain. 'She got the results of the DNA test on Bobby?' They'd needed to prove paternity before King could adopt the boy. If Josiah was his father, then Micah had a claim to the child. 'Josiah was not his father.'

'So the Cross family has no claim on the boy.'

'None.'

'Do you know who the father was?'

'No. And likely never will, seeing as the boy's mother and grandmother are dead. Social Services see no reason why King can't adopt Bobby.'

Eva let out a yelp and hugged him. 'You're the best.'

His grin sparkled in his eyes. 'I didn't do anything. I just delivered the news.'

'You did more than that. I know you pushed things along.'

'Maybe a nudge.'

Absently, he ran his thumb over her collarbone. Even under the shirt he could feel the rough edge of the scar Sally had left on her skin. He frowned. 'You're one tough gal, Eva. I'm not sure I'll ever forget that day.'

She captured his fingertips and kissed them. 'Eyes forward, Detective Garrison. Eyes forward.'

Deacon smiled, but a ghost of worry had crept into his expression. 'I'm working on that.'

She kissed him and smiled. 'I've had lots of practice. Keeping my eyes on the future. I'll help you stay focused on what matters.'

'Sally's trial is slated for November.'

Eva nodded, unable to suppress a shiver. Sally had recovered from her gunshot wound. She had written several letters to Eva, always enclosing an old article from Eva's trial a decade ago. 'The sooner it's over, the better. What about Micah?'

'We've not been able to link a single crime to him.'

'He had to know she was back. Someone had to have been helping her.'

'I know. We've just not figured out who yet.' He tucked a stray strand behind her ear. 'I don't want to think about them right now. Just us.'

He hugged her and she held him tight. 'Just us.'

Read on for an extract from
Mary Burton's next novel, *Merciless*,
coming soon from Penguin.

Chapter One

The foul odor of decaying flesh roused the woman from her drugged haze, burning her nostrils and lungs like a freshly snapped ammonia capsule.

She blinked, clawed toward consciousness, searching the pitch-blackness for a landmark to anchor time or place. However, there was nothing except the stench that grew more potent with each hitching breath. She coughed and gagged. The contents of her stomach churned and rose up her throat.

She lifted a trembling hand to her mouth but discovered the slight movement drove a cutting pain through her muscles and ribs. She froze, didn't want to move, fearing more agony, but nausea overruled everything and had her rolling to her side. Tears burned her eyes as she gripped the edge of the metal table and vomited until her throat burned.

When the worst of the retching stopped, she collapsed on her back, allowing only small shallow breaths as she stared into the darkness. She closed her watery eyes and gently swiped her fingertips across her lips. The odors still hovered but the worst of the nausea had passed.

With the sickness satisfied, there was only the pain. *Only.* Every square inch of flesh pulsated. Throbbed. Burned.

Fear rose up, but she quickly wrestled it down. Now was not the time to crumble.

She blinked. Once. Twice. But the fetid darkness didn't

diminish. It could have been the middle of the day or night, winter or summer. She couldn't tell.

She tried to rise again but her insides screamed. Again, she collapsed.

Where was she? What had happened? She had to get free.

Think back.

In the last few weeks, she'd sensed that she was being watched. At first she'd clocked up the feelings to an over-active imagination. But as much as she denied the feelings, they grew stronger whenever she'd stepped out of her apartment, whenever she arrived at work or whenever she took a Pilates class. Soon she'd started to think twice before she went anywhere. She'd stopped going to the gym and her favorite nightclubs. Her world shrank to the small path between home and work.

And then the notes had arrived. I LOVE YOU. TOGETHER ALWAYS. YOU ARE NEVER OUT OF MY MIND.

The notes had been a relief. In fact, she'd laughed when she'd received the first. *Of course!* Her ex had been her stalker. It had been three weeks since they'd shared a bed or seen each other, but she knew he was the one watching. He enjoyed dark, erotic games. He liked scaring her. Keeping her off balance.

Knowing he was watching, she'd wore tighter skirts and sweaters, proudly strutting and hoping she tortured him with jealousy. She met a younger man and took pleasure kissing him, knowing he was lurking in the shadows.

When she'd found the red velvet box and she'd discovered the ivory pendant nestled inside, she'd known she'd won. She'd been energized by her power over him, knowing soon he'd beg for forgiveness. Men were so easy. So weak.

'Oh, God,' she whispered.

Someone had been stalking her. Watching. Planning. But it had not been her lover.

Pushing through pain and sickness, she sat up. 'I'm alive. And that counts for something.' She repeated the words like a mantra.

She blinked again and again, willing the blackness to fade and the stench and pain to vanish. But no lights magically flicked on. It hurt to breathe and her thoughts moved like thick muddy waters.

Where had she been last? The theater? Her apartment? The club?

And then she remembered. She'd been at the Duke Street Cafe. There'd been an impromptu party. Someone had decided to celebrate another large donation to her theater. The donation ensured that the theater would be able to make its payroll and mount a grander, more expensive production in the spring.

The party had been a glittering, exciting affair and she'd been happy. There'd been lots of champagne; so much so, that she'd lost count of how many times the waiter had refilled her glass. Of course her ex had not come. He never met up with her at public events. But another old boyfriend had hit on her and because she'd felt so good she'd flirted back. It had been fun. Intoxicating.

How had she gone from such magical moments to this cave of horrors?

She ticked through the evening's events. Wine. Music. Singing. A bite or two of food. Some guy, one of her ex-boyfriend's buddies, had offered her coke, but she'd turned him down, knowing the drug would keep her wired most of the night and make her look too puffy for tomorrow's photo call.

Had the actor and his friend slipped her something anyway?

Thoughts blurred in her mind. She couldn't cut through the misty mosaic to access the right memories. All she had was the party and then this dark, dank hole that smelled of death. The middle had vanished.

It didn't matter how she got here. What was important was escaping. And if she was good at anything, it was cutting her losses.

As much as she strained to see, she couldn't make out the room's details. The place was as still as a grave until suddenly she heard a tap turn on and water trickle.

She cocked her head. 'Is someone there?'

Water gurgled and bubbled, but no one answered.

Struggling with a choking fear, she swung her legs over the side of the metal table. Her head spun, pain slammed her and her stomach threatened another revolt. She hesitated and waited for her body to calm.

Gingerly, she set bare feet on a floor made of cold, wet stone. Her toes curled. She hated the slimy surface so much like a lake bottom.

Wobbly limbs screamed under the protest of her weight as she stood. Every muscle ached. Her dress felt damp but she had no idea of the cause.

The soothing *drip, drip* of water remained her only reference. It sounded as if it were off to her right. At least now she had a direction.

Get to the water and she'd figure out her next move.

She took a tentative step away from the table. Sweat dampened her body. Her dress clung to her breasts, hugging her nipples in an intimate way that left her feeling exposed. But as tempting as it was to cover up with her arms, her outstretched hands were all that kept her balanced.

With each step, the stench grew worse and the urge to turn away increased. Still, she kept shuffling toward the water. Without warning, her knee bumped painfully into the side of what must have been a giant metal tub. Bolts of pain shot out and reverberated up and down her leg. She gasped and the smells nearly overpowered her.

Instinct had her turning from the tub. 'Shit.'

She didn't have the strength to retrace her steps to the table now swallowed up in shadowy obscurity.

Tears filled her eyes and rolled down her cheeks. It would be so easy to surrender. But she'd never been a quitter. Ever.

Summoning her most imperious tone she said, 'I demand to know if anyone is there.'

The shadows hovered around her, mutinously silent, still and unmoved by her practiced sternness. Her only answer was the steady, quiet trickle of water dripping into the tub.

'I shouldn't be here,' she said. 'This is a terrible mistake. People are expecting me to show up at work. They'll call the cops if I don't show.'

She shoved a shaky hand through feathered curls and righted her hunched shoulders. Body and bones creaked as if she'd just passed her ninetieth birthday and not her twenty-sixth. What had happened to her? 'I demand to know where I am.'

This time a shadow in a corner shifted. 'You demand? If I were you, I wouldn't demand. I'd beg.'

The rough, clipped voice had her head jerking around. 'Why should I beg?' Even as she asked the question, she saw the absurdity. She'd beg or do whatever was asked of her to get out of here. 'What do I need to beg for?'

'Your life would be a good start.' His voice was so silky and gentle. And for a moment, it sounded very familiar. Had he been at the party? Where had she heard his voice before?

She leaned against the tub, fearing her legs would give way and she'd fall to her knees. 'I am not afraid.'

A soft chuckle snaked through the gloom, unsettling her more than if the shadow-man had hurled threats. 'You should be afraid.'

Tears streamed down her cheeks but she raised her chin. 'What is that smell?'

'Rotting flesh.'

This time her knees did crumble. She dropped to the ground, digging long fingers into the stone. 'Why?'

'Why? Why are you here? Why is there rotting flesh in the room? Why what?'

His voice sent fear knifing into her. 'Why me?'

She heard the clip of his shoes on the stone floor as he moved away. For a panicked second she thought he'd leave her alone in this room of horrors. Instead, he flipped on a light.

In a blink, overhead fluorescents clicked on, flooding the room with light and forcing her to wince and shield her eyes from the burning glare. Carefully, she cracked open her lids, letting the light leak into her pupils.

When her gaze finally focused on her jailer, she saw he stood directly in front of her. He wore crisp jeans, a dark sweater and rubber gloves. He looked so normal. Handsome even.

'Who are you?'

'Doesn't matter.' He clapped his hands. 'Want to have a good look around before we get to work?'

The source of the smell had her turning back toward the tub. It was a vile putrid concoction of greasy, black water. Loose fatty deposits floated on the surface. Oh shit! Was it flesh clinging to bone?

She screamed and lurched back. 'What is that?'

'It's where the polishing process begins. Flesh must be stripped from the bones before I can polish them.' The lightness in his voice told her he was truly enjoying this moment. 'Now, we better get moving. We've got work to do.'

'Work? Where is this place?'

'Far enough from anyone that can help you.'

Tremors started to move through her limbs. 'Where *am* I?'

'It's where I do my work. My art.'

'What kind of art?'

'Look behind you.'

She turned and saw a workbench. Equipped with saws, screws and buffing pads. It reminded her of a jeweler's workstation. Until she saw it – the polished white femur.

'That's not art!'

'You seemed to like the cameo I gave you.'

Her hand rose to her throat where the broach had rested just days ago. 'That was bone?'

He winked. 'I love the way the light glistens on the bones, don't you? Human bone carves like sandstone.'

'You are demented.'

Blue eyes sparked. 'To each his own.'

'Please, don't do this to me.'

'No going back now.'

'Of course there is. I won't tell.'

And then as if she hadn't spoken, he said, 'If we get started now, we'll be done by this time next week.' He hooked a steady, gloved hand under her elbow and pulled her to a standing position. 'Let's get you back on the table.'

Her legs wobbled and her insides ached with fire. When she glanced down, she saw that blood stained her skirt and legs. Crimson droplets covered the ground around her feet. 'What have you done to me?'

He guided her toward the table. 'I haven't done anything. Now up you go.'

'My body hurts.' She'd been invaded, assaulted. Flickers of what had happened flashed: an attacker shoving into her with such force she'd screamed. He'd laughed. Pushed harder and then he leaned down and bitten her shoulder until her blood had spilled. He'd taken pictures. 'You did this to me! You did this!'

'Not me. Him.'

Her head spun and her pain paralyzed her muscles. 'There are two of you?'

He ignored the question. 'You know, you have the most perfect bone structure. Your cheekbones are symmetrically perfect. It's as if an artist sculpted them.'

'Please,' she whispered.

'Mother Nature can be so haphazard and fickle but with you she really outdid herself.'

She lay back against the cold metal, her body collapsing with exhaustion. Whatever reserves she'd possessed had vanished. She was empty. 'What are you going to do?'

Out from the shadows stepped another man. She knew this man. She'd run her fingers through his hair. She'd kissed his face. Gotten to know the feel of his broad shoulder blades under her hands. 'You did this to me.'

Smiling, he snapped another picture. 'I'm finished with her. She's yours now.'

'No, please,' she said.

He didn't answer, but simply turned and left her alone with The Other, who grinned as he selected a knife from a table.

'Don't leave me here with him!' she screamed.

A door closed.

The Other picked up a knife. Light glinted from the steel. 'I'm going to make the pain go away.'

As much as the pain scorched through her body and stole her breath, it was proof of life. Without the pain, she feared, she'd be lost. 'I want to leave.'

Gently, he smoothed his fingertips over her forehead. 'Shh. We can't do that.'

The gentle touch detonated shivers. And then he dragged the razor-sharp blade over the tender flesh of her neck. The pain was sudden and searing. Warm blood drained so quickly from the wound.

She inhaled but her lungs didn't respond. She tried to pull in a second breath. Nothing. Panic exploded as she directed her energy toward her lungs.

Breathe! Air!

A gurgling sound rose in her chest as the air already in her lungs seeped out through the wound. More blood pooled around her shoulders. She gripped the table, clinging to her final hold on life.

He kept smoothing gentle fingers over her head. 'Don't fight it. Fighting only makes it worse. It will just be a few more seconds, then it will all be over and I can get you in that tub with the others.'

Her vision blurred. Her lungs and flesh howled for air. Gentle fingers stroked her hair and her cheeks.

'So pretty.'

Delight danced in his eyes. The more she struggled to breathe the greater his enjoyment. In these last moments of her life she realized bliss for him was watching her die.

The blackness returned to the edges of her vision and with each second her constricting pupils squeezed out more light.

She had no breath to scream.

And then, like the final curtain call in the theater, the blackness dropped.

He stared down at her, his gloved hand stroking her hair. It was a miracle that she'd gotten up off the table. After what the First One had done to her, it was a wonder she was alive. But he'd have been furious if she'd died. The killing was his treat. His well deserved reward.

He'd not expected she'd be such a fighter. She was a beautiful woman accustomed to using her looks to get what she wanted. She'd never tasted the harshness that life really could offer.

But she'd faced him with a hoity arrogance that he

found a bit charming. It was always more fun to bring the bossy ones down a peg.

He clicked on an overhead light and studied her face. Her flesh had been torn and bruised. If anyone saw her now, they'd be appalled by the damage. He didn't like it when skin was mauled and ruined.

But thankfully, the injuries were only skin-deep. Flesh had been torn but her bones were sure and strong.

She would make a fine addition to his collection.

MARY BURTON

DYING SCREAM

NO ONE WILL FIND YOU
An aspiring artist. A high-school senior. A stripper. Three women who seemed to have nothing in common except their sudden disappearance. But one man knew them all. Wealthy, privileged Craig Thornton even claimed to love them. And for that, they paid the ultimate price.

NO ONE WILL SAVE YOU
When Adrianna Barrington receives an anniversary card from her husband Craig, she assumes it's a sick joke. After all Craig is dead. But then come the whispered phone calls and beautiful flowers, all reminding her how much Craig misses her. While Adrianna begins to doubt her sanity, grisly remains are found on the Thornton estate. Detective Gage Hudson is convinced the bodies are linked to Craig. But the biggest shocks are yet to come.

NO ONE WILL HEAR YOU
A psychopath has taken up his chilling work again, each death a prelude to the moment when Adrianna is under his control at last. And the only way for Gage and Adrianna to stop him is to uncover the truth about a family's dark past and a twisted love that someone will kill for again and again . . .

He just wanted a decent book to read ...

Not too much to ask, is it? It was in 1935 when Allen Lane, Managing Director of Bodley Head Publishers, stood on a platform at Exeter railway station looking for something good to read on his journey back to London. His choice was limited to popular magazines and poor-quality paperbacks – the same choice faced every day by the vast majority of readers, few of whom could afford hardbacks. Lane's disappointment and subsequent anger at the range of books generally available led him to found a company – and change the world.

'We believed in the existence in this country of a vast reading public for intelligent books at a low price, and staked everything on it'
Sir Allen Lane, 1902–1970, founder of Penguin Books

The quality paperback had arrived – and not just in bookshops. Lane was adamant that his Penguins should appear in chain stores and tobacconists, and should cost no more than a packet of cigarettes.

Reading habits (and cigarette prices) have changed since 1935, but Penguin still believes in publishing the best books for everybody to enjoy. We still believe that good design costs no more than bad design, and we still believe that quality books published passionately and responsibly make the world a better place.

So wherever you see the little bird – whether it's on a piece of prize-winning literary fiction or a celebrity autobiography, political tour de force or historical masterpiece, a serial-killer thriller, reference book, world classic or a piece of pure escapism – you can bet that it represents the very best that the genre has to offer.

Whatever you like to read – trust Penguin.